Sign up for our newsletter to hear
about new and upcoming releases.

www.ylva-publishing.com

OTHER BOOKS BY ANDREA BRAMHALL

Norfolk Coast Investigation Story:
Collide-O-Scope
Under Parr
The Last First Time (Coming December 2017)

Just My Luck

ROCK
AND A
HARD
PLACE

ANDREA BRAMHALL

DEDICATION

"To see what others cannot...
You must climb the mountain"

— **Ron Akers**

As on the mountain…as in life. Not all mountains are made of rock, and most do not have the safety of ropes attached.

We all have our own Everest, my friends, so climb
yours, then relax and enjoy the view.

ACKNOWLEDGMENTS

Astrid, Daniela, Michelle, and the wonderful team over at Ylva—thank you for all your help, your faith in me, and your steadfast dedication to producing great books. You've helped me improve as a writer in more ways than I can tell you.

Streetlight Graphics—for the wonderful cover, thank you.

Louise—thanks for putting up with me when I'm supposed to be talking to you and instead I'm thousands of miles away climbing a rock wall in Patagonia.

For those of you who pick this up—I truly hope you enjoy reading it as much as I enjoyed writing it. This was a wonderful adventure!

PROLOGUE

JAYDEN HARRIS FLIPPED UP THE collar of her fleece, rubbed her hands together, and ducked inside the cavernous mess tent easily capable of seating a hundred people at a time. Coffee and a spot of lunch sounded like a good plan, then a little more sleep before she had to get everything ready for her group to head out of Everest base camp at midnight on the start of their summit bid.

She checked her watch. 11:35 a.m. Okay, maybe it was a little early for lunch. But she couldn't help but smile when she noticed the date on the chronograph: April 25, 2015. Three years. Damn, the time had gone so fast.

A gust of wind through the open door tugged at her hair. She quickly gripped the long, dirty-blond curls that whipped about her face and secured them with a band at the nape of her neck.

"Hey," a familiar voice called.

Jayden turned and smiled when Rebecca stepped in line next to her, but Rebecca didn't smile back.

"What's wrong?" Jayden asked.

"Pain in the arse Pete wants to go out and drill his self-rescue skills again."

"That's not a bad thing, babe." She supressed a groan of mutual frustration. So much for her afternoon of relaxation, but on the mountain safety always came first. A nervous climber meant a dangerous one. If an afternoon of skill drills put Pete at ease, it could save more than just his own life down the road.

"Yeah, I know," she replied with a heavy sigh. "I just wanted to spend the rest of today with you, that's all."

Jayden's smile widened. "I know the feeling, but we can always celebrate our anniversary when we get back."

This time Rebecca did smile as she stepped onto her tiptoes to close the six-inch height difference between them and kissed Jayden's cheek. Her eyes twinkled with a seductive mischief when she stepped back and whispered, "I'm going to hold you to that," before pressing her lips firmly against Jayden's.

When Rebecca finally pulled back, she took the coffee mug from Jayden's hand, took a long swig, then handed it back. "Thanks." She sighed and ran a hand through her shoulder-length brown hair. "You stay here and finish your coffee. I'll take him out this time."

Jayden shook her head, loath to shirk her responsibility. She was the team leader and company owner; the safety of the clients was hers to ensure, not Rebecca's. No matter how capable and experienced she was, the buck stopped with Jayden, and she knew it.

"Thanks, but I should really do it."

Rebecca frowned. "Look, I don't want to argue with you, *babe*." She spat out the endearment like an insult. "Not today. But it really pisses me off when you do this."

"Do what?"

"Treat me like I'm just another pretender on the mountain. I do know what I'm doing, you know?"

Jayden held her hands up in supplication. "I know that. I'm not trying to do that to you, I promise. It's just that—"

"Yeah, I know. There's only the great Jayden Harris who can teach anything to anyone about survival in the mountains." She turned to leave the tent, but Jayden caught her arm before she could walk more than two steps away.

"That's not fair, Becks. I have a responsibility to them."

"What about your responsibility to me? Don't I matter? I'm your girlfriend, your partner, I thought. Yet you continue to treat me like one of the other lackeys."

"That's not true."

"Actually, yeah, it really is."

2

Jayden shook her head. So much for not wanting to fight today. She didn't want to do this again. Jayden knew that Pete was a capable climber, who carried the skills he needed well embedded in muscle memory. His insecurities were in his head. And Rebecca was a good, strong climber and a competent teacher. For all her worries about the elements of their unpredictable environment, Jayden was probably micromanaging.

Did Rebecca have a point? Was she treating her like some underling rather than the equal partners she professed they really were? She wouldn't insist like this if Rebecca were Fen, would she? Were the escalating problems in their relationship all her doing after all?

"Fine. I'll take a nap this afternoon while you take him out on the ice."

Rebecca's frown morphed into a triumphant grin as she slipped her arms around Jayden's waist, holding her close. "Thanks."

A shiver crawled up Jayden's spine, making the hairs on the back of her neck stand up. She grimaced, trying to place the draft, and quickly turned about her, looking for an open tent flap. But there was nothing. She shook her head and ran a hand over the back of her neck.

"Becks?"

"Yeah, babe?"

"Be careful out there."

Rebecca wrinkled her nose again, her brown eyes dancing in the dim light of the mess tent, and her lips quirked into that cheeky, half-cocky, half-sexy grin that Jayden loved so much. "Always am, Jay. Always am."

Jayden watched her go, still unable to shake the feeling that something wasn't right. She felt itchy, restless. The peace she always felt in the mountains, even on the busiest peaks, was missing. She sipped her coffee and took a seat at one of the tables, determined to forget her uneasiness and focus instead on the challenge before them: guiding a group of first-timers to the summit of Everest.

Their route was well planned; ladders were lashed together to provide bridges across deadly crevasses, and ropes were bolted into the rock and ice to give them some protection up the exposed faces they needed to conquer as they went. Provisions were waiting for them at Camps One and Two, along with oxygen to help them all resist the effects of altitude sickness and the devastating result that was pulmonary oedema. Drowning in one's one bodily fluids while trying to breathe was not a pleasant way to die. But it was certainly one of the most common on the mountain. Yeah, it was risky. That's what made it exciting. It's what got the blood pumping. And they were ready for this. She was ready.

Nevertheless, she couldn't sit still. She downed the rest of her coffee and stepped outside. Row upon row of small yellow dome tents ran down one side of the encampment. Red ones ran in another direction, and a scattering of multicoloured ones dotted the rest of base camp. Each colour represented a different trekking company. The blue tents of her own Adventure Trekkers company were close to the middle of the encampment. A good, safe place in a safe camp. Not much about a tour up Everest could be classified as safe, but base camp was.

Was her uneasiness about the state of their relationship what had her on edge? She frowned. *I'll go and apologise to her again. Maybe we can make a plan to take some time off, go somewhere romantic, and see if we can sort everything out.* She checked her watch again to see if she had time to catch Rebecca before she set off with Pete. It was already 11:50 a.m. Probably too late, but she checked their tent anyway. It was empty. *Damn.*

The red, yellow, and blue triangles of the bunting around camp fluttered on the breeze as she decided how to use the restless energy. She was within two minutes of the medical tent, and picking up their first aid kits and medical supplies would save a job later.

"Hey, Jay," Jost Clabben said as she walked in.

"Hey, Doc. How's it going?"

"Quiet day today." He shrugged. "Lots of people have already headed out to the higher camps."

"I saw that. What was it—110 at Camp One tonight and 70 at Camp Two?"

"Yah. Crazy. This mountain gets busier and busier every year. I came out here for a quiet life, you know?" He laughed and clapped her on the shoulder.

"I hear ya, Doc. I'm not so much of a people person myself."

"You climbers, you never are. That's why you're crazy enough to go chasing all those summits."

She chuckled. "Truer words."

"So what can I do for you today?"

"First aid kits and basic med supplies, please. We're heading out tonight."

"Ah, of course. I'll just—what the hell...?"

The ground beneath her feet shook. No, it was more than that. It felt more like it was rocking, pitching from side to side like a boat rolling on a wave. First one, then a second, the pitch and fall growing as one moment slipped to another.

"Earthquake!" she shouted. The doctor's eyes opened wide, and they both ran for the tent flap. But the grey sky above them shook, then Jayden realised it wasn't the sky that was shaking. The ground beneath her quaked so violently, she struggled to keep her feet beneath her; she grabbed on to the doctor's shoulder for stability. He, too, stumbled against the tremors and jostled against her. Just a little. Just enough to see it. She tapped him on the shoulder and pointed as words failed her.

A curtain of white tumbled down the mountainside. The worst nightmare of anyone on the mountains.

"Avalanche!" she yelled into the sonorous rumble that split the air.

Ice and snow and rock careened towards them with a speed and ferocity she could never have imagined. Base camp was days away from the summit, days of gruelling walking, climbing, and suffering, surely too far away for the angry torrent of ice to reach them, right? But what about those already on the way to Camps One and Two? And Rebecca?

"Oh God, Rebecca." She didn't know if she shouted the words or whispered them. She couldn't hear it over the growing rumble splitting the sky like it had erupted from the bellows of the earth and shot straight up to the heavens. "She shouldn't be out there. It should've been me. Oh God, please."

The doctor tugged on her hand, his mouth open, his lips forming words she couldn't hear.

She shook her head. "I should never have given in to her." She tore her eyes away from Jost and glanced up at the sky. She'd never believed in God or heaven. It didn't matter. She'd gladly sell her soul to trade places with Rebecca right now. "Please let her be okay." But even as she pleaded, she knew the odds were against her. Really, it would take a miracle. The wall of ice charging at them was going to claim lives on the mountain today.

They stared in silent horror as the roar of hell grew louder, and it became terrifyingly clear that base camp was never going to be far enough away. Not by a long way. A tsunami of snow and rock rained down towards them.

Rocks heavy enough to crush bones became missiles, hurtling towards them at the speed of a bullet.

They needed some sort of shelter against the oncoming avalanche. Canvas offered little protection…but it was the best they had. Without it, they'd be relying on luck alone in a billion-to-one shot at survival.

If they weren't buried alive and frozen to death.

So Jayden did the only thing she could think of: she pushed Jost in front of her, shoving him back into the medical tent behind them and down under one of the gurneys as far from the door as they could go. The ice was right on their heels.

She tried desperately not to think about Rebecca, out there, too far away to find even the limited protection a tent could offer. "I should never have let her go," she whispered.

The tent rocked under the force of the avalanche smashing against the fabric, tearing it apart under the pressure. The wall closest to the to the door gave way under the torrent; poles flattened, gurneys crushed, and the two nurses and a doctor sheltering under them were buried alive. Jayden raced forward, only to be held back by Jost.

"Wait!" he screamed into the thunderous noise that surrounded them.

Then, in an instant, the sound was gone.

An eerie silence filled the half-crushed tent as the last of the debris settled. Slowly, Jayden wiggled her fingers, flexed her toes and ankles, and pushed herself into a sitting position. Her eyes took in everything, but her brain couldn't comprehend what she was seeing. She couldn't grasp that there were nurses and doctors—people she knew—buried under the snow and ice in front of her.

A whimper brought it all rushing in.

She shoved Jost's hand from her shoulder and rushed towards the mound of debris. Careful not to climb on it, lest she stand on a person and crush them further, she started at the side, clawing through it with her bare hands, determined to release those she'd seen buried in there. They might have a chance at surviving if she could get them out of that frozen tomb.

She pushed at rocks that were too heavy for her to lift and nodded her thanks when Jost joined her in the effort. She scraped at snow and sharp shards of ice. Finally, she reached a hand, outstretched and gloved, with the strap of an ice axe wrapped around the wrist. She didn't recall seeing anyone dressed for the outdoors inside when the tent had collapsed, and the only explanation her mind could grasp was that someone out on the paths had been swept back in along with the rest of the debris.

She worked swiftly, freeing the form until she could drag it out of the hole and turn it over. Then she screamed.

"No!"

Rebecca's head hung at a sickening angle, her throat severed in a jagged cut more than halfway through. Blood dripped from the ice axe hanging from her wrist. The brown eyes that had laughed at her concern less than half an hour ago were open and stared up at her, unseeing. They'd never see anything again.

CHAPTER 1

Rhian Phillips spun her pen on the desk while she waited for her colleagues to filter into the room and take their places. Her boss, Rachel Webster, would be there exactly on time for the meeting. She always was. And as always, Rhian tried to be there five minutes before. Not that it had curried any favours with the intimidating woman, but, still, it hadn't done her any harm either. Sometimes that was the best you could hope for in the cutthroat world that was marketing and advertising at Webster, Spencer, and Cline—London's leading advertising company—and when the managing partner was not only your boss but your stepmum. Impressions had to be made to the rest of the staff. Not to Rachel.

"Hey, Rhi. So what's this all about?" Joe Gert asked as the conference table and the twelve chairs around it slowly started to fill up. He was one of the senior account managers and had been her mentor when she'd first started.

Rhian shrugged. "No idea. I got the call to come up same as you and everyone else, Joe."

"No insider scoop?"

Rhian snorted a quick laugh. "'Fraid not." If anything, Rhian was always the last in the know. Rachel didn't divulge anything so she couldn't be accused of giving her privileged information. Yet the rest of the staff shied away from her because they all suspected she knew more than they did or was reporting back to Rachel all the time. It was…irksome. Tiring. *Maybe it's time to spread my wings and move on*, she thought—not for the first time either. Trying to live up to Rachel's expectations and standards was just as exhausting as trying to ignore the stigma of non-existent nepotism from her workmates.

"We've got good news and bad news, people." Rachel straight-armed the door open and let it swing shut behind her with a loud bang. She blustered through the room to the head of the table and dropped a heavy stack of files onto the veneer-covered surface. "Where do you want me to start?"

She cast a slightly menacing look around the room. Her brown eyes looked so fierce that Rhian had always been just a little scared of her as she'd grown up—first spending weekends, school holidays, and special occasions with her dad and this woman, and then living with them permanently after her mum had died. Still, she wasn't all bad. Rachel had been there for her when her dad hadn't.

Rhian shook her head and snapped herself away from the hurt. Not going there again.

"Start us off with the bad news, Rach," Joe said.

"Right-o. Joe's going to be a daddy."

"I said the bad news." There was a grin on Joe's lips.

"I know," Rachel shot back and her expression dared him to dispute her. He sat quietly, his grin broadening. "It means the rest of us are going to have to work harder to make up for you being brain-dead from sleep deprivation and hormones."

"I thought it was women who got hormones when they were pregnant?" Dave Roper sat at the far end of the table.

Rhian snorted, tucked her hair behind her ears, and started doodling on her pad. Her interest in the workplace banter had long since fizzled away to nothing. But she dutifully kept sneaking glances around the room, waiting for Rachel to get to the point.

Rachel pointed to Joe's face and the sloppy grin there. He looked a little stupid and a lot happy. "Do I really need to say any more?" She waited for the titters around the table to subside. "Seriously, Joe, congrats. I know this is something you and Stacey have been trying at for a long time. I'm really happy for you." She patted his hand. "You stupid idiot."

Joe laughed loudly. "Thanks, boss."

She dipped her head and cleared at him and cleared her throat. "So, on to the good news. Patagonia." She met everyone's gaze around the table. "Who can tell me about Patagonia?"

The silence around the room was deafening.

"No one? Really?" Rachel asked incredulously. "Rhian?"

Rhian looked up, eyebrows raised in question. "Huh?"

"Are we distracting you?"

Rhian's cheeks burned. "Sorry, I was just making some notes about something I have to do after the meeting." She cleared her throat and hoped Rachel couldn't see the crappy sketches of climbing knots all over the paper in front of her. "What did you ask me?"

The look on Rachel's face said she knew Rhian was lying. "Patagonia."

"What about it?"

"Seems no one here knows anything about it. Do you?"

"It's the region of South America that bridges Chile and Argentina down the length of the Andes mountains to the southern tip," Rhian said. "It's the southernmost point of the world outside of Antarctica. It's made up of glaciers, mountains, volcanoes, forest wilderness, marshes, lakes, desert, and steppes. It's vast, it's wild, and it's desolate. The weather's extreme, and the winds ferocious. And the glacier is one of the very few left on earth that is still expanding."

"Thank you. What about the company?"

Rhian frowned again, as did everyone else at the table. "You mean the clothing company?"

Rachel nodded.

"They make some awesome outdoor equipment. I've got one of their down jackets. Brilliant. Why?"

Rachel slid files across the desk surface to everyone. "Patagonia, the company, has hired us to run a new marketing campaign. They want to grow their appeal to women. As we all know, when it comes to clothes, women spend more and more often than men do. Also, women are becoming increasingly active in extreme sports and the outdoors. This expansion makes a lot of sense. So they're sponsoring a reality TV show that will be based in Patagonia, the country, and will feature their gear. The Argentinian tourist board is putting up the other half of the funds needed as a way to promote tourism in Patagonia."

"Is this an existing TV show that they're starting to sponsor?" Claire Sheffield, Dave Roper's assistant, asked.

"It's brand new, people." Murmurs went around the table. Rachel ignored them and pointed to the files. "Page one," she said, flipping open her own file and holding up the A4 page with the title *The Amazing Climb.*

Rhian cocked her head to the side, opened the folder, and quickly scanned the first few pages as Rachel carried on talking. Her excitement and curiosity grew with each detail. *Oh my God. This is...brilliant.*

"The show will feature climbers from all over the world competing for a fantastic prize—"

"Which is?" Dave asked.

"Yet to be disclosed," Rachel said. "And it will feature climbs and challenges in Patagonia—"

"Where and how many?" Claire asked.

"Yet to be disclosed," Rachel said again.

"There are too many unknowns, Rach. I say it's too risky for them," Joe said.

"Riskier than you know, Joe. There are still lots of details to work out—which we will—and lots of things to be sorted—which we'll take care of. But what you all need to know now is that we've been hired to produce this TV show."

Rhian grinned. A climbing TV show in Patagonia. Heaven.

"Are you insane?" Claire, Joe, and Dave demanded at the same time.

"We're a marketing firm," Claire continued, "not a production company."

"Yeah, we don't do this kind of thing, Rachel," Joe said. "We're not geared up for it."

"That's not entirely true, Joe," Rhian said. Rachel glanced at her but didn't interrupt. Rhian wasn't sure what that meant, but she'd had a point, so she was going to make it. "We do commercials and infomercials all the time. The idea of producing or creating in the medium isn't a foreign notion for us."

Rachel's lips slid into a satisfied smirk as she offered Rhian a nod of approval. Rhian squared her shoulders and straightened her back.

Joe scoffed. "That's not even in the same league as this kind of shit. You're talking months of prep, months of filming—on location. You're talking... Shit, I don't even know half of what you're talking about to pull off a project like this."

"Sure you do. We break it down into chunks like we do with every big project we take on. We all have our strengths, Joe." Rhian looked at him steadily, assessing his real concern about the project. It didn't take much to figure it out. He was about to become a father. He didn't want to take on a huge project that might take him away from home.

One less for me to compete with, then.

The thought struck her out of the blue. Compete with? She didn't compete with these people. She just did her job and kept her head down. Why was she even thinking about competing with them to take this on?

"Yeah, we do have our strengths," Joe retorted. "In marketing and advertising, not TV production. Not in making films. Not in distributing them to the masses."

"We don't need to worry about that," Rachel said. "Patagonia has signed a deal with Amazon for the worldwide distribution of the show."

Dave whistled. "Nice."

"Exactly. This is going to be big, ladies and gentlemen. Massive. It's an opportunity for us to take the company in a new direction. To try something new, something exciting, something that will put Webster, Spencer, and Cline on the map in a whole new market. Media markets are changing at lightning pace out there, people. This is our chance to stake a claim in it."

The energy was rolling off Rachel in waves, and for the first time she could remember, it didn't make Rhian want to jump out of the way. She was being swept along with it. She was thinking about her colleagues as competition because she wanted this project. She wanted it to be hers. She wanted Patagonia, and she wanted the chance to show them she could do something they were all afraid to try.

"What's the format of the TV show?" Rhian asked.

"Sixteen contestants. Amateur climbers from all different backgrounds. International pool, not just UK climbers." Rachel's gaze locked on Rhian as though no one else in the room.

"Recruitment method?"

Rachel hitched her eyebrow. "Social media would probably be the best place to start."

Rhian scribbled some notes across her pad, the first time in a long while she'd used her pen in a meeting for something other than spinning it or doodling. "Timescale?"

"It's March now. Filming starts in a little over six months, and we have to get this together by then."

"Six?" Joe cried. "You've got to be joking. We'd need at least a year to do this. If we even could."

"We've got six months," Rachel said again. Her tone made it perfectly clear that there would be no negotiation on this. It was a done deal. Rachel had decided, and the steely look in her eyes told them all she would damn well pull it off by herself if they didn't get on-board with it. Rhian had no doubt she could. She couldn't remember a single thing Rachel had failed at once she put her mind to it. But this time, she wouldn't have to. This time, Rhian was going to pull it off. *What was it she used to say when I was little? 'Shoot for the moon, kid. Even if you miss, you'll land amongst the stars.'*

"We can't do this, Rachel," Claire said from the other end of the table.

Rachel frowned and opened her mouth to speak—

"Yes, we can," Rhian said. "We can do this if we work together as a team." She pointed to the packets in front of them. "If we all take on different aspects of the project, there is nothing in it that we haven't done before. On a smaller scale, granted. But we have done it all before."

A crowd of scowling faces stared back at her. No doubt they were wondering just who the fuck she thought she was, talking to them like this. Trying to convince them. That was Rachel's job. Rachel, who was currently sitting back in her chair, hands clasped behind her head, and watching Rhian like the cat that had got the cream. And the tuna. And the catnip. *What the hell's going on with her?* Rhian shook her head to focus on the group, rather than Rachel. She didn't have time to worry about that. She didn't have time to worry about anything if they were going to pull this together.

"Joe," she said, "you've had the most contact with crews doing infomercials and the like. I'll need you to pull together the film crew. We need people who are capable of climbing the mountains with our contestants and guides too. They'll be filming on ropes, across the glaciers, and camping side by side with everyone else."

"Do not land us with any divas, or I swear to God the baby won't be the only thing keeping you awake in six months' time," Rachel added as Joe stared at Rhian, his mouth hanging open. She held his gaze, but she could see Rachel grinning out of the corner of her eye. "Okay?" she asked with just a flicker of a glance to check in with Rachel. Was she really okay with her taking charge like this?

Joe also glanced at Rachel, obviously waiting for her to react. She didn't.

"Joe?" Rhian asked again, her voice a little softer. She licked her lips. She needed the team to agree, and Joe was the most senior team member in the room. If he went along with this, if he agreed with her, they all would. She knew it.

Joe sighed and scribbled some notes. "Got it."

The thrill of victory skittered down her spine. She felt like whooping and dancing in her chair, but restrained herself. That kind of behaviour wouldn't help her cause any, no matter how much her inner self was running laps around the room and singing "The Eye of The Tiger".

"Thank you," she said in the most professional voice she could muster before turning to Dave. "Your expertise on branding, product placement, and selection will be invaluable."

Dave smiled and nodded. "I can do that."

"Every one of our contestants will need to be kitted out in Patagonia products. Their sales department should be able to tell which are the best ones for the task ahead and to start putting it all together."

"Do they only produce clothes?"

"No," Rhian said. "They do some awesome packs and sleeping bags too."

Dave nodded.

"We'll need to showcase every product we possibly can," Rachel added.

"Of course," Dave said as though it went without saying. To his credit, Rhian agreed. He'd done this stuff long enough.

Claire and most of the others around the table were scribbling notes on their pads as fast as they could.

"Well, Rhian, since you seem to be taking charge of this project, you'll need to get started on the recruitment drive and find the right guide, as she'll have to host it too. But most importantly, find me the right contestants."

"Me? You don't want to do that part?" Rhian was shocked. Contestants. Guides. The host! This show, and therefore their entire campaign, was going to live and die based on the people on camera. It didn't matter how beautiful the landscape was going to be or how good the products were if no one watched because the show turned out to be boring. "You want me to take on such a critical role? Why?"

The bigger question was why was she balking? She wanted this project, yet her natural inclination to fall into Rachel's shadow was once again

14

asserting itself. That and the fact she'd never taken on such a major, project-defining role as this one. Nerves were a bitch.

"Because no one else here's even climbed a ladder much less a wall or a rock face," Rachel said.

"Hey!" Dave groused. "I climbed a ladder to go into the loft the other day."

"You told me you fell off coming back down and nearly ended up at the bottom of the stairs," Rachel said.

Dave grinned sheepishly. "You don't forget anything, do you?"

"Never." Rachel wagged a finger at him before turning her attention back to Rhian. "So, Rhian, that makes you our resident climbing expert. You've been climbing rock faces and indoor walls as long as I've known you. I've listened to you talk about climbing until chalk dust was coming out of my ears, and I know you go off and join climbing tours every time you go on holiday. Wasn't it Alaska you just got back from?"

Rhian nodded. Just a couple of weeks ago, as a matter of fact.

"And Spain the time before that?"

She nodded again, slightly taken aback that Rachel remembered so many details. She always seemed so disinterested when Rhian was talking to her about it.

"Well, since you're the only one of us that knows the difference between a grade 5 and a grade 6 ice wall, that makes you the right person for this task." Rachel's eyes softened a little as she looked at her, and Rhian saw what she needed. Belief. Rachel believed she could do it.

"Shoot for the moon," she whispered under her breath. Rhian cleared her throat and met Rachel's gaze. "Okay."

Rachel's smile spread across her lips slowly. "Good." She waved her hand, palm up, for Rhian to continue.

Rhian swallowed. "Dave, we'll need to liaise about climbing and safety equipment—"

"Surely that's the health-and-safety guy's responsibility!" Dave protested.

Rhian lifted the packet Rachel had given them. She'd only scanned most of the contents, but she'd picked up more of the salient details than the rest of the team while they'd been arguing with Rachel. "The guide—who I'll recruit—will be in charge of health and safety on and off set," Rhian said, her cheeks burning. She was so unaccustomed to being the centre of attention, it made her uncomfortable. It was something she had to get over. "I'll be working with them directly. I'll have to, and so I'll have the requirements for you before long. I can probably work up a rudimentary list for you right now, to be honest, but there's enough to be going on with before we start on the shopping."

Dave scribbled on his pad with a nod.

"Thanks." She turned to look further down the table. "Mellissa, logistics? We'll need travel schedules for each of our applicants and then the contestants, film crew, and all equipment, vehicles in Patagonia, etc. You know the drill."

"I do," Mellissa said in a clipped, efficient voice. She'd been with the company since almost the beginning, working first as Rachel's assistant and then as Rhian's upon returning from maternity leave a few years back. Organisation and logistics were definitely her specialities.

"Martin, web design. Can you liaise with Dave about the rebranding?" She pointed to the file. "It looks like we'll need to give Patagonia's website a complete overhaul. The online shop they've got at the moment is looking a little dated and heavy. Pics need streamlining. The usual."

"No problem."

"It would also be a good idea for you to liaise with Rhian about the promotion and recruitment drive," Rachel said. "Social media will be a great way to get the message out for applications. Can you help her set that up?"

"With pleasure," Martin said.

Rhian ran through the rest of the file. Rachel had already broken the project down into the relevant tasks to get started with. All she had to do at this point was dole them out and make sure everyone was happy and ready to walk out of the room and start running with the project. They didn't have any time to waste.

"Okay, people, let's get this ball rolling," Rachel said when Rhian reached the end. "I want progress reports on my desk...and Rhian's...by Friday lunchtime." Everyone got up, shuffling their papers and scratching their heads. "Rhian, you got a minute?"

Rhian nodded and hung back in her seat while the rest of the team almost ran out the door.

"You okay?" Rachel asked.

Rhian smiled. "Yeah. Thank you for the opportunity—"

Rachel waved her hand. "Don't. You earned it. If you'd worked anywhere else, you'd have had the chance a long time ago. You know that, I know that, and now none of those idiots can dispute that. So don't thank me for holding you back." She smiled fondly at her. "In all honesty, I've been waiting for years for you to show me what you did in that meeting. That you want to be here. I needed to see that fire in your eyes, that excitement, and the desire to win. I've been waiting to see that you wanted more than just clocking in and clocking off, kiddo." She sighed. "I was about ready to give up on you."

The euphoric thrill of the meeting vanished, replaced by a feeling she was much more familiar with—that she never quite measured up, that she wasn't good enough, that she was unworthy.

"I almost thought you were ready to up sticks and take off for pastures new."

Rhian blinked but met her gaze. "I almost was."

Rachel's mouth twisted into a knowing half-smile. "Well, you were always brutally honest."

"I wonder where I learnt that skill."

"Touché," Rachel conceded. "I'm glad you didn't. When they first approached me about this project, I knew it was perfect for us. For you. I wanted this for a lot of reasons, but mostly, I wanted it because I knew you'd love it."

"A gift? Not like you, Rach."

Rachel lifted an eyebrow. "Am I such a wicked stepmother?"

Rhian chuckled. "Only when you wanted to be."

"My, my, you have put on those training claws, haven't you?"

"Sorry—"

"Don't apologise." Rachel's fond gaze hardened. "You'll need to grow more than training claws for this project, kiddo. If you apologise for the slightest thing, you'll never get through it. So, on that note—" She opened the folder in front of her and pulled out a piece of paper before sliding it across the desk to Rhian. "This is a list of tour companies and guides in the area that Patagonia would be willing-slash-happy to work with."

Rhian took the page and looked it over, giving herself a moment to adjust to Rachel's typically whiplash-inducing change of pace. Very few names were on it. "Only three? Is this it?"

Rachel nodded.

"Why so few? What's the politics here?"

"Nothing political. Gender. These are the only women with good reputations who lead groups of climbers close by. They know the area and get people up and back safely. On an expedition like this, that's important. We need to minimise the risks where we can."

"I know. The inherent risks are great enough as it is."

"Exactly."

Rhian looked at the names again. "They're really serious about appealing to the female market?"

"As a heart attack."

Rhian let the corner of her lips slip into a small half-smile. "Looking at them and their stats online is all well and good, Rach. But I think I'm going to need to go and meet them before I commit to anyone."

Rachel smiled. "I wouldn't have it any other way." She slid an envelope across the table to her. "You leave tomorrow afternoon. Returning in a week's time. That should be enough time to meet with these three and make a decision. I'll feed Rufus for you while you're gone." She grimaced even as she offered to feed Rhian's podgy, ginger tomcat.

"What would you have done if I hadn't agreed to this crazy scheme of yours?"

"I'd have thought of something." Her eyes seemed deadly serious. "You fought for this. Are you telling me now that you don't really want it?"

Rhian looked at the page in her hand and the envelope sitting where it had stopped on the wood. Patagonia—the place she'd longed to visit for years. The climbing, the adventure, the outdoors...and all while getting paid. Nah. This job was made for her. "I want it."

"Good. Now, on that note, we've both got a lot of work to do. What're you doing for dinner tonight?"

Rhian ran a hand over her face, then her fingers through her hair. "Probably a burger on my way home to pack."

"Pft. Come to the house. I've got a lasagne defrosting for tonight."

"Erm, no thanks."

Rachel scowled at her. "He misses you, you know."

Rhian clenched her teeth. "He made the choice, Rach. You know he did. He can't pick and choose the parts of my life he has a hand in. If he can't accept me as I am, then he doesn't accept me at all. He threw me out of the house and told me not to come back until I wasn't a perverted freak anymore." She covered her hand over her mouth and held her breath a moment before she said, "I'm still a perverted freak, Rach. I'm still gay, and I'm still me, so why should I go back there?"

"Because he loves you, and he's sorry." Rachel's eyes were soft, brimming with tears.

"Then he needs to tell me that, don't you think?"

"How can he if you won't even talk to him? If you won't even let him show you he's trying?"

"Is he? Is he trying? Because I haven't seen or heard anything from him since."

"He's tried to call. At least half a dozen times."

"In five years. That doesn't even make every birthday and Christmas, Rachel."

"I know. But you haven't even picked up the phone whenever he's tried. And he's too proud to do any more, Rhi."

"Then he doesn't love me enough." Rhian slid the page through her fingers from one end to the other, then back again. Her eyes stung, but she refused to cry about it anymore. It was done. Her father had made his choice, and now they all had to live with it.

He couldn't accept that she was a lesbian, and no amount of badgering by Rachel was going to convince her that he'd changed his mind about that. Not after the things he said that night. Not after what he did. He was probably only making the token effort to keep Rachel off his back. He always called her a nagging harpy when she got on a roll. Well, that wasn't the kind of apology that would make up for what he did.

She had her pride too, and she refused to be someone she wasn't to keep him happy. It wasn't a sacrifice he'd made for her when he'd fallen in love with Rachel despite being married and having a family. He'd done what he wanted, been the man he was, and sod 'em all. Well, she was his daughter. So sod him.

"Every time you rebuff him it... Well, it's like another piece of him dies."

"And you think it doesn't kill me too? You think it doesn't rip my heart out a little more every time, knowing that my own father can't stand me? That he hates me because of something I can't change, that I can't do anything about?" She shook her head. "He made his choice and his feelings perfectly clear when he hit me and threw me out of the house." She lifted her hand towards her face but let it drop before she could touch the cheek her father had slapped. In the dead of night sometimes, she could still feel the way her flesh had burned under that blow. "I love him. Despite knowing that he hates everything about me, I still love him. But I can't trust a word that comes out of his mouth anymore."

Rachel's hand closed over her own, stilling her fingers. "It's okay, honey."

"I'm sorry if it's causing you problems with him."

Rachel barked out a harsh laugh as she wiped at her eyes. "Rhi, I'm big enough and ugly enough to take care of myself. And I'm more than capable of handling your twat of a father. Excuse the language."

Rhian sniggered. "Don't worry. I've heard the term before."

"I'm sure." She chuckled along with her. "I'm sorry."

Rhian shrugged. "Not your fault. He—"

"No, I'm sorry for how I froze that night. I've wanted to say that ever since you came out to us and all I could do was sit there and stare while your father turned into a man I didn't even recognise." She ran her fingers through her dark hair, now shot through liberally with silver, letting the strands ripple down her shoulders.

"It was more than five years ago," Rhian said quietly.

Rachel leant back in the chair next to Rhian and ran a hand down her back as she hunched over the desk. "Long overdue, then." She continued to rub Rhian's back in small, soft circles.

Rhian couldn't look at her. She knew there'd be tears in her eyes, and she knew she wouldn't be able to hold back her own if she saw Rachel all emotional too.

"I'm so proud of you." Her hand disappeared from Rhian's back as she stood, then she felt the pressure of Rachel's kiss on the top of her head. Rachel's hands curled over her shoulders and squeezed tight. "I know this is a huge project, kiddo. And I know I haven't always been the best when it comes to giving you the chances you should have had in this place. But this is it, Rhian. This is your chance to shine, and to show not just me but the rest of the bastards in this place exactly what I know you can do. Because you can. I'm sure of it."

Rhian put her hand over Rachel's and pulled until she was hugging her from behind.

"There's so much riding on this, I can't… Doesn't matter. I know you'll do your best and you'll make it work."

"Thanks." When Rachel squeezed her shoulders tighter, Rhian hung her head and drew in a shuddering breath. They stayed like that for a few minutes before Rachel nudged her and pulled her arms back.

"Okay, enough of the mushy stuff. Get back to work."

Rhian chuckled. "Yes, boss."

"Make me proud, kiddo," Rachel murmured.

Rhian looked up, tears spilling onto her cheeks.

Rachel sniffed loudly and blustered out of the room again, muttering *bloody kid* under her breath. Rhian wiped her face on her sleeve and determinedly pushed away the emotions threatening to engulf her. Rachel had faith in her. Rachel. Her Rachel thought she could pull off a project. And not just any old project. Just the biggest, most amazing project the company had ever landed.

"Fucking hell," she whispered, popped open the envelope, and peeked in at the tickets and travel itinerary. She wriggled around in her seat.

"I'm going to Patagonia!"

CHAPTER 2

"Northwest Electrical, may I take your name, please?"

"Jim Brown."

"Good afternoon, Mr Brown. I'm Jayden. How can I help you today?"

"The 'leccy's gone off."

"Your electricity is off. When did it go off, Mr Brown?"

"About two minutes before I got on the phone to you. I've been on hold for half an hour now."

Jayden glanced at the screen and saw he'd been on hold for only ten minutes. *The muzak's bad, mate, but I've heard worse.* "I'm very sorry about that, Mr Brown. I need to ask a few questions to try and figure out what's happened. Is that okay?"

"If it gets someone out here to sort it, fire away."

"Is it all the electricity or just say the lights or just the plugs?"

"Everything's dead, love."

"And if you look outside, can you see street lights, or lights or appliances on in other houses?"

"Hang on." Crackling down the line indicated he'd put the phone down. Distant muttering and cursing followed before his voice was clear again. "The street lights are on, and it looks like the woman across the street's trying to compete with Blackpool's Illuminations over there. Every light in the house must be on. That enough?"

"Yes, thank you. Do you know where the fuse box is for your house?"

"Under the stairs."

"Okay. We need to take a look at the fuses and see if they've tripped. If that's what's caused your power to go off, then we should just be able to reset it, and you'll be good to go again."

"Bloody hell. Hang on a minute."

Jayden glanced at the clock. 4:45 p.m. Only fifteen minutes until she was finished for the day. *Let's hope I can drag this call out that long. I don't fancy any more today.*

"Right," Mr Brown said, huffing. "I can see all the fuses, and they're all where they should be. The lights and the telly are still off. Now what?"

"Okay, Mr Brown, let me just check a few details with your account to make sure there aren't any issues or any problems in the area." She quickly paged through several screens and closed her eyes when she located the problem. "Mr Brown?"

"Yes. You sending an engineer round?"

"No, I'm afraid I won't be able to do that. When was the last time you topped up your electricity?"

"Eh? You what?"

"You're on an electricity metre. You go to the shop to put money on the key and then top up your account, right?"

"I don't. That's bloody daft, that is."

"Your account's been on a metre for four years, Mr Brown. Does your wife normally take care of the top-up? Or someone else in the house? Perhaps you could ask them when it was last loaded up?"

"Can't ask the bitch. She's gone and fucked off with her fancy fella."

Shit. "I'm really sorry to hear that, Mr Brown. Looking at your details, though, and given what we've looked at, it looks like your metre just needs topping up with credit to bring your electric back on."

"How the bloody hell am I supposed to do that?"

"You take the key and go to the nearest shop that does top-ups." She tapped a few keys on the computer. "There's a shop about a hundred metres from your house that does them. If you go there with the key, they'll put the credit on it, then you insert it into the metre, and your electric will come back on."

"And the heating?"

"Are you on electric heaters?"

"No, gas."

"Erm, then you'll need to speak to the gas people about your gas problems, sir."

"Bitch. I bet she's got that on one of these bloody metre things an' all, hasn't she?"

"I'm sorry I couldn't be more help to you, Mr Brown."

He sighed heavily down the line. "Not your fault, love. I'm sorry I'm being a grumpy old bastard. I just don't know where anything is or how it all works. She took care of everything in the house, you see. I went to work and earned the money. Now she's gone off and left me, and I don't know what to do without her."

"It must be really hard for you, Mr Brown."

"Listen to me blathering on. You don't need to be hearing my sob story."

"It's all right. We're a help desk after all. Here to help."

He laughed, but it sounded sad. "Not this kind of help. Anyway, sorry to bother you. And thanks."

"Not a problem. I hope you get everything sorted out."

"Aye."

She rang off the call and watched as the clock ticked over to five o'clock. She signed out of the phone system, logged off her computer, and slung her bag over her shoulder as she made her way to the door.

"Jayden, we've talked about your call times before," Steph, the twenty-one-year-old office manager, said before she could open it.

Jayden turned and looked at her. "And?"

"You know we have targets we need to meet."

"And customers who need to be satisfied. Sometimes that takes longer than five minutes."

"Not if you follow the script."

"Yes, if you follow the script. Sometimes they have junk blocking access to the metres they need to read, or fuses to flip. Sometimes they're old, and they don't move very quickly."

"Then you should gently encourage them."

Jayden shook her head and turned her back on the young woman. "Whatever," she said as she shoved open the door and left the petty issues of the office behind her.

The evening sun on the rare spring sunny day beat down on the busy pavement, and the odour of tarmac, diesel fumes, and sweat hung in the air. She crossed the road to the bike rack, slipping her helmet and sunglasses on as she glanced across the street for traffic. She quickly unlocked her bike, put the saddle back on, and clipped into the pedals as she set off.

Manchester in rush hour was no place to be. Manchester in a car in rush hour was a hell she couldn't stand. She cranked the pedals hard, building momentum as she clung to the curb down Piccadilly, and within a few minutes she was coasting around the roundabout and onto the A6. She had places to be and people to see. Well, one person, actually. But an important one.

The nursing home had sprung up from the swimming baths she and her sister had played in as children. A place they'd begged her mother to let them go every chance they had. A place their mum had eventually told them to stop bothering her about. Now it was an expensive private care facility for those suffering from dementia and Alzheimer's disease. It was clean. It was well decked out. But it was still clinical, as all care facilities were. It was still sterile and had the lingering smell of antiseptic wherever you turned. Still, that was better than the other odours that could be dominating the place.

Jayden pulled up outside the front door, secured her bike to the fence rails, and stowed her helmet and gloves in her bag. She used the corner of her T-shirt to wipe her sweaty brow, re-secured her hair with a band at the nape of her neck, and pushed the buzzer for entry. One of the nurses waved at her as she signed in at reception and slinked over to her.

"Don't you drive?"

Jayden frowned at her. "I'm sorry?"

"Every time I see you, you're on your bike. Don't you drive?"

"Oh, well, I have a license, but I don't see the point in having a car. I like being on my bike. It's easy to get around everywhere, and it keeps me in shape." She shrugged, wondering what else the woman wanted to know. Her inside leg measurement, perhaps.

"I can see that." She smiled wickedly and held out her hand. "I'm Debbie, I've just been assigned as your mum's primary care worker."

Jayden's cheeks warmed under Debbie's direct gaze as it flicked up and down her body long enough to both make her feel uncomfortable and help her ignore the empty feeling in the pit of her stomach. The one where happiness used to be. The one that had sat empty for almost a year.

"Oh, right." Jayden shuffled her bag to her other hand and took Debbie's hand. "Jayden Harris."

"The mountain climber, I know."

Not anymore. Not since she'd flown out of Everest base camp and walked away from the Nepalese branch of Adventure Trekkers, much to her sister's—and co-owner's—dismay. But Fen simply couldn't be in two places at once—Patagonia and Nepal—and Jayden wasn't fit to be in any place at all. So Adventure Trekkers Nepal was no more. It wasn't the only outfit that had ceased operating out of Everest's base camp in the wake of the avalanche. Far from it.

"So you're working with my mum?"

Debbie cleared her throat. "Yes, yes I am. She's had a good day today. She wanted a bath earlier, and she had a walk around the garden after lunch. She seems happy."

"That's good."

"Yes. I'm sure she'll be glad to see you. Want me to show you through?"

Jayden shook her head. "I'm good, thanks." She pulled open the door to the corridor that led to the main sitting area. The patio doors onto a small walled-in courtyard were open. The scent of lavender and roses drifted in on the warm breeze. People sat in chairs around the edges of the room, and she couldn't help but think how it looked more like a doctor's waiting room than the place where every one of these people lived. A young carer wandered around the room with a trolley full of plastic cups, a big jug of water, and a kettle full of tea. She asked everyone who was awake if they wanted a drink and supplied them. Most were asleep. Or pretending to be.

Can't blame 'em. I'd want to sleep through this life too.

Michelle Harris was asleep—really asleep—in the far corner, her back to the open door, her hands wrapped around a Maltesers box, and a scowl painted on her face. Jayden snickered as she sat in the empty chair beside her and pulled her phone out of her pocket. While her mother slept, she replied to a message from her sister with a picture of their sleeping mother and started to scroll through Facebook.

Over the past nine months since Michelle had moved into the nursing home, Jayden had quickly learnt not to wake her mother. It never went well. It was far better to let her sleep. Even if she slept through the whole visit. Jayden had long since come to the conclusion that it really didn't matter. Not to her mum, anyway. She didn't remember she had a visitor from one moment to the next, and increasingly Michelle didn't recognise her. The visits were for her own sake. Both Jayden and her sister knew it.

A message popped up on her screen.

Don't let her sleep through the whole visit. I wanna Skype with you guys. I'm back at base, waiting.

Jayden rolled her eyes. Half a world away, and her big sister was still trying to boss her around.

You know what she's like if I wake her. She gets in an awful mood. I'm not doing that to her just because you've finally gotten your arse back to semicivilisation at a decent hour!

Bitch.

And?

Seriously, is she okay?

Jayden looked at her mum with a critical eye. She looked thinner. The tall, wiry frame she and her mother shared was beginning to look little more than skin and bones. Her dirty-blond hair, also like Jayden's, was normally full of curls, long, and a little wild. Today it looked lank, perhaps a little greasy. Strange since she'd supposedly had a bath earlier. But maybe she'd bathed and not let them wash her hair. It wouldn't be the first time the stubborn woman had done something like that. Her clothes were clean, even though her cardigan was on inside out. It was highly likely that at some point throughout the day, Michelle had taken it off and put it back on herself that way.

She looks fine. They're taking good care of her here.

Good job. It costs a fucking fortune.

Good job your company's doing so well then, isn't it?

It isn't just my company, Jay, and you know it. Whether you're out here working with me or not, it's still half yours. Argentina, me, Nepal, you. Remember? So, when are you getting your arse back outside?

Ten past never gonna happen.

LMAO. I'll believe that only on my deathbed, Mogo.

Jayden scowled at the use of the nickname Fen had christened her with when they were kids and started out climbing. Mogo—short for Mountain Goat—had stuck around longer than any of the other nicknames they'd used for each other over the years. And way longer than Jayden wished it had.

Fuck off.

Come out here and make me. You need these mountains just as much as I do.

Jayden chuckled at the familiar yet childish banter. But Fen was right, and as much as the thought of stepping foot on the ice again terrified her, Jayden knew it. She did need them. Almost as much as the air she breathed. She wasn't going to admit it. But she knew it.

Leave me alone, I'm doing important work here.

What? Playing games on your phone?

Bitch.

Get your own insults, Baby Sister, and stop stealing what's mine.

Ignoring you now.

Yeah, yeah. We'll see.

Jayden shook her head and switched apps, opening up her games. She smiled as she made sure her mum was still asleep. Fen was right. She was over in Argentina, running their company and sending back all the funds they needed to keep their mum in the facility Jayden had chosen. Fen was working tour after tour to make ends meet. Jayden worked for just enough to cover her own rent and food money while she sat and watched it all drift by. It wasn't fair to Fen, and Jayden was honest enough to admit that. But when was life ever fair?

"Who are you?"

Jayden snapped out of her reverie and looked at her mum, a big smile slipping onto her face as she turned. "It's me."

Michelle scowled, flailing out and catching Jayden's cheek in a noisy slap. "Get away from me! You're robbing me! Help! Help! She's robbing me! Help me!"

Jayden jumped up from the chair and moved away quickly as her mum's fists and feet set into attack mode. "It's all right. I'm not robbing you. I'm not going to hurt you. It's okay."

"Help! Help! Someone please help me!" Michelle rolled her head against the back of the chair, screwed her eyes shut, and held her hands out in front of her in a gesture of surrender. "Please don't hurt me!"

"Mum, it's okay. It's just me. No one's going to hurt you. No one, I promise."

Debbie appeared at her side. "Maybe you should move out of sight. I'll try and get her to calm down a bit."

Jayden nodded and moved away. She backed up as far as the doorway and stood so that she could see into the room but not be easily seen by her mum. It took Debbie half an hour of gentle coaxing to get Michelle to calm down enough that she could leave her.

It wasn't the first time her mum hadn't recognised her, and it wouldn't be the last. It was quickly becoming the norm. She swallowed heavily and pushed away the feelings. There was more than enough time for those when she was alone.

Debbie approached her slowly, a gentle smile on her lips. "I'm not sure it would be a good idea to go back in tonight."

Jayden shook her head. "No, I'm sure it wouldn't." She didn't look away from her mum, now wandering about the room, picking up anything she could lift and looking at it against the light. "Thank you for calming her down."

"It's what I'm here for. Can I get you something before you go? A drink, maybe?"

"No thanks. I'm good." She pushed the strap of her backpack higher up her shoulder and slid her other arm through. "Thanks again for helping Mum." She didn't wait for Debbie to answer; she just strode off down the hallway and out the doors.

The sun was starting to set, but grief clung to her. She needed to shake it off, to get away from it. She needed the silence and the vastness she'd never found anywhere but the mountains. But the mountains were no longer her refuge. Now they were the stuff of her nightmares.

She clipped into her pedals again and zipped out of the car park, then turned off the direct route home to take a detour, turning and riding with no direction in mind, no destination to reach but exhaustion. The night held little allure for her anymore, and sleep was an infrequent visitor.

The roads had quietened somewhat, but traffic was still everywhere as she rode the miles until her thighs ached, her lungs burned, and her mind was blissfully quiet. Then, and only then, did she make her way to her flat. She shouldered her bike, climbed the stairs, and opened the door.

"Hi, honey, I'm home," she whispered to the empty, lonely space.

CHAPTER 3

Rhian was tired. The business-class seat on the plane was comfy enough, but even her headphones couldn't block out the wailing baby behind the bulkhead to the economy-class seats. For twenty non-stop hours. Rhian had no problem with children, as long as they were quiet and didn't approach her unless asked to. Okay, so she was fairly Victorian in her approach, seen and not heard, and all that. But what the hell? She hadn't subjected the world to her spawn, so why should she have the spawn of others thrust upon her?

The airport at El Calafate was a small one compared to Heathrow, but it had everything it needed. Passport control, duty-free, luggage carousels, and a clean toilet. Bonus.

She ran in to use the facilities. She swilled water over her face and peered into the mirror assessing the damage. Her grey eyes were bloodshot, and the sandpaper behind her eyelids wasn't helping. She gripped her shoulder-length blond hair, fastened it with a band, and slid it through the back of a baseball cap she'd stashed in her backpack.

She'd changed into dark blue denim shorts and a light green button-up shirt while still on the plane. They fit well over her slim frame, but the creases of travelling were impossible to miss. Ah well, not much she could do about it now. Not convinced she'd pass for human, she walked out of the bathroom and out of the airport and to seek her transportation.

Rachel had been thoughtful enough to organise her a Jeep and driver for the duration of her stay, so she didn't have to wait for a taxi or the bus to take her to El Chaltén, 220 km away. She would be forever grateful for this act of kindness. And the sleep.

Her driver, Carlos, seemed content to let her be after loading her bags in the back of the Jeep and offering her a bottle of water. She'd almost emptied it before succumbing to the gentle sway of the vehicle as they sped along the national road around the south-eastern shore of Lago Argentino—the largest freshwater lake in Argentina, fed by glacial meltwater, and a stunning turquoise blue—before turning onto Route 40.

"Miss Phillips."

Rhian shook awake slowly.

"Miss Phillips." Carlos's heavily accented voice broke through her weariness and tugged her back to the crisp sunshine that beat down on her. A swift wind tugged her hair all over as the topless Jeep motored along the ribbon of tarmac towards—

"Oh my God." Rhian stared ahead at her first glimpse of the towering sentinel that was Mount Fitz Roy. Streams of snow and ice clung to the cliff, and the formidable shadows of crags and overhangs disappeared into buttresses and crevasses. Its massive stone bulk stood tall and proud eleven thousand feet and growing over the flat plains of the steppes as they sped closer.

"The massif, Miss." Carlos pointed through the windscreen.

"So I see."

"I thought you would want to see."

"You thought right, Carlos. Thank you." She smiled but couldn't manage to tear her eyes away from the majestic beauty of Cerro Fitz Roy and the surrounding massif. It was spectacular. The sun was setting behind them and reflecting onto the jagged monolith, and its surrounding peaks turned the orange granite a palette of rose-pinks and golds. Slowly, the sun dipped lower until only the tip of Fitz Roy was lit, the jewel in the crown of the Chaltén massif.

"Does it always do that?" she asked, barely able to make herself heard over the roar of the wind.

Carlos laughed. "No, miss. Often you cannot see it for the clouds."

"Then I'm very lucky."

"Are you hungry?"

"Now that you mention it, yes. I'm starving."

He flashed her a smile. "I had my wife pack some things for us for the journey. Can you reach the blue bag on the back seat?"

Rhian turned in her chair and leant over to grab the bag and heft it forward. "It's heavy." She grunted. "What did she pack? The whole cow?"

Carlos chuckled. "No. But maybe the whole sheep."

Rhian opened her eyes wide and popped her mouth open in a comical mask of shock. "Please tell me she cooked it first."

"How do you like empanadas?"

"Never had one before."

"Sandwiches de miga?"

Rhian shook her head and started lifting packages from the bag. "I've had sandwiches from all over the world, though, so I'm guessing that'll be fine. What's the other one you said?"

"Empanadas?" he asked, and she nodded. "They are little pastries. Isabella makes the most delicious empanadas, with beautiful sweet lamb or cheese and corn." He waved at the little packet she was holding close to her nose. "Take one out. You'll love it, I'm sure."

The little pastry looked very similar to a small Cornish pasty. The filling was completely encased in a pastry crust with a sealed edge, like a circle folded in half. It smelled delicious. And Carlos was right. The meat inside was so tender it melted in her mouth. She moaned her appreciation before swallowing. "Carlos, if you ever divorce your wife, tell her I'll marry her if she'll make these for me."

He chuckled and picked one up from the open paper in her hand. "Maybe I ask her to teach you how to make them instead."

Rhian shrugged. "That could work too, I suppose." She popped the remaining bite of the pastry in her mouth and hunted through the bag for one of the sandwiches. The crustless, thin white bread was stuffed with wafer-thin slices of meat, lettuce, and tomato. "What kind of meat is this?"

Carlos took his gaze briefly off the road. "Wild boar. Do you like it?"

She nodded. "It's just like ham but a bit, I don't know, stronger maybe. More meaty or piggy. God, I must be tired. I'm not even talking sense anymore."

"I understand what you mean. When I was in England, I had your bacon and ham, and you're right. It does taste weak compared to this. This is full of flavour. Proper meat."

"When were you in England?"

"Hm, many years ago now. Maybe ten or twelve. It was before I married."

Rhian finished her sandwich and picked up another of the small pastries. "Were you there for work?" She bit into the cheese-and-corn-filled empanadas. "Oh my God, this is so good."

Carlos smiled again. "I will tell my wife how much you enjoyed her cooking when we get to El Chaltén tonight. She will be very pleased and no doubt send me with breakfast for you in the morning."

"You won't hear me complaining."

"Yes, I was in England to work. My family were sheep farmers for many generations, I went there to learn different ways of farming. I stayed for two years. After the second winter, I decided to come home and find a wife. It was time to, how you call it, make roots?"

"Yup. And she's called Isabella?"

"*Sí.*"

"Do you have children?"

He shook his head. Rhian thought he seemed sad. "Not yet. We have been married now for eight years, but still no little ones for us to spoil."

"Do you still farm?"

"No. My father left the farm to my elder brother when he died. He was a drunk with very bad luck at cards."

"So now you're a driver?"

He shrugged. "Now I do whatever I can to pay my bills and feed my wife. Today that is driving. Next week, who knows?"

"That's sad." Rhian grasped her water bottle and took a sip.

"That's life."

"Hm." She took another small drink, then put the lid back on. "It's still sad. Do you want me to get you a drink?"

He leant forward and pulled a small bottle out of the pocket on his door. "I have one, thank you."

"How long have you lived in El Chaltén, then, Carlos?"

"For five years now."

"And what's it like?"

"How do you mean?"

"Well, is it a good place to live?"

His smile stretched across his lips. "It is a wonderful place to live. It is a new town. It was only founded in 1985, and it is still growing. Still developing. There are around two thousand settlers in the town now, and many, many more during the summer when the tourists come to hike and climb. We are very proud of our town, and we work very, very hard to make sure it stays, how you say, pristine?"

"That's right. Pure, clean."

"Yes, pristine and preserve for the future. Only native species of plant and animal are found. There is not, how you say, dirt…no, ref…reuse… what is word?"

"Refuse? Rubbish?"

"*Sí*. No refuse. We recycle and have program to take away all refuse. Thank you."

"That's great. It sounds wonderful."

"It is beautiful. Did you know that Chaltén means 'smoking mountain'?"

"No."

"Most often times when you see Cerro Fitz Roy," he said, pointing to the magnificent giant, "it has snow or mist billowing from the summit in the wind and it looks like it is smoking. That is where this whole area gets its name from. El Chaltén. The smoking mountain."

"I can't wait to see your town."

"Tomorrow, weather will be good, and you can see El Chaltén. Tonight, not so much. Too much darkness when we arrive."

"No street lights?"

"*Sí*, some. But only very little."

"How much longer till we get there?"

"An hour or so. Maybe a little longer."

"I think I might take another nap." He nodded and kept his eyes ahead as she let her heavy eyelids slowly close to the sight of Mount Fitz Roy glistening in the moonlight.

CHAPTER 4

RHIAN SAT AT THE WINDOW in her room, sipping her coffee and staring out at El Chaltén. Low bungalows, Alpine-style lodges, and apex houses dotted the landscape, and the Fitz Roy loomed over them all. It reminded her of some of the great Alpine towns she'd been to over the years: Grindelwald or Zermatt. Not just places where the tourists stopped on their way to conquer the peaks they lived in the shadow of, towns that actually lived, breathed, and grew. El Chaltén was the same. It had an energy about it that crackled and made her feel alive.

Of course, that could be down to a good night's sleep and a great cup of coffee. But she was willing to give the town the benefit of the doubt.

It was almost eight a.m., and Carlos was due at any moment to take her to the first guide on the list, Sarah Matthews. She'd been leading groups over the Chaltén massif for the past eight years and had a sterling reputation. Four and a half stars on TripAdvisor, according to the notes Rachel had given her. Instead of setting her mind at ease, the ratings from the Internet site set her on edge. People were subjective, and websites with reviews were too easily manipulated, if you were canny enough to do so. No small business was good enough for eight years to maintain a rating that high. Not in the tourism industry. All it had to do was rain at the wrong time, and someone would complain on the Internet.

You're getting cynical in your old age, Rhi. She smirked to herself. Not that twenty-eight was old. Some days it just felt like it.

Carlos's Jeep pulled up outside, and he honked, waved at her window, and held up a bag.

Rhian chuckled. "Looks like you convinced your wife to feed me again," she said to herself then finished her coffee and grabbed her bag, plucked her key card from the switch beside the door, and hurried out to meet him. "Yum, yum, Carlos. What did you bring me?"

"Medialunas."

"And what's that?" She tossed her backpack on the back seat and climbed in.

"A little like a croissant, but shaped a little different. More like, how you say, 'tie'? They are sweeter too."

She opened the package. "Oh, cool. They look like bowties."

"Sí, bowtie. Medialunas." She bit into one as he shifted into gear and pulled out onto the road. "You like?"

"Lovely," she said around a mouthful of the sweet pastry. She held one out for him, but he shook his head.

"I ate already. My wife send these for you and tell me to invite you for dinner tonight."

"Really?"

He nodded. "Sí. She say she show you proper Argentine meal. If you think empanadas and medialunas is good food, you see what she make for you tonight." He grinned and turned left at the end of the road. "You will come, no?"

"I'd love to." She ate the second pastry and sat back as he drove through the quiet streets. When he pulled to a stop outside a wooden Alpine-styled shack, he pointed.

"Mrs Matthews is inside. I will wait here."

"That's great, Carlos. But I might be a while."

He shrugged and reached between the seats, grabbing a newspaper from the back. "I will be fine, Miss Phillips."

"Thanks." She stepped out of the car and into a muddy puddle, grimacing at the cold water that splashed up her leg as she shook off her shoe and grabbed her rucksack. The door swung open easily as she entered the building and buzzed at the reception desk.

"Yeah, yeah. Just a minute," a low female voice called from the back of the building.

"Okay." Rhian took the time to look around. Posters filled the white-painted walls, and uncomfortable plastic chairs clung to the walls. A leaflet rack stood in the far corner, filled, messily, with tourist information, trekking guides, and hotel adverts. A leaflet advertising horse riding treks around the area caught her attention. She was glancing through it when a short, powerfully built woman with dark, spiky hair and dark eyes strode out of the back room.

"How can I help you?" Her smile sported slightly crooked front teeth and enhanced the creases at the sides of her eyes.

"Sarah Matthews?"

The smile faded a little. "Who's asking?"

Rhian stepped forward and offered her hand. "My name's Rhian Phillips. I'm here from the London advertising agency—"

"Why would I want an advertising agency based in London?" The smile dropped completely, and she ignored Rhian's extended hand. "I don't need any advertising. I've got more than enough business as it is. Thanks, but no thanks and all that."

Rhian stared at her. It wasn't the first time someone had turned down a proposal. But in the past, she had at least been able to make the proposal before being thrown out. *Four and a half stars on TripAdvisor, my arse.*

"That isn't why I'm here, Mrs Matthews."

"Right. What do you want, then?"

Rhian produced her most professional smile despite her growing annoyance at the woman's rude and dismissive attitude. "I wanted to talk to you about a job."

Sarah Matthews rolled her eyes. "I'm not hiring either." She folded her arms across her chest. "Look, honey, I'm not interested in taking on some gap-year student wanting to bum around for a year knocking up climbs and doing diddly-squat."

Rhian gaped at her. "I'm not a student!"

Mrs Matthews looked her up and down, a sceptical look on her face.

"I told you I work for a marketing firm."

"Right, right. So you're what? An intern or something? What do you want a job here for, then?"

Rhian clenched her teeth in an attempt to maintain an even temper in the face of such an obnoxious woman. This was who they'd approved for the show? They'd be off air in a week! "I'm not asking you to hire me in any capacity."

She was more than a little aware that she was looking not just for a guide but for the host of the show. They needed someone with genuine warmth, humour, and wit. Someone who could befriend the audience through the camera lens with a gleam in her eye and a smile on her lips. In short, not some grumpy, rude woman who wouldn't give you the time of day.

"Then what do you want?"

Rhian debated trying again. She didn't want to go back to Rachel and tell her that she'd failed to get this woman to cooperate, but in all honesty, even if she could, she didn't truly think it could work out. *I'll be the one who has to work with her, after all.*

Decision made.

"Nothing." She turned on her heel and let the door slam in her wake. "Nothing at all," she muttered to herself. Rachel wasn't going to be happy, but then again, when was Rachel happy? She climbed into the Jeep as Carlos looked up in surprise, crumpling his newspaper between his fists.

"Next, please, Carlos."

He frowned. "You okay, miss?"

"No. I'm afraid I don't really like rude and arrogant people."

He closed his mouth with an audible click and turned on the engine. "*Sí*, that is Mrs Matthews." He glanced over his shoulder and pulled out into the road, ignoring the woman as she strode towards them. He smirked and flicked his gaze up to his rear-view mirror. "She no nice lady."

"So it would seem. The others on the list—are they like her?"

"Who is on your list?"

"Fen McCash and Chris King."

"No, they both nice ladies. Not like her."

"Okay, good."

"We are closest to Ms King office here. You want to go there first?"

Rhian shrugged and tried to loosen the tension from her shoulders. "Sure, why not?"

The building he pulled up to looked very similar to the one she'd met Sarah Matthews in, but the paint on the front was fresh, and there were flowers in window boxes, adding a touch of colour to the dark wooden boarding.

The meeting with Sarah Matthews had not gone at all like she'd planned. That wasn't going to happen again. She took a deep breath and squared her shoulders. *You're an intelligent, articulate, and successful woman, Rhian. You can talk to a climber about offering her a climbing job.*

She walked up the path and reached out for the handle. Her hand was shaking. *Okay, plan B. WWRD? What Would Rachel Do?* She smiled. *She'd have knocked Sarah Matthews into next week, that's what Rachel would do.* She shook her head. *Matthews is the past. Let it go. Now we're on to King. Focus on King, and channel your inner Rachel.*

She plastered on a smile that she hoped projected confidence and charm and pulled open the door.

A tall woman with blond hair smiled at her from the reception desk when she walked in. "Good morning," she said.

"Morning." Rhian held out her hand. "I'm Rhian Phillips. I'm looking for Chris King."

The woman stood and shook Rhian's hand. "You found her. How can I help you, Miss Phillips?"

"I work for an advertising agency in London," she said and waited to see if Chris King would react. She didn't, so Rhian continued. "I'm meeting with some of the guiding companies here with a view to hiring someone to help us run a new reality TV show as part of a multi-layered marketing campaign. Would this be something you'd be interested to discuss with me?"

The woman's eyebrows hiked up her forehead. "Marketing what?"

"A well-known clothing brand, as well as the area here on behalf of the Argentinian tourism board."

Chris whistled. "Yes, I can discuss it." She rounded the desk and crossed the floor to the door. She quickly flipped the *open* sign to *closed* and locked the door. "Let's go through here, and we can talk." She showed Rhian through to what seemed to be the living space of the building. A small kitchenette in the far nook, a TV and sofa in front of the patio windows, and a large wood burner in the centre of the room filled the space. There was a ladder against one wall, leading up to a loft space. Presumably it was the sleeping area.

Chris pointed to the sofa. "Please take a seat."

Rhian sat while Chris placed a chair in the middle of the floor and sat on it backwards. "When would this all start?"

"Six months from now. The crew would arrive in September to coincide with the start of the season. The contestants then would be in from October. We'd do a month of training and assessments with them, and filming will begin in November over a twelve-week period."

"And what do you want me to do?"

"We'll be setting them challenges to accomplish. Every challenge leading up to it will determine if they are capable of the final challenge. If they aren't, they won't make it there."

"And if the weather does what it does here and blows all your plans to shit?"

"We'll have contingency plans in place."

"Okay, but that doesn't really answer my question. Would you want me to lead the climbs?"

"In some instances, to begin with, yes. As they get better, which they would, I'd need you more to help with the film crew, placing cameramen on safety ropes to get the shots they need of the contestants. I need local expertise to scout locations and keep both the contestants and crew safe, while we make the best damn challenge show TV has ever seen." She leant forward and rested her elbows on her knees. Something in Chris's demeanour held her back from mentioning the final part of the job. She couldn't put her finger on it, but there was something. "I know you've completed the traverse. I've seen the video of you on top of Fitz Roy. You're capable, and you haven't been rude to me, not like the last person I tried to talk to about this."

"I'm not the first one on your list?" Chris frowned, and Rhian watched as her insecurity peeked out from behind the façade of bravado.

"No. There were three people on my list of potential guides when I came here. I don't have a preference. It's more important to me to find someone I can work well with and who will keep people safe. You're the second person I've met with simply because you're the second closest to my hotel. I still have one more to visit."

"So this is more like an audition than a request."

Rhian chuckled. "If that's how you want to see it."

"Hm. I think I need to think about it."

Rhian pursed her lips. *Shit.* What was wrong with people today? She was offering the chance of a lifetime—maybe. This could be a golden opportunity for this woman, and she wasn't jumping at the chance. Rhian grimaced, but hoped she hid it well. *Rachel would have charmed or manipulated her into signing the dotted bloody line by now.*

She stood and held out her hand. "Then thanks for your time." A flicker of indecision rippled across Chris's face, and Rhian wondered if her ploy was going to work.

"That's it?" Chris held her hand limply.

Rhian frowned. "I'm leaving you to think about it. I don't have any more details I can share if you're not on board." It wasn't entirely true, but she was hoping that curiosity and the fear that the job would disappear would get the woman to show some sort of...commitment, or at least the desire to fight for the damn opportunity. "Plus, I do have other places to go. I'm sorry."

She held her breath waiting for Chris King to make her choice. *Come on, come on. Tell me you want this.*

"Do you have a card, then, so I can get in touch with you?"

Shit. Rhian fished one from the pocket on her backpack and handed it over. "It was nice to meet you."

She slipped the card into her shirt pocket. "Yeah, you too. Thanks."

"You were very quick again, Miss Phillips," Carlos said as she got back into the car. "She no nice to you too?"

"She was nice enough. She just wasn't sure she wanted what I'm offering. And please call me Rhian."

He nodded but neither agreed nor disagreed. "Ah. Is a complicated job, no?"

"Yes. But very lucrative too."

He nodded and pulled away. "Sometimes, though, is no money that is important."

"True." She tucked her bag into the foot well by her feet. "Last one, then. Let's hope Fen McCash wants what I have to offer and isn't rude along the way."

"Fen is good people." He smiled.

"Friend of yours?"

He waggled his hand from side to side. "I work with her during the season sometimes. Driving her groups in and out of the mountains, moving gear, and such like. She's a nice lady. Good, fair."

"Sounds like the kind of person I'm looking for. Why didn't you bring me to see her first?"

"I didn't want you think I play favouritism. Only take you see my friend. Only take you where I get work out of the deal too, most probably."

Rhian snorted a quick laugh. "Fair point." She relaxed back into her seat. "Since you know her so well, why don't you tell me a little about her?"

"Trying to get, what you call it—insider information?" He grinned wickedly and drummed his fingers on the steering wheel.

Rhian laughed. "A girl's gotta work her sources, Carlos."

"Well, since we are already here, I do not have time to divulge critical information."

Rhian scowled at him. "Fine, fine. I guess I'll just have to make up my own mind, then." *Damnit, that was too fast. I haven't even had chance to formulate a plan.* She fiddled nervously with the door handle.

"You okay, Miss Rhian?"

She swallowed her nerves and turned to offer Carlos a grin. "Absolutely." She exited the car and was surprised by a woman standing at the door and waving at them. She had long auburn hair that was pulled back to a ponytail at the nape of her neck, a wide smile, and laughing eyes.

"Morning." She headed towards them. "To what do I owe the pleasure, Carlos? Come on in. I told Mark to put the kettle on for coffee."

"Thank you, Fen, but no. No coffee for me today. I'm working."

She nodded to Rhian and offered her hand. "I'm Fen McCash. Are you a friend of this here reprobate?" She tossed a playful wink at Carlos and joined him in laughter.

Rhian took the offered hand. Her grip was firm, no-nonsense, and warm. "I'm Rhian Phillips. Carlos is being kind enough to chauffeur me around for a while."

"Ah, I see. Well, then, nice to meet you, Rhian. Are you here on holiday?"

Rhian slipped her bag over her shoulder and shook her head. "I'm here to meet you, actually."

"Me?" Fen asked, surprise clear in her voice. "Why on earth would you be here to meet me?"

"Do you have a few minutes to talk?"

Fen indicated the house behind them. Like others she'd visited that morning, it was a dark, boarded, Alpine-style apex house, but this one was probably twice the size of the others and had a corrugated sheet metal annex on the side. "As long as this isn't some crafty American ploy to try and serve me some bogus lawsuit, we can chat in there."

"They send Brits to do their dirty work now?"

Fen nodded sagely. "Like I said, crafty." She winked again and led Rhian through the door.

A tall, wiry man with dark hair and eyes stuck his head from around a door frame and held up a mug. "Coffee?" He frowned. "I thought you said Carlos was here?"

"He is. He's on the clock, though, so he's staying in the Jeep." She nodded towards the road. "Obviously trying to make a good impression."

"Oh, right. I'll take him one out, then." He smiled at Rhian. "Can I get you one while I'm at it?"

"That would be great. Thanks. I'm Rhian, by the way."

"Mark McCash. Milk? Sugar?"

"Just milk, thanks."

Fen waved her hand in the direction of the comfy, low-slung sofa against the back wall of the reception area. The feeling of comfort and homeliness was already so different to the other two places. Rhian already felt much more comfortable with the McCash style of doing things.

"So what can I help you with?"

"I need a local guide, a woman who will work with me to create a reality TV show to showcase a leading outdoor-gear manufacturer as well as the Patagonia region. It's a marketing campaign that will run worldwide, feature contestants from all over the world, and take up pretty much the entirety of your next summer."

Mark came in and put their drinks on the coffee table. "I'll just go and give this to Carlos."

Fen nodded but didn't take her eyes off Rhian. "What's your objective with the contestants?"

"Ultimately, the five-day Fitz Traverse."

"Bloody hell."

"Each week there would be a challenge, each one getting tougher and tougher. The two worst performers each week go up for the public vote to leave the competition. So by the time we get to the final, only those capable of doing it will be left. Sixteen climbers. Twelve weeks."

Fen shook her head. "You can't do the traverse solo. It needs to be in pairs."

"They will be."

"So you'd have two winners at the end of the series?"

"Yes. We'll work out who to pair together to get them across the traverse safely, and on one week, there'll either be a double elimination, or we'll lose someone to injury at some point."

Fen smiled and nodded. "Contingency plan number one."

"Yes."

"And if you lose more than one to injury?"

"Then we get a non-elimination week."

"Who would be setting the challenges?"

"You and me."

"Other than challenging the contestants, what is your objective with them?"

Rhian smiled. She got it. "Showcasing Patagonia off to its fullest."

"All well and good when the weather's lovely. But that isn't always the case."

"So I hear. We're trying to show Patagonia in all its glory, but the reality has to be there too. If we're promoting the area to tourists, then they need to know that the sun doesn't always shine. Otherwise the tourist board, who is putting up half the money, will be inundated with complaints."

Fen laughed, then took a sip of her coffee. "You said most of next season. When are you looking at starting this project?"

"The film crew will arrive in September. Contestants in October and filming for the series in November."

"Over twelve weeks?"

"Yes."

Fen nodded. Her gaze flicked about the room, but Rhian didn't think she was looking at anything outside her head. She bit her lip. "I have a few conditions, Rhian."

Rhian cocked her head, her attention completely focused.

"No one goes up a mountain I don't think they can handle, no one goes up alone, and they don't go up without a rope. If they do, they're out. Safety has to be my main concern. Not getting a better shot, not pushing another limit. Safety. That's my priority. If they don't make the traverse, I don't care. I'll do whatever it takes to make sure they make it home alive. I'll be battling those bastards every step of the way." She tossed her thumb over her shoulder to indicate the mountains that loomed through the windows. "I won't battle you or obnoxious cameramen or arrogant climbers either. Clear?"

"What? No promises to get me the best shots possible or unmissable TV?" Rhian asked.

Fen shook her head. "I don't play around when it comes to getting people home safely. You want someone who will offer you promises of gold and bring you home body bags, go and see someone else."

Rhian shook her head. "I don't. I need someone like you, because there will be more than enough hotheads running around the place, just like you said."

"I take it you're talking to a number of people." She stared into her coffee cup. "I'd be surprised if you didn't. Big project like this, you need to be sure you've got the right people, the right team, in place. If you do decide to go with my company, can you give me as much notice as possible? I've got bookings in for the summer already that I would have to hire on extra guides to deal with or farm out to another company."

"You're the third person I've spoken to today."

Fen nodded. "Then I expect you'll need to think about your decision." She picked up a card from the table and turned it over. She patted her pockets until she found a pen and scrawled on the back of the small card. "My mobile number. I'd appreciate it if you could let me know either way." She offered a crooked smile. "Then I'm not wondering until next summer and seeing who gets the job if you make the wrong choice."

Rhian took the card, and slid it into her pocket. "There is one other part to the job."

"What's that?"

"Hosting the show."

Fen's eyes widened. "You're looking for me, or rather your guide, to be the host too?"

Rhian nodded. "We want a someone, a woman, with knowledge, skill, and a personable approach to host the show. We need credibility as much as watchability, and someone like you, who has a vast experience in the mountains, a stellar reputation—and if you don't mind me saying so, who is attractive as well—will certainly go a long way to making the show work."

Fen was watching her closely, a small smile tugging at her lips.

"Still interested?"

"Well, I can't honestly say I ever thought that would be something I'd end up doing, and I'm not sure I'd be any good at it, but I've always said I'd try almost anything once." She shrugged. "So yeah. Why not?"

Rhian grinned. That was what she was looking for. Fen's attitude, her manner, and her wit struck the tone and balance she could see in the host for the show. She also needed someone who would stand up to the hotheads who were undoubtedly going to try to push every limit they could on this project. Fen would shut them down in a heartbeat. She could already see it.

WWRD? She'd sign her up before she walked out the door.

"Any chance you could show me around a little bit?"

Fen frowned. "Around where?"

"This place. Adventure Trekkers. If it's going to be headquarters for this project, I need to know what we've got to work with."

"You're offering me the job?"

"Looks like it."

"Just like that?"

"There were three names on my shortlist. Three women who have completed the traverse—"

"There are a number of guys out there who've done it."

"I need a woman as the face of this project, the leader of this motley crew we're putting together."

"Why?"

"Because that's what our client wants."

Fen threw her head back and laughed. "And what the client wants, the client gets, right?" Fen stood, held out her hand, and tugged Rhian to her feet.

"It's the name of the game, Fen."

She smiled and led Rhian through to the annex. Racks of gear were hung in orderly lines from pegs all along the walls. Pulleys suspended from the ceiling racks and rails full of lengths of ropes, sleds, snowshoes, and skis. Shelves bisected the room into four long corridors filled with labelled tubs. Tents, sleeping bags, harnesses, rock boots, chalk bags, anchors. It was a climber's treasure trove. Everything she could've wanted or needed was tucked away in this room.

"Since this project would take up the entire season next year, I presume the money's good."

"Very."

"Excellent."

"Can I make a condition of my own?" Rhian asked.

"Maybe."

"I would like Carlos on-board for the project. We'll need transportation a lot, both for people and gear. Through the winter as well as when September rolls around."

Fen smiled and clapped a hand on Rhian's back. "I've been thinking I could do with a full-time driver on my staff for this. Who's recruiting the contestants?"

"I am."

"You're going to be a busy girl."

Rhian nodded and ran her hand reverently across one of the gear racks. "You climb?"

"Yes."

Fen grinned. "How long are you here for?"

"I've got four more days before I have to leave."

"Want to do some scouting with me? We can take a look at some of the easier routes, and you can see the beast." She pointed out the window to Mount Fitz Roy. "Up close and personal, as they say."

Rhian beamed. "That would be awesome."

CHAPTER 5

"WE NEED TO TALK ABOUT your efficiency, Jayden," her supervisor, Steph, said from the head of the table. Twenty-one years old, full of her own self-importance, and slathered in fake tan. Jayden had had just about all she could take of her.

"Your average call time is way over the five-minute target. You need to buck up, or I'll have no choice but to put you on report for it. Then all your calls will be monitored."

Jayden ripped the headset from her head. She threw it onto her desk and pushed her chair back. Enough was enough. Almost six months of listening to customers complain, staff bicker, and this stupid woman go on and on about the bloody targets was driving her insane. The late August sun was shining outside the windows, but the air inside the office was suffocating her.

Jayden grabbed her backpack from under the desk and slung it over her shoulder. She didn't say anything as she stalked towards the door.

"Hey! Get back here. You're gonna get yourself in trouble."

Jayden threw her head back and laughed. "I don't give a fuck." She sorted her bike, fastened her helmet to her head, and set off. It felt good to pump her legs and crank the pedals. The sun warmed her skin and the breeze cooled the sweat on her brow. She wasn't made to sit at a desk day in and day out while she rotted away. She needed to breathe.

Thirty minutes later, she hopped off her bike and slid the key into her front door. She grabbed a bigger pack and her bike panniers and quickly filled them with her camping gear, food, water, and a spare set of clothes.

She needed to get away from people, from cars, and street lights, and everything else that made up the suburban rat race she'd been dragged into.

Space. That was what she needed. Wide-open, empty space.

For just a few hours, she needed not to feel or to think. She needed to not blame herself for not taking Rebecca's place. For just a second, she needed not to wish she were dead instead of her. She rubbed her stomach in a futile attempt to settle it and continued to ignore the band constricting her chest that made it harder and harder to breathe.

"I was the leader," she whispered to the empty room, swiped at the tears on her cheeks with disgust, and gritted her teeth. "It should've been me, Becks. It should've been me."

Back on her bike, she pointed her nose for the hills and headed out of the town centre.

Stockport was many things; pretty wasn't one of them. But its proximity to Manchester city centre and all its work opportunities were pluses. Today it was the other direction that called to her. The one she'd refused to let herself look at before today. The hilltops and moors of the Peak District had always been Stockport's greatest draw—to Jayden, at least. And today, they drew her like a mother calling her home.

The hour's ride helped clear her head as she fell into the rhythm and cadence of the hills. The monotony of suburbia slipped away. The dark shadows of the gritstone crags hugged the lush peat landscape filled with flowering heather and pheasants cooing from the scrub. She reached the roundabout on the A6 offering her Castlefield or Buxton, then veered left and climbed through the village of Sparrow Pit—a tiny hamlet with little more than a half-dozen stone cottages and a pub. Mam Tor and Kinder Scout were but a few miles further on, and she itched to sleep under canvas tonight.

She wouldn't bother with a campsite. Too many people around. Too many kids screaming. It was the last weekend in August, and the schools' summer holidays were nothing but a curse to everyone but teachers. No, tonight she planned to sleep out under her tarp and watch the stars from the top of the Kinder Plateau. She wanted nothing more than to feel the midnight wind on her skin and to feel. Just feel. She was sick of the crushing emptiness inside her, and she needed to see that reflected outside. Just for tonight. Just this one night. Then she could go back inside and lock the doors again. Put all the emotions back in the boxes and lock them all away again. She just needed one night.

The final push up the road at Barber Booth had her out of her seat, panting, and sweating before she sat back on her brakes the whole way down to Edale. She stowed her bike in one of the lockers at the train station, knowing it would be safe there, gathered her gear, and headed towards The Rambler's Inn. A good meal would set her up for the night. It was busy, even though it was only just five p.m. She ordered the steak-and-ale pie and pulled her phone from her pocket as she sat, sipping a pint of Hobgoblin while she waited for her food.

Three missed calls. Number unknown. Fucking Steph, no doubt telling her she was fired. As if her walking out hadn't been indication enough that she had quit. Two text messages. One saying she had voicemail. The other was from her sister. She groaned. She was not going to enjoy telling Fen she'd quit her job. Again. She opened the app and stared at the message. It was from Fen's number, but it wasn't from Fen.

Jay, hon, it's Mark. When you get this, give me a call. There's been an accident.

Jayden's palms began to sweat. Her heart pounded, and blood roared in her ears. Her food was put in front of her, but the delicious smell made her feel sick. She swallowed the bile down and connected to Fen's number.

"Jay, thanks for calling so quickly." Mark's voice was gruff. It sounded thick with tears.

"Is she…?"

"There's been an accident."

"I know. You said that in your message. Is she okay? Is Fen okay?"

"What? Oh, well, yes, I suppose so."

Jayden let out a sigh of relief. "What happened, then?"

"We were out scouting some of the early routes for this job."

"The TV one?"

"Yes. It's a massive thing, Jay. I mean, massive. This woman we're working with, Rhian, she's been awesome. And the gig… Well, if the ratings look as good as she hopes, this could become an annual thing."

"Got it, big deal. What happened out there today?"

"Oh, yeah. Sorry. Anyway, it's still winter here, as you know, but we were crossing the glacier—"

"Roped up?"

"Of course." He sounded offended. "This isn't my first fucking hike on the ice, you know?"

"Sorry, sorry." She did know. It was Mark who'd taught her so much when she was just a kid learning her way on the mountains. She liked to think she was responsible for getting him and her sister together in the end. "But you're waffling. Just get on with it."

"Rip off the plaster, right?"

"Always."

"A crevasse opened up underneath her. She dropped thirty feet and smashed into the wall."

The ice wall inside a crevasse could be as hard as polished marble and just as slick. Trying to get out of one was like trying to climb up a diamond. Ice tools could barely get a purchase. Without a rope…you had no chance. "How bad?"

"She's got two broken ribs, a broken arm, a broken leg, and a dislocated knee."

Jayden breathed out again. "So six weeks in plaster and then rehab. She'll be okay."

"And a fractured spine."

The air escaped Jayden's lungs in a mighty whoosh. "Fuck."

"I made it worse, Jay. When I pulled her out, I… It's my fault she might never walk again."

"It's not your fault, Mark. It's not. Accidents happen on the ice."

"I heard it. She was okay till I pulled her up. She would've healed."

"She still might. Mark, you pulled her out and saved her life. That's more important than anything else."

A sob reverberated over the line. "How do I tell her she won't walk again?"

Jayden swallowed hard. "Is she awake?"

"No. She's in theatre. They're operating on her arm and her leg. The breaks were bad. They need to put a plate in her leg."

"Okay. Then don't tell her. She'll be out of it for a while. I'll be there tomorrow, Mark. We'll do it together, okay?"

He sobbed again, and she wasn't sure if it was relief or fear she heard in it. Maybe both. "Thank you."

"No need. Now get off the phone. I need to book a flight."

"I love you, Jay."

"Yeah, yeah. You say that to all the girls."

He chuckled through the tears she could still hear. "Only the pretty lesbians. Otherwise your sister would kill me."

"Meh. She still might. She's a bitch like that."

"Where are you? It sounds noisy there."

"I'm in a pub getting something to eat. Now, let me go so I can get my arse on a plane to you." Her mind was already racing with the plans she needed to make. First thing was the last train out of Edale back to Stockport. She checked her watch. She had an hour. She started to shovel her food into her mouth with one hand as she scrolled through her phone with the other.

She felt nauseous, and the last thing she wanted to do was eat, but who knew when the next meal would be coming. Mark's cry for help had flicked her into emergency mode, survival mode. Energy meant function, and that was what she'd need to do now. She had to function. For Mark's sake. For Fen's.

CHAPTER 6

ARGENTINA WAS JUST LIKE SHE remembered it. Beautiful. But after thirty-four hours of travelling, Jayden was in no mood to appreciate it or the first day of the Patagonian spring. She bustled through the airport, absentmindedly bumping into the back of a short blonde who was talking on her mobile while looking for a taxi. "Rude," the woman said.

"Sorry," Jayden muttered and pushed open the door before she hopped into a taxi at El Calafate airport and asked the driver in Spanish to take her to the hospital—as fast as he could. He nodded and broke every speed limit as he zipped through the busy streets. She fired off a quick message to Mark so he'd be waiting for her at the front entrance.

He pulled her into a tight embrace as soon as she'd paid the driver and her bag hit the concrete.

"Has she woken up yet?"

He shook his head against her shoulder. He still hadn't let her go. She wrapped her arms about his waist and held him. "Come on, don't squeeze so tight. I need a pee."

He snorted and loosened his grip, wiping his eyes with one hand. He kept the other arm wrapped around her waist. He stooped to pick up her bag and led her into the cool interior of El Calafate Hospital, pointing out the ladies' bathroom as they went. When they reached the private room in the intensive care unit, he pushed her into the room's only chair and perched his six-foot frame on the edge of Fen's bed.

"So what's the latest?" Jayden asked as she tried to adjust to the sight of her unconscious big sister looking so small and frail. This wasn't like

Rebecca. Fen was still here, still alive, and she would heal. She repeated it over and over in her head.

"The operation went well. There should be no real issue with the arm or leg in the future. But her spine…"

"Where it is?"

"T4."

"Which means?"

"The fracture to the T4 vertebra is causing pressure on her spinal cord, and we can't tell if the nerves are damaged or just inhibited because of the swelling right now." A young woman walked in and held out her hand. "I'm Doctor Hernandez."

"Jayden Harris." She shook the woman's hand. "I'm Fen's sister."

"Ah. It's good you're here, then."

"What does all that actually mean, Doctor?"

"Well, if the nerve is severed or damaged, then your sister is looking at a wheelchair most likely. Incontinence would be expected, and depending on which nerves were affected, she could have muscle issues with the trunk— her chest area too."

Jayden swallowed hard and tried not to throw up.

"If the nerve is merely impinged because of the swelling protecting the vertebra, then in time she should regain sensation and eventually movement in her limbs. At the moment, she is unresponsive to painful stimuli on both sides."

"So you don't really know, right?"

The doctor shrugged a little. "It's a tricky injury. But she is alive, and she's strong. You need to help her focus on both of those things when she wakes up. She's going to need it." She scribbled a few notes on the chart at the bottom of Fen's bed, nodded at them both, then left the room.

"Ray of sunshine, that one," Jayden muttered.

"We need to know the facts, Jay."

She nodded and twisted her head from side to side, trying to get her neck to crack. "I know." She closed her eyes and scrubbed her hand over her face.

"Why don't you try and get some sleep? I'll wake you if she wakes up."

She nodded, but didn't bother to open her eyes.

CHAPTER 7

RHIAN WAS JOSTLED FROM BEHIND as she headed for the front of the airport. "Rude," she said to the rapidly disappearing back. The tall woman with long dirty-blond curls muttered an apology as she shoved past her.

She sighed, hitched her bag higher on her shoulder, and walked out of the building. It was the first of September, and the first day of the next stage of the project. Carlos was waiting for her. A huge grin on his face, a bottle of water in one hand, and a brown paper bag in the other.

"Isabella sends empanadas for you again, my friend."

She wrapped her arms around him like he was an old friend and kissed his cheek. "It's good to see you again, Carlos. I can't believe it's been six months already."

"*Sí*, right? So much has happened, yet it feels like yesterday you were eating with my Isabella and me while we make plans for this very big adventure of ours."

"My thoughts exactly." She threw her rucksack on the back seat while he slid her suitcase into the back of the Jeep. "So how are the plans coming?"

"Good. I think." He nodded as he climbed into the driver's seat. "Yes, I think is all on track. I've been speaking very much to your assistant, Mellissa. She is very good to be getting me all the details of the equipment arriving, and the people too. We have just one week before the film crew begin to arrive." He pulled onto the road and began manoeuvring them through the city.

"That's right. And she's been a godsend. She'll be coming out with the contestants."

"Good. It will be nice to meet her face-to-face, then."

"Yes. And what about the routes and challenges? Has Fen told you anything about her work on those?"

Carlos frowned. "I do not know. I'm sorry. You should be speaking to Mark, I think."

"Mark? Not Fen?"

Carlos nodded.

"Why do I need to speak to Mark? What's happened?" Carlos glanced around him, his discomfort evident as her voice rose and a shrillness crept into it. "Sorry, you've just got me a bit panicked here." She chuckled and forced herself to relax. After all, if it was anything serious, Fen or Mark would have been in touch with her. "I mean, I'm sure everything's okay, right? We're ready to do this, and Fen said the scouting's been going really well. She's got almost all the challenges sorted, so what can possibly be wrong?"

"I think, maybe, you should be speaking with Mark."

She pulled her phone from her pocket and scrolled through, intent on doing just that. Of all the fallback plans she'd made for the project, this was the one she hadn't been able to prepare for. If Fen backed out, she was fucked. The whole project was fucked. She couldn't believe there was something so wrong that Carlos looked this worried about it yet neither of them had called her. What the hell was going on? She needed to get to the bottom of it all and get answers, and preferably a solution, before she went to Rachel. Or this would not "make her proud". Not at all.

"Actually, I think I'd rather speak to him face-to-face, Carlos." The drive to El Chaltén would give her plenty of time to get her temper under control and figure out a possible solution if Fen was backing out on her. That was the only reason she could come up with that Carlos would look so worried. "Can you drive me straight there?"

Carlos's frown deepened. "I'm not sure that would be best. Not right now."

Rhian turned to him, her nerves at fraying point. "Carlos, my company is paying them a small fortune—actually not that small a fortune—so when I ask to speak to them, I expect to be able to speak to them. I haven't made any unreasonable requests, but you've scared the crap out of me right now. And this project... Well, we can't stop it now. Too much money has been invested by too many people. If Fen's having cold feet about it, at too-late-o-fucking-clock, then I'm damn well going to speak to her about it right now."

"Is no so simple, Miss Rhian."

"It is to me. Now take me to the bastards." Carlos opened his mouth but clearly thought better of it. Instead he nodded and flicked on his indicator.

Six months. She'd wasted six months developing the show, the routes, the challenges, and now they were dropping out on her. She could have spent the time finding someone else to do this with. But now everyone else was in place. Everything rested on Fen leading the groups—safely— through the next five months and on her hosting the show. She was the right person for the task. Rhian was sure of it. But one thing she was even surer of was that there simply wasn't the time to start again. The contestants were chosen. The bloody film crew was arriving in less than a week. *Maybe I can go back to the rude woman—what was her name again? Sarah? I could go and see if she'll do it. It'll cost more, no doubt, to get someone in at the last minute, but at least then we won't have to cancel everything. And waste or lose the millions that have already been invested.*

She clenched her teeth, her jaw muscles flexed, and she drummed her fingers on her thighs.

"Is no what you think, Miss Rhian."

"No? Then what is it?"

Carlos stopped the car and pointed. El Calafate Hospital. Rhian's mouth popped open. "Oh God." She'd been so annoyed with Fen and Mark that she hadn't even noticed Carlos not getting onto the road to El Chaltén.

"Fen hurt very bad, Miss Rhian."

"But I only spoke to her a few days ago."

"Was two days. Mark and she look for route, for show, and ice open. Crevasse, no?"

She nodded, still staring at the building. "How bad?"

"Mark say arm, leg, ribs broken. Knee out of joint and back broken."

She swallowed. "Bloody hell." She closed her eyes and tapped the contact on her phone.

"Landed safe and sound, then, hey?" Rachel's voice was light and sounded happy.

Well, that won't last long. "Rach, we've got a problem."

"Fuck. Don't tell me problems, Rhian. Give me solutions."

"Don't know if there is one for this."

"Let me just close the door." A loud bang, followed by a much quieter background followed. "Right, hit me."

Rhian quickly outlined what Carlos had just told her.

"Bollocks," Rachel said. "She's okay, right?"

"I don't know anything other than what Carlos has told me."

"Fuck."

"I know."

"We're too far down the line to stop this thing now."

"I know."

"There's too much money gone in."

"I know."

"The company would be bankrupted if we have to pay out the penalties for not getting this done."

"I know."

"Stop saying 'I know' like that. It's annoying."

"I know," Rhian added. She couldn't resist. "Sorry. So what do you want me to do? See if one of the other two from the list can fit in instead?"

"No. If you'd had confidence they could have done it six months ago, you'd have gone with them then. There's no way they're going to be able to do it on a month's notice." *Tap, tap, tap.* Rachel's nervous tic of drumming the desk with her pencil echoed on the line. "Isn't there another climber with this company?"

"Mark? Yeah, sure. But I thought Patagonia wanted a woman's face, plus I'm not sure what state he'll be in. It sounds like he was out there with her, and she's his wife. I don't think—"

"No, another woman."

Rhian frowned. "I never met another woman, and I don't recall—"

"Let me get the details and call you back. You go and see Mark and find out what's going on."

"You want me to go into the hospital and interrogate him about a TV show while his wife's in bed injured?"

"Sounds a bit callous when you put it like that."

"You think?"

"Look, kiddo, I know this is where the shit gets real, but we need information before we can move forward and figure out if we've got a canoe and a paddle down this river of shit, or if we're just drowning. You're my eyes and ears out there, and I need to know. I need to know if Mark could work with another woman to make the work he and Fen have done useable. I need to know if he'll second whoever it's going to be, to make sure it's safe, because I do not, I repeat, *do not* want one of our contestants to get hurt. I don't care what disclaimers they've all signed."

"You're all heart, Rach."

"No, I'm honest, Rhi. You know that. Now stop moping, and go find me some answers. I'll try and have some info for you when you come back to me. Okay?"

"Sure," she said, but Rachel was already gone.

"You want me take you to El Chaltén now, Miss Rhian?"

Rhian shook her head. "Unfortunately, I really do have to go and see Mark now." She held up the phone. "Boss's orders."

"Your boss, she—how you say—big bitch?"

Rhian chuckled. "She can be." She dialled Mark's number. "She's also my mother."

Carlos's eyes opened wide.

"Mark, hi, sorry to bother you, I know this is a really bad time, but is there any chance I can talk to you for a few minutes?"

"Rhian? Oh, yeah, okay. I'm glad you called, actually. There's something I need to tell you."

"I know about Fen's accident."

"You do? Oh, right. Well, that's what I was going to tell you. I didn't call before because, well, she's only just come out of surgery a little while ago, and I'm waiting for her to wake up so I can...so we can tell her..."

"Oh, Mark. I'm so sorry. How did she take it?"

"She hasn't been awake since the accident."

"God."

"Yeah. It's a mess."

"I know. Listen, I'm in the car park with Carlos at the moment. Is there any chance I can see you for a few minutes? I know it's an awful time, but, well, my boss is already pressuring me to get info so we can figure out how to, well, work around this, I guess."

"Oh, right. Well, I guess that would be okay. Jay's here, so Fen won't be alone if she wakes up. I'll come down. I could do with some fresh air."

"Thanks. And, again, I'm really sorry."

"Not your fault. See you in a minute."

She ended the call and tapped the edge of the phone against her knee, her mind whirling, trying to see a way through the maze of obstacles that now littered her project. How could everything turn to shit so fast?

Mark looked worn out. Usually his eyes sparkled and energy radiated from him. Today it felt as if a cartoon character of him—flat and colourless—were walking towards her. He seemed to be merely an addition to the background.

Some days I really fucking hate you, Rachel. She climbed out of the car and walked towards him. The least she could do was meet him halfway.

"Hi," he said quietly when they met.

"How is she?"

"Like I said, still asleep. The doctor said the surgery went well. Now all we can do is wait till she wakes up, then see if the spinal cord is damaged or just impinged because of the swelling."

"Can't they do a scan or something to tell?"

"They have. There's so much swelling they can't get a clear image of the spinal cord."

"Are you okay?"

He shook his head and let it fall forward, chin to chest. "I did it, Rhian."

"What do you mean?" Rhian asked with a frown. "It was an accident."

"I pulled her up on the rope. I broke her back." Sobs tore through him.

"No, it wasn't your fault." She pulled him into her arms and stroked his back while he sobbed. "It was an accident. If you hadn't pulled her up, she'd be dead. It's not your fault."

"I should've done it differently."

"Mark, she had a broken arm, a broken leg, ribs, and a dislocated knee. She was never going to be able to pull or climb out of there on her own. You did what you had to do. You saved her life."

"What will we do if she can't walk again?"

"You adapt. You find new ways to live."

"But she won't climb again."

"Then you'll carry her. You'll find new adventures together."

"It's not that simple."

"No, I imagine it won't be. But maybe it should be."

"Yeah." He pulled away and sat on the stone edge of a raised flower bed. "Sorry for blubbing all over you."

"Don't be silly. What else could a little girl like me expect of a big strong bloke like you?" She bumped his shoulder and sat next to him.

He chuckled softly. "Yeah, doing my hard-man-of-the-mountains rep no favours, am I?"

"I'd say that ship's sailed."

"So how come you got here so quickly, anyway?"

She frowned. "It's the first of September. This was always my arrival day."

His face paled further, and his mouth popped open. "Fuck. The show. Oh my God. What're we gonna do? She can't...I can't...oh fuck."

She shook her head and held her hand up to stop him. "We'll figure it out. Will you help me as much as you can? I know you're going to be here with her a lot, but if you can show me some of what you've put together when I find a new guide, it would really be a massive help, I'm sure. I hate to ask. I really, really hate to ask this of you now—"

"Rhian, you have to. It's your job. I get it. And of course I will. Just let me know what you need when you've found someone else." He pointed to the doors with his thumb. "I should be getting back. She might be awake now, and it isn't fair to leave it all to Jay."

"Jay?"

"Jayden, Fen's sister. She flew in from the UK today. You must have been on the same flight."

"Oh, okay. Well, go on, then. You best get back in there."

"Yeah. And thanks."

"No worries." Rhian watched him go, knowing he'd do what he could, but he wouldn't be up to leading this event now. His heart wouldn't be in it, and that could get people killed. Even if she did shave his beard off and stick him in a dress. She called Rachel to let her know she had no good news to add.

"Well, lucky for you I do."

"What's that, then?"

"The trekking company is owned by two people."

"Yes, Fen and Mark McCash. I told you neither of them is in a position to do what we need now."

"Wrong. It's owned by Fen McCash and Jayden Harris. Her sister. She's another climber. I've run her name by the tourism board and the clothing company. They're both fine with her taking over and being the face on this. They said she's an even better climber than Fen is. I'm reading her CV right now. Everest, K2, Annapurna. In fact, it says she's done all the 8000s, as well as the Seven Summits. Is that good?"

"Yes."

"It also says she's one of the few women in the world to ever climb Cerro Torre too."

"Really?"

"That's what the bio says."

"Wow. That's really impressive."

"Good. So, anyway, they're all happy with this solution. And she's the company director too, so she's already contracted to us as well."

"I can't believe you've spoken to the clients already."

"Gotta be on the ball, kiddo. We've just been on Skype now. Should have seen their faces when I mentioned her name. Seems she would have been first pick for the Patagonia dudes, anyway."

"Then why wasn't she on the list?"

"Don't know. Maybe she wasn't in the country."

"Mark did say she just flew in from the UK today, so that must be it."

"She's there?"

"Well, yeah. Mark said she was with Fen. So I presume she's in the hospital."

"Then go in there and talk to her. Get her on board, and get to work."

"Rachel, you have the sensitivity of a hippo's arse. I will not march into that hospital room and tell a stranger that she's under contract to me, to leave her injured sister's bedside, and come and get to work. They're waiting for her to wake up to tell her she may never walk again."

Rachel sighed. "Fine. Speak to her tomorrow, then." And then she was gone.

Rhian smacked the phone to her forehead and growled her frustration at the flower bed. "Bitch."

CHAPTER 8

"Everything okay?" Jayden asked when Mark walked back into the room.

He gave a funny little combined half-shrug, half-nod and perched on the edge of the bed again. "It was Rhian. The woman we've been working with about the TV thing."

"She came here? Fen's been in the hospital less than forty-eight hours. Fucking vultures."

Mark shook his head. "It wasn't like that. She was worried about her."

Jayden snorted. "Worried about all the money she's got riding on this project, more like."

"No, Rhian's not like that. She's really nice. She was really awkward when she asked if I'd work with whoever they get to take over on the stuff me and Fen have already put together."

Jayden barked a short laugh. "See? Trying to pick over the carcass already." A soft moan from the bed stopped her cold, and Fen's eyes fluttered open.

"Hey, babe." Mark ran to the head of the bed. "You're okay, babe. I'm here. You're in the hospital. Look who I found lounging around doing nothing as per usual." He pointed in Jayden's direction. "The prodigal sister's returned."

"Christ, I must be dying, then," Fen said, her voice little more than a croak.

"Not quite, but I can probably arrange something if you want?" Jayden stooped over the bed from the other side. "The lengths you'll go to get your own way."

Fen's eyes had closed again, but there was a grimace of a smile touching her lips. "I always win the bet, Mogo."

Jayden was too relieved to see Fen's eyes open to even care about the hated nickname. She smiled and hoped it didn't look as sad as it felt. "That's cos you cheat."

"I'd take offence to that, but I can't be arsed right now." She licked her lips. "Can I get some water?"

Jayden eased a straw between her lips and held the small glass over Fen's chest. "Slowly."

Fen nodded and sucked a small sip through the straw. By the time she was finished, she'd drunk half the glass and laid her head back against the pillow to catch her breath. "Better give me the bad news, then," she said, her voice stronger than it had been before. Mark looked away, tears gathered in his eyes again. "Jesus, I really must be dying after all." Fen grimaced as she tried to lift one hand to touch him. "Why can't I move my arm?"

Jayden glanced down and saw it was stuck under the blanket. With a tiny chuckle, she moved and untucked Fen's uninjured arm so she could lift it. "Sorry about that."

"You scared the crap out of me. I thought you were gonna tell me I was a quadriplegic or a paraplegic or something. Christ..." She stopped, her gaze fixed on Mark's fallen face. Her eyes widened, and she looked over to Jayden. "Since Laughing Boy over there's gone all quiet, I guess it's up to you to do the dirty work, Baby Sis. What's the story?"

"Maybe we should hang on a—"

"Just get on with it. I'm still here, still breathing, still looking at your ugly mug, so it can't be all bad."

Jayden schooled her face, reminding herself this was about Fen and helping her through it all. She could be strong for her now. *God knows she's been strong for me our whole lives.*

"What do you remember?"

Fen concentrated, her brow wrinkled with the effort. "We were walking over the glacier. Oh God. A crevasse opened up right underneath me." She swallowed and flicked a glance over at Mark. "What's the damage, then?"

She took hold of Fen's hand and gently squeezed her fingers. "Broken bones that will heal. Arm, leg, ribs. Dislocated knee." She tried to find the right words. How did you tell someone—someone you love—something like this?

"Okay, none of that's too bad. And I must be on some shit-hot painkillers. I can barely feel a thing."

Mark shook his head and swiped at the tears on his cheek. "I'm so sorry, babe. I'm so sorry."

"What're you sorry for? It was an accident. I'll mend." He sobbed and hid his head against his shoulder. "Come on, then, out with it. Like a plaster, remember? Hurts less if you do it quick."

Jayden took a deep breath, sucking in the air that would divest her sister of the freedom she still thought she had. "You have a fracture of the T4 vertebra. They can't tell if the spinal cord's damaged or not right now."

Fen closed her eyes. "That plaster analogy's a load of shite, isn't it?"

"I always tried to tell you that."

"Remind me of this next time." A tear snaked out of each eye and rushed for her hairline. Jayden reached over and wiped away the one in easy reach. Fen offered her a weak smile. "So what's the prognosis?"

"They don't really know yet. Until the swelling goes down, they can't see what's really going on in there. At the moment, though, you're stuck in here, on your back, to make sure it doesn't get any worse." She stroked her finger down Fen's cheek. "I mean it. No moving. I don't want this to be fixable now, and you go and fuck it all up because you're impatient."

"Glad you're here, Mum." Fen offered her a watery smile and a cheeky wink.

"Ha bloody ha. I'm being serious here."

"I know." She sniffed. "That's when you most remind me of her." She squinted. "You need a haircut. You look like a wild woman."

Jayden sniggered. "Now who sounds like Mum?"

Fen stroked Mark's back and flicked her eyes towards the door, then back to Jayden. Jayden was more than happy to give them some space. It was going to be hard. But Fen was strong. Not just physically, but mentally too. She'd be okay. She could get through this.

The wall in the corridor was cool against Jayden's back. The heating system made an attempt to stir the air, and the lights hummed overhead, even though it was the middle of the day. Hospitals were the same the world over. Too many sick people, too many drugs, and too much sorrow.

Well, at least she won't be pissed with me for quitting my job. Again.

CHAPTER 9

RHIAN HAD STAYED IN A hotel in El Calafate rather than go back to El Chaltén with Carlos. She needed to speak to this Jayden Harris, and she figured she wouldn't be leaving the hospital anytime soon. Rachel had e-mailed her everything she could find on Jayden, and she was right. The woman certainly was impressive, probably the best female climber in the world and one of a handful of women to complete all fourteen of the 8000ers—the highest mountains on the planet: Everest, K2, Broad Peak, Nanga Parbat, Shishapangma, Cho Oyo, Manaslu, Kangchenjunga, Lhotse, Makalu, Dhaulagiri I, Annapurna I, Gasherbrum I, and Gasherbrum II. There were only fifty women in the world who had ever climbed the Seven Summits—the highest mountain on each of the world's seven continents—and Jayden Harris was one of them.

Then, eighteen months ago, she just dropped off the radar.

Why would someone do that? What would make a person give up a passion like that? Because it had to be a passion, a commitment, a love affair, to keep someone striving to reach those feats, to keep pushing yourself further and higher than you ever thought possible. *She's been to fricking Antarctica, for God's sake!* She made a mental note to research next time she was free what had happened.

She wiped her hands on her pants and tucked them into her coat. It was cold. Spring had arrived in Argentina, but clearly someone had forgotten to pass on the message to the sun. Her breath fogged as she walked from her hotel to the hospital.

As well as Jayden Harris's professional history, Rachel had e-mailed her the contract Fen had signed on behalf of the company, and it clearly was on behalf of the company, Adventure Trekkers, and not just Fen McCash. So, legally, Jayden was now responsible to uphold the deal on their behalf. She'd spent the night studying pictures and interview footage of Jayden Harris, and she could see why the sponsors were so happy with her. Long, dirty-blond curls with sun-streaked highlights gave her a slightly wild look. She had blue eyes that shimmered with the same humour and intelligence Rhian had seen in Fen, and a reputation and climbing history that would make even the most hardened climber stand up and take notice of her.

Rhian opened the door to the hospital and followed the signs to the cafeteria. She typed out a quick message to Mark, bought a coffee and a few pastries, and sat down to enjoy her breakfast. And wait.

She didn't have to wait long.

She'd barely finished the medialunas when Mark slunk into the room. She pushed her untouched coffee towards him. "You look like you need this more than I do."

"Thanks," he said and quickly guzzled it. "What can I do for you?"

"First tell me how she's doing."

He shook his head and rested one elbow heavily on the table. "She had a bad night. The pain in her arm and ribs kept her up or woke her up throughout the night."

"I'm sorry to hear that. What about you? Have you gotten any sleep yet?"

"No. I can't find a comfy place here, and I can't leave her. It's too far to go home just to get a few hours' sleep and then come back."

Rhian didn't think, she just fished her key from her pocket. "I'm a five-minute walk away from here. Go and get a few hours at my hotel room. Shower, get something to eat, and then you can come back."

He started to shake his head. "No, I can't—"

"You'll be no use to her if you make yourself sick. She's going to need you to be strong. To help her, you need to look after yourself too." She pushed the key into his hand. "Go on. Tell me where she is, and I'll go keep her company for a while."

He frowned. "I'm too tired to even argue with you." He quickly gave her directions to Fen's room and held up the key. "Thank you for this. I can't tell you how much I appreciate your help."

"No need. Just go and get some sleep. You look like death."

"You forgot the warmed-up bit."

"No, I didn't."

He snorted. "Funny."

"I aim to please, Mr McCash. See you later." She watched him stumble through the cafeteria and out the door before getting herself a fresh coffee and a spare and following his directions to Fen's room.

Monitors bleeped, and a drip hung above the bed. She could barely see Fen over the footboard. She was laid flat on her back with one side of the blanket raised for the cast on her arm and leg and the other hand clasped around that of a woman sleeping in the chair beside the bed. Jayden Harris—her long, lean form stretched out in the high-backed chair, a coat tucked about her shoulders, and one hand on the edge of the bed—was instantly recognisable.

"If you wake her up to give her another goddamn sleeping pill, I swear to God I'll shove it up your arse." Her voice was a low, menacing whisper.

Rhian chuckled softly. "I come bearing gifts, not weapons," she said just as quietly, but without the menace. One blue eye popped open warily, glanced at her, then fixed on the coffee cup she was holding out. "It's black, but I've got some whitener and sugar packets in my pocket."

Jayden's eyes opened fully, and she glanced at Fen before slowly pulling her hand from her sister's grip. "I don't care right now." She stretched her arms over her head, and Rhian heard the vertebrae pop softly back into place. She stepped further into the room and held the cup out. "You don't sound Greek to me." Jayden took the paper cup from her hand and took a sip.

Rhian frowned. "I'm not. Why...oh, the gift thing. Trojan Horse and all that. Right. Sorry."

Jayden shrugged and sat back in her chair. "So who are you, then, if not a Greek?"

"I'm Rhian Phillips. I've been working with Fen and M—"

"I know what you've been doing with them. Why are you here? Surely you can see she can't help you anymore."

Rhian nodded. "She can't be the guide, no. I wanted to see her, talk to her. But I'm also here to talk to you."

"Me? Why? I've got nothing to do with it, and I don't want anything to do with a stupid, bloody TV show."

"Wow, okay." She held her hands up in surrender. "I'm not sure how I've pissed on your chips, but I just want to talk to you."

"The only thing you could possibly want to talk to me about is picking up where Fen left off. Right?"

"Well, that's a bit of an assumption—"

"We don't know each other and we've never met. The only reason you could have to talk to me would be about this ridiculous scheme of yours. So tell me I'm wrong?"

"You're not."

"Then get the fuck out."

"Can you at least let me explain?"

"I'm not interested. I don't want anything to do with it. I don't want anything to do with climbing." She pointed to Fen in the bed. "It gets people hurt. Sometimes it gets people killed. And I don't want any part of it."

The way Jayden phrased it set alarm bells ringing in her head. *Sometimes it gets people killed. But Fen's okay. She's alive, she'll recover. So who...?* Rhian shook her head. She didn't have time to be distracted by questions about words that could just as easily be throwaway lines. Everyone knew climbing was a dangerous sport. Of course it killed some people. She needed to focus. She needed to get this project back on track, and she needed to protect the company—protect Rachel.

"I understand you're emotional right now. And I really am sorry I had to come here and speak to you at this time. I wish it could wait. But it really can't." She pulled the contract out of her bag. "This is the contract Fen signed on behalf of your company." She flipped the pages and pointed to the bit she'd highlighted. "Your company. Not just her personally. So that means as half-owner of the company, you're now responsible for fulfilling this contract."

Jayden rose out of the chair like a wave folding in on itself before it crashed against the shore. Rhian wasn't sure if she was the grain of sand about to be washed away by the tide, or the wall that would halt its progress.

"So sue me."

"Jayden, stop." Fen's voice cut through the crackling air and grounded the electricity that seemed to spark about them. "We can't afford for them to sue us, so don't try and dare them into it. Rhian doesn't want to do that, do you?"

Rhian shook her head. "No. God, no. I truly wish I could have come here today just to see you and make sure you're okay. I swear, Fen."

Fen was quiet a moment as she studied Rhian carefully. "I believe you. We've gotten to be friends over the past few months. So sit down, the pair of you, and talk like civilised human beings." Fen tapped one hand on the bed. "Rhian, come and sit here. Let the ogre stew over there." She smirked and grimaced as it turned into a yawn.

"How are you feeling?" Rhian asked as she perched next to Fen on the bed. "You look better than Mark did when I saw him earlier."

"I think I got about twenty minutes more sleep than he did." She lifted her head from the pillow. "Where is the big lump, anyway?"

"I sent him to get some sleep."

"Good."

"And a shower."

"Even better."

"In my hotel room."

Fen chuckled. "Well, since you're here, I can't see the harm. Thank you. He needs a kick up the arse sometimes." She clasped Rhian's hand. "Now, tell me what the problem is?"

Rhian let out a deep breath and quickly filled her in on the issue as Rachel had laid it out to her.

"You're telling me that if Jayden doesn't take on my project, the one I agreed to—"

"On behalf of the company," Rhian interjected.

Fen stared silently. Rhian let her mouth close with a click.

"As I was saying, if she doesn't take on my project, this Rachel is going to go bankrupt because the big companies will sue her, and she's the kind who likes to take the whole ship down with her. If she goes, we go. Is that right?"

"Effectively…yes."

"Bitch," Jayden said.

Fen silenced her with another glance. "And what about you?"

"What about me?"

"What would you be doing if Jayden wasn't involved?"

"I was going to see if the rude one would take over."

"The rude one?"

"Oh, sorry. Sarah. The guide I spoke to first. She was so rude, I never even told her exactly what it was I was after. But at least I think she'd be decisive enough to make the calls that were needed, rather than Miss I-Need-To-Think-About-It."

Fen squeezed Rhian's hand. "So why are you doing what she wants? Is your job that important to you?"

Was it? Yes, her job was important to her, or at least this project was. But was it important enough that she would do this simply to keep it going? No. What was important to her was Rachel. And if Rachel lost this project, she lost her company. And the company meant everything to Rachel. Almost as much as winning Rachel's approval meant to Rhian. Those three parting words still echoed in her head: "make me proud". She had to deliver.

Rhian shook her head. "Rachel's my mum."

Fen's eyebrows rose. "Glad I didn't put voice to what I was thinking about her, then."

"It's okay. She can be a bitch. And I know that this is a really bad time, the worst possible time, and that I'm asking an awful lot—"

"More than you'll probably ever know."

Rhian frowned and followed Fen's gaze to Jayden. Her hands were shaking as she sat in the chair, elbows on her knees, and her head bent forward. Her hair cascaded around her shoulders, hiding her face.

"Can you give us few minutes, please, Rhian?" It was a question, but not one that needed an answer and not a request she could refuse. She stood and closed the door behind her. Jayden didn't move, yet she seemed to crumple in on herself as Rhian watched through the small window. Just for a moment. Then it felt too intimate, too private, and she turned away.

"Please don't ask me to do it." Jayden's voice was a whisper.

"Listen to me," Fen said softly. "The routes are all scouted, and the challenges written up. Mark and I have been working closely with Miguel and Santiago. They can do the climbing to set lines for the cameramen, and the rest of the crew can do the heavy lifting. All you need to be is the face for this. You lead them out on the hikes in the early days, you speak in front of the camera, and you send the weakest players home. You stop anything dodgy from happening. It's that simple. Honestly, the hard stuff's done."

"That's bullshit and you know it." She ran a shaky hand through her hair, then clenched her fist, trying to work out the tingling pins and needles as her fingers turned cold and the blood drained away. "Anything can happen out there. Anything. Look at you!"

Fen nodded. She held her uninjured hand out for Jayden to take. All Jayden could do was stare at it. Fen wiggled her fingers, and Jayden saw her hand grip them without even realising she'd moved.

"I know. And I know this is only adding to your fears, honey. What happened to you, to Rebecca, is more than I can imagine. It's every climber's worst fear and the ultimate reminder of who's in charge out there—a reminder that we're not all-knowing or all-powerful, and that no matter how skilled we are, we also need a bit of luck on our side every time we step foot out there."

"She died, Fen. So many of them died." Jayden laid her head on the sheets, next to Fen's arm, and tried to hold back the tears as Fen stroked her head.

"As callous as it sounds, hon, people die every day. People die in their beds, while crossing the street, while sitting in restaurants eating salad. It happens."

"I can't risk it. I can't let them risk it. I shouldn't have let her risk it. I should have gone out with Pete, not her. It was my expedition; I was the leader. It should have been me. Not her."

"Rebecca knew what she was doing out there, Jay. She was doing what she loved."

"She went out there, and she died."

"Yes. She died doing what she loved. What about you?"

"What are you talking about?"

"Rebecca died doing what she loved. I got hurt doing what I love."

"Exactly my point. It's too dangerous."

"Pft. Personally, I'd rather die young doing what I love, having lived every single day of my life, than die in bed, a hundred-year-old, toothless hag never having seen or done anything."

"I'm not you."

"No, you're not. But if you don't get back out there, you're going to die a little more every day anyway. You feel the call of it even more than I do. It pulls you, doesn't it? Even as much as it scares the living shit out of you right now, it's still drawing you in."

Jayden frowned and sat back in her chair, staring down at the floor. She didn't want to admit that she'd been ready to give in to that temptation just to feel something beyond the ache, beyond the void that sat in her chest.

"The freedom. The quiet." She reached out for her hand. "The peace that fills your soul when you sit on top of a mountain and look down. How have you managed to stay sane without it?"

"Who says I have?" she whispered.

"Fair point."

Jayden still couldn't lift her head. The tiled floor had a crack along one edge of a white tile, curving around one corner in a perfect arc. "I can't."

"I know how much Nepal took from you. I know how much losing Rebecca tore you apart. But it's time to stop hiding from the world."

She snorted a bitter laugh. "I haven't been hiding. I've been a part of more of the real world these last eighteen months than at any other time in my adult life—"

"But you don't *live* in the real world. You just exist in it. You *live* in our world. The world of ice and rock. That's what you've been hiding from. What you're still hiding from."

"You weren't there, Fen. You didn't see… You don't know what it was like."

She was quiet a long time. So much so that Jayden looked up, half expecting her to be asleep.

"No, I wasn't. And I hope I never have to see what you did. But I'd like to think that if I did, it wouldn't change me. That it wouldn't keep me from the people I love or the places that feed my soul. That it wouldn't kill me slowly, one day at a time." Fen held her gaze as she carried on. "I could tell you that if you don't do this, we'll go under, and Mum will end up in an NHS care home. We both know what they're like. If you don't do this, I'll never be able to pay for my medical expenses, never mind what I'll do after the company we spent fifteen years building is gone and I have no income to support myself. If you don't do this, Mark will likewise be fucked too. And he's worked just as hard as we have."

"I don't need to listen to this guilt-trip shit." Jayden started to stand up.

"Sit down!" Fen shouted. "I am not done."

The tone of her voice was as demanding as Jayden had ever heard, and the effect on her wobbly legs was immediate. She dropped heavily back into her seat.

"I could tell you all that, and every word of it's true—we both know it." The look in her eye gentled, and her voice softened. "But that isn't why you need to do this. That's why *we* need you to do it. Do you want to know why I want you to do it?"

Jayden shook her head.

"Because I miss my sister."

Jayden's eyes stung with the tears that welled and slipped down her cheeks.

"I want my best friend back."

Jayden hung her head again and tried to push back the emotion she'd held inside since the ice had cascaded down the mountain and frozen her soul.

"She was so strong and capable and talented. She was my hero. She might've been my little sister, but she was the person I looked up to most." Fen's voice cracked, her own emotions slipping through the crevices. "She was my rock, the one person in this whole world I knew had my back no matter what."

Jayden turned her head, trying to get the words to miss her ears. But each one landed and gripped hard, like an alpine heather clinging to the granite the avalanche had forced her to become. Each word dug into the cracks and took root.

"I really need her now. To be my strength. My heart. To be my hero again."

"You don't know what you're asking of me."

Fen nodded. "Yes, I do. I'm asking you to be everything for me that I would be for you. That I am for you."

Jayden couldn't hold it back anymore. She let the grief and the tears flow.

Fen tugged her until her head was resting beside her on the bed again and stroked her fingers through Jayden's hair. It was softly soothing as her grief began to release.

"You're really gonna make me work with that stuck-up little bitch out there?"

Fen chuckled. "Rhian's nothing of the sort."

"She came barging in here, threatening to sue us, Fen." Jayden spoke with a lacklustre voice. The passion and fire had drained from her with her tears. "She knows what's happened to you, and she still—"

"You're generalising and taking things out of context. Rhian's become a friend over the past six months that we've been working together. She truly has. Telling us everything today was as much a warning as anything else." Fen carried on, stroking her fingers through her hair. "She doesn't want anything bad to happen to anyone. She's a good person." She tugged on a lock of Jayden's hair. "Give her a chance. I think she'll surprise you."

"Pft," she said and turned her head to look at Fen. "I'm sorry I've been so shit."

"You don't need to apologise. You had shit to deal with. But it's time to stop wallowing in it and come back home."

"I know you're right. I do." Jayden closed her eyes and tried not to feel the fear and panic that had gripped her from the instant she'd seen Rebecca's eyes staring up at her. Dead, unseeing eyes. "I just don't know how to do it."

"The same way you got up your first wall, Mogo."

Jayden looked up at her.

"One grip at a time."

CHAPTER 10

JAYDEN OPENED THE DOOR AND stepped through. She met Rhian's eyes and nodded to get her to follow. She wanted coffee. No. She needed coffee. Rhian fell quietly into step beside her through the long corridors filled with people and noise and the smell of antiseptic and sweat. The hum of the lights overhead felt like an itch on her skin, and the regurgitated air made her lips dry. She licked them and felt the cracked skin on her lower lip. She made a mental note to pick up some salve as soon as she could.

She ordered a cappuccino from the barista in the hospital cafe.

"Two, please," Rhian said and fished change out of her pocket.

Still Jayden said nothing as she led them, with drinks in hand, to a table in the far corner of the room. She watched as Rhian stirred it before taking a sip. She felt drained, her eyes stung, and she wanted nothing more than to curl up in a corner and let the world carry on without her. But that wasn't an option. Not only would Fen kill her, but also something was niggling, wheedling inside her, demanding...*something* from her. Something she didn't have the time or the inclination to decipher right then. She had Rhian Phillips to deal with. She sipped her coffee. *So let's start dealing.*

"Would you really sue?"

Rhian looked uncomfortable. "I wouldn't, no. But it isn't my company, and I do believe that Rachel would feel she had no choice."

"Why do you call your mother by her first name?"

Rhian sighed. "Long story short, she's my stepmum. She married my dad when I was three. My parents had joint custody, but Mum died when I was five. So I lived with Dad and Rachel after that. I call her Rachel, because that's what I've always called her. But in real terms, she's the mother who raised me. And the mother I love."

"Yet you call her a bitch."

Rhian smirked. "On occasion. And usually she's quite pleased with the appellation."

"Strange woman."

"Driven woman." Rhian sipped again and twisted her cup around on the saucer. "She built her company from nothing and has succeeded in a cutthroat business for almost thirty years. She'd argue that getting called a bitch meant she was doing her job right."

"Screwing people over is doing her job right?"

Rhian shook her head. "That's not something she sets out to do, nor does she enjoy it. But she doesn't shy away from making the best situation for her clients and herself in any given situation. She's very honest about that. She has no hidden agenda. She wears it on her sleeve. And that makes her easy to work with in many ways."

"You always know where the knife's coming from?"

Rhian snorted a humourless laugh. "Yes, I suppose that's one way of putting it." She stirred her coffee again, tapped the spoon against the lip of the cup, then put it back on the saucer. "Will you work with me?"

Jayden watched her for a long moment. Watched the way she tucked her blond, shoulder-length hair behind her ear and the way her grey eyes seemed to be darker in the softer light of the cafeteria. The way her fingers twisted a napkin or played with the spoon or spun her coffee cup. She was never still. Her leg bounced on her toes, vibrating her whole body gently. Nervous? Hyperactive?

"If I tell you something's too dangerous, will you threaten to sue me to get it into the show?"

Rhian shook her head. "No, I don't want anyone getting hurt. This has to be as safe as it possibly can be." She held Jayden's gaze. "Climbing's inherently dangerous. I know that, and everyone coming here knows that. But I don't want anyone taking unnecessary risks. I need someone there who will see them and stop them before they can occur. That's not about anything but being a sensible, decent human being. I haven't come to this as a producer or director. I'm in marketing. To me, dying and broken people aren't something that's easy to market and sell to the public. No matter what the producers and director might say it will do for the ratings."

Jayden nodded. "Very well. The moment you violate that, our contract is null and void, and you can take me to any court you want. Clear?"

"Crystal."

She reached for her cup and swallowed half the contents. "I need a couple of days here before I go to El Chaltén and we get started."

"No problem. What do you want me to do in the meantime?"

"Whatever marketing executives do."

Rhian frowned. "I was supposed to be going over the routes and challenges with Fen. Everything else I have to do is as done as I can make it right now."

"No e-mails you've got to send or people to bug on the phone?"

Rhian chuckled. "I'm very efficient. I've already bugged everyone who needs bugging and set the Internet ablaze with correspondence. So what can I do to help you?"

"Christ," she muttered, and swallowed the rest of her drink. "I'm not leaving here. I suppose you could go to the office and pick up the paperwork Fen's already done and bring it here. We can go over it here, and ask her anything while we're at it. That would probably be a big help."

"I can do better than that." She pulled out her phone and tapped the screen. "Carlos, hi. Are you busy today? You are? When? Fantastic. Listen, I need you to do me a favour on your way over. Have you got a pen?"

Jayden chuckled. Efficient indeed. The paperwork would be here in a third of the time and save a full round trip in fuel. She had to appreciate the economy as well as the effective planning. She closed her eyes for a moment, letting everything sink in. Trying to ground herself and not think about what this was going to mean. What she'd just agreed to.

"So Carlos is heading out to the airport in a couple of hours to pick up a load of gear that's coming in today," Rhian said. Dragging Jayden's attention back to the present. "He's going to swing by the office beforehand and get the files Fen's put together. He said he knows where it all is because he helped her build some new shelves or something to hold them all. I also asked him to bring a few things for Fen and Mark. Just some clothes and stuff for Mark, and some bits and pieces for Fen. I hope that's okay?"

Jayden nodded, touched by the unexpected gesture. "That's very thoughtful of you."

Rhian ducked her head as a faint tinge of pink stole across her cheeks. "I thought you probably came straight from the airport and had whatever you needed already, but if you want to get some sleep, you're welcome to use my hotel room. As you know, Mark's there now, but if you want to go after, or I can see if they have another room. If you're going to be here for a little while, you may as well get to sleep in a bed instead of just that chair all the time."

Jayden held up her hand to stop the words. Rhian's mouth closed with an audible click. "Do you always talk so much?"

Rhian blushed again. "Only when I'm nervous."

Jayden's eyebrow hiked up her forehead. "I make you nervous?"

Rhian sighed. "Incredibly. I mean, you've been to frickin' Antarctica! You've done the 8000ers, and the Seven Summits." She put a hand over her mouth. "Sorry, I'll stop now."

Jayden chuckled. "The offer of your hotel room is another very kind gesture. Are you sure you don't mind?"

Rhian shook her head, hand still in place. She seemed determined not to speak again...for a few minutes, at least.

"Then, thank you. When Mark gets back, I will take you up on it. No need to go to any additional expense. We'll be here more than we'll be away, so hot-bunking should be fine. However, right now, I could do with some food and another coffee."

"I can get that. What do you want?"

"I'm capable of getting something—"

"I know. My treat. For saving my hide."

Jayden clenched and unclenched her teeth. "Fine. I'm not fussy, just food, preferably warm, and plenty of it."

Rhian grinned. "That I can do."

CHAPTER 11

THE SNOW HAD FINALLY CLEARED from the streets of El Chaltén. There was still a week of prep work before the contestants arrived, and Rhian had to go over their accommodation to make sure everything was ready. All their gear had been delivered and should have been added to each assigned room. Contestants were only allowed to bring with them a small amount of personal essentials for the duration of the shoot.

The crew had taken to calling it the conclave, as in the contestants' enclave. Even though the crew were already living there, the name had stuck. The Hotel El Chaltén, which they were taking over for the season, was different to those around it. The outside was the standard dark wood, Alpine style of all the buildings that surrounded them, but on the lower floor, the walls were made of glass to offer views of the surrounding mountains from every aspect. The roof was a single slope, rather than the apex, giving the front of the hotel four floors, while the back just had three.

It had a huge bar and dining room on the lower floor that they'd cleared out to make into a comfortable space for the contestants. They'd left some tables in one corner to provide work and eating spaces. Comfy sofas were scattered around a huge wood burner that sat in the middle of the room, the flue disappearing out the roof, four storeys above it. The bar itself was still there, stocked with the bare essentials—beer, wine, and whiskey. And the catering staff would run the kitchen at the back, as they were to feed the crew as well as the contestants.

She already knew those areas were good to go. She'd been over them three times already, checking and rechecking that everything they needed was there and that the contestants' food requirements were catered too.

They had two vegetarians, a celiac, and a diabetic in the mix of sixteen. Eight men and eight women who were to battle it out for the prize and the title of *The Amazing Climb* Champions. None of them knew what the prize was yet, and she was looking forward to explaining it all to them when they arrived. Or maybe when filming started. She and Rachel were still discussing it.

She rubbed her hands together like an excited child and climbed the stairs to the second floor of the conclave. The second and third floors had sixteen rooms on each. The crew was on the third floor, and contestants had been assigned the second. The four rooms on the fourth floor were for the director, Angela Parrot; the assistant director, Simon Gert; Rhian's assistant, Mellissa; and Rhian herself. She was due to move out of her tiny hotel room tomorrow. She couldn't wait.

Her new room had a view straight up to Cerro Fitz Roy.

She shook her head to bring herself out of her daydreaming. She had work to do and only an hour before she was due to meet with Jayden to go over some more of the route plans. This afternoon, Jayden was going to drive them out as far as she could towards the massif, then they would hike for a couple of hours to check out some of the approaches to the lesser satellites in the range. Guillaumet was the first they needed to look at, as it was the first the contestants would have to climb.

Jayden had suggested throwing in as part of the training challenges some of the climbs that would make up the traverse of the final. Fen and Rhian had thought it a brilliant idea and had seized upon it, even though it meant reworking a number of the challenges they'd already worked long and hard on. Her reasoning for it was simple. If they couldn't make a single climb, they didn't stand a chance of completing the traverse.

She opened the first room and ran through the inventory that had been folded and stacked neatly on the single bed. The room was cool, the window was covered by a long net curtain, and a dark wood wardrobe stood in one corner. The en suite sat off to the left, with a small table and single chair next to the door, and the room's only free electrical outlet. There was no TV, no phone, just a radio alarm clock on the bedside table next to the lamp.

If they wanted to use a laptop, and many of them would to check weather forecasts and research climbs, they'd have to do it on the desk, or else downstairs. The rooms were meant to be functional, not luxurious. After all, if they could sleep out on the mountain, on glaciers and sheet ice, how many mod cons did they need?

She quickly inventoried the contents of each room and moved on. She finished with five minutes to spare and jogged out of the conclave and down the quarter-mile to the Adventure Trekkers headquarters. Jayden was already loading up the Jeep with packs and a cooler.

"Ready?" Jayden asked.

"Yup. Need me to grab anything else?"

She shook her head. "I've got everything. Some snacks too." She tapped the cooler. "Carlos tells me you're a fan of Isabella's famous empanadas."

Rhian grinned. "Guilty as charged. On that note, you better take me out there so I can work them off."

Jayden shook her head. "You'd need to eat more than I've got in this cooler for you to have to worry about that." She pulled keys out of her pocket. "Come on. The day's a wasting."

Rhian climbed in and secured her hair with a band she'd taken to keeping on her wrist. The wind and her fine hair were not a good combination. She was sick of having to pull out knots every night. Jayden had her own hair wrapped under a buff with a cap on over the top. Her sunglasses covered her eyes, and she wore a deep blue tank top and cargo shorts that clung to her thighs. Rhian pulled her own sunglasses off her head and slipped them on.

"So what's the route today?"

"We're headed for Paso Guillaumet. We have to cross a bit of the Piedras Blancas glacier, and there's a little climbing involved, but Fen tells me you can handle that."

Rhian nodded. "I take it you have gear back there. I don't fancy going over the glacier in my shorts." She pointed to her bare legs.

"Yup. I've got everything you need. I thought we could give some of this new clobber a trial."

"How long is the hike?"

"Around thirty kilometres. Should take us about nine hours there and back. You'll get some great views, but better than that, we can get a decent look at Guillaumet."

"And what exactly are you looking for on it?" Rhian asked.

"Any changes to the rock after the winter. I want to see what the ice pack looks like and assess the avalanche risk, see if any of the edges have sheared. If there are any significant changes, I might have to climb it to see if we need to add or replace any bolts. We'll need them to be secure for the camera crews. Your director doesn't want to do it all with body cams or helmet cams. Seems to think the audience would end up with vertigo if we did."

Rhian chuckled and decided to ignore how white Jayden's knuckles were on the steering wheel and how her voice had cracked as she spoke. "Yeah. Have you seen any footage from those things? They make me seasick."

"Maybe she does have a point, then."

"So, thirty kilometres, a glacier, and some rock climbing today. Anything else?"

"Hm, a crystal-clear river, a glacier-fed lake, and sunshine. What more could you possibly want?"

"Well, when you put it like that, nothing. Nothing at all."

Jayden gave her a tight, uncomfortable-looking smile and changed gears as she turned into the El Pillar Hotel. "A friend of Fen's runs this place. He's letting us leave the Jeep here for the day so we can do this in the single day, as long as we get moving."

Rhian nodded and climbed out of the car. The gear Jayden had packed for her was perfect. A thin base layer, a pair of light pants, a hooded pullover, and a lightweight shell jacket.

"You've got a down belay jacket in the pack as well as all the other gear we'll need for the climb section. The temp could get down to about two degrees Celsius on the glacier today. Crampons and axe on the outside, emergency kit at the bottom." She patted her own bag. "I've got a sat radio in my bag too, just in case." She hauled a long length of rope out of the back of the Jeep and wound it around her body like a bandolier. "We'll rope up across the glacier."

Rhian nodded. *Are you nervous about the glacier?* She wanted to ask, but she didn't dare. Jayden's attitude towards her had softened over the past three weeks, but she still wouldn't classify it as "warm and fuzzy". She wasn't sure sometimes how much she could ask about professional matters. Personal stuff... Well, she was certain that shit was off the table.

It was weird. She watched Jayden around the crew, around the other guides, and around people in town, and she was always cracking a joke or offering a friendly ear. She was everyone's best friend, and everyone seemed to love her. She didn't behave that way around Rhian, though. She still seemed to blame her for putting them all in this situation, for forcing herself on Jayden.

She pulled on the pants and the long-sleeved top, pulled the sleeves up over her elbows, and tucked the rest of the layers into easy-to-reach pockets. She wouldn't need them until she got to the glacier. Maybe she wasn't even what Jayden felt had been forced on her. Maybe it was the situation. She shook her head and slid the heavy pack onto her shoulders.

"After you." She waved her hand and followed Jayden down the dirt trail signposted *Laguna de los Tres*. The five-inch height difference between them was definitely not playing to Rhian's advantage as she tried to keep up with Jayden's long stride and easy, rangy style, and she tried not to think that maybe, just maybe, she was doing it on purpose, pushing Rhian to punish her for her "crimes". She huffed out breaths, but she didn't slow down. If that was Jayden's goal, she was going to be disappointed.

But then Jayden slowed her step and fell into line next to Rhian. "Sorry," she said. "I've not really walked with anyone for a while. I need to get used to going at someone else's pace."

Rhian frowned. *So much for the punishment theory.* She shook her head again and resigned herself to a day full of wondering and questioning. *Never gonna figure her out, so just get on with it. Not everyone's going to love you. That's not a surprise, now, is it? You're a big girl and no stranger to being on the receiving end of the cold shoulder or whatever.* She pushed away thoughts of her dad and the last time she'd seen him. That wasn't going to help. It was time to figure out how to live with rejection.

Whatever she had to live with was so worth it as they cleared the forest path and got their first clear glimpse of Laguna de los Tres and the Piedras Blancas Glacier, with Cerro Fitz Roy and Guillaumet directly behind them. The pristine white of the glacier lay in perfect counterpoint to the dark gritstone of the mountains and the ice blue waters of the lake.

"Bloody hell."

"Gorgeous, isn't it?"

Rhian nodded mutely as she stood still, staring at the beauty that was nature's own work.

"In a way, it's a shame so few people get to see the world like this," Jayden continued. "But in another way, if they did, they'd probably ruin it."

Rhian snorted a quick laugh, still unable to tear her eyes from the view. "So cynical, Ms Harris."

Jayden shrugged. "I like to think of myself as a realist."

"Hm. I still say cynic."

"Well, you're the boss. I guess you can say what you want."

Rhian turned and caught the twisted smile on Jayden's lips. *Are you teasing me or letting slip your problem with me? Both?* She decided to take a punt in the hopes of diffusing any animosity that still lingered. "I wish. I've never been the boss, and you know it. Fen was, and now you. And back home, Rachel calls the shots. All I am is a glorified secretary and bean counter." She laughed. She didn't care what her job was right now. She was in one of the most stunning places she'd ever seen, and she was getting paid to be there—to hike out and climb a mountain and cross a glacier. Life just didn't get any better than that.

"Oh, you're more than that, Miss Phillips. And I'm pretty sure you're well aware of it." She strode off down the slight hill towards the lake. "Come on, we don't have time for standing around doing nothing."

Rhian laughed. "See? I told you. You're the boss."

The hill didn't go down for long, and soon they were heading up a steep eight-hundred-metre climb to the lake. Around ten kilometres of their hike were completed. Rhian swung her bag off her back and tugged out her water bottle, emptied it in one, and refilled it from the lake. She scooped a handful of the water straight into her mouth, delighted at the fresh, clean taste and the icy-cold temperature as it slid down her throat. She put on her pullover as the increased height brought with it a chill. Despite sweating now, she knew she would quickly cool in the breeze. It was much easier to keep warm than it was to get warm again once she was cold.

Jayden pointed down the length of the lake and across to the expanse of ice that stood in front of them. "We'll stop for a quick bite and to put on our ice gear as soon as we get around the shore." She checked her watch. "We're making pretty good time, so we'll have a few minutes to stop then."

Rhian nodded, shouldered her pack again, and followed behind. The view was no less spectacular now that she'd reached the glacier, but it was considerably more intimidating. What had looked like a flat sheet of ice they'd have to walk across now was clearly a sheet of ice they'd have to climb. Though not particularly steep, it would be hard work.

They rounded the rocky edge of the lake to the south side, covering the ground quickly. When Jayden reached the start of the ice field, she slung the rope from over her shoulder and dropped her pack to the rock. She had her crampons on and fastened while Rhian was still untying them from her pack.

"Need a hand?"

Rhian bit her lip as she concentrated. "I'm good, thanks." She finally managed to get the last buckle done and secured the spikes to her boots. She pulled on her jacket, and climbing harness, tying on when Jayden handed her the end of the rope, the other end already attached to her own harness.

"Ready?" Jayden clipped Rhian's helmet closed under her chin and tapped the top. "For luck," she said to Rhian's quizzical look.

Rhian chuckled and looked up the sheet of ice. "Let's do it."

———— ✦✧✦ ————

The climb was long, and Rhian's calves were burning from the walk across the glacier by the time they reached the Paso Guillaumet, but she stood and looked out over the ground they'd just covered…and she wouldn't have missed it for anything. Jayden held her hand up to shade her eyes as she scanned the rock face of Guillaumet.

"How does it look?" she asked.

"Pretty good, I think. From the pictures Fen took before the winter kicked in, I'd say there were no significant changes, so the routes and timescales we're looking at should be fine." She pointed to a large slab of ice and snow clinging to the rock face. "If anything, that looks smaller than it was in the pictures. Looks like there's already been some avalanche activity to bring down the risk."

"Good." Rhian pulled a protein bar out of her pocket and ripped open the wrapper. "I've got another one, if you want it."

Jayden shook her head. "I'm good, thanks." She skipped across the ice to get a better view up one of the gullies, a frown marring her beautiful face.

Beautiful? Since when did I think she was beautiful? Since you saw her asleep in the hospital...before she started shouting at you. Remember, idiot?

"Problem?" she asked, more to distract herself than anything else.

"No. The crag's fine. I'm just cautious."

"That's what you're here for, right? To be our safety monitor when we're all ready to be daring and fearless." She smiled.

"Yes." Her jaw seemed tight, and her fists curled at her sides.

Rhian could feel the anger radiating from her. "Did I say something wrong?"

Jayden shook her head and seemed to put herself back together, carefully stacking up the blocks of her self-control to form that bloody wall that surrounded her.

"Whatever I said, I'm sorry."

Jayden ignored her and moved to the other side of the wall's base, staring up at finger holds that looked tiny—because they were—and toe holds that were like standing on air.

"Okay, then," Rhian said with a deep sigh and finished her bar before she pulled the second from her pocket. She grimaced a little. Peanut. She preferred chocolate, but it was still edible. She wanted to demand a response of some sort, an acknowledgement that another person had offered an apology for some imagined wrong. But no. Miss I-Can't-Give-a-Fucking-Inch couldn't even do that. She wanted to demand that Jayden tell her what her problem was. Demand that she explain why she acted like a best friend to the rest of the world but couldn't string together two fucking words that weren't all business for her benefit.

But she already knew. Jayden was never going to forgive her for making her do this job. Clearly she hadn't wanted to. Clearly she had a reason she hadn't been on the circuit for a while. Clearly it was Rhian's fault that she was here now, having to deal with whatever demons were haunting her. Clearly.

Never mind that it wasn't Rhian's fault Fen had fallen into a crevasse. Never mind that it wasn't Rhian's idea to run the stupid TV program in the first place. Never mind that she hadn't even picked the potential guides—that was the bloody clients' choice. But Rhian was the face she could pin all that anger on. Rhian knew it. And Jayden was never, ever going to forgive her.

"Are you going to eat that or just mangle it?" Jayden pointed to the mutilated bar in her hand.

"What does it matter to you?" she snapped back.

Jayden held up her hands in surrender. "I'm sorry. I'm an arsehole, okay? I shouldn't have ignored you. That was rude." She tapped her boot against a rock, knocking snow and ice from the sole. "I'm usually quite nice."

"Not to me you're not." Rhian spoke quietly.

Jayden nodded. "I know. There's just some...stuff...I'm trying to get my head around. It's taking a while. That's all. I shouldn't take it out on you, though. Please accept my apology."

"I will, on one condition."

Jayden raised an eyebrow and waited.

"You'll try to be nicer to me from now on. I'm quite nice myself, you know."

Jayden's lips quirked into a smile. "I had noticed that, actually." She turned quickly, and Rhian could feel her cheeks heating up. "Come on, we've only got about five hours of daylight left. How do you feel about rappelling down the ice? Shorten our journey time."

"Okay. Sure."

CHAPTER 12

RHIAN STARED INTO SPACE AS she went over the details of the afternoon. Again. Carlos would meet her at the car park at 5:00 p.m., and they would travel to the airport to collect the contestants. Hopefully the plane would be on time. The catering staff had packed snacks and water for the journey for everyone, and they would be back at El Chaltén by ten. Then tomorrow the real stuff would kick in, when they all would meet for breakfast and the egos would really start to—

"Am I that boring?" Fen asked from the bed beside her.

"I'm sorry, what?"

Fen laughed. "I said, am I that boring? Clearly I am."

Rhian shook her head. "Sorry, just got so many things whizzing through my head." She rubbed her hand over her face. "Right, start again. How are you doing? I haven't seen you in a week."

"I'm doing good. They managed to get a clear image of my spine yesterday."

Rhian watched her. She didn't seem happy or sad about the results. "You've got a poker face of stone. Now, spill."

Fen laughed again. "The cord looks to be intact."

"That's great news."

"Yes, it is. Even better, they're going to let me start sitting up again in a day or two."

"Oh my God," she said quickly, slapping her hand to her forehead and opening her eyes comically wide. "Like, so, for sure, we should, like, totally have a party or something—like, yeah."

"Sarky bitch." Fen laughed along with her. "I swear, I never would have thought I could be so excited at the possibility of sitting on my arse for a few hours."

Rhian clasped her arm. "Seriously, Fen, I'm so pleased for you. I take it they're hopeful, then, that you'll be okay?"

"Yeah. Hopefully."

"Ah. Still hedging their bets?"

"Yeah. Everyone's frightened of getting sued these days." She sniggered.

"Aw, for fuck's sake. How many times do I have to apologise for that?"

Fen laughed loudly. It was good to see her so happy. She was so vibrant and full of life. Seeing her lie in bed had been like watching a plucked flower slowly wilt and fade away.

"I'm just messing with you. So tell me, it's the first of October. Are you ready for them all to arrive?"

Rhian scrunched her face up like she smelt something bad. "I guess so."

"You guess so? Rhi, you've been working on this for seven, nearly eight months now. You guess so?"

"Okay, okay. We're as ready as we're going to get."

"You look nervous."

She laughed. "I am."

"Why? This is so exciting. It's the start of everything really getting going."

"Exactly." She crossed her arms over her chest like a shield. "All these people are depending on me to get this right. They're all expecting me to know what I'm doing here, and I don't. I've never done anything like this before. How am I supposed to make this work? What do I know about TV shows? Or how to keep everyone safe up there?"

"That's Jayden's job, not yours. All you need to do is follow her lead, and she'll keep everyone safe. So you can stop worrying about that one."

No, I can't, because there's something bugging her that she won't tell me.

"Secondly, you've watched enough reality TV shows—"

"I've only ever watched *The Amazing Race.*"

Fen scowled at her interruption. "You've watched enough reality TV shows to know how these things work, what viewers want to see, what your clients want out of it, and what you know you can get out of your contestants. You've got a good crew in place to take care of the technical aspects, hon. Let them do their jobs, and everything will fall into place."

"You don't know that."

"Yes, I do."

"How? How can you know that?"

"I have faith in you."

"You don't know me."

Fen shook her head. "Yes, I do." She reached for Rhian's hand. "I know more than you think, and more than you, probably."

"Definitely."

"Precisely."

Rhian sniggered, then let out a hearty peal of laughter. Fen joined her, and slowly her confidence began to return.

"You can do this, hon. I wouldn't have agreed to do this in the first place if I hadn't believed in you."

"We'd only met for like five minutes."

"I know when I know." She shrugged. "Simple as that."

"And you never question it?"

"Of course. But that's when something always goes wrong. If I trust my gut, nine times out of ten, it works out. If I don't, nine times out of ten, I'm fucked."

"Right. Well, on that note, I think I need to be off."

Fen chuckled again. "Crisis of faith over?"

Rhian shrugged. "Maybe. But I really do have to run." She pointed to the clock. "I told Carlos I'd meet him at five. It's quarter to now, and this place is a maze." She leant over and kissed Fen's cheek. "Thanks for the pep talk."

"Hey, that's what I'm here for."

"See you in a few days."

Fen shook her head. "No, it's going to be manic for you now. You and Jayden. See me when you can, but don't kill yourselves over it. Mark will be around, and Carlos said he was going to bring Isabella to see me a few times when he comes into town for supplies and whatnot. So don't fret. I'll be fine."

"But you're my friend. I want to."

"I know. But it'll give me more incentive to get my arse into gear and get out of here."

"Hm. I don't know about that."

"Do as you're told. Now, go. Don't keep the man waiting."

Rhian shook her head. "Yes, boss."

Carlos couldn't park where he normally did to pick her up. Instead, he was waiting in the bus at the far end of the car park. Rhian jogged over and hopped up the steps. He handed her a clipboard and a cap with the company logo on it and grinned at her.

"Suits you," he said with a snigger.

"Careful or I'll tell your wife you're hitting on me."

He laughed. "You wouldn't."

"I would. And we both know she'd make earrings out of certain parts of your anatomy if I did." She grinned widely when he shuffled uncomfortably in his seat. "Just kidding. You know I like Isabella too much to let her risk jail time." She snickered at the look of outrage on his face before he crumpled into laughter with her.

"You ready to go pick them up?" he asked.

"Yeah, let's go make sure we've got 'em all."

"You think some no show up?"

She shrugged. It was a worry that played on her mind. But in all reality, she'd be shocked as shit if that happened. These people had fought tooth and nail to get picked for this show. The prize was awesome, an all-expenses-paid trip to climb Mount Vinson on Antarctica. Probably the most difficult and expensive of the world's Seven Summits to get to. And without being cynical, for any amateur climber looking to turn pro or make a career out of their passion, this was a platform they'd be stupid to miss.

"I hope not, but it'll be okay. We have a male and a female alternate if there is a no-show."

"Ah, Miss Rhian's contingency plans strike again." He chuckled and drove them out of the car park. "So much with the organisation."

"Well, Carlos, Rachel would have my guts for garters if I fluff this project up by not anticipating a simple problem." It had become something of a running joke, how many contingency plans she'd put into place for what she hoped was every possible eventuality. Barring a major disaster, everything should be just fine. And if she was truly honest, her contingencies could probably deal with a couple of major disasters too.

"It's good. Makes people feel safe. Makes them trust you."

She smiled widely. "Thanks." She took her seat just behind his chair and clapped a hand over his shoulder. "Keep the compliments coming, and I won't tell your wife how you like to flirt with me after all." She smiled innocently at him when he met her gaze through the rear-view mirror. "Let's go pick 'em up."

Twenty minutes later, she pushed open the door to the airport and saw Mellissa holding a clipboard. She stood on her tiptoes, trying to see over the crowd staring out towards the arrivals gate. Her blonde hair was pulled up into a tight bun, and her red, faded T-shirt and denim shorts were neatly pressed. *Who irons shorts and a T-shirt?* Rhian quickly dismissed the thought and checked the arrivals board. The plane from Heathrow had landed on time—a minor miracle—and they were therefore expecting the first faces through the doors any second.

"Perfect timing, boss," Mellissa said as she stepped up beside her. "I'm pretty sure that's the first one there." She pointed to a tall, wiry-looking guy with dreadlocs hanging from under his red skull-and-crossbones-covered bandana. A loose-fitting wife-beater vest in canary yellow hung off his frame, and basketball shorts hung well past his knees.

"Ah. Luiji Mantessori," Rhian said. "Twenty-two years old, Italian, six foot two. I watched him pull himself up a hold with one finger on the indoor wall. Born and raised in Valle di Fassa."

"Dolomites?" Mellissa asked.

Rhian nodded and waved at the tall man. A smile spread on his face. "Yup, the north-east part of Trentino."

"You've been there?"

"A long time ago, yes. Great climbing."

"So he's good?"

Rhian nodded and held out her hand. "Luiji, good to see you again."

Luiji dropped his bags at his feet and wrapped his long arms around Rhian's shoulders. He kissed both her cheeks and squeezed so hard she was almost lifted off her feet. "It is wonderful to be here, Rhian. Wonderful to see you again."

She tapped his sides and wriggled in his embrace. "Okay, okay. You can put me down now."

He chuckled and let go, then held out his hand to Mellissa. "You must be Mellissa." He took her hand, bowed theatrically, and kissed the back of it. "I am at your service."

Mellissa giggled. Rhian rolled her eyes but held her tongue as another of their climbers arrived. Taylor Blackshaw: five foot three inches, Canadian, with a skill for off-width climbing that had made her a legend in the field. She climbed up cracks in a rock face so wide she had to use her whole body as a wedge, and she did it so fast that she held record upon record, something the tall, muscle-bound guys who usually participated in the extreme-climbing niche hated with a passion. Rhian loved it and the quiet way Taylor just seemed to fill a space without having to say anything.

Slowly they all gathered. Mellissa ticked off names on her clipboard, and Rhian chatted with them all about the flight and the shocking food they'd been served. She made little attempt to corral the high spirits that were flowing when a group of adrenaline junkies got together. They were still waiting for the last climber to come through from baggage claim when a piggyback race broke out at the length of the arrivals hall, and Rhian just shook her head as Luiji and his "piggy", Killian O'Leary, celebrated their first win.

Mellissa waved her over as she stood at the security desk. Rhian quickly pointed them all outside to the bus and instructed them to head over and get their bags loaded.

"What's up?" Rhian asked when she got to Mellissa.

"There was no one else on the flight."

"Shit. Who's missing?"

"Karen."

Rhian shook her head. Karen had seemed quite timid at the trials, but she'd e-mailed back and forth with her up until two days ago, and she'd seemed keen. "Right, I'll e-mail her and see what happened, but can you contact the alternate and get her here as quickly as possible? I don't want anyone to miss training if we can help it."

"Who is the alternate?"

"Brooke Shields."

Mellissa raised her eyebrows, and a slow grin spread across her face. "You wish."

Rhian chuckled. "Oh God, I know, right? Seriously, though, she really is called Brooke Shields, just not *the* Brooke Shields."

"Some parents are cruel."

"Could be worse. At least it's a nice name and a gorgeous woman to be named after."

"True. Where's she coming from? I need to get looking at flights for Miss Shields."

"South Africa."

"Right, well, I've got the Jeep here, and it'll be easier for me to sort things here with better Internet than on the road. I'll catch up with you back at the conclave and let you know what the score is."

"Good plan."

Mellissa nodded and headed for the service counter. Rhian headed for the bus. Unexpected circumstances, nil. Contingency plans, one. She scored her finger down the air.

She could hear the raucous laughter and lewd comments coming from the bus when she was still twenty feet away.

Did I remember to ask the caterers to put the sleeping pills in the water?

CHAPTER 13

THE SMELL OF EGGS, BACON, toast, and coffee assaulted Jayden as she walked into the communal room of the conclave. It was just six thirty in the morning, but there was a lot to be done, a lot to be dealt with. A month was not nearly enough time in which to do it all. Not as far as she was concerned, anyway.

Thirty or more people sat around long tables. The chatter and clatter of cutlery scraping on plates was so loud, she wanted to turn around and walk right back out again. She didn't. She'd promised Fen she would do this. She'd committed to the project. Everyone was here. It was too late to back out now. No matter how much she might want to.

Rhian was sitting at one of the tables, alone, a stack of papers in one hand, a cup of coffee in the other. Her attention glued to the tablet on the table in front of her. A frown marred her forehead as she bit her lower lip.

Jayden crossed the room and pulled out the chair next to her. When she didn't react, Jayden shrugged, sat down, and waited. And waited.

Her blond hair was tucked behind her ears, as usual, and it brushed the collar of her shirt at the nape of her neck. A small pair of sleeper earrings caught the light, and Jayden was mesmerised by the way the it reflected from the surface. A subtle pattern had been cut into the metal to enhance the effect, casting tiny light patterns across the soft, downy skin at her jawline.

Jayden was enthralled by the way the shadows shifted as her jaw worked. The muscles bunched and relaxed under her skin as whatever she was reading clearly pissed her off more and more. She was about to question how she knew Rhian was pissed off, but before the thought was fully formed, she realised the answer: she knew a lot about Rhian.

She knew that the coffee in her mug would have milk but no sugar in it. And milk, not cream. She knew she'd have had a breakfast of medialunas and that this was probably her third cup of coffee already. She also knew that, by the look of the shadows under her eyes, Rhian hadn't slept.

She shouldn't be noticing all these things. Rhian was a work colleague, not a friend. She sighed deeply, then cleared her throat to get Rhian's attention. "Good morning," she said. "What's got you so engrossed there?"

Rhian looked up from her tablet, eyes wide. "Hi there. I didn't see you come in."

"I know." She smiled. "I've been sitting here for five minutes, waiting for you to spot me."

"Really?" She put the papers on the table. "I'm sorry. I was just trying to figure something out." She took a sip and put the cup back on the table, empty.

"Anything I can help with?"

"No." She turned her head one way, then the other, until the vertebra slid into place with a pop. "Just one of the climbers who didn't get on the plane, so we have to fly in an alternate. It's proving difficult to get a straight answer as to why Karen didn't want to come on the trip she fought so hard to get on in the first place."

"Ah, I see." She wiggled her finger, pointing at Rhian's face. "This is your I-don't-understand-what-the-idiot-was-thinking face." She narrowed her eyes. "It's a workable look, but be careful of the lines those furrows will leave."

"Funny."

"I try my best. When will the alternate get here?"

"Day after tomorrow."

"Now I get it. We should all be out on the glacier at base camp by then, and you're not sure if we should delay that trip to wait for her or if she should be brought out after she gets here."

Rhian laughed. "Since when am I that obvious?" She turned the tablet towards Jayden and pointed to the screen. "I don't think we can afford to wait." She slid her finger across the screen and let the graphic of the area and a long-range weather forecast play. The storm system was set to blow in within the week and would likely have them stuck in for another week. Outside training would be slowed to low-level hikes, as the wind forecasts were just too high to risk being up on the mountains. They'd have to stick with distance work and the indoor training systems they'd set up in the climbing gym.

"I saw it before I left this morning. You're right. We can't wait. Once the storm digs in, we'll be losing a week of mountain prep as it is. It's part of what I wanted to talk to you about. If we can, I'd like to try and get these guys out of here today rather than wait till tomorrow."

"Short notice?"

Jayden shrugged. "On the mountain, you have to be adaptable. This will give us an insight into who is and who isn't up to that challenge."

Rhian looked at the screen again and nodded. "Good point. And it's not like you were planning to take them up any of the mountains."

"No, I just need to see these guys establish a base camp on the glacier and then pair off to find a high camp for one night. I need to know they can handle the conditions and what skills they have out there. We both need to know they have enough knowledge to keep themselves safe."

"Okay. Will you pair them off?"

"Yes. For this first challenge. They don't know each other very well, and we should see if they can work together and learn to trust each other too. I'll also be able to see how they handle the quick start and the hike, and we'll get a sense of their attitudes at base camp before I send them out. By the time they start, I'll know who will work best together. But I want to keep switching up the pairings. That'll help them cope when pairs change after eliminations."

Rhian nodded. "Then go amass your troops, General Harris." She tossed in a jovial mock salute.

"You're not coming? I thought you were with us on this expedition?"

She shook her head. "I think we need to adapt the plan." She offered Jayden a lopsided grin. "I'll bring Brooke out and meet up with you when she arrives."

Jayden shook her head, uncomfortable with the idea of Rhian heading out onto the ice without her. "No, you can come out with me and the rest of the group. I'll get Miguel or Santiago to stay back and bring—Brooke, was it?" She waited for Rhian's nod of confirmation before continuing. "Well, one of them can bring her out when she gets here." Jayden inclined her head, settled on the newly formed plan. Not letting Rhian be out there alone was just good safety protocol, protecting the project and all that other good crap.

"That leaves you short a guide out there, Jayden. I'm a decent climber, but I'm not Miguel or Santiago. You know that. You need them and their expertise from day one. Plus they're stronger and can carry more than I can." She shook her head. "No, my plan makes much more sense. I'm the least useful person to you on this expedition. Therefore, I should stay behind and bring her when she gets here."

"You're not useless," Jayden protested.

"I didn't say that. I said I was the least useful. That's different."

Jayden had to concede the point. "Then it should be one of the other crew members that brings her out."

Rhian frowned. "I am perfectly capable of walking out there with her. The more crew members you have with you to start with, the more training you can get through before this storm system hits. Neither time nor the weather is on our side right now. We'll head out first thing in the morning after she arrives. I'll be able to prep her one-to-one when she gets in from the airport. You know this plan makes the most sense."

It did, and Jayden knew it. But she was also acutely aware of the last time she'd given in to a request like this. A request to trust in someone else's judgement, someone else's skills. *Rhian is not Rebecca, and this isn't Everest. This isn't an earthquake hot zone, and the route is one she's already walked most of with you.* She knew if she was going to refuse this plan, she'd have to explain why she couldn't let Rhian do it. And she couldn't do that without telling her far more than she wanted Rhian to know about her.

She's a big girl, Jay. She's also your boss. So take a deep breath and let her call the shots. There's no increased risk to her plan that warrants a safety intervention.

"You're right, it does. It's a good plan. And thank you."

"You're welcome. See? My contingencies are paying off already."

Jayden chuckled as she shook off her uneasiness and stood, clapping her hands to get everyone's attention. "Good morning, ladies and germs," she said to a round of titters. "I'm Jayden Harris, and I'm the chief guide around here."

"Does that mean you're gonna hold our hand up there?" The thick Irish accent of Killian O'Leary cut through the crowd.

"It means that health and safety out there is my number one priority. If I tell you not to climb something, you don't. If I tell you to go back to camp, you go. If I tell you to pair up with someone, you pair with them.

And if I tell you to get the hell off my mountain, you get out of my sight." The room was silent. "Are you clear, Mr O'Leary?" She couldn't make out his mumbled response. "I asked you a question. Are we clear, Mr O'Leary?"

"Yes," he said louder. "How the fuck did she know who I was?" he whispered to the tall black man in the room—Luiji Mantessori—loudly enough to be overheard. She chose to ignore it and move on.

"Every one of you has experience in the mountains. Every one of you has climbed at least one of the Seven Summits or one of the 8000ers, many of you more than one. But right now, you have to prove to me that you're capable of this challenge. We have a month of training before we start filming. A month to get yourself as ready as you possibly can be for the challenge ahead of you. And we're not going to waste a minute of it. It's 6:30 a.m. At seven thirty, the bus outside will take everyone on it to the Adventure Trekkers office to gear up. We'll be spending six nights on the glacier. Our objective is to establish our base camp and for each person to be paired up and spend at least one night on a high camp."

Low whispers and comments flittered about the room. Chairs scrapped away from tables, and a couple of people stood. Not sure if they were ready to go and pack or ready to object, she carried on.

"Gather any personal kit you need for the six nights. Technical gear is at the office. I will brief everyone on the bus as to what we need in our base camp. This is a mandatory training exercise. Clear?" She looked around the room at all the nodding heads. "Carlos will close the doors to the bus at seven thirty exactly. If you aren't on the bus then, you won't be coming." Wide eyes and stunned faces greeted her proclamation. "Clear?"

More nods.

"I said, are we clear?"

A chorus of "yes, ma'am" filled the room.

"Then what the hell are you waiting for?"

Fifteen chastened men and women almost ran from the room to gather their kit. She could see them cataloguing lists in their heads as they burst through the doors and away from her. She sat back down and cast a questioning look to Rhian, who was sniggering behind her empty coffee mug.

"What?"

"I know I called you General, but I didn't realise you were going to go all boot camp on them."

Jayden shrugged. "I wouldn't have done if Killian hadn't started up like that. This is too big a group with too many egos to let him get away with something like that and think I can still control this group."

"Makes sense. You going to be able to keep it up the whole time?"

"I won't have to. By the time we get back, this group will have bonded, and they'll have either learnt to respect me and my skills, or they won't. If they don't, it won't matter how heavy-handed I come down on them, they'll never listen to me. If they do, then I won't have to be heavy-handed with them."

"A clever tactic."

Jayden smirked. "I've been around the block a time or two."

"I just bet you have," Rhian said. Jayden lifted an eyebrow, and Rhian seemed to realise what she'd just said. Her face turned bright red, and her mouth popped open. "I...erm...I didn't mean that the way it sounded," she stammered. "I meant all your experience climbing. That's all. I wasn't—I didn't—I mean...oh, bloody hell." She scrubbed her hands over her face and sighed. "It's no use. Go ahead and kill me."

Jayden laughed. "Why? Then I wouldn't get to watch you squirm, Miss Phillips."

Danger! Danger! Back away now! She cleared her throat. It was becoming a habit around Rhian, it seemed. "Anyway, I should go speak with the crew. They don't need to set up their ice base until the week before we start the filming."

She got up and walked away but not before she caught the smirk that now accompanied Rhian's blush. "Oh, what the hell. It's just a bit of friendly banter," she whispered under her breath. "She's a big girl."

Her conversation with Angela Parrott and Simon Gant took less than five minutes, and she decided to wait for the climbers on the bus. It would be interesting to see who arrived first, what little cliques had begun to form already, who sat next to whom on the bus. And, more interesting yet, who sat furthest away from each other.

She spent the next half hour planning the drills she needed to cover this week with each of them. Self-rescue skills. Rope skills. Risk-assessment skills. Navigation skills. All of which she had to test before she could assess what each of them required individually to ensure their safety.

The first contestant on the bus was Kimi Shizuma, the twenty-year-old Japanese free-solo climber from Hida, in the Japanese Alps. A tiny five foot two inches of muscle and power. Rhian had shown her the footage they'd taken of her climbing at the trials. Her movement across the indoor walls had been awesome to watch. Lacking the wingspan of the taller climbers, she relied on dynamic movements to race up walls, jumping from hold to hold with no contact on the walls at all, grabbing and securing herself in her new position with a grace and ease Jayden hadn't seen in a long time. Kimi nodded as she passed Jayden, swung her pack off her shoulder, dropped into the window seat, and parked her bag on the aisle seat. Clearly not bothered about company.

Jayden filed the information away and marked a note to watch her group work carefully. Lone wolves weren't always good at climbing in pairs.

She wasn't the only lone wolf in the pack, apparently. Three more got onto the bus alone and occupied seats by the windows, using their packs to deter any visitor who might think to join them. Hunter Jones and Lonnie Brown were the first people to leave the conclave together and board the bus. They glanced at each other when they saw how others were sitting, shrugged, stowed their packs in the rack overhead, and sat next to each other with a fist bump.

By 7:28 a.m., they were only waiting for two people—Luiji and Killian. Half of her hoped they didn't make it in time. She'd love to see the looks on their faces when she had Carlos pull out just as they came running out the doors. But at seven thirty, she had no such luck. They weren't on the bus, but they weren't even visible in the distance behind the bus as Carlos pulled away. The rest of the passengers were quiet. *Time for a little damage control.*

She stood to address them all. "I'm a bitch on wheels, right? Gonna ride your arses to the edge of the earth, then push you over the edge, right?" She met the eyes of every person on the bus. "Maybe. But everything I do will be with one single goal in mind. Anyone want to hazard a guess what that might be?"

She waited, the groan of the old diesel engine the only sound until a small voice piped up. "Keep us safe."

She smiled at Kendal Richards, the tall, rangy blond from New Zealand. *A little timid, but at least she offered her opinion.* "Exactly. You're all experienced climbers. You've all taken on and conquered some really difficult climbs. You wouldn't be here if you hadn't. But experienced climbers die on mountains every day. Climbers with more experience than you all put together die on mountains because they get complacent. They get cocky. Arrogant. Their skills get rusty—their basic skills.

"This first week is about making sure that you aren't rusty, that you aren't arrogant. And that you aren't going to get yourselves killed doing something stupid. To do that, I need discipline, and I need attention to detail. You give me that, and you'll go home a better climber than you are right now. Whatever the outcome of this contest, that's got to be worth something, right?"

Everyone nodded, and relaxed back in their seats.

"You going to let them back on expedition?" Kimi asked from her seat.

Jayden smiled. "Depends what they've got to say for themselves." And how they said it. She was pissed that her phone hadn't rung yet. It was now seven forty, and they were pulling up at the office. "Right, everyone off the bus. The annex at the side is where all the gear's kept. It's a lovely, tidy place at the moment. I know because I organised it. I want it to stay that way at all times. You'll be sharing three-man tents, so get yourselves organised. Split heavy gear and share loads. You'll need a full climbing rack and a full length of rope each. Take enough water for the day and food rations for the week. Any questions?"

Kendal raised her hand.

"Shoot."

"How long a hike to the glacier today?"

"Fifteen kilometres, then you've got to cross the glacier until you find a suitable spot for base camp." She waited for any further questions. When none were forthcoming, she clapped her hands together. "Right then, kiddies. You've got an hour. Let's get a move on."

It was after eight before her phone rang. Rhian's number. She slid her thumb across the screen. "I warned them," she said with a smile.

"I know. They didn't seem to think you were serious."

"So I gather. And now?"

"They look like naughty little schoolboys outside the headmaster's office waiting for the cane or something."

"What's their excuse?"

"I didn't ask. Didn't think it mattered. Everyone else made your deadline with time to spare. There's no reason why they couldn't."

Jayden nodded. Exactly. "What time did they make it downstairs?"

"Ten to."

Twenty minutes late. "Did they see you?"

"No."

"Okay, thanks. Stick Luiji on, please." She waited as Rhian handed over the phone. "Well?" she barked at him.

"I had to use bathroom. I was only a minute after half past seven, but you had already gone."

"Bullshit. You came downstairs at ten to eight. Twenty full minutes after I told you I'd be gone. Want to try that again?"

There was silence.

"Give the phone back to Rhian."

"Hello?" Rhian said.

"Seems he thinks it's a good idea to lie to me."

"I heard. Want to give Killian a shot?"

"No point. I think they need to stew in their own juices for a couple of days. Can you bring them out with Brooke when you come?"

"Sure. But aren't you worried about what they'll miss in the meantime?"

Jayden sniggered. "If I've judged these guys right, they'll bring their A game when they get back here. They'll have something to prove."

"Isn't that the problem? The chip on their shoulders is the size of the bloody mountain they're supposed to climb."

"No. They'll have something to prove to me. They'll know I think they're the bottom of the pack, and it will make them work twice as hard. They'll complete the skills training with Brooke. I was going to have to split sessions anyway. I'll spend the time with them to make sure it'll be fine. They'll just be backloaded like she is."

"You sure?"

"Yes."

"What do you want me to do with them for the next two days, then?"

"Nothing."

"Nothing?"

"You aren't their babysitter, Rhian. They're big boys. They can either find themselves something constructive to do, or they can get themselves into more trouble. It's up to them."

"You're the boss."

Jayden laughed. "If only that were true." She hung up and went inside to check her pack and share gear with Miguel and Santiago.

CHAPTER 14

"I CAN'T BELIEVE THE FUCKING BITCH just left us!" Killian towered over Rhian as she sat at the table.

"Why not? She told you she would," Rhian said, her eyes locked with his, refusing to back off. Jayden was right. These two needed to learn a little respect, or they were going to get themselves, or someone else, killed.

Discipline was an essential tool for survival when operating in extreme conditions. If you didn't have enough to arrive at a designated meeting on time, you didn't have enough to be a part of a team. While there would be only two winners in the end, they would have to work as a team to stand any chance of getting there.

"But she isn't the one calling the shots here, darlin'." His Irish accent was getting thicker and more pronounced the angrier he got. "You're the boss. Call her back and tell her to come and pick us up. Now."

Rhian slowly rose out of her chair. Killian wasn't a tall man, only five foot five, if he was lucky. She topped him by a good inch, and she had no qualms about using it to her advantage. "No."

"What?" He tipped his head back to meet her gaze, and clearly resented having to look up at her. "You can't do that. I signed up for this fucking challenge. Signed every fucking bit of paper you and those stinking lawyers put in front of me. I'm here to win this thing. And you're trying to put me at a disadvantage. You know I'm the best climber here. You know I can run rings around the rest of these arseholes, so you're trying to give them a better shot at it." Spittle caught at the corner of his mouth.

You owe me for this, Jayden. But, damn, he was obnoxious, and, to her surprise, standing up to him actually felt good.

He wasn't finished. "I'm gonna fucking sue you when this thing is over and I've won it. I'm gonna sue you and that fucking lanky bitch."

Rhian merely waited until he stopped talking, well, shouting. When he did, she said, "Since you signed every piece of paper, you can try to sue us all you like. But you'll find in those documents an agreement to abide by the terms of conduct as set out by myself or the head guide, Jayden Harris."

"That bitch had it in for me from the start. Everyone could fucking see it." He balled his fists at his sides. "I don't know what her problem is, but she's got it in for me." He sneered. "Maybe she's afraid of a little competition." He held his arms out to indicate the kind of competition he thought he represented in a crude display of macho insecurity.

Rhian frowned. "Killian, trust me when I tell you that Jayden would never be afraid of you. In any way."

He growled low in his throat, and his arms moved so quickly she didn't have time to react. One hand wrapped about her throat, and the other whipped back to strike.

The stinging slap of his hand across her cheek brought tears to her eyes and memories clamouring to the forefront of her mind. It was no longer Killian who had her by the throat. Eyes wrinkled slightly with age that had once gazed at her with affection now blazed with malevolent intent. Spiteful words filled with hate spewed from his lips, and the rejection in his blow scarred her so much deeper than the flesh that throbbed.

"Who's afraid now, bitch?"

Killian's heavy Irish accent snapped her attention painfully back to the present. This wasn't her father. Killian stood there with one hand gripped around her neck and his other in a fist, cocked and ready. She closed her eyes as she lifted her hands to grab the fingers pressing into her throat, even as she waited for the next blow to strike.

There was a roar of frustration and a jerky movement, followed by her quick release and a loss of balance. She landed on her backside on the dining room floor. A burly security guard stood at one side of her, a second twisted one of Killian's arms up his back, while Luiji held the one that had been about to strike her by the fist.

Killian roared again, trying desperately to break the hold. Rhian stared at him, heart pounding, chest heaving as she dragged one lungful of air after another into her body. Swallowing heavily, she tasted blood on her tongue.

She wiped her lips with the back of her hand and stared for a moment at the smear of scarlet across her skin. Summoning all her willpower, she gulped back the sob that threatened to tear itself from her aching throat. Rhian would not let him see that. She was the one in control here. Not this pathetic excuse for a human fucking being.

The more he struggled against the restraint, the more detached she began to feel. Slowly but surely, she got her emotions and her breathing under control and levelled him with a glare she knew Rachel would've been proud of.

"Pack your crap," Rhian said, balling her own hands into fists, determined not to let Killian see her shaking. "A driver will be taking you to the airport. Today."

"You can't fucking do that!" Killian raged and struggled against the two men holding him.

"I think you will find, my angry little friend, that she can," Luiji told him.

Rhian pointed to the CCTV camera overhead. "Every second of that has been recorded, Killian." She pointed to the stairs. "You get on a plane, or you can meet the Argentinian police. Your choice."

"Ma'am, I think we should call the police and report this regardless," the security guard said.

She knew he was right. She should report Killian to the authorities, but she was equally sure she had more than enough to deal with as a result of this, never mind the time she'd waste with the police. Plus, Rachel was going to go apeshit about this anyway. Add to that the bad publicity a call to the police would probably cause… Having to explain how she'd let the situation get so out of control was going to be humiliating enough. Containing her fuck-up was definitely the way to go. That meant getting him out of the country was the quickest and cleanest solution to the Killian issue.

She shook her head at the guard. "I'd prefer not to."

"But he assaulted you, Ms Phillips."

She nodded.

"I'm supposed to call in the police in the case of any incident like this."

Rhian offered him a small smile. No doubt the man was worried about his job. *I'll have to make sure Rachel knows it wasn't his fault.* She grimaced internally and hoped it didn't show on her face. *It was my fault after all. I just have to remember not to insult angry little men in the future.* "I understand what you're saying. But I'm a busy woman, and I think Mr O'Leary will learn that his actions have consequences, regardless of police involvement. He's lost his chance at this show, and with it any hope he might have had of using this to further his career."

Luiji pulled Killian away from Rhian and pushed him roughly into a chair. Killian started to get up, but Luiji pinned him in place with his hands on both shoulders from behind. "Learn when you're beaten, man. Do you think she's fucking around with you? Haven't you learnt anything? You're getting off easy. So stay down, or it won't be the airport you are going to."

"Who the fuck do you think you are, Rasta man? Fucking brown-noser. You were all for teaching that frizzy-headed bitch a lesson, same as me."

Luiji nodded. "Yes, I was. But it is I who am learning the lesson from her. It is a shame you cannot learn it with me, but I fear it is beyond you, no?"

"Fuck off."

"Indeed." He shook his head and looked at Rhian. "Are you okay?" he asked her quietly.

She nodded but didn't say anything. The adrenaline of the moment was wearing off, and the shock of it was hitting her. Sweat ran down her spine even though she felt cold inside.

Luiji cocked his head to one side. He clearly didn't believe her, but instead of calling her on it, he twisted his hands in Killian's shirt and tugged him to his feet. "Come. You have a flight to prepare for." He hauled a kicking Killian towards the doors. "Would I be able to discuss matters with you later today, Rhian?"

Rhian nodded. Just once. And watched them disappear out the door and up the stairs. She shook her head again in an attempt to clear it and refused to let her legs give way. The urge to sit in a chair while the world carried on around her was strong, but there was no way she was going to let a tosser like Killian O'Leary see how much he'd gotten to her.

Determined, she put her anger and the grain of fear into a box in her head, labelled it "to be dealt with later", and crossed the floor to the reception desk. After requesting a driver to be outside waiting to take

Killian immediately to the airport and sit with him until he was checked in and through security, she called Mellissa.

"Need you to make some more arrangements. We'll be needing the male alternate ASAP and a flight back to Dublin for Killian O'Leary."

"Bloody hell. What happened?"

Rhian quickly filled her in on the details. Sparse details. No mention of hands-around-throat details.

"He hit you?"

Yup, no question about it. "It was just a slap, Mel." Mellissa didn't need to know how close it had been to being more than that. It would only make her worry. The older woman had long since taken on the role of big-sister-slash-aunt in Rhian's life, and she knew without question that Killian would find himself on the end of some elaborate revenge scheme if Mel thought Rhian had been in real danger. They didn't need any more aggravation. Well, Rhian didn't. Better to play it down and brush it off.

Mellissa giggled. "I'm glad Luiji stepped up."

"Me too. Sounds like they're coming back. I'll let you get the flight sorted. I don't care how indirect a route he has to go. I just want him out of Argentina before the end of the day."

"No problem. I think there's a route that goes via Nairobi. I can get him stuck on a nice long layover."

"Christ," Rhian said. "Remind me never to piss you off."

"What would be the fun if I reminded you?"

Rhian chuckled. "Good point. Speak to you later." She ended the call and watched as Luiji, with Killian's bag on his back, manhandled a now-sullen Killian out of the hotel and pushed him into the waiting car. He handed the bag to the driver and shook his hand. Rhian couldn't hear the conversation between them and didn't really want to know what Luiji might have to relay about the passenger they were both watching through the car window. She made a mental note to make sure the driver got a tip for this job. A big one.

When the car had gone, Luiji straightened his shoulder and walked back into the conclave. "Is it convenient to speak with you now, or would later be better for you?" he asked politely.

"Now's fine, Luiji." She waved her hand to the empty communal area and the table she'd sat at before. Taking her seat, she waited, ignoring the throbbing in her cheek. She could tell by the way Luiji's gaze kept dropping that it must be bright red, and she wondered if an actual handprint was visible.

He sat opposite her and leant his elbows on the beech-wood surface, clasping his hands. "First of all, are you really okay?" He gazed into her eyes, and he seemed to read her.

She couldn't hold his gaze. Not if she wanted to keep herself from crying on him. "I'm fine. Thank you for what you did. I appreciate it. A lot. I know you'd become friends with him, so that couldn't have been easy—"

"He was not a friend. I am ashamed to even be associated with a poor excuse of a man like that." He reached for her hand but stopped himself before he took it and instead clasped his fingers on the table. "I am a man with four sisters, with two young daughters and a man who expects every man to do what I did this afternoon without thought or question. Not for thanks or reward or recognition, but because it is the right thing to do."

"That is a wonderful sentiment and an ideal I think every decent human being shares. But we both know that isn't always the way the world works. And even if that was, I'd still want to thank you for your intervention this afternoon. Because that's also what decent human beings do."

Luiji grinned. "This is very true." He clapped his hands on his thighs. "Good, that is one matter resolved. Next, I must apologise. For myself, my behaviour has been nothing short of arrogance itself. I was overexcited and allowed my machismo, my—how you say—bravado?"

"Yes, bravado. Ego."

"Yes, that is the word. I let my ego do my talking for me. I must let my climbing do it instead."

"I'm very glad you realise that, Luiji."

He nodded, his face still serious and solemn. "I have much to learn and would wish to learn from Jayden Harris. I have looked at her on Google and on YouTube." He drew in a deep breath. "There is much, much I can learn from a climber like her. I was too eager to show her I was worthy of her respect to remember that I had first to earn it. Will it be possible for me to rejoin the group? Please."

"Not today."

He stared at his hands and nodded. "I understand. I will try to make amends with her when she returns with the group." He started to push his chair back.

"We'll be heading to meet her and the group the day after tomorrow. There will be two alternates coming with us. We'll be carrying additional supplies to supplement the team already out there, as we won't need to take some of the technical equipment they already have. For example, there are enough tents already, same with cooking equipment, and so on." She stopped, hoping he would follow what she wanted and seize upon the opportunity he was being offered.

"If you can show me where the stores are, or direct me, I will make sure we have all we need ready for the trip. I can prepare the equipment for each pack too."

"Good. That will help me a great deal."

He smiled for the first time since he had walked out of the conclave to see the empty parking space. "Is there anything else I can do to help?"

She shook her head. "Not for me. But you could see if the camera crew need anything. They always seem to have heavy equipment that needs humping around."

"Of course." He stood and reached for her hand. Instead of taking it to kiss, as he seemed to do all the time, he shook it. "I will redeem myself. You shall see."

She watched him go. The bounce was back in his step, but the arrogant swagger was gone. "Jayden," she said to the empty room, "you sure handled that one right." She paused. "Come to think of it, Rhi, you didn't handle that pile of shit too badly yourself." She stretched her right hand over her left shoulder and giggled as she gave herself a little pat on the back.

CHAPTER 15

PACKS FULLY LOADED AND STOWED in the belly of the bus, thirteen pumped-up climbers waited—five full minutes before her deadline—for Jayden to board and get moving. She was happy with the way they'd all worked together. They'd been efficient and practical. They weren't carrying anything they didn't need, though she felt they'd be taking one or two items with them in the future as soon as she showed them exactly how the small items could save their lives.

Carlos parked up at El Pillar Hotel, and she led them down the path she had taken a couple of weeks earlier with Rhian. It had been cooler then, but temperatures on the glacier would drop quickly, and they'd need the full gear she'd insisted they all bring with them. They walked quickly, covering the ground to the lake at least an hour faster than she had managed on her earlier outing, and Rhian had been far from slow. Water bottles filled and cool-weather gear donned at the far end of the lake, they began the climb onto the glacier.

When they reached the glacier plateau, she led them east, away from the route she'd taken with Rhian and, instead, onto the glacier proper. In front of them all was the horseshoe-shaped arc of the Fitz Roy massif. She gathered them all around her and pointed out each summit in turn.

"Ladies and gentlemen, that is your goal: to start with your ascent of Guillaumet, and then from the summit you will traverse the ridge, rappelling and climbing each mountain until you descend from de l'S a week later." She waved her arm in a huge sweeping arc. "Pick your base camp location. Bear in mind that while we aren't climbing any of them this week, we will be soon."

"I thought you said we were going out to do high camps," Taylor said.

"You will be, but you don't have to summit a peak to camp high. Simply climbing from the glacier up to Passo Guillaumet is high enough for what needs to be accomplished this week." She pointed to the low point of the ridge line that still towered over their current position by several hundred metres. "Anyway, as I was saying, choose your base camp with care so it will suit your needs and the weather conditions that are so prevalent here."

She stood back to watch and listen as they discussed the merits and pitfalls of each possible location. In the end, they chose a site halfway between Guillaumet and de l'S.

"Sure, it's a good spot," Hunter Jones offered. "But this location will be open to the wind blowing across the glacier. That's gonna make for cold and difficult conditions."

Voices of assent chimed in.

"Is true," Felix Romero said. "But we could build a wall of ice blocks around the perimeter to protect the camp from the worst of the conditions."

"That's a lot of work." Sky pointed to the landscape. "There isn't a lot of fresh fall. We'd have to cut the blocks."

Felix shrugged. "It would be worth it, I think. We're going to be using this camp for much time. Effort now would prevent us work later when we are not so fresh."

"That's a good point," Hunter agreed. "I think it makes sense." He met Sky's gaze and grinned. "It doesn't have to be the Great Wall of China or anything."

Sky laughed. "Good job. Shall we get over there, then, guys, and see what snow we can find for our wall?"

Jayden was impressed. They were taking the task seriously and setting up a proper base camp. Not just some makeshift, "it'll do" kind of affair.

"Let's go and get the temporary sleds put together to give them a hand transporting the ice and snow bricks they plan to make for their wall," she said to Santiago and Miguel. "Since they're going to keep us warmer and out of the wind with it, I don't see any harm in helping with a little transportation."

"*Sí,*" Santiago agreed.

"Not the construction, though, guys. They do that themselves."

"And if the wall no hold?" Miguel asked.

"Make sure we put our tents out of the line of fire." She grinned. "It won't be the first time we've slept through the wind on the glacier."

"Is true. Would be nice to have a nice barrier, though." Santiago sighed. "Let us see what they come up with." He dipped his head and took off after the group, quickly gaining on them and offering their assistance with transportation.

The work went quickly, and within four hours, they had the tents set up and a four-foot-high arc of ice blocks along the western edge to protect from the prevailing wind. Jayden knew it wouldn't be long enough or high enough at the thirty feet they'd completed, but they'd figure that out overnight. She smirked to herself. They could add to it or not tomorrow, if they had the energy. Tonight, they needed to prepare water for the upcoming day, feed themselves, and get a decent night's sleep. None of which was easy on the ice.

Jayden surveyed her motley crew of sleep-deprived climbers as they huddled around mugs of coffee and bowls of eggs and beans. The wind had howled all night, and the clear, blue sky of yesterday had given way to the grey clouds that lurked above them and clung to the summits of the mountains around them. The glacier valley looked an uninviting and fearsome place.

"Perfect," she whispered to herself as she sipped on her own coffee.

Conversation had already begun about raising the height and doubling the length of the ice wall. She planned to give them till lunchtime to do it. That would give her enough time to scout around for the locations she wanted for the afternoon's training. But that didn't mean she had to waste the time they had now.

"Who can tell me the six principles of self-rescue?" A hush descended, and she fought to restrain the laughter in her throat. It really was like being a teacher in a school. "Come on. What's the first step in rescuing yourself when the shit hits the fan?" She glanced around. "Felix?"

"*Merde*," he muttered under his breath. "Survey the scene. Prevent further injuries by identifying potential environmental factors to yourself or a potential rescuer."

"Textbook answer. Good. Second step?" No one spoke. "If you don't volunteer, I'll pick someone again. You should all know this."

"Determine first aid requirements," Hunter said.

"Good. Three?"

"Plan your course of action," Sky offered.

"Excellent. Four?"

"Build system for rescue," Kimi added.

"Exactly. Five?"

"Double-check your system," Tomasi, the Colorado-based Fijian climber, said.

"Exactly. No point using something that's going to make the situation worse. And finally, number six?"

"Initiate your plan. Administer first aid, rescue yourself, and or locate aid," Taylor responded.

Jayden grinned. "See? You did know it." She checked her watch. "It's just after six now. Lunch is at twelve. You've got till then to finish what you want to do with your wall. After lunch, we'll be working through a selection of scenarios for self-rescue and the various techniques and skills we'll need to save our own skins should accidents occur."

Murmurs of assent greeted her words, and she quickly finished her coffee and donned her daypack. She and Miguel roped together to cross the glacier and search out the various crags and outcrops that would suit her purpose. There were plenty at the base of Aguja Mermoz, the peak between Guillaumet and Fitz Roy. She chose a route on the west face of the peak called the Hypermermoz, a 350-metre, 6c-rated climb that met the famed Argentina route to the summit of the peak.

She didn't need to climb that high. She only needed to go twenty metres or so to place her anchors and fix the rope she needed. Miguel was a competent climber, and she trusted him on the belay as she climbed the sixty feet, placing nuts, chocks, and cams as she went. She fixed her quick draws and slid her rope home to buy as much protection as she could.

After a long ten feet without a good place to slip a nut into the rock, she found a good-sized crack, used a cam at the narrowest part, and placed a stone chock at the widest part of the crack. Wrapping a girth hitch around the conveniently shaped rock, she heard a sound she hadn't in quite a while—humming, a gentle melodic tune that reverberated off the rocks and echoed in her ears. It was her own voice. Had it truly been eighteen-plus months since she'd done that? Since she'd felt the music inside?

She rested her forehead against the rock wall and breathed in the scent of earth and chalk and snow. She was part of the rock. It was in her. And she was never satisfied unless she could slake this thirst in her soul. It didn't matter that she was only climbing sixty feet. It didn't matter that she wasn't leading a daring attempt on a summit or racing for a record. No. She just needed to feel the rock beneath her fingertips and smell the earth in the air, and she was home. This was what Fen had been trying to tell her, not just in the hospital when she made her agree to this job but every day since she got off the plane from Nepal.

"Okay, Jay?" Miguel shouted up to her.

"I'm good. Just smelling the rock for a minute." She could just picture the frown on his face at the crazy English woman smelling the rocks, but that was okay. She was a little bit crazy. Always had been. It was part of what pushed her to do the things she did. "I think we're high enough here for what we need to do. I'm gonna rappel down. You got me?"

"*Sí*. I have your weight. Go."

She sat back in her harness and walked down the wall as he slowly let out the rope. She looked about her as she descended. The clouds were still hiding the sun, making the day grey and murky, but inside, she felt lighter and freer than she had since Rebecca...since Rebecca had died. She closed her eyes. She didn't want to picture Rebecca's dead eyes again. She couldn't stand to see them. Not here. Not when she was just finding herself again. Surely that would just be too cruel.

A lunch of dried sausage, rice, and rehydrated vegetables was waiting for her when they got back to base camp. The wall was now a little over five feet high and more than double its previous length. The worker bees had been busy, and they all looked exceedingly pleased with themselves. They sat around the camp, down to shirts and pants. The exertion had warmed them all up nicely, and the wind break certainly helped keep their little encampment a lot warmer. She accepted her plate and a mug of coffee and found a bench that had been built from ice blocks. A few of them were dotted around the camp now. They'd been very busy indeed.

She tipped her head back, pointing it at where the sun should have been and smiled. Today was a good day.

CHAPTER 16

RHIAN SWIPED THE TIP OF her pen around the page. The image that began to appear beneath her fingers was lost in the concentration of creating it. A bold line here, a shadow there, and a beam of light reflecting in the foreground.

"Are we boring you, Rhi?" Rachel's voice cut through the static-laden Skype connection as well as her daydream, shocking her back to the reality of the conference meeting she was supposed to be paying attention to. Angela, the director, and Simon, her assistant, sat on either side of Rachel, watching Rhian with smirks on their faces, and the six tiny windows of faces on the call from the far corners of the world were fixed on her too. Well, as fixed as they could be when they were looking at her tiny little square on a computer screen.

"Sorry, no. I was just making some notes. A couple of things I've remembered I need to organise before the alternates arrive."

Rachel gave her a look that told Rhian she knew she was talking bullshit, but Rachel let it go. "And on that note, we've had a very unhappy phone call from Killian O'Leary."

"And?" Rhian asked.

"He could make life uncomfortable and create some unpleasant media attention," Angela suggested.

"He can try. He's got no chance after what he did, though."

"He's claiming he was provoked," Rachel said.

"Fuck off."

Rachel's eyebrow shot up. "Excuse me?"

Rhian glared and reached over. She opened a file and clicked the *play* button. The CCTV footage of Killian's assault on her, and his clear intention to strike again before Luiji physically stopped him played on all their screens. When it finished, there was a series of uncomfortable grunts and shuffles from the callers. But as Rhian expected, Rachel reacted first.

"That little fucker!"

"That's the whole scene. How did I provoke him?"

Rachel shook her head and put on a masterful show of remaining professional, even though she was pissed. Really pissed. Rhian cringed. She wasn't looking forward to the bollocking she was going to get later.

"Not you," Rachel replied. "He's claiming Jayden provoked him by abandoning him and causing detrimental damage to his training and that she had been aggressive and bullying in her manner towards him prior to that."

Rhian laughed angrily. "The only time he ever met her was that morning where he tried to show her up and she called him out on it. I can get you that footage too, if you like."

"It might be worth it to have all our bases covered."

"You are joking, right?"

Rachel cocked her head to the side and said slowly, "Would I joke about something that could result in legal action against my company?"

Shit. Rhian swallowed. "No. But it's ridiculous. Jayden did nothing wrong. This is a case of sour grapes after he got himself kicked off the show for being a wanker. Pardon my language. But he was. You saw what happened with me. That isn't just high spirits or a bit of showing off. He hit me. He physically assaulted me. Now, even if someone else had provoked him—which she didn't—that would still not make this behaviour acceptable, or defensible. He'd still be going home even if she had wound him up to it."

Rachel hiked her eyebrow up. "Precisely, kiddo. You're right—you are absolutely spot on. Thanks to this footage you've turned up, we've got him precisely where we want him, and we have nothing to hide. So why not be completely up front about it and show that?" Rachel's smile broadened.

Rhian wanted to think it was because she was proud of her, maybe even impressed with the way she'd handled the incident herself, as well as the shitstorm they were currently sitting through. But it was more than likely because Rachel knew she couldn't lose this particular battle. Killian might as well say goodbye to his kneecaps.

"From our perspective, it looks well on the show and our company if he does try to make a meal of this and we have to leak this footage. Puts our clients right at the forefront of protecting women's rights and taking a stand on violence against women."

Rhian pressed her thumb and forefinger against her eyes to give herself a moment. Trust Rachel to already have a spin for this little incident. She shook her head. "Fine," she said and dropped her hand back to the table. "I'll dig out the footage of his earlier interaction with Jayden and send it all over to you too."

"Great. I suspect as soon as Mr O'Leary and his counsel see that, they'll slink back to their hole."

"He has counsel already?" She glanced at her watch. "He won't even be back in Ireland yet."

"Whether he is or isn't, we've had two calls from the man himself and one from a Dermot O'Leary, purporting to be his legal representative in a suit he plans to bring against us, Patagonia, and the Argentinian tourist board if his position on the show isn't reinstated immediately."

"On what grounds?"

"Bullying, sexual discrimination, and sexual harassment."

Rhian stared at her. "Are you kidding me?"

"Nope."

"Who's supposed to have harassed and discriminated against him?"

"Not curious about the bullying?"

Rhian waved a hand. "Clearly he's aiming that at Jayden."

"Yes. The rest is levelled at you. Says you're pissed and ordered him off the show because you came on to him and he wouldn't sleep with you."

Rhian laughed. One loud, harsh bark of a laugh.

Rachel offered her a half-smile. "I know, I know. But it would still be awful if you had to defend it in a court."

Angela frowned. "What are we missing?"

Rhian glanced away from the computer screen and met the gaze of her face-to-face colleague. "I'm a lesbian. I've been out for almost six years now. As you can see, Rachel knows all about it, so we can easily put this particular claim of his to sleep."

"Yes, but it might strengthen his sexual discrimination claim."

Rhian tipped her head to one side.

"You're a man-hating dyke after all, right?" Rachel said with a derisive laugh that Rhian suspected was to soften the insult that Killian would hurl at her.

"Perfect. Just perfect."

"That's life, kiddo." Rachel sympathised.

Rhian paused and tried to visualise the best way forward. She had contingencies for when her contingencies went wrong. But she didn't have a plan for this. She didn't know what the best decision was or how the fallout would affect the project or their clients. She was sure of one thing, though.

"I'm not letting him back on set. Whatever else he claims happened, I have cast-iron evidence of his assault and the way he had to be restrained from continuing his attack on me. That gets anyone a plane ride home."

Rachel nodded. "Your project, your call. Get me that other video file, and we'll take it from there."

She didn't know if it was the right call, in terms of PR. And she equally couldn't tell if Rachel truly agreed with her decision. Maybe Rachel was supporting her decision publicly to not undermine a project leader in front of those working under her, and Rhian would hear more about it in that private bollocking she was expecting later. The uncertainty of it all made the self-doubts creep in. *Maybe I should just swallow my pride and agree to have him back. Is that what Rachel wants me to do? But then the cocky little shit would be unbearable and make it a living nightmare for everyone else. Not to mention me. Unless he got voted off quickly. Given how this has played out, the little bastard would get out of that too.*

The conversation shifted to the logistics of getting the camera crew and equipment out to the glacier. They decided upon horse transportation and then sledding the gear across the ice. It would be a laborious, energy-sapping, time-consuming process. But it was seemingly the only realistic option with such heavy gear.

Her mind wandered easily from the discussion of logistics and planning. She and Angela had already been over this numerous times. She went back to her simple line drawing, adding a small patch of shadow under one sweeping line.

Rachel's voice drew her back to the real world again.

"I think that's everything for now, people," Rachel said. "Rhian, would you mind staying on the call a few minutes with me?"

Rhian swallowed but nodded and said her goodbyes to the rest of the callers. *Right. One bollocking coming up.* As if they sensed what was about to happen, Angela and Simon wandered away to give her some space.

"Thanks," Rachel started. "Since I know you've got your trip to organise for tomorrow and the two alternates to pick up, I won't keep you long."

"Okay."

Rachel's gaze was glued to her cheek, and the anger she'd held in check was evident in the tightness of her jaw and the flush on her cheeks.

"I'm sorry, Rachel. I know I fucked up—"

"Are you okay?" Rachel's voice was quiet and husky, and her eyes shone with tears in the light of her computer screen.

Tears? Christ, this must be worse than I thought. "Yes. It was nothing—"

"Nothing? Nothing?" Rachel's eyes were wide, her mouth hung open slightly. "That was not nothing. I can see the bruising from here, and I'm in fucking England! Christ."

"I'm sorry. I don't know how things escalated so quickly. I just never saw it coming."

"How could you?" She exhaled loudly, clearly reining in her temper. "Why didn't you call the police and let them deal with him?"

"I didn't want the negative publicity." She laughed derisively. "Guess that's just another way I fucked this one up."

"Stop."

Rhian looked up at the screen.

"You didn't fuck this up. I wouldn't have gone to the police either, if it were me. For the same reason. There was no reason to expect that this little dickhead would try to blackmail his way back in after what he did. So as the business owner, I understand your instinct and thank you for it. You did exactly the right thing."

Rhian stared at her. "I did?"

Rachel nodded. "Yes. Couldn't have done it better myself, kiddo."

"Thank you."

"Don't thank me. As your—as your mother, I want to rip his fucking bollocks off."

Rhian chuckled. That ferocity in Rachel's voice was for *her*. It was defending her. And when was the last time Rachel had so definitively praised her like this? *Rachel must be feeling pretty sorry for me for taking a smack in the face for her to be so supportive.*

Rachel visibly calmed herself and slid her professional persona back into place.

"Stop looking at me like that. I need to go and be a bitch again."

"Sorry."

"Bloody kid." She smoothed her hand over her hair. "Right, you get back to work. Send me those video files as soon as you can, and I'll take care of it all on this end."

"Okay." Rhian clicked the mouse to end the session. *Well, that went better than I expected.*

Simon and Angela walked over to the table as she closed the lid of her laptop.

"You okay?" Angela held out a wet cloth.

Rhian nodded and took it. It felt so good against her sore cheek.

"Bastard," Simon said. "I can't believe what a wanker he turned out to be."

Rhian shrugged. "Nothing we can do about it now." She tried to ignore the pang of guilt at the trouble she was causing everyone. After all, she'd picked him to be a contestant. They had wanted some conflict in the show, after all. Ratings and all that. She hadn't expected it to backfire on her quite like this, though.

"We'll leave you to it, hon. Just wanted to make sure you were okay after that shower of shit." Angela leant over and tapped Rhian's pad. "Nice sketch, by the way." She twisted her head as she looked at it. "You've captured the look in her eyes just right."

Rhian frowned and leant back in her chair, looking consciously for the first time at the image she'd drawn. "Fuck," she whispered under her breath as Simon and Angela crossed the room and the door swung shut behind them. "That's not good."

Jayden's face stared back at her from the page.

CHAPTER 17

JAYDEN SCRUTINISED THE EAGER FACES around her in a small semicircle. Three pairs waited to be given the scenario they would have to safely navigate. Three ropes hung from the rock faces close by them.

"Okay, scenario one: your lead climber's unconscious and with a limb jammed in a crack, but his weight is still loading your belay. You need to escape your belay and effect a rescue. You have approximately twenty-five feet of slack in your line. Do not let your casualty drop. They'd break the limb and in all likelihood end up dead from smacking their heads on the rock wall, or if they came loose, they'd fall to their deaths. But I'm sure I don't need to reiterate all that to you, do I?"

Six bobbing heads greeted her mutely.

"Okay, Sky, Jake, Felix, you're our casualties. Hunter, Liv, and Lonnie, let's see what you can do."

The three casualties quickly climbed the twenty feet she needed of them to weight the lines and find a sufficient crack to cling to. No real stuck limbs…just in case. But close enough for the simulation to be effective.

Hunter went quickly into action as soon as Felix stopped moving. He tied a Mule knot to free his hands from holding Felix's weight on the loose line. He used the slack on his line to tie on to his anchor point with a figure-of-eight knot before slipping a cordlette over his shoulder and securing it to the loaded line with a Klemheist knot above his Mule knot. The final step in releasing himself from the belay was to attach the carabiner in his Klemheist knot to the remaining slack fixed to the anchor behind him.

Jayden glanced at her watch. Less than two minutes. "Good. What're you going to do now?"

"Use the line to ascend and assess his situation."

"How?"

"Prusik foot loop to help me up the rope that I know is safely anchored at both ends. I'll use a carabiner to keep me attached to the line and use another strap through my harness with a couple of Prusik knots on either side to slide up the line."

"Do it."

He clearly knew what he needed to do. Quickly. She was happy to leave Santiago watching his progress while she turned her attention to Lonnie, who was still struggling with his Mule knot to secure the load from his hands. She walked over, her crampons biting into the ice as she moved, and spoke quietly to him. She walked him through the movement step by step as he finally managed to secure the knot he needed and begin to secure his anchor. She ignored the flush of frustration that coloured his cheeks. There was no place for pride or ego when it came to survival.

Liv started to scoot herself up the rope towards Sky, only a minute or so behind Hunter. Another impressive show from the shy climber who had had little to say for herself in the two days they'd been on the ice, yet had put in solid performances around the camp, including her skills on the rope and on the wall.

Overall, they'd all put in some solid performances. Lonnie was the one who had struggled the most with this exercise, but he was managing now. Every one of them had managed to successfully rescue their beleaguered lead climber. So far, anyway. And most of them had done so with practical ease that spoke of much repeated practice of the skills. Pete's knotwork was simply a little rusty. Not unusual for a free-solo climber who didn't climb with a buddy or a rope most of the time. She had a feeling he'd be sitting around the camp after dinner tonight with his practice cord, tying and retying knots until he could do them without looking. Exactly as she wanted. This was playtime. This was a chance to figure out where they needed work and to put that work in.

Once each of them had freed their climber and returned them safely to the ground, they switched roles. They moved quickly through the skills. No one wanted to be standing around, or hanging on a rope for too long. The wind was picking up, and the chill was chapping at their noses and cheeks.

They ran through four scenarios in total, completing each one successfully with no pretend fatalities.

As far as Jayden was concerned, it was another good day on the mountain. She'd missed this part of her job, of her old life. She loved teaching people the skills they needed to survive out here. She had those skills. She had the knowledge. People were drawn to the mountains, to the ice, to the thrill of the challenge. It was something primeval and instinctive that called to the adventurer inside. It always would.

New people would always be attempting new challenges; it was human nature. And the mountains would claim their share of souls as payment. Not everyone who sought the summit would come down safely. But she had the skills to give those who tried the best chance they could get of accomplishing it. She could help most of them return home safe at the end of the day. She could. In her head, she knew it. Seeing Lonnie's triumph as he successfully negotiated the last three scenarios only made that clear to her. The image of Rebecca's dead eyes would always haunt her. But running from that wouldn't ease the burden of guilt she carried. Only using it to fuel her desire to bring home safely as many people as she could would do that. Preventing as many people as possible from having to live with the nightmare that still woke her at night was the only good thing she could ever hope to achieve from that disaster.

This place, this job…this was what she was born to do. She just had to keep her heart believing it.

CHAPTER 18

Oh. My. God. The picture you've got of Brooke Shields going up that climbing wall does not do her justice.

Rhian read the text message from Mellissa for a second time while she was sorting her gear and harness in the annex of Jayden's office. Luiji was on the other side of the room, packing extra provisions in his already-heavy pack. It seemed he was intent on making up for his arrogant behaviour and planned to do it with a show of brute strength. She quickly responded to the text:

???

Mellissa wasted no time replying.

Why didn't you tell me she could be the real Brooke Shields's daughter or something! She's stunning!

Rhian shrugged at her phone's screen.

I don't really recall thinking that when I met her.

Are you blind! And you call yourself a lesbian. I'm straight and married, and I'd sleep with her.

Rhian laughed and tried to imagine strait-laced Mellissa chatting up a woman. It wasn't happening. She replied again:

Don't do that. We're in enough trouble as it is. Just bring them back here so we can get ready for our hike tomorrow.

sigh. Whatever.

She tossed her phone onto the counter and started clipping quickdraws, cams, and nuts to a sling to make them easier to transport. She doubted she'd be doing any climbing, but Jayden insisted that anyone going out to base camp was going prepared. The last thing Rhian was going to do was break any of Jayden's rules and undermine her authority. Her mind was drawn back to the sketch she'd done of her while she was supposed to be listening to Rachel during their meeting. What had driven her to draw that—to draw her? The question kept buzzing inside her head, an answer sitting on its wings. But she sure as hell wasn't going to acknowledge it, no matter how many times she asked herself the same stupid question.

It's just clearly been too long since I got laid. She ran her fingers through her hair and grabbed another handful of gear before securing it in place, trying to remember exactly how long too long had been. Three years. On a holiday to Spain. She'd been with another climber on the tour from America. It had been a little holiday romance, short and sweet. *Bloody hell. No wonder I'm doodling every pretty face I see.*

Satisfied, she finished packing her gear and called out to Luiji. "Dinner?"

"Absolutely." He poked his head up from the pack he was hunched over. "I just need to wrap that rope over there, and I am ready."

"Need a hand?"

He shook his head. "I can do it." He was already half-done wrapping the long length by the time she crossed the room. He really was engaged in a supreme effort to make amends. She just hoped Jayden would appreciate it when they met up tomorrow. She wasn't looking forward to telling her everything that had happened with Killian since she'd left, but there was no getting around it. Jayden needed to know. And besides, she'd know something was wrong the instant she saw that Killian wasn't with Rhian's little entourage.

They walked back to the conclave in comfortable silence, and dinner was dotted only with conversation about the next day's hike. It was... companionable. And, indeed, Rhian found herself enjoying his company, something she hadn't expected when they'd first met. Like Killian, she'd accepted him on the show not just for his climbing skills—which were formidable—but because his personality was polarising. You either loved him—which she suspected many of the young female viewers would with his long dreadlocks, chiselled jawline, muscled abs, and his perfect puppy-dog look. Or you hated him—many of the slightly older male viewers probably would, for the exact same reasons. He would become a talking point, and that would start to generate some buzz. She couldn't help but wonder if he suspected as much.

The door to the common room opened, and Mellissa walked in, a scowl on her face and the two smiling newcomers on her heels.

"Wonder what that look's about," Rhian whispered to herself too quietly for Luiji to have heard.

"Our new team members," Luiji cried, jumping to his feet and hurrying across the room to greet them. He wrapped his arms around Brooke—who did look remarkably like her famous namesake—and kissed her on both cheeks. "A pleasure to meet such a beautiful lady."

Rhian sniggered to herself. "And that's exactly why you'll either love him or hate him," she said, again under her breath.

Brooke, for her part, swiftly yet diplomatically backed out of his grasp, took hold of his hand, and shook it. Rhian was impressed with the way she handled the young Lothario and established her level of comfortable contact. Luiji just laughed and pumped her hand vigorously.

They'd made good time from the airport, and Rhian smiled as she welcomed them all. She held her hand out to shake with Brooke as she had done with Luiji and was taken off balance when the young woman tugged her into a tight embrace. Luiji's eyebrows rose and a knowing grin spread across his face. He offered Rhian a subtle thumbs up. *Great. Just fucking great. Now I remember why I didn't put her in the main team.*

During the trials, Brooke had been friendly—overfriendly—towards her. At first, Rhian had been more than a little flattered. She was gorgeous, after all. And Brooke Shields—the real one—had been her first crush. She'd watched *The Blue Lagoon* until the damn tape wore out. But it had quickly become evident that Brooke wasn't acting upon a natural attraction. Her actions and words didn't really match up. The look in her eyes was just a little…off. When she was supposedly unable to tear her gaze from Rhian, she'd seemed distracted. Rhian had quickly come to the conclusion it was a ploy, an attempt to curry her favour in order to ensure Brooke's place in selection. Instead it'd had the opposite effect: Rhian had hated the way

Brooke had tried to manipulate her so blatantly. And Brooke seemed to think the tactic would have some benefit now she was here.

Rhian quickly pulled away and departed to the kitchen to ask the staff for meals for the three of them. Within ten minutes, they were sitting down to plates of spaghetti bolognese, a fresh loaf of garlic bread, and a pot of coffee.

"What? No wine?" Brooke ripped a piece of bread from the loaf and took a hearty bite.

Rhian frowned and shook her head. Mellissa was supposed to explain tomorrow's schedule to them. "Not with such an early start. We need to have had breakfast and be ready to leave by seven."

Brooke waved her hand. "Yah, yah." She clicked her fingers and looked towards the kitchen door. "The service here isn't what I was expecting."

"This isn't a five-star hotel." Mellissa's clipped tone took Rhian by surprise.

"You're not joking," Brooke replied.

"Staff and crew aren't here to wait on you. If you want something, you've got legs. Go and get it yourself." Mellissa's hands were clasped tight, her lips were pulled into a thin line, and her eyes looked as hard and angry as Rhian had ever seen them.

What the hell happened between these two?

Brooke scraped her chair back and stormed into the kitchen. After only moments, they heard loud voices, then cajoling laughter. Eventually, the doors swung open again, and Brooke reappeared with a bottle of wine tucked under her arm and four glasses in her hands. *Four?*

Brooke put the glasses down in front of everyone except Mellissa, and started to pour. Rhian held her hand over her own glass and just managed to stop herself from calling her out when she caught Mellissa shaking her head at her, and mouthing, "Don't." Brooke shrugged and poured into the remaining three. She told stories about the flight and about her own experience learning to fly, how she could've made a much better job of the landing than the pilot had done. Oskar, the other alternate, was as quiet as Brooke was brash and annoying. This was the other reason Rhian hadn't chosen her to begin with. While she was making reason number two perfectly clear to everyone, she was busy reinforcing reason number one under the table by squeezing Rhian's knee.

Rhian sighed and moved away, crossing her legs so they were as far away from Brooke as possible without making a scene or getting up. When the conversation stalled, Rhian pushed her chair back and faked a yawn.

"Well, ladies and gents, I'm afraid it's time for me to head up. Like I said, we've got an early start in the morning and a long hike ahead of us."

Mellissa, Luiji, and Oskar all followed her lead. Luiji gathered Rhian and Mellissa's plates. "I'll take these in for you both and see to the cleaning up," he said. "See you in the morning."

Rhian smiled gratefully. "Thanks, Luiji."

"I'll give you a hand," Oskar said and grabbed the extra glasses alongside his plate.

"Good plan." Luiji pushed open the door with his foot and held it ajar for Oskar to go through first.

"Goodnight, everyone." Rhian crossed the room and began climbing the stairs to the top floor with Mellissa next to her.

"I'll come with you, ladies," Brooke called after them, then knocked back a half glass of wine and practically raced to the foot of the stairs and climbed up alongside them.

Mellissa frowned. "You need to take care of your plates."

Brooke scowled. "The boys offered to do the cleaning."

"I don't recall them making that offer to you," Mellissa said, a growl in her voice.

Rhian schooled her face not to react, but the behaviour was most odd. Mellissa had been her admin assistant for four years. She was a good fifteen years older than Rhian, married for more than twenty years, and the embodiment of a competent, capable, and willing assistant. They'd worked together on countless projects, travelled to many places, and become friends in that time. And this was the first time she had ever seen Mellissa react this way. To anyone. She was without fail placid, friendly, demonstrative, and easy-going. Seeing this...fiercely protective...behaviour from her was like seeing her childhood teddy bear grow fangs.

"Besides, Luiji can show you where your room is. You're on the same floor as him. We're not." She slipped her hand through Rhian's arm and tugged her away and up the stairs.

Rhian caught the scowl on Brooke's face out of the corner of her eye but didn't say anything. As soon as they reached the fourth floor, Rhian followed Mellissa into her room and waited as Mellissa flopped down on her bed and smacked a fist into the pillow.

"What happened?" Rhian finally asked.

"Doesn't matter. Just don't get sucked in by her."

Rhian perched on the edge of her bed. "Do you really think I'm so desperate I'd let someone take advantage of me?"

Mellissa turned over and stared up at her. "You knew?"

Rhian nodded. "Question is, how did you know before you even got her back here and saw her behaviour towards me?"

"Simple. She explained her strategy for winning this show to us in the car on the way back here."

Rhian frowned and bit her lip. The show would be won by a combination of successfully completing challenges, public vote, then being the first pair to cross the line on the final traverse. Getting onto the show was the last time Rhian would have any bearing on the possible results. From here on out, it was up to the climbers to prove themselves, win popularity, then give everything they had to win. "I don't see how she thinks seducing me would ensure her winning the show."

"She figures you'll keep her out of the public vote if she's sleeping with you, that you'll want to keep her around as long as possible."

Rhian shook her head. "It's not up to me."

"I know that, and you know that. Seems little Miss Thinks-a-Lot-of-Herself doesn't."

"And that's what's got you wound up like this?"

"Of course it does."

Rhian stared at her.

"I hate women like that. She thinks all she's got to do is flash her tits, or suck on…whatever…and she'll get everything she wants. Bitch gives the rest of us a bad name. And to think she thinks you'd fall for that sort of crap…God, she makes me so mad." Mellissa frowned. "What? Why are you staring at me like that?"

Rhian shook her head. "Nothing. Sorry. I've just never seen you this upset before."

"Well, you didn't have to listen to her in the Jeep. She was going on and on about how she… Well, never mind. I'm sure you can fill in the blanks."

"A bit descriptive, was she?" Rhian wiggled her eyebrows, ready to try to lighten the mood.

"Well, let's just say, if I'd recorded it, I could've given it to Todd. It would've been a present to myself."

Rhian burst out laughing. "That good?"

Mellissa nodded through her own fit of giggles.

"Maybe I should get Oskar to tell me."

"Don't you dare. I'm amazed that boy could look you in the eye after everything she said she was going to do to you."

"Aw, come on. You're seriously not going to tell me?"

"Nope."

"It's been three years since I got laid, Mel. You gotta give me something."

"Three years?"

Rhian nodded solemnly.

"Then I definitely can't tell you. It'd kill ya." She fell back on her bed, laughing, wrapping one arm around her waist and pointing at Rhian's crestfallen face. She was at least in a better mood now.

"Bitch."

Mellissa kept laughing for a few seconds before she put her hand on Rhian's arm. "Seriously, what she was saying, the way she was saying it, she made me sick. You're a good friend, Rhian. I want better than that for you."

"Don't worry, Mel. By the sounds of it, I want better than that for myself." She grasped Mellissa's arm and pulled her into a gentle hug. "Thanks for sticking up for me and defending my honour."

"All part of the secretary's code." She squeezed her tight before pulling away and heading for the door. "It's the best way to ensure bonuses."

"Bitch!" Rhian yelled at the rapidly closing door. Mellissa's laughter rippled easily through the thick wood.

CHAPTER 19

Jayden was leading a pair of climbers through crevasse training when she saw Rhian and her three contestants crossing the glacier, roped together in pairs and spread out across the ice for safety, exactly as she'd instructed Rhian to do. They still had a decent walk ahead of them before they reached base camp. Enough time for Jayden to finish the crevasse session and get coffee made before they sauntered in.

When they finally arrived at the encampment, Rhian pulled off her hood and neck gaiter and grinned. "Damn, it's nice to be out of that wind for a bit. I'm loving that ice wall."

Jayden helped her lift her pack off her back and lowered it to the ground as the others followed her into a semicircle of people gathering around.

Luiji shook hands with Hunter and Lonnie, tugging them in for the obligatory man hugs before chest-bumping Tomasi and tipping his head to the rest of the team. Jayden filed the information away for later use, as she did with every detail she learnt about her team. She looked around to where Killian stood on the edge of the group, only to find it wasn't Killian. A new face smiled at her alongside the woman she hadn't met before. She strode over to them.

"Hi, I'm Jayden. You must be Brooke." She shook Brooke's hand first then held it out to the new guy.

"Oskar Nowak."

"Well, nice to meet you, Oskar." She waved her arm out wide. "Welcome to base camp. We've got coffee just brewed, so help yourselves. Dinner shouldn't be but a few minutes, right, Felix?"

"Yes, ma'am," he shouted from over at the camp kitchen. He had a smile on his face, clearly enjoying his turn as camp chef as he tossed the contents of one pan and stirred another. It smelled gorgeous, and Jayden couldn't wait to get a bowl full of it, whatever it was.

"How long?"

"Twenty minutes," Felix shouted back.

"Plenty of time. Hunter, Lonnie, over here." She called and waited for them to arrive. "Guys, this is Oskar. He's gonna bunk with you two." She turned back to Oskar with a smile. "This afternoon they were busy tidying it up to make space in their tent. We thought it would be for Killian, but now it's for you, so you should at least be able to get your sleeping bag in there." They all laughed and sauntered off, Hunter leading the way. "Follow me," she said to Brooke.

"You're the head honcho around here?" Brooke asked.

"Nah, that's Rhian. I'm just the guide." She stopped in front of the group of women chatting with Rhian. "Sky, Kimi, this is Brooke. She'll be sharing with you ladies."

"I'm not sharing with Rhian?" Brooke asked with a frown.

Jayden shook her head, surprised, and a little unsettled by the question. "No, you'll be sharing with Sky and Kimi." *Rhian will be sharing with me. It's my turn to spend some time with her now. What the hell? Where did that come from?* She pushed aside the intrusive thoughts and focused on the sneering woman in front of her. "You'll partner Kimi for your training tomorrow. It'll do you good to get to know each other a little bit. Luiji!" she shouted and turned on her heel, dismissing Brooke and her annoying dissatisfaction. Her covetous attitude towards Rhian made Jayden want to put her in her place, and enjoy doing it.

Luiji ran across the ice to her faster than she thought wise, but she didn't say anything. She wanted to see what he was going to do. He checked himself to a loping jog and slid to a halt in front of her, then held his hands up.

"May I speak?" he asked politely. She nodded and waited for him to continue, aware of Rhian arriving at her side the instant she got there. "I wish to apologise for my behaviour. I do not blame you for banning us from the trip. I would have done the same in your position. But I have had much time to reflect on my attitude, and I give you my word that I will show you I have learnt the lesson you were trying to teach me."

"And what was the lesson?"

"That it takes more than ability to survive out here. I must have strength, not just in body, but in mind, in will, and in heart." He tapped his chest. "I must have discipline, and control. And above all else, I must have respect—respect for you, for myself, and, most importantly, for the mountain."

Jayden smiled. "I'm very glad you're still with us, Lui. You mind if I call you Lui?" She offered her hand.

"I think I like Lui." A wide smile broke across his lips. "Thank you, Jay," he said with emphasis.

She threw her head back and laughed. "Okay, you'll have to crash with Miguel and Santiago."

"No problem. I have extra provisions for stores in my pack. I will unload those first and then make up my sleeping space. Which tent is it?"

She pointed to the yellow-and-black dome on the far side of the encampment. "They're out scouting a location for me right now, but they'll be back in a few. If I know those guys, it'll be as neat as a pin in there. You shouldn't have any problems."

He nodded and scooted off.

"He's been a different guy the last couple of days," Rhian said.

"Good. Do I want to know why Killian isn't here?"

"Probably not, but you need to."

Jayden glanced at her and nodded. "Well, since the only tent left with space in it is mine, you can tell me later."

"Thanks. I'll save the gory details for you, then." She cocked her head to one side.

Jayden frowned as the change in light showed the faint outline of a bruise on her cheek. She touched the tip of her finger to Rhian's chin, turning her head a little further so she could make it out better.

"How did this happen?"

Rhian pulled her head away. "I'll fill you in later. How's the training been going?"

Jayden didn't like the sound of that but allowed her to change the topic. They would have plenty of time to talk later. In private. "Very well. They're all working hard and improving quickly. You picked good climbers. Some of them just need a few reminders, but very few of them are learning new skills here. You've made my job a lot easier. Thanks."

Rhian's face flushed under the praise, and she turned away, her gaze flicking from one contestant to another.

Jayden took pity on her discomfort. "So tell me what I need to know about our two newbies."

"Well, Oskar's a twenty-year-old Alpine specialist—"

"At twenty? No one's a specialist at twenty."

Rhian scowled playfully. "Do you want me to tell you or not?"

Jayden sighed, but quirked her lips. "Go on, then." She rolled her hand in a circular motion.

"He's been based in Chamonix since his parents moved him there when he was twelve. Skis like a demon and has scaled the Eiger, the Matterhorn, and Mont Blanc this year."

"Originally from?"

"Poland."

Jayden nodded. "Explains the odd accent he has. Polish-French mix."

Rhian chuckled. "But at least his English is good."

"True."

"And then we have…"

Rhian sighed heavily. "Brooke Shields," she said and paused.

"You're joking, right?"

"Everyone asks that. And, no, I'm not. I didn't name her," Rhian replied testily.

Jayden held up her hands, eyes opened wide. "Sorry."

Rhian sighed again and shrugged off her annoyance. "No, I'm sorry. She's just…doesn't matter. Anyway, she's from South Africa—Cape Town. Twenty-three. Mostly a sport climber with trad climbing experience."

"And?"

"And what?"

"Why's she pissing you off? Bad attitude?"

"No, not bad. Just…" She sighed again. "Give it an hour. You'll see for yourself." She snorted a bitter laugh. "If you even need an hour." She nodded in the direction of the tents. "Which one's home, then?"

"The black-and-red one."

"'Kay. Thanks." She picked up her pack and set off for the small dome tent at the far edge of the encampment, close to Miguel and Santiago's. Jayden's frown deepened. She didn't like the sound of it. The woman had already set her teeth on edge, questioning where she'd be sleeping and who she'd be sleeping with.

Then the penny dropped. *Shit.* Clearly Brooke was hitting on Rhian. And just as clearly, Rhian was uncomfortable with it.

She tucked her hands into her pockets and made her way over to the camp kitchen.

They'd been working together for five weeks. They'd shared some great hikes, done a few climbs, and had more working dinners together than she could remember. They'd talked about a lot of things. They were becoming... friends. Though neither of them had spoken much about their pasts, she'd gotten the distinct impression that Rhian was gay—just little comments, off-the-cuff remarks that had led her to the conclusion. And Jayden wasn't usually wrong about these things.

Despite the rocky start, and Jayden's admittedly uncharacteristic harshness towards her, she could admit her initial assessment of Rhian as a vulture had been wrong. She'd proven herself to be kind, considerate, intelligent, and with a sense of humour that constantly caught Jayden off guard. She enjoyed being around her, working with her, talking to her. And the idea of Rhian being uncomfortable, for any reason, well, that really pissed her off.

Felix handed her a large bowl of pasta with chunks of chorizo and peppers and a spicy tomato sauce all over. "There's garlic bread on the board there." He pointed to the end of the makeshift table and went back to ladling out another portion.

She was sitting on one of the ice benches, chewing thoughtfully, when Rhian sat next to her.

"Mind if I join you?"

Jayden shook her head and swallowed. "Not at all. On one condition."

"What is it with you and conditions?" She chuckled. "Go on. What's the condition?"

"You tell me what's bothering you about Brooke."

Rhian rolled her eyes and nodded as the lady in question walked towards them with her own bowl and a cocky grin. She plopped down on the other side of Rhian, and Jayden instantly noted how Rhian's jaw tensed when Brooke put her hand on Rhian's knee and patted it before stroking it. The action of a lover, intimate. Too intimate for the situation unless… Had Rhian and Brooke had a fling? Or a one-night stand? A little fun, thinking she'd never see the rejected climber again? Is that why Rhian looked so uncomfortable?

An image of Rhian cradled in Brooke's arms popped into her head and stubbornly refused to leave. She pictured Rhian, eyes closed, lips parted in surrender as Brooke plundered her mouth with her tongue. Brooke's hand, wrapped in Rhian's blond hair, tugging her head back to give her access to her delicate throat. Rhian's hands grasping at her shoulders as her hips pressed into Brooke's body.

Jayden's heart smacked against her ribs like an out-of-rhythm bass drum, low and deep and threatening to crash through at any moment. Jealousy wasn't an emotion she was familiar with, and it wasn't one she liked the flavour of now.

The soft press of Rhian shuffling closer to her snapped her out of that torturous daydream. But Jayden wasn't even sure Rhian was aware she'd moved. Her eyes were fixed ahead, and her fingers were clasped tightly around her fork.

Whatever the reason, Rhian was uncomfortable, and Jayden couldn't ignore it. She couldn't let Rhian sit beside her like a stone while Brooke ran her hands possessively over her body. She just couldn't. It wasn't right. Jayden shifted her bowl to her lap and her fork into one hand and slid the other around Rhian's shoulders. *In for a penny, as Mum used to say.* She leant over and kissed her cheek.

"It's really good to see you again, babe," she said loud enough for Brooke to hear. Two things happened at the same time: Brooke's hand stopped stroking Rhian's leg, and Rhian's head spun to look at her so quickly, their lips touched. Jayden used the momentum to tuck her cheek against Rhian's and whisper in her ear, "Play along if you want her to leave you alone. Slap me if you don't." She could feel Rhian's throat work as she swallowed.

"I missed you too," she said quietly.

Jayden smiled and held her position a moment longer. "We can talk about this later as well. Okay?"

Rhian nodded and eased away from the embrace. Brooke's hand had moved from her knee, and she'd slid across the ice bench until she was no longer touching Rhian. Jayden smiled and decided to have a little fun with the game they'd started. She reached over and tucked a strand of hair behind Rhian's ear. She didn't miss the way Rhian's eyes fluttered shut, or the way she leant her face into Jayden's palm before she pulled away and started in on her meal. Her body relaxed as the group all gathered.

She relaxed even more when Oskar sat beside her, putting a whole other body between her and Brooke. Jayden caught his eye over the top of Rhian's head and nodded to him. He winked and tucked into his food with gusto.

"So tell me all about your little fan, Miss Phillips," Jayden said when they lay side by side in their sleeping bags.

Rhian groaned and pulled the hood over her face. "Why do I have to? You saw what she was doing."

"Yes, I did. I guess I'm wondering why."

"A girl could get offended, you know."

"What?" Jayden frowned. "What do you mean?"

"You ask that question like it's beyond the realm of possibility that a woman could find me attractive and want to hit on me, or something."

Jayden laughed before she realised Rhian was serious and looked more than a little offended. She looked upset. "You can't be serious? Rhian, you're gorgeous. Any woman would be stupid not to—you're playing with me, aren't you?"

Rhian grinned. "Little bit."

"Child."

"Hey, I'm not the one who pulled the fake-girlfriend stunt."

"No. You seemed content to stew on it. What's up with that?"

"I was about to slap her and was working out just how much trouble it would get me into."

"See? My plan worked much better, then. No trouble at all."

"Hm. I wouldn't be so sure about that." Rhian sighed heavily. "If everyone thinks we're sleeping together, it could make our other issue worse."

"What other issue?"

"Killian."

"Ah. The missing Killian. He's not here, so why is he still an issue?"

"He's threatening to sue for bullying, sexual harassment, and sexual discrimination."

Jayden sat up in her sleeping bag, twisted so she was facing Rhian, and stared at her. "Are you kidding me?"

Rhian shook her head. "Wish I was."

"Bullying? I gave everyone the same treatment. Everyone had the same deadline. That's just bullshit. As for discrimination, he's a white bloke. All he needs to do is live to be an old one, and he's hit the jackpot. How does he get discrimination—oh. You mean I'm discriminating against him because I'm a man-hating dyke?"

Rhian chuckled.

"I thought this wasn't funny."

"It isn't. It's just that that was the same phrase that Rachel used. And he's not claiming you discriminated against him. He's claiming I did. After he refused my sexual advances."

"My, my, Miss Phillips, you sure are getting around a bit on this tour. Wait, your mother called you a man-hating dyke?"

Rhian sniggered. "Told you she was a bitch."

"Yes, you did. I don't remember disagreeing with you. Is she right?"

"What? No. I don't hate men. Well, some of them I do, but I hate some women too. I don't discriminate in that way."

"At least we know where we stand now. I'm a bully."

"And I'm a sexual predator."

"Well, won't Brooke be disappointed when she finds out." The uncomfortable thought wormed its way into her brain. "Wait, does she already know? Is that why she was so keen to bunk up with you?" She tried to keep her tone light, make a joke of it. But it stunned her how much she needed to know the answer.

"What are you talking about?" she asked with a frown.

"You know...you and Brooke—you've met her before at the trials, right?" *Please don't let them be lovers. I'll never get that image out of my head if she confirms she slept with that bitch.*

Rhian nodded but still didn't respond.

"Well...is there history?" Jayden hoped she was hiding the very real anxiety that gripped her, but she could hear the quaver in her own voice.

"History? Are you kidding? The only thing she wants from me is a ticket to the final, and she thinks sleeping with me is the way to get it."

Thank fuck for that! "Ah. And you're stuck on how much you can tell her to back off because of the situation with Killian."

"And the fact I'm now out of alternates. If she quits, we're kinda screwed."

"And I came along and dropped us both in it." She slapped her hand to her forehead. "I'm sorry."

"Don't be. Like you said at the time, I could've slapped you."

"But you didn't."

"No. I liked her reaction."

"And how do you think she's going to react now?"

"Don't know. She doesn't have a lot of choices out here, but once we get back to El Chaltén, she could well decide to quit. I might have to try and talk Mellissa into being our reserve alternate."

"We could fix it so she lost the challenge and got kicked out first."

"Yeah," she said and yawned. "Still think she'll kill me first."

"So what do you want to do? We could play it like we've had a fight and are no longer, erm..." She waved a hand between the two of them.

"A couple?" Rhian supplied.

"Yeah. A couple. And then she'll think you're available again, and—"

"Then I'm stuck fending her off for as long as she remains in the competition. No thanks. You started this, you're stuck with me now, sweetheart." She patted the sleeping mat. "So lie back down and share some of that body heat. My toes are freezing." She rolled onto her side away from Jayden.

"Oh, so you're the bossy kind of girlfriend," she said, lying down and turning to face Rhian's back.

"That'd be telling." She shuffled back until their sleeping bags were touching.

Jayden took a moment to enjoy how their bodies spooned together so easily before she asked, "What's happening with the Killian situation, then? Do we have to give statements or something?"

Rhian shook her head. "No, I gave Rachel the CCTV footage of the time you met the group and told them the plan and the deadline, and the footage of when he hit me—"

"He hit you?" Jayden sat up and rolled Rhian onto her back. She wished she could see her but it was too dark. She wanted to look at that bruise again. "When? What happened?" Jayden's head swam with anger, and the strangely satisfying image of a dismembered Killian scattered across the ice. She reached above her head and turned on the small lamp suspended from the centre of the tent. She squinted a little against the dim light and turned back to study Rhian's face. The bruise was barely visible in the low light, but it *was* visible. And Jayden seethed.

Rhian glanced away and tried to turn her head. "Erm, didn't I mention that bit before?" Tears clung to her lower lashes, and she desperately tried to blink them away.

Jayden cupped her cheek and stopped her from turning away as she forcibly smothered her rage. "Erm, no, you didn't. I'd remember if you told me the little twat hit you." Whatever had happened, Rhian was here, she was okay, and she didn't need Jayden flying off the deep end about it. Clearly she'd already handled it. Even if the little bastard had left a bruise. And some tears.

Rhian giggled. "So you're the protective kind of girlfriend."

Jayden paused, then laughed herself. "Sorry, it's just...I mean, I knew he had a chip on his shoulder but I didn't think he'd go that far. I'm so sorry."

"It's not your fault. You weren't even there."

"I wish I had been, though." She smiled to herself, thinking about the ways she'd like to make the little fucker suffer for daring to touch—

"You're growling. What are you thinking about?"

She chuckled. "Entertaining fantasies of making him a eunuch."

"Rachel said she wanted to do the same thing to him."

"Hm. Maybe I was wrong about your mum being a bitch after all."

Rhian took hold of her hand, and Jayden realised she'd still been stroking her cheek. "No, you were right. She's just the bitch you want to have on your side."

"I'll bear that in mind." She squeezed Rhian's hand and said softly, "Tell me what happened."

Rhian sighed heavily and tucked her hands back in her sleeping bag like she was trying to hide herself before she started to speak. Slowly she told Jayden what had happened, and Jayden battled another homicidal urge.

"I'm glad the little bastard's gone now," Rhian said when she finished her story.

"I'll bet. I'm sorry I left you to deal with my mess."

"That's why they pay me the big bucks. Apparently."

"Rachel tell you that?"

"Nah. Rachel tells me I do this because I love it, not for money."

"Is she right?"

Rhian shrugged. "Sometimes." She yawned and closed her eyes, snuggling deeper into her sleeping bag. "You're different out here."

"What do you mean?"

"You've changed. You seem happier, more playful. I mean, would you have contemplated pulling this fake-girlfriend thing with me a month ago?"

"No."

"Exactly. Even a few weeks ago, you were still treating me like the enemy. You've changed."

"I am," she said quietly after a few minutes. "Happier, I mean. I don't think I've changed, though. More like I've started to become me again."

"Why?"

Jayden didn't want to relive the past. She wanted to enjoy feeling connected again. So she debated how much to say. "I'd stopped climbing. I was working in a call centre."

Rhian giggled. "I can't picture you in an office."

"Neither could anyone else, but there I was. 'Hello, Northwest Electrical, how can I help you?'" she said with a nasally affected voice. "It was awful."

"So why were you there?"

Jayden shrugged. "It was where I needed to be for a while."

"But now you're back in the mountains, and you feel happy."

"Yes. I feel more alive and yet at peace at the same time. I know that's a contradiction, but—"

"It's okay. I get it."

"That's good. I was worried I was starting to sound like a total nut."

"Starting?"

"Hey, be nice. I'm your girlfriend, and you haven't seen me for days, remember?"

"Oh yeah. Right. Sorry."

"I should think so." Jayden snapped off the lamp and snuggled deeper into her own sleeping bag.

"I like it," Rhian said quietly.

"Like what?"

"This new you."

Jayden couldn't help but think how much she liked it too.

CHAPTER 20

RHIAN WATCHED AS BROOKE CONTINUED to glare at Jayden while she spoke to the group, handing out the day's tasks and sending the first two pairs off to their high-overnight camps. She went over the use of the emergency sat phones as she handed them out to Lonnie and Hunter and Liv and Sky. She also handed out assignments, from kitchen cleanup to crevasse training, were handed out, and the group quickly scattered. Jayden came over and squatted in front of her, gently putting her hand on Rhian's knee.

"Is this all right?" she asked quietly so no one else would hear.

Rhian nodded, charmed that Jayden still felt the need to check the limits of their new "relationship", despite Rhian having given her the go-ahead the night before. After all, she was doing this for Rhian's benefit, and all she seemed to be getting in return were glares from a certain someone. "I'm sorry she's being difficult."

Jayden chuckled. "Just wait till she's had to climb out of a crevasse on her own. She won't have the energy left to blink at me, never mind give me dirty looks like that." She sniggered. "Speaking of crevasse training, I want you to join us for this one. I plan to make all the crew who will be out on the ice complete this training too. Next to avalanches, crevasses are the most dangerous part of being out on the glacier. Anyone out here is at risk, especially as the weather warms and the ice begins to melt. These huge moulins—"

"What's a moulin?"

"It's a glacier mill. Meltwater rushes through a tunnel or a crevasse and through the glacier. Sometimes they find their way to the lakes or the sea, and other times they don't seem to go anywhere. They must run into a space inside the glacier and refreeze or find some other escape route. No one really knows, because no one's gone into one and come out again—not alive, anyway."

"Sweetheart, you need to work on your gentle delivery of bad news."

Jayden laughed and ran her hand a little further up Rhian's thigh. "Is that so, babe?" She squeezed her leg gently, then stood. Rhian's gaze followed her, and she held her hand over her eyes to block the sun as it created a halo around Jayden's mane of dirty-blond curls. "We're leaving in twenty minutes, and you'll need to pack your gear. Luiji's in this group, so don't keep us waiting."

"Yes, boss," she joked. "Anything else, boss?"

"Not right now." She offered her hand and tugged Rhian to her feet. "I'm sure I can think of something later."

"For God's sake, get a room." Brooke's voice shocked Rhian. She hadn't realised she was nearby, but clearly Jayden had and had played their little ruse to the hilt for her benefit.

Rhian swallowed the pang of disappointment that Jayden's actions had been for the crowd and not for her. But she knew that. She knew it was all for the benefit of the others. She just wished it wasn't. She wished so much it wasn't a game that she allowed herself to forget, just for a minute, that Jayden wasn't really hers. So much so that she didn't even have time to try to rein in the impulse to stand on her tiptoes and press her lips to Jayden's.

She didn't expect Jayden to respond to her tentative kiss. But she did, with arms wrapped tight about her waist as Jayden's lips parted against her own. Rhian moaned, slid her hand into Jayden's hair, and opened her mouth beneath the gentle pressure of Jayden's lips. The skim of hands up her back felt like they were burning through the layers of her clothes until Jayden eased away from her, trailed a finger down her cheek, and gave her a smile that Rhian had never seen before, one that spoke to her.

She swallowed and tried to breathe. "I should go get ready."

Jayden just nodded and let go of her. "Fifteen minutes."

"You said twenty."

"That was five minutes ago. Chop, chop, you're wasting time." She jogged away, leaving Rhian dizzy and staring after her.

"You led me on."

The harsh, guttural quality of the words were like ice down her back. "Excuse me?" She turned to see Brooke still staring at her.

"You heard me."

"I did, and at the risk of repeating myself, excuse me? I did nothing to invite your frankly creepy innuendo and stalker-like advances, Brooke. I'd go so far as to say you'd decided what you were going to try to do before you even met me. I tried to be subtle. But you didn't take the hint. I'm not interested, and I'm not available to you. How much clearer do you need me to be?"

"You weren't so clear when your girl wasn't around."

"Yes, I was. Like I said, you can't take the hint." Arguing would have no further benefit. All they were doing was drawing a crowd, so she turned on her heel and went to grab her gear. Behind her, Brooke was still shouting to anyone who would listen how Rhian had teased her and led her on.

"That's bullshit." Oskar had apparently finally decided to speak his mind. "She didn't lead you on. She was trying to get away from you the first night at the conclave, and you got yourself too drunk to notice. Last night, she was clearly uncomfortable when you sat next to her trying to feel her up in front of her girlfriend. Talk about tacky."

"You didn't see her when you went to wash dishes like a little manservant."

"No, I didn't. But I heard Mellissa tell you to clean up after yourself and send you packing to your own room. Like the lady said, you just can't seem to get the message."

His voice dropped when Rhian stooped into the tent to grab her bag, but it was still loud enough for her, as well as everyone in the camp to hear.

"You're forgetting, Brooke, that I was in the car with you on the way from the airport to El Chaltén. I heard every detail of your little plan to seduce her to book yourself a one-way ticket to the final."

Rhian crawled out of the tent in time to see him look Brooke up and down.

"And I thought only men were supposed to be sexual predators. I've got three sisters. If I heard a guy talk about one of them the way you talked about Rhian, they'd still be picking their teeth up off the floor." He spun away, and his gaze caught Rhian's. She mouthed "Thank you" to him. He nodded and disappeared into his own tent.

148

The crowd dissipated until only Brooke stood in the middle of the encampment. Her face was beet red with rage, or embarrassment. Rhian didn't know. And quite frankly, she didn't care. Instead, she tried to figure out what she was going to do about getting another climber in to take her place. Rhian could see only two options for her: quit or brazen it out.

"She won't quit," Jayden said, appearing heretofore unnoticed beside the tent.

"How do you know?"

"She wants to win too bad."

"God, can you imagine having to hand the prize to her?"

"That won't happen."

"I repeat myself: how do you know?"

"Audiences are going to hate her. The second she's in the bottom two of a challenge, she'll be gone."

"You don't think the young guys will vote to keep her in because she's gorgeous?"

"Even a pretty face looks ugly when you see the warts on the soul."

Rhian tore her gaze from Brooke, still standing in the middle of the camp, and stared up at Jayden. "Very poetic, sweetheart."

"Very true." She crouched down and whispered softly, "you don't have to call me sweetheart when no one else is around."

Rhian couldn't stop staring at her lips. Those soft, beautiful lips. So much so that she didn't notice that Jayden was striding away from her until she was already gone.

"But I want to," she whispered to her retreating back. She closed her eyes, and the image of her sketch floated before them before it morphed into Jayden's smile after their kiss.

"I'm fucked. I am so fucked."

CHAPTER 21

RHIAN TOOK A DEEP BREATH, readied her ice axe, and aimed at the ice just above her shoulder. She put as much swing and force into the blow as she could generate, but the tip of the axe merely glanced off the rock-hard ice face and skidded away, refusing to take hold. The precarious purchase her crampons had on the slick surface shifted and released under the movement of her weight, and she was once again dangling on the end of a rope. Meltwater was raining down over her head to further complicate matters, and the roar of water tunnelling through the ice cavern below only added to the fear.

Jayden's account of climbers dying after encountering such moulins had not helped. The thought of being swept away by the rushing water and drowning in the icy chambers of the heart of the glacier made her palms sweat and her fingers tremble. It didn't seem to matter that she knew that two people were anchoring her rope to the surface. Nor did it matter that this was a drill. She looked down the hole into the blue, then black, heart of the ice, and her mouth went dry.

Stay calm, Jayden had told them in the briefing. *Your greatest weapon is your brain, not your muscles.*

"Brains don't do you much good if you don't use 'em." With her eyes closed and her fists wrapped around the rope, she caught her breath. When she finally opened her eyes, she touched the impenetrable surface and watched a water droplet roll down—gravity and the slick plane of ice doing their work. Then it hit her: gravity. She needed a better way to fight gravity than trying to plant her grip against something that just wouldn't give.

She glanced up the rope, her lifeline to the world, and realised *it* was her best way out of the watery chasm. She just needed a realistic way of climbing it.

Jayden had only allowed them to do this exercise carrying what they normally carried when walking on the ice. She'd told them that being able to self-rescue when you had all the right gear was great, but what did you plan to do when you got caught without the best gear to hand?

"Die, most likely," Rhian said as she left the ice axes dangling from the straps about her wrists and searched her pockets to see what she had to hand. Trying to get to the gear in her backpack was a last resort. It would cause her to shift her balance, and the chances were good that she'd lose her bag and kit to the moulin. Besides, getting it on and off again while dangling on the end of a rope was probably more difficult than trying to pull herself up the rope hand over hand would be.

She had an idea, but to make it work, she needed a piece of cord she could make a loop out of, and nothing in her pockets would do. Her boot, however, looked promising. She kicked her leg up and planted it against the ice. She used one hand to hold herself against the rope, to keep herself in a seated position rather than lying back, and used her right hand to loosen the crampon buckle, then untie her shoelace. She quickly pulled the long bootlace through the eyelets and tightened the buckle on her crampon again. It would keep the boot on her foot. She hoped.

She doubled the lace and tied a flat overhand knot to secure the two ends together. Her head was freezing. She could hear her teeth chattering, even if she could no longer feel her jaw working. Her fingers began to feel clumsy and heavy, like sausages on the end of her hands, not the nimble digits she was used to. She flexed them, opening and closing a fist quickly for a few seconds to get the blood flowing and to give her a little more dexterity. She put the shoelace between her teeth and rubbed her hands together in the hope of generating a little friction heat. It wasn't much, but it was just enough.

She used the shoelace to create a Prusik knot, wrapping it around the rope several times before feeding it back through on itself and creating a sliding knot she could slide up the rope but that would not slide down on its own. She carefully fitted her booted foot through the loop, avoiding touching the sharp edges of her crampon against the fairly thin cord her lace had made. Slicing it in two would, well... That would be bad. When she had her foot in place, she shifted her weight and used the loop as though it were a rung on a ladder and stood up as tall as she could. Using the rope and her left hand to hold her body weight, she slid the knot upwards until it was above her knee, then stood up again.

The rim of the crevasse already looked so much closer. The exertion was getting her blood going, and she was feeling warmer. She smiled. She was getting out of this frozen hellhole. It didn't take long for her to make her way up the rope and get her hands over the lip of the ice, but she carried on grabbing at the rope. She lifted the Prusik knot one last time to get her shoulders and torso over the edge and allow herself greater leverage to get out of the hole.

She fell onto the ice and rolled onto her back, panting and spread out like a snow angel. She chuckled and reached for the hand being offered.

Jayden was grinning and pointing down at her boot. "Shoelace Prusik?"

Rhian nodded and scrubbed her hands through her hair to try to ruffle out some of the ice water. "Couldn't find anything else to make a cordlette without going into my pack."

"It's a great idea. Easy to reach, less chance of losing your gear, and a shoelace is just as good a tool as anything else. Especially when you make your bootlaces out of five-millimetre paracord. Well done," she said and led Rhian to the cooking burner Miguel was using to make coffee. The warm drink that was pressed into her hands was welcome, as was the towel Jayden draped over her head.

"Well done?" Brooke sneered. "It took her fifteen minutes to drag herself out of there. If this was a real survival situation, there wouldn't be a towel or a hot drink. She'd be dead."

"Enough, Brooke," Jayden said. Her voice had a cold edge, and her eyes dimmed from the warm enthusiasm of Rhian's success to the ice blue of the moulin she had just escaped. "Rhian did what I asked her to do." Jayden's gaze never shifted from her face, and Rhian wondered what she was looking for. Signs that she wasn't doing okay? "She used her brain to get herself out of the situation. If she hadn't, we'd have hauled her up and discussed techniques she could have implemented to help herself. She didn't need that. Some people would have done it quicker, others slower. Had it been a real-life situation, Rhian is still capable of functioning and would've been able to take care of her needs." She smiled at Rhian. "Wouldn't you?"

Rhian nodded and sipped her drink. The warmth seeped back into her body as it crept back into Jayden's eyes.

"You're only saying that because you're fucking her. You wouldn't let any of us off that easy."

Brooke spoke so quietly, Rhian could barely make out the words. Apparently, Jayden's hearing was much better than hers. She whirled around and strode into Brooke's personal space.

"I've already sent one prick home because of his attitude. You looking for a quick exit too?" Brooke's eyes were open wide as she shook her head. Jayden stepped back and signalled Santiago. "Let's see how you like the moulin. And since you think it's such a race, we'll put you on the clock, shall we? Miguel?"

"*Sí?*"

"Get your watch handy. If Brooke isn't over the edge in fifteen minutes, she gets to make her own coffee."

"*Sí.*" Miguel turned away from them all in what Rhian recognised as an attempt to hide a smirk. She was pretty sure everyone else had caught it too. But at least he tried.

"Let's go, then," Jayden said. "Oskar, Luiji, I want you two anchoring the rope this time, please." The guys nodded and set about attaching themselves to belay devices, MBD's—or manual braking devices—and the bolts and ice screws that had been set up to make this exercise as safe as possible. And it was still potentially fatal. A flaw in the rope or a poor swing from an axe cutting through it and there would be nothing they could do to help the climber fifteen metres below them.

While they were all busy, Rhian put her hand on Jayden's arm and tugged her gently to one side. "You didn't need to do that."

Jayden frowned. "Do what?"

"Stand up for me like that. She had a point."

Jayden chuckled. "No, she didn't. You were still functioning—"

"I meant the other bit. That you were standing up for me because of our supposed relationship. Are you sure it's a good idea to antagonise her? Setting her a challenge like that? Showing her up in front of them all—"

"She's showing herself up."

Rhian nodded. "I know that, you know that, and everyone else in the camp knows that. Except Brooke. Right now, she thinks we are the only people responsible for making her look foolish."

"I see your point, but if I didn't stand up for you, then she wouldn't believe in our supposed relationship. You want to go back to fending her off?"

Rhian shook her head.

"Didn't think so. Second, if I let that go after everything that happened with Killian, then it makes his discrimination case stronger again because I let a woman get away with the kind of behaviour I pulled him up on, in front of witnesses."

"Killian was kicked off for attacking me."

"Yes, but I still called him on his bad attitude. Just like I'm doing with Brooke. She can argue that it's because of you, but the rest of the team need to see that my behaviour is consistent with all of them. And this is me being consistent, not me playing the overprotective girlfriend."

Rhian scrubbed the towel over her head. "Christ, this is all getting so complicated."

Jayden chuckled. "Isn't that what relationships are? Complicated."

"Guess that means you're not the romantic type, then." Rhian smiled up at her.

"Guess you'll just have to wait and see." She bent forward and kissed her cheek. "Now, I better go and check on the kiddies, make sure they don't kill themselves and all that."

"Okay," Rhian whispered to her retreating back as she covered her cheek. Brooke's gaze met hers across the ice field, and a sneer curled the corner of her lips. How was this situation getting so out of control? And how much worse was it going to get?

CHAPTER 22

THE CLOUDS WERE GATHERING AS they made the last two kilometres back to El Pilar and the bus waiting for them. Jayden surveyed the ragtag group she was returning with. She was proud of them. With only one exception, they had formed a tight-knit team over the seven days they'd been out on the ice. They'd worked together to maximise each other's skills and minimise each other's weaknesses. It might not make for good TV, but it would make for a safer show. That was her priority.

She hung back to speak with Rhian as Luiji, Oskar, Hunter, and Lonnie loaded bags into the belly of the bus as the others arrived. Taylor and Sky passed out water and sandwiches from the crate Carlos had brought with him, and one by one, they climbed on board. Except for Brooke. She stood fifteen metres from the bus, arms crossed over her chest as she leant against a wall. She'd dumped her bag at Hunter's feet and moved off without a word.

"Any ideas on what to do with our problem child?" Rhian asked.

"Plenty. But I don't think you'll let me do any of them," Jayden said with a grin.

Four days. They'd spent four days pretending to be a couple, sleeping in the same tent, touching each other, giving each other the occasional peck on the cheek. And, of course, that kiss. Jayden licked her lips. She could still taste Rhian on them. Going back to normal was going to be hard.

"Will you join me for dinner tonight?" she asked. "I could make us something back at Fen's house. We could discuss it away from the group."

Rhian smiled sadly. "I'd love to, but we've got that Skype meeting set up with Rachel and the investors, remember?"

She'd completely forgotten. "I'm supposed to be there too?"

"Yes."

She wrinkled her nose. "But I hate things like that, and I've got so much to do. I need to make sure all the kit is cleaned and packed away properly—"

"And the guys already know what they have to do. They'll be doing it while we have the meeting. You can check it afterwards. Besides, do you really think Miguel or Santiago will let them get away with mishandling your equipment?"

They wouldn't.

"I don't exactly want to be at this meeting either, but the investors want to meet you."

"Why? I'm just the safety girl."

Rhian laughed. "You're so much more than that, and you know it. Now, stop whining, and get on the bus."

"Okay, then. How about after the meeting?"

Rhian cocked her head to the side.

"Dinner. After the meeting?"

Rhian smiled shyly, and Jayden wondered if someone was watching them. "I'd love to." She quickly glanced down at the ground and slipped her backpack off her shoulders. "I think they're all waiting for us."

Jayden held out her hand. "I'll put that away for you. You go make sure everyone's ready to go."

"Thanks." Rhian gave her the bag and sauntered towards the bus. Jayden watched the sway of her hips as she went. The way she tugged her fleece over her head and tied it about her waist before she skipped up the steps made Jayden very glad that Rhian had agreed to her impromptu dinner invitation. When Jayden finally climbed onto the bus with Carlos, Luiji, and Oskar, she took the seat at the front of the coach next to Rhian.

"I thought you might want a sandwich." Rhian handed over a cling-wrapped package and a bottle of water.

"Probably a good idea." Jayden unwrapped a corner and took a big bite. "Stop me from passing out with low blood sugar during this meeting."

Rhian chuckled. "My thoughts exactly."

Jayden nudged her shoulder and swallowed the food. "Thank you," she said quietly.

"You're welcome," Rhian said just as quietly.

———— ✦⊂◇⊃✦ ————

"You ready for this?" Rhian asked as Jayden sat down at the table. They'd been back in the resort less than an hour, and the scheduled meeting wasn't supposed to be for another couple of hours. But Rachel apparently needed to talk to them both. Yesterday.

"Nope, but you might as well do it anyway."

"That's the spirit." Rhian hit the tracker pad on her laptop, and the picture appeared. Rachel was sitting behind her desk, wearing a red blouse and a scowl.

"About time you two showed up," Rachel began, not even looking away from the tablet in her hand. "We've got problems."

Rhian rolled her eyes. "Good to see you too, Rach. This is Jayden Harris. Jayden, Rachel Webster."

"Nice to meet you, Mrs Webster." Jayden tapped two fingers to her forehead and offered a mini salute with them. Rachel, of course, missed it, as she was still staring at her tablet, but Rhian thought it was cute.

"Yeah, you too. And Rachel will do, Jayden. Now, Killian O'Leary has filed suit against the firm, the show, and you both personally."

"Fucker," Jayden spat out.

Rachel looked up at them for the first time, a smile on her face. "Quite. So this is set to be a long drawn-out battle with the little prick. I've got the videos, and our lawyer has them now. He's confident that they guarantee any case going in our favour, so he doesn't want to settle. It will make us look like we have something to hide if we do."

"But if we don't, this will likely have negative repercussions anyway, won't it?" Rhian asked.

Rachel nodded. "I have a plan, but first we have to tackle something else that has only added fuel to the fire this afternoon." She flipped the tablet so they could see the image on the screen.

Rhian stared at it. How the fuck—Brooke.

"It's not what it looks like," Jayden said.

"It looks like you're in a lip lock and groping my daughter." Rachel moved the tablet and glared at them over the miles. "Am I wrong?"

"She wasn't groping me!" Rhian shouted.

"I mean, there's a good reason for—" Jayden started.

Rachel held her hand up. "Rhi, you're a big girl. If you want to screw someone, I'm not going to lecture you about it. But this picture was taken by a contestant, and said contestant is now splashing this on social media. This, in conjunction with the Killian O'Leary suit, does not look good for you. It strengthens his case. And you already knew about him before this picture was taken. What were you thinking?"

"Rach, I—"

"It was my fault." Jayden ran her fingers through her hair. "I kissed her before I knew about the situation with Killian O'Leary, and I did it to try and help Rhian."

Not one hundred percent accurate, in regards to the lip-lock part, but she did start the ball rolling before she had the facts about Killian. Boils down to the same thing in the end, I suppose.

Rachel's eyes narrowed. "Help her? What are you talking about?"

Rhian took a deep breath. "Brooke Shields has been hitting on me since she got here. Before that, really, at the try-outs. It's one of the reasons, actually the main reason, I didn't accept her in the first place."

"So you decided to get in there first?" Rachel said to Jayden.

Jayden shook her head. "No, it wasn't like that. Brooke was being really…predatory about it. Really over the top. It was clearly making Rhian very uncomfortable, and she didn't seem to know how to handle it. I thought if we pretended to be a couple, she'd leave Rhian alone. It wasn't until after this that I learnt about Killian and that Brooke had made it perfectly clear that she planned to seduce Rhian, not for a genuine reason but because she thought it would guarantee her a ticket in the final."

"Is that right, Rhian?"

"Yes."

"So you and this Brooke, there's no history between you?"

"Other than me trying to keep away from her, no."

"Why didn't you shut her down? I've never known you to say no when you weren't interested."

"In all honesty, I was trying to figure out the best way to avoid any chance of there being repercussions. We've got enough going on with Killian causing trouble. I didn't want to be at the centre of any more."

Rachel cocked her head to the side, her lips twisting in to a quick smile. Rhian knew that smile. It meant Rachel appreciated the thought because it was something she hadn't thought of herself. Rhian supressed the grin tugging at her lips. Now was not the time. She could celebrate the little win later.

"So you weren't screwing her before you got to the ice camp?"

Rhian narrowed her eyes at Rachel. *And then she has to go and spoil it.* "I've already told you I wasn't."

"And you aren't screwing Jayden?"

Rhian huffed. "Do you have to be so crude?"

"Answer the question."

"No. There's nothing going on between the two of us. Why does it matter?"

"Because Miss Shields has tagged this picture with the caption *when the woman you shagged last night sees her girlfriend again and ditches your ass to save her own.* Then she's tagged everything to do with the show, our sponsors, and pretty much everything else you can think of."

Rhian was speechless. How was this all going so wrong?

"That's bullshit," Jayden said from beside her. "It's sour grapes talking. Everyone, and I mean everyone here, knows that Rhian has been trying to stay away from her. Oskar, the other alternate, told everyone what Brooke was saying on the trip from the airport to him and Mel. Apparently, she went into explicit detail of how she planned to gain a place in the final, and it had nothing to do with her performance on the rock."

Rachel's jaw worked. That twitching muscle meant Rachel was beyond pissed off. She was entering rage stage two, and Rhian could practically hear the cogs in her brain whirring.

"Right, I need a couple of people in that group that you trust a hundred percent, and I'm hoping you're going to say this Luiji fellow and the new guy Oskar." Rachel started scribbling notes on the pad in front of her.

"I trust Luiji," Rhian said.

"And I trust Oskar," Jayden added. "He made it very clear where he stands on Brooke, and he put himself in between the two of them on a couple of occasions."

Rachel nodded. "Okay, Jayden, can you get them here for me now? We need to get going on this ASAP."

Jayden nodded and left the room. Rhian knew she'd run to Adventure Trekkers and run them back. She smiled at the thought of how Jayden hadn't hesitated to stand up for her again.

"Is Mel around?" Rachel asked.

"In her room, I think."

"Can you get her down? I'll need her help with this."

Rhian nodded and sent Mellissa a text.

Need you on conf with Rachel now. Can you come down ASAP?

She didn't have to wait long for the response.

On my way.

"She's coming down." Rhian put her phone back on the table.

"You okay, kiddo?" Rachel asked, her jaw still tight. Her eyes, though, wore the look only Rhian ever saw: kind, compassionate, caring Rachel looked at her. Her mum.

Rhian shook her head. "It's so fucked up, Rach. I don't know what the hell I've done to deserve all this, and I don't know how I'm going to fix it all."

"Let me worry about the fixing. And you didn't do anything wrong. You know there are arseholes in the world. You've just met a couple of 'em on this trip. That's all."

"Yeah."

"Sounds like you've met far more good ones, though."

Rhian frowned a little.

"First Luiji stands up to this Killian. Then Jayden stands by you to protect you, and this Oskar chap too. Sounds like the good folks are outnumbering the bad ones."

Rhian smiled. "That's true."

"So suck it up, buttercup. Besides, despite evidence to the contrary, I think you're doing a brilliant job, kiddo, and these little bastards could end up doing us a favour if we play this right."

"What do you mean? What are you going to do, Rach?"

Rachel grinned wickedly. "Watch, and learn from the master."

Rhian groaned. "Please don't do anything that's going to mortify me for life."

"Tsk. You know me better than that. I wouldn't do anything that would put the company in jeopardy."

"Gee, thanks."

Mellissa bustled through the door. "What's the emergency?"

Between the two of them, they quickly filled her in on the details, and Rhian was gobsmacked when Mellissa reacted.

"That fucking skanky little bitch. I told her to stay the fuck away from you, or I was going to kick her arse back to South Africa from here."

Rachel held up her hands in surrender. "Whoa there, sailor, where's the mild-mannered Mel gone, and what did you do to her?"

Mel stared at Rachel through the screen. "You didn't hear what she was saying."

Rhian sighed heavily. "Neither did I. You wouldn't tell me. Oskar wouldn't tell me. What the fuck is so bad that you've all reacted like this but can't even tell me what it was that she said?" Rhian's voice rose sharply. She was getting sick of people protecting her as if she were a child.

Mel closed her eyes and breathed in deeply. "I'm sorry, Rhian. I can't bring myself to say the things... I don't want to. And I don't see how it will benefit you to know. Not since you've still got to work with her."

"I don't have to work with her," Rachel said. "And I fucking well *do* need to know."

Mel clenched her fists. "I have a recording of most of the conversation. When she started on the way she was... Well, I don't know. I just knew there's something wrong with that girl."

"I need that recording," Rachel said.

"I'll send it to you."

"Good. Now, in the meantime, this is what I need you to organise for me, Mel..."

Rachel was clear and precise in the instructions she gave Mellissa before she left them. It was also clear what Rachel intended to do. All she needed were two people who could legitimately have the details they were going to leak to social media to burn Killian and Brooke.

"Can this work, Rachel? I mean, we all know social media's a great marketing tool, but can it really undo the damage these two can cause?"

"Kiddo, it has just given the world Donald Trump as US president. I think we can safely say at this point that Twitter can do fucking anything."

Rhian rolled her eyes. "Fair point."

"The bigger question is whether or not your two new friends will be open to what we need them to do."

"They've shown themselves to have a lot of integrity, Rach. Don't try to appeal to anything else, or they'll think you're no better than Killian or Brooke."

"High road, got it."

"And don't try to force them. If they aren't happy to help me...us... then that's it. Okay?"

Rachel nodded but didn't say anything.

"I mean it."

"Fine. But you and Jayden have to keep up the couple act for the duration."

"We know. At least until Brooke's out of the show."

"No, I mean the duration of the show. You're still together at the finale. You got me?"

"What? Why?"

"If people believe that Brooke was trying to split you up for her own nefarious ends, they hate her as long as you guys are all in love. As soon as it's over, her commentary on this comes back to bite you on the arse, and you're the cheater who breaks Jayden's heart."

"For God's sake. It's like a soap opera, and none of it's true."

"It doesn't have to be, and you know it. It's what pulls in readers, generates click-throughs, and generally titillates. That's it."

Rachel cocked her head to the side and twisted the tablet towards her again. "It looks pretty convincing to me. And I know you."

Rhian scowled. "So?"

"So I saw how you looked at Jayden when she defended you. And I've never seen that look on your face before."

Rhian looked away from her mother's penetrating gaze. "Don't."

"Don't what?"

"Don't start seeing things that aren't there."

Rachel nodded when Rhian finally looked back at the screen. "And if you're the one who isn't seeing what is?"

"Then it'll be my problem to deal with."

Rachel sighed. "Rhian, I'm not asking as your boss."

"It'll still be my problem to deal with."

"You're as stubborn as your bloody father."

Rhian cracked a smile. "Surely that's not a surprise to you?"

Rachel laughed. "No, it isn't. But will you promise me one thing?"

"What?"

"You'll pick up the phone and talk to me when you're ready to see what's in front of you."

"There's nothing to see. She was trying to do me a favour, that's all. Now, can we drop it? They're coming back."

Rachel nodded. "Just tell Jayden she needs to keep it up, all right?"

Rhian nodded too and smiled as Jayden waved and the three of them came jogging in.

"Gentlemen," Rachel said when they were seated and Rhian had introduced them all. "How are you enjoying Patagonia so far?"

"*Fantastico*!" Luiji said enthusiastically.

"I'm very glad to hear it. I wanted to thank you both for your assistance in the last week."

They both frowned, but Luiji was seemingly the spokesperson for the pair. "We have done nothing so special."

"You have to me. You see, Rhian's my daughter, and I hear you've been good guys and helped her out a couple of times."

"Ah, I see." Luiji shrugged. "Is nothing we would not do for everyone else."

"Well, I wanted to say thank you anyway. And to apologise."

"Apologise? For what?"

"For putting you all through this. It looks like the show may get cancelled because of this pair."

"Excuse me?" Luiji leant forward in his chair.

"Killian is suing us all for discrimination and harassment."

"That bastard hit your daughter!"

"I know. I've seen the footage. That's how I know I have you to thank for her pretty face still being as beautiful as ever."

"So you know that he has no grounds to win a case."

"We do, but the problem is he's screaming about it on social media sites, and the publicity, between him and Brooke, is likely to get this canned before we even start recording."

"But you have the tape?" Luiji said.

"What's Brooke got to do with it?" Oskar asked.

Rachel held up her hands to stop them. "Sorry, fellas, I can only deal with one at a time. With regards to Killian, our lawyers have the tape, so I can't release it. No one who works for my company can."

"Because of the lawyers?" Luiji clarified.

"Yes. As for Brooke, she's posted a picture of Rhian and Jayden kissing on Facebook, claiming that Rhian cheated with her the night before and that the kiss was her attempt to cover her own backside with her girlfriend."

"Fucking bitch," Oskar said. "You didn't sleep with her." He turned to face Rhian. "She was down here drinking still when Luiji and I went to bed. Brooke was alone and calling Mel to hell and back for taking you away from her and the first stage of her plan. That bitch. She's going to get this thing sunk because she can't compete fair and square and her game isn't working." He folded his arms over his chest and looked back at Rachel. "I take it you have a plan, and you need us to do something to make it work?"

Rachel smiled. "You're smart. I like you."

He cocked his head. "What do you need us to do?"

Rachel quickly outlined her plan for them. "Will you do it?" she asked into the silence that followed.

Luiji and Oskar looked at each other, slow smiles spreading across their faces. "Oh yeah," Oskar said.

"With pleasure," Luiji added. "How are we supposed to have come by this footage, though? It may be questioned, and I need to have an appropriate response."

"You're going to film the footage on your phone from the camera bank."

"I don't understand."

"Officially, we can't give you this footage. You have to 'steal it'." She twitched her fingers in the air, to put the words into air quotes for him. "Then, if you are asked how you got it, you can say you stole it because you didn't want a rat bastard like Killian O'Leary ruining your shot at winning the show. We'll put out a response to this that the matter is under internal review. And then it will just go away. As to how you know it's a problem, tell them you're a clever guy and you saw Killian's social media posts when you got back from the glacier trip."

Luiji nodded. "I can do that."

"Good. Oskar, you won't need anything but the knowledge that you already have. You heard everything Brooke said in the Jeep with Mellissa, correct?"

Oskar nodded, glancing quickly at Rhian. "I won't have to go into detail, will I?"

"Just as much as you need for her to be unable to wriggle out of it. But be accurate, and don't make anything up."

"Trust me, I couldn't make up that shit if I was paid to."

"You are also privy to the events that happened at the hotel and out on the ice."

"I get it. I saw more than enough, don't worry. Are you sure this will help?"

"Yes."

"And it won't backfire on us?" he asked.

"How do you mean?"

"It won't have a negative impact on us that will get us voted off the show?"

Rachel shook her head. "I don't see it. You're standing up for women's rights, you're standing up to a bully and a sexual predator. This is all brownie points for you guys with the general public and with women in particular. And you know that on these shows women vote three times as often as men, right?"

Luiji shook his head. "I did not know this."

"That's why it's so hard for a woman to win one of these things. Women don't like to vote for another woman. Sad fact, but borne out time and again."

"So this could help our chances?" Luiji asked.

"With the public, yes. You still have to be good climbers to win, though. This is about skill as much as popularity," Jayden said. "No one can win this on public vote alone."

Rachel smiled. "Exactly."

Luiji and Oskar nodded. "We get it. So when do you want us to start?" Oskar asked.

"Now," Rachel said. "The sooner, the better. We need to get out in front of this thing and start making some impact of our own, or there will be no competition to win."

They agreed and quickly said their goodbyes.

"Jayden, Rhian, I've got a lot of work to do, and you two look like you need some sleep. I'll see you later." Rachel hung up without waiting for a response.

Jayden chuckled and lifted one eyebrow at Rhian. "Quite the piece of work, your mother."

"You don't know the half of it."

"I'm sure. Now I can see why at the hospital you felt you had no choice but to come and ask me to do this."

"I'm still sorry about that."

Jayden waved away the apology. "No need. I get it now that I've met my mother-in-law." She laughed.

"Ah, yeah. About that."

Jayden cocked her head to the side. "What about it?"

"Well…let's go get that dinner we discussed and talk about it."

"I don't like the sound of that." She followed Rhian out of the door. "Why don't I like the sound of that?"

"Because you're smart."

"I'm not going to like this, am I?"

Rhian's shoulder drooped. "Probably not. And I'm sorry."

"Maybe you should just tell me now."

"Dinner. Please." Rhian wasn't sure how she was going to react to having to continue playing her girlfriend. But since Jayden hated being forced to do anything she didn't want to do, Rhian suspected she was going to lose the burgeoning friendship they'd developed. And she really wanted to hold on to that for as long as she could. Even if it was only for another ten minutes.

CHAPTER 23

JAYDEN MOVED AROUND THE KITCHENETTE with ease, glad that Mark had kept the freezer stocked with pizza. She unwrapped one and quickly threw it in the oven. There was a bottle of wine in the cupboard that she held up for inspection.

Rhian nodded. "Why not?"

"Why not, indeed." Jayden grabbed two glasses and poured them generous measures. She sat beside Rhian, twisted in the chair so she was facing her, and tucked one leg under the other. "So what am I not going to like?"

Rhian took a deep breath. Then a large gulp of wine. Then put her glass on the table. Then threaded her fingers together and pressed her clasped hands between her knees.

"Is she firing me or something?"

Rhian turned to her quickly. "What? Who?"

"Rachel. Is she firing me? Is that what this is?"

Rhian shook her head. "No. Nothing like that. Though you might quit when you hear, I don't know. It's, I mean, I wouldn't blame you if you did. Want to quit, I mean. It's just that…I hope you don't."

Jayden reached across the couch and touched Rhian's hand. "Just tell me what's going on. Then we can figure out the rest."

Rhian's face paled further, and Jayden could feel her hands trembling beneath her own. "She—Rachel—needs us to keep being a couple for this to work."

"Okay," Jayden said slowly. Jayden had set the wheels of this in motion herself. Why was Rhian so nervous about this request? Had Jayden's attentions been making her uncomfortable all this time? Was she only tolerating them as a lesser evil compared to Brooke's? She'd thought that perhaps Rhian was enjoying what they were doing. Maybe even looking at this being more than just pretend. Or was that just wishful thinking? Were those shy glances just in her imagination? She went over that kiss in her mind, as she had done repeatedly since it happened, loving the way Rhian had trembled in her embrace. Had she gotten it wrong? Had she miscalculated so horribly? "I figured that would be the case at least until Brooke was no longer around."

"You did?"

Jayden affected a casual air that belied her surprising amount of investment in the question. "Of course. Didn't you?"

Rhian shook her head. "I guess I didn't really think that far ahead in all this."

"Ah." Jayden felt the stab of disappointment. "Then I guess I'm sorry you're now caught up in my lie and it's making you uncomfortable."

"It's not your fault. You were trying to help me."

"But all I did was make things worse." Jayden put her own glass down and took hold of Rhian's hand. Well, no matter what Rhian thought of her, they were now in this, for better or for worse. "Look, we're friends, right?"

Rhian nodded, her gaze fixed on their joined hands. She seemed rattled. Jayden needed to fix this.

"So as friends we can spend time together without there being anything awkward about it, right?"

Rhian nodded again, her gaze still fixed.

"What more is there to a relationship that other people actually see anyway? I mean, I'm not in the habit of inviting people into my bedroom to watch me and my girlfriend. Are you?"

"No," Rhian said with a small smile.

"So we hold hands out there a little bit, maybe kiss on the cheek every now and then. But we just carry on being friends. Nothing too different, really."

"And you'd be comfortable with that—with being my pretend girlfriend—for the duration of filming?"

"The whole time?"

Rhian nodded yet again. "The whole time"—she finally managed to look Jayden in the eyes—"spend the next four and a half months pretending to care for me."

Jayden looked at her. Really looked at her, at her grey eyes that changed with her mood and reflected the tumultuous passion and…anxiety…that simmered inside her. Those pink-tinted lips that had tasted so sweet were parted, moist, and inviting. Her blond hair was tucked behind her ears, the short fringe slipping over one eye when she moved. And the truth hit Jayden: She didn't have to spend the next four and a half months pretending to care for Rhian. She did care for her. The real question was, could she spend the next four and a half months only *pretending* to care for her?

Clearly Rhian would return to the UK when this show was done. And Jayden would be here—alone—taking care of the business while Fen recovered…or not, as the case might be. Rhian would return to her life, to her mother, her firm, her friends, maybe even a girlfriend.

She broke the silence that had suddenly developed between them. "Do you have a girlfriend back home?"

"Excuse me?"

"I never thought to ask before, I'm sorry. Is that why you don't want to do this? You don't want to hurt someone you care about back in England?"

"No." Rhian's voice was quiet. "No girlfriend."

"So it's just that I'm repulsive, then," she said with a smirk.

Rhian chuckled. "Yeah, turning women to stone wherever you go."

"Hey, that's my signature move."

"Then you really need to work on those moves, Jay."

"Don't need to now." She reached over and tugged gently on Rhian's hair. That was allowed with her officially-sanctioned pretend girlfriend, right? "I've already bagged me a babe."

Rhian groaned. "Ew. *Bagged a babe.* That's an awful phrase."

"Okay, I'll give you that. But—" An alarm sounded from Jayden's phone. "—shit. Hang on. I need to get the pizza out of the oven." She stood. "Don't go anywhere."

"I won't."

Jayden took two minutes to throw the pizza onto a plate, slice it, grab paper towels, and get back to the sofa with their dinner. She pushed the plate under Rhian's nose. She snatched a slice and took off the tip with her teeth.

"Okay, where was I?" Jayden asked.

Rhian swallowed her pizza and said, "Babe-bagging."

Jayden chuckled. Things seemed to be easing up between them. "Right. So, ignoring the awful phrase, why do you seem so against this idea?"

Rhian shrugged.

"No, don't do that."

"Don't do what?"

"Try and avoid the question. Clearly you have a reason. So be honest with me."

"I don't want to say anything that will be...I don't know...taken the wrong way or something."

"You're worried about offending me?"

"Well, yeah."

Jayden laughed and swallowed a good mouthful of her pizza slice. "You won't. Just tell me what's going on."

"I'm not sure I can do this." She tossed her slice back onto the plate and wiped her hands with the napkin.

"Pretend to be attracted to me?"

Rhian nodded, still wiping grease from her fingers.

Jayden chuckled and tried to swallow the bitter taste of hurt that laced the sauce on her slice. "Well, I know I'm not exactly a stunner, but I can't do a great deal about that. This is what we've got to work with—"

"No. That's not what... That's not the way I meant it."

"Then what did you mean?"

"This is why I didn't want to say anything." Rhian shook her head. "We've got to work together, and we've got to pretend to be a couple. I don't want to make anything any more awkward than it already is." She covered her face with her hands.

"Rhian, I'm a big girl. I don't expect every lesbian I meet to find me attractive." She shrugged and took a tiny bite. "We're pretending, remember—a couple of friends doing what we have to do for work purposes."

Rhian cocked her head to the side and looked Jayden in the eyes. Jayden felt she was staring down into her soul when she asked, "Is that what you want?"

Jayden cleared her throat and shrugged. "It's what we have. And don't feel bad that you don't fancy me. It's not like you're my cup of tea either. So it's all good." Her voice didn't sound like her own. It was deeper, and seemed to come from somewhere far away. She tossed her own slice of pizza down and finished her glass of wine before reaching to pour another. She tried to pinpoint what had actually changed in the last half hour. She'd walked into the house with her friend and pretend girlfriend, who, granted, she'd acknowledged was hot. She wasn't blind. But now she was sitting on the sofa with the same friend and pretend girlfriend, and everything *felt* different. Everything suddenly felt very wrong. She felt like a crevasse had just opened beneath her, and there was nothing but air between her and the ice below.

"You're not?" Rhian whispered. Her eyes remained downcast, hands clasped between her knees, and her hair skipped forward from behind her ears, shielding her from Jayden's gaze.

"Sorry, what?"

Rhian peeked out from the curtain of hair obscuring her face. Her grey eyes seemed to whirl with emotion and restrained energy. Like a storm approaching on the horizon. "You're not attracted to me?"

"No," she said quickly. The denial was vomited from her lips, hastened by the bitter energy of rejection. She hated lying, but what else could she do? She had a little pride. "Of course not," she added a little more softly.

"That's good." Rhian's smile looked painful, like she was forcing her skin to move despite resistance from her muscles.

"Yeah." Part of her wondered at the smile of Rhian's face. Was she nursing her own bruised ego too?

"That's okay, then." Her voice sounded an octave higher than normal.

Why wasn't she acting relieved? She'd got what she wanted. Jayden hadn't quit, and she was going along with the charade—had even made it seem like it was no big deal. "Yeah."

Rhian sighed. "I should probably get going now. Since we're all good, and we know what's going on."

"Probably a good idea."

"I'll see you tomorrow, then."

"Probably."

Rhian stood and dropped the napkin on the table next to the plate with the unfinished pizza on it. "Okay. Well then, goodnight, Jayden."

Jayden looked up from the sofa. She couldn't seem to make her legs move. She knew she should stand and see her out. Walk her home, even. But she couldn't make herself do it. "Night," she said.

She listened to the door close and the silence that filled the room. She hadn't lied when she'd told Rhian that she didn't expect other women to find her attractive. But she'd hoped Rhian did, even just a little. Her feelings for Rhian ran deeper than she'd realised. As did the hurt. She closed her eyes, then quickly put her hand to her mouth as she ran for the bathroom.

Rebecca's eyes burned behind her eyelids as Jayden gave up the pizza she'd consumed. Guilt twisted her gut until there was nothing left.

"I didn't even think about you. Not the whole time." She wiped her mouth with some tissue and started the tap running. "I'm so sorry, Becks, I forgot. How could I forget?" She leant back against the wall, knees pulled up to her chest, arms wrapped tight around them, and let herself remember.

She replayed that last smile in the mess tent. The cocky, sexy grin, the promise to be careful. She remembered the chill up her spine, the hairs on her neck standing on end as apprehension walked along her soul, offering her the warning she hadn't listened to. Every minute between that and the moment the avalanche had hit ticked away as she sat on the cold tiles. Every second flayed her until she was staring again at Rebecca's lifeless corpse, as cold and rigid as the ice and rock she was encased in.

"How could I forget?"

She picked up the phone and dialled Fen's mobile number.

"Hey, Mogo," Fen said after the second ring. "What's up?"

Jayden sniffled and tried to control her emotions enough to speak. She couldn't.

"It's okay, hon. I'm here."

Fen whispered quiet words through the outpouring of grief and guilt. Never asking her to explain, never asking for more than Jayden could give. She was just there. And Jayden felt her presence as clearly as she would have felt her embrace had they been in the same room. For those few minutes, it was enough.

CHAPTER 24

"Push," Jayden said. "Come on."

"I am fucking pushing," Fen replied through gritted teeth as she pushed her plaster-cast-covered arm against Jayden's hand as hard as she could. She managed to move it an inch before she gave up and breathed heavily.

Jayden grinned. "That's progress. When are they letting you out of this shithole?"

"Don't know yet." She used her uninjured arm and the pull-bar hanging over the bed to raise herself into a seated position. "It's only been five weeks since the accident. I think they want to wait until the casts are off my arm and leg before they let me loose on the world at large."

Jayden crinkled her nose. "S'pose that makes sense. But you are making progress, right?"

Fen nodded. "The cord looks to be intact, so they hope it's just a matter of time before I regain some sensation in my legs."

"Did they give you any idea of how long that might be?"

"No. They can't make any promises on that. But we have hope, Jay. It's just a matter of time, and I'll be walking around again."

"Climbing again?"

Fen's smile dropped a little. "One step at a time."

"Is the only way to get yourself up the mountain."

"So they say."

"So you say. You always told me that, sis." Jayden was grateful Fen hadn't asked her about the late-night phone call and her emotional breakdown. She knew it would come. It always did. She just wasn't sure how to explain herself. She wasn't sure she could.

"Tell me about the week of training," Fen said. "I've been dying to know how it's all going."

Jayden gave her a rundown on each contestant—strengths, weaknesses, performance in the tests they'd already conducted, expectations in the ones still to come. Fen knew each climber they had been expecting. She'd long ago gotten their names and CVs from Rhian. When Fen asked about Killian, Jayden screwed up her face but gave her the run of the full story.

Fen's face turned red and blotchy when she saw the footage of Killian attacking Rhian. And Jayden refrained from telling her about the hole that she still needed to repair in Fen's kitchen from when she'd first seen it. She knew she could blame the damage to her hand on a rock wall rather than one made of plaster and wood, if Fen asked. The messages back and forth between Killian and Luiji had been blowing up social media since he'd posted the video of the attack and his message to Killian:

> Is this what you call discrimination against you, man? Because here in the real world, we call it assaulting a woman.

It was three hours before Killian had responded, claiming the footage was faked by the studio to try to get him to drop his lawsuit. Luiji had posted a photo of himself with a caption:

> Can't fake me, man. And I'm more than happy to tell the world and the courts, because I saw everything you did. And I heard everything you said. On camera and off camera. Would you like me to share those words too?

> Why are you doing this to me? That bitch treated you like shit too.

They'd traded back and forth for hours, Killian's feed slowly devolving to a series of insults and impotent threats as Luiji fired barb after barb, telling Killian his claim of sexual harassment was bogus because no lesbian was going to try to harass his ass.

Fen whistled after she reached the end. "Christ, you don't do things by halves, you lot."

"Apparently not."

"And is this working like the boss lady wants?"

Jayden nodded. "Looks like it. Rachel's e-mail this morning said they've had requests for interviews about the company's stance on women's rights issues, violence against women, and LGBTQ rights. Looks like the client is getting the platform it was looking for in a very positive way."

"Wow. Well, that's something positive at least. How's Rhian dealing with all this? It must be getting her a lot of attention. Is it causing any other problems in the group?"

Jayden sighed. "This isn't, but there is one other issue."

Fen waited, her expression asking the question she didn't need to voice.

"It's the other alternate. Brooke."

"What about her?"

Jayden found herself stuttering as she told Fen about Brooke's behaviour towards Rhian. About Jayden's impulsive decision to offer her protection in the way she had. The way it had backfired with Brooke's social media posting.

"So far, Oskar's only put one comment on the picture."

"Saying?"

"See for yourself." Jayden brought up the Facebook picture on her phone and let Fen see it.

"'When the woman you shagged last night sees her girlfriend again and ditches your ass to save her own.'" Fen read the caption out loud. "Classy piece, then."

"You have no idea."

"'When the woman with a girlfriend turns down your ugly, trying-to-cheat ass, and you can't take it. Hashtag sour grapes, hashtag needs to learn to take no for an answer, hashtag sexual predators aren't just guys.'" Fen whistled again. "Ouch, he went for the jugular."

"Yeah."

"And she hasn't responded yet?"

"No. Nothing."

"Watch your back, sis. Okay?"

Jayden nodded. "Don't worry about me."

"Of course I worry about you. You look like shit, after all," Fen said with a grin.

"For fuck's sake." Jayden threw her hands up in the air. "Not you too. I've had about enough of women telling me how crap I look lately."

"Hey, hey, hey. I was pulling your leg. Chill."

Jayden saw the look of confused contrition on Fen's face and scrubbed her hands over her own. "Sorry. I overreacted. You're right. Sorry."

"It's okay. It's not like you to go off like that. What's going on?"

Jayden shook her head. "Nothing. It's just me. Just been a long week with a lot going on, I guess."

Fen nodded and watched her. "Bullshit."

Jayden snorted a quick laugh.

"Come on, you forget I'm your big sister. I taught you how to lie, and I taught you badly so I'd always know. Besides, I still remember that call from last night. I know I was pretty groggy from the sleeping pill they gave me, but I know I wasn't hallucinating. Now, spit it out before I have to use my cast to beat it out of you."

Jayden laughed. "Go on, then, I could do with a laugh."

Fen quickly rolled her magazine with one hand against her leg and swatted Jayden on the head with it. "You shouldn't take the piss out of the disabled."

"Ow. You're not disabled. You're just…recovering."

"Tell me."

"It's nothing. Honest."

"Tell me, or I'll get one of the nurses to spill laxatives in your coffee."

Jaden stared at her, a perfect picture of shock on her face. "That's just evil."

Fen grinned wickedly. "I know. I've had to get creative since none of you will take my threats seriously anymore."

Jayden eyed her coffee cup suspiciously before draining it.

"So who's been telling you you're butt ugly?"

"Rhian."

"Rhian's too nice to tell you you're butt ugly."

Jayden didn't say anything.

"No way. She's your pretend girlfriend. She wouldn't say that."

"You're right, she didn't. She just said she isn't attracted to me. She didn't think we could pull it off."

Fen's gaze dropped to her phone, and the picture of the two of them kissing was still on the screen. "Looks pretty convincing to me."

Jayden shrugged one shoulder and leant back in her chair. "Anyway, we're friends, so we're going to show everyone that we're friends who are going to hold hands sometimes to make people think we're a couple."

Fen tipped her head to the side and watched her. "And which bit bothers you more?"

"What do you mean?"

"Which bit bothers you more? That you're pretending to be a couple with a woman who isn't attracted to you? Or that you're pretending to be in love with a woman who you really are in love with?"

"I'm not in love with her. I barely even know her. She's just a friend."

Fen waved a finger in circles in front of her face. "You don't look like this when a friend tells you they're not attracted to you. You look relieved. You take the piss out of them. You don't look like you lost your puppy."

"I'm not in love with her." Jayden crossed her arms over her chest. She could feel her mouth forming a pout and knew she was behaving ridiculously.

"Fine. You're not in love with her. But you do like her."

Jayden opened her mouth to deny it.

"And don't you dare lie to me, because I'll know and spike your coffee."

Jayden narrowed her eyes. "It's people like you that get disabled people discriminated against, you know."

"Yeah, yeah. Spill it." She wiggled her fingers in a come-hither motion, beckoning for Jayden's confession.

"Fine, yes. I do like her."

"A lot."

Jayden ground her teeth.

"The truth, now."

"Yes."

"Excellent. I like Rhian too."

Jayden rolled her eyes. "Hoo-fucking-rah. We all love Rhian, whoop-di-doo. Let's throw a party."

Fen grinned. "You just said you love her."

"It was a figure of speech!"

"Yeah, yeah."

"Oh, for God's sake. What does it matter anyway? She's not even attracted to me, so it's a moot fucking point."

Fen scratched her head a minute. "Do you remember when you first introduced me and Mark?"

Jayden frowned. "Yeah. What's this—"

"Do you remember what I said to you about him?"

"Yes, you said he was an arrogant prick and that if I ever let him in the house again, you'd rip off my arm and beat me to death with it. You've always tended towards violence."

Fen ignored the barb. "And what did you do?"

"I invited him for dinner the following week."

"Why?"

"Because I knew he wasn't an arrogant prick and that you'd like him when you got to know him a bit."

"And do you remember what I said after that second meeting?"

"I believe it was something along the lines of 'he's all right but not my type'."

"Exactly. Why do you think I said that?"

"You do know we've already had this conversation, don't you?"

"Answer the question."

Jayden rolled her eyes again. "Because you thought he was interested in me and therefore not available to you."

"So what was I trying to do?"

"Protect yourself from getting hurt, oh wise and wonderful sister."

"Smart-arse. And do you remember me saying I wasn't even attracted to him?"

"Yup."

"And that he was just going to be a friend?"

"Yup. But this isn't like that."

"How do you know?"

"Well, she doesn't have a girlfriend. I asked. And she knows I don't. We've talked about that before. See? Not like that."

Fen shook her head. "Have you told her?"

Jayden twisted the hem of her fleece between her fingers. "Told her what?"

"Don't do that. You know what. Have you told her about Rebecca?"

Jayden didn't respond.

"Jay, honey, you do know that the way you behave, it's clear that there's something you're hiding, don't you? That there's something buried in you that hurts so much." She reached for Jayden's hand. "You do know that, don't you?"

Jayden shook her head and pinched the bridge of her nose. "Not around Rhian, I don't."

"Sure you do. You do it all the time. You never let go of that pain, and, honey, that's truly understandable. Is this why you were so upset last night?"

"No, I really don't do that with her."

Fen wiggled her hand. "You're still grieving, Jay."

"You don't get it. Last night I was like that because I *wasn't*. I forgot her, Fen. I was sitting there sharing pizza with Rhian, listening to her tell me that she wasn't sure she could even pretend to be my girlfriend because she wasn't attracted to me, and I wasn't thinking, *Oh goody, that lets me off the hook with my dead girlfriend*." She leant forward in her chair. "I wasn't thinking about Becks at all." She swallowed hard. "All I was thinking was *Shit, I finally found someone I could really fall for, and she doesn't even want me*." She pulled her hand from Fen's and scrubbed them both over her face. "Does that sound like someone who's grieving to you? Does it sound like someone who lost their partner less than two years ago? Does that sound normal to you?" She got up from the chair and started pacing the room, the restless energy inside her far too much to be contained in a chair. She ran her fingers through her hair, cursing when they got stuck in a tangle.

"You finished?" Fen asked quietly.

"Humpf. I think I've made my point, don't you?"

"Yes, I think I see things pretty clearly."

"Well, do you care to share, or should I just get the fuck out of here now?"

"You're scared."

Jayden laughed. "No shit. Glad you didn't decide to be a shrink, Dr Freud." She wrapped her hand around the door handle and started to turn it.

"You're scared because this is the first time in almost two years that you've let yourself feel something other than pain. You're scared because this is the first time in your life you've felt something as deep as you already feel for Rhian."

She turned back to face Fen. "I loved Becks!" she shouted.

"Yeah, you did. But Becks was easy for you to love. She was everything you imagined a partner of yours would be, and on the surface, you were perfect for each other."

"Exactly. I loved her."

"But that was only on the surface."

"Fuck off."

"No, you'll hear me out. You loved the easy relationship you had with her, but Becks, as much as I loved her too, was never going to be enough for you. Not in the long-term. There wasn't the spark with Becks that would've kept you together. I'd go so far as to bet that you even knew before she died that there was something wrong in that relationship. That it was failing. Didn't you?"

Jayden replayed that last argument in her head. Those last words. But she couldn't speak them. To admit Fen was right would be a bigger betrayal, surely. "I loved her," Jayden repeated. But the fire of the statement was gone.

"I know you did. But you know I'm telling you the truth."

Jayden let the words penetrate. Let them start to sink in.

"And that makes you feel even more guilty that she's gone. That you survived that awful fucking mess and she didn't."

Jayden's knees buckled, and she only just managed to stumble to the chair at the bedside.

"I forgot her."

"No, honey. You'll never forget her. Not really. But you will move on. You can."

"It's too soon."

"Only if you make it too soon." Fen reached for her hand again. "You can sit and wallow in this, or you can decide to move forward and pursue what's in front of you. What, or rather, *who* I think we both know is right for you."

Jayden shook her head. "Even if you're right, and I'm not saying you are, she's made it clear she doesn't want me."

"So you told her you didn't want her, to protect your fragile ego and give yourself an out. Right?"

Jayden sat in silence.

"There's just one problem, Mogo. It's too late for that already, isn't it?"

"What?"

"You've already laid yourself open to her by agreeing to this plan of pretending to be her girlfriend for the next four and a half months. Do you really think you can spend that time with her, pretending to care for her, really caring for her, and still protect your heart at the same time?"

Jayden wiped her eyes. "I don't really have a lot of choice, now, do I?" She closed her eyes and tried to pull up Rebecca's cocky, sexy grin. Tried to remember the feel of her lips against her cheek that last time. But she couldn't. All she could see was Rhian's shy smile, feel her fingers on her cheek, and her lips pressed against hers out on the glacier. That one moment of utter perfection that had caught them both off guard and unawares.

She glanced down at her hands, staring at the fingers that had trailed over the bruise on Rhian's cheek, the hands that had touched Rebecca but now only felt the warmth of Rhian's flesh. She waited for the guilt to crush her chest and twist her guts. She waited for the agony to start. But when it came, it was already less than the night before.

She closed her eyes and tried to picture Rebecca's face, her eyes, but the image of them was blurring at the edges. And the stab of pain that hit her had already lost its potency.

In place of the emotions she'd expected was desire. The desire to run to Rhian. To touch Rhian. To hold her, speak to her, smile, and laugh—to just be with Rhian.

Jayden groaned, then linked her fingers with Fen's and sighed. "I'm fucked, aren't I?"

Fen chuckled. "No, but you want to be."

"Crude. Just crude."

Fen sat quietly for a moment while Jayden absorbed the feelings. The depth of emotion that washed over her when she thought about how right it had felt just holding Rhian's hand scared the shit out of her. But she craved more. The next four and a half months were going to be hell. She knew by the end of it she would be hopelessly in love with Rhian and that the woman would fly back to England and take Jayden's heart with her. Without even knowing what she was doing. She sighed again.

"You could always do something about it, you know."

"What are you on about now?" Jayden sat with her eyes closed.

"Well, the way I see it, you've got the perfect opportunity to...well, to let her fall in love with you, I suppose."

Jayden snorted a bitter laugh. "She's not even attracted to me, dummy. Did you miss that part of the conversation? Besides, you can't make someone fall in love with you."

"I'm not saying you can make her. We don't practice voodoo-doodoo or witchcraft. I'm talking about giving her every opportunity to see how fantastic a person you are and then to do the right thing."

"And that would be...?"

"Fall in love with you, of course."

"Of course. How stupid of me to forget that, since I left my wand at Hogwarts."

Fen chuckled. "That was funny. You can be funny. That's attractive."

"Gee, thanks."

"I'm not done, yet. What's the most attractive thing about a person?"

Jayden stared at her.

"Their personality. Their sense of humour, intelligence. Their sense of adventure."

Jayden rolled her eyes again. "That's the kind of thing they always say about ugly people."

"Maybe, but think about this. Looks attract a person or not, but it's the person they prove to be that either keeps them together or tears them apart. Correct?"

"Yeah, I guess."

"You like her. I mean, really like her."

"That's not always enough, Fen."

"Jay, I know how hard it was on you. Base camp. Losing Rebecca. Fuck, it damn near killed you. But since you've been back here, since you took this project on, I've seen you again. Just like I asked. Just like you needed."

"But you still want more from me."

"No." Fen shook her head. "I want more *for* you."

"Semantics."

"Not at all. I want you to be happy. Really happy. And I think Rhian could do that for you. She's helped you get back out in the mountains—"

"That was blackmail."

"She makes you laugh."

Jayden crossed her arms over her chest but didn't dispute the point.

"She stands up to you when you're being unreasonable."

Jayden scowled at her and wished she'd never confided in Fen how shocked and surprised she'd been when Rhian had held her ground about staying behind to bring in the stragglers. Nor how much it had helped her.

"And she makes you smile more than I've seen since you first conquered Everest."

Jayden ground her teeth, determined not to think about the way Rhian coaxed so many smiles to her lips.

"So, if you like her—and, I mean, really like her—then court her. Show her how wonderful you are. Give her every opportunity to fall in love with you."

"I can't do that. Even if I wanted to."

"You do want to. And you can. You have to pretend to be her girlfriend, right?" Fen waited until Jayden nodded. "So do all the things you would for your girlfriend. Show her what a brilliant girlfriend you'd be for her. Don't pretend to be her girlfriend, Jay. Be her girlfriend. Don't play games. Just be it and, like any relationship, see where it leads you both."

Jayden closed her eyes and tried to picture what it would be like. Would Rhian notice that Jayden wasn't playing a game with her? Would she pull the plug if she did? No, Rhian couldn't. She had to do this. Her mother's company was at stake. Jayden pictured herself holding out flowers and kissing the back of Rhian's hand. Not because other people were around, but just to see Rhian smile. She imagined making them dinner and pouring her wine, learning all the little things that made Rhian laugh. Then walking her home. Would she dare to kiss her on the doorstep if no one else was there to see?

They'd spent six weeks becoming friends. And the past four days, they'd spent twenty-four hours a day together out on the ice, eating, working, sleeping side by side the whole time. And she wanted more.

Could she really play the role of her girlfriend? No, Fen was right. If she was going to do this, she was doing it all the way. No half measures, no games, no pretence. *I'm going to be Rhian's girlfriend.* She tried the thought on. She should have been surprised by how comfortable it felt, but she wasn't. Not really. She should have felt scared by how comfortable it felt.

But she wasn't.

"What have you got to lose, sis?"

What did she have to lose? She was a woman with deep feelings for someone who didn't return them. She had the opportunity to see the woman of her affection every day, to show her every day that there was something there. And if she couldn't convince Rhian of that, she was still a woman with deep feelings for a woman who didn't feel the same. What would change? Nothing. But if she could convince Rhian to take a chance on her...then everything could change.

What did she have to lose? Jayden blinked, a smile tugging at the corner of her lips.

"Absolutely nothing."

CHAPTER 25

RHIAN RUBBED HER EYES AND tried to focus on the weather report on her tablet. The storm that had kept them all inside for the past three days was still blowing and looked set to remain for at least another three. She'd missed seeing Jayden the day before but admitted to herself it was probably a good thing. She'd barely slept since their pizza dinner, and the thought of seeing Jayden again in front of everyone, pretending in front of everyone, twisted her stomach into knots. She lifted her coffee cup, only to find it empty. She tutted and went to get another cup, hoping this one would be more successful at removing the sandpaper from her eyelids.

Oskar pulled out the seat next to her, a wide grin on his face. She rested her cheek on her hand, elbow on the table, and waited and watched.

"You look lonely over here, boss lady. Wanna hit the wall with a few of us?" he offered.

She smiled ruefully. The indoor climbing gym was the best offer she'd had all day. "Wish I could. I'm afraid I've got boring work to do, though. Instead of lightening my workload, the weather adds to it."

He nodded. "Shame. You look like you could use a break."

"You saying I look like shit?"

He chuckled. "Wouldn't dare." He rapped his hands on the table like a drum roll and stood. "Catch ya later, then."

"Later." She waved him off, turned back to her tablet, and opened her e-mail program. She scanned the contents of a report from Rachel declaring Luiji and Oskar "the bomb", then shook her head and sniggered. She could just picture Rachel in her black suit and red blouse, dark hair piled up on her head, her glasses perched on her nose as she mouthed the words in her office, trying out the phrase beforehand.

Rhian sent her a quick reply, asking if she had counted the number of times she'd practiced saying "the bomb" while writing that e-mail and hit *send.*

There was another e-mail in her inbox. One she wasn't expecting. She held her breath as she clicked on it and read:

> My darling daughter Rhian,

"Like I believe that shit."

> I know things between us have been difficult, and I accept that that is my fault. Entirely. I do not blame you for refusing my calls. I can't. Not anymore. Not now that I have seen what I did to you.
>
> Rachel showed me the video.

"Rachel, I'm gonna fucking kill you." She wanted to just press *delete,* the same way she did on her answering machine on those few occasions he'd left her a message telling her to call him. Not asking. Telling. Her hand hovered over the red cross, but she couldn't bring herself to push the button. The tone of this was so different to those demanding messages, so conciliatory, so apologetic, so…not her dad, that she couldn't stop herself from reading on.

> There was a time, when you were a little girl, that I put myself above what was best for you. I betrayed you and my duty as your father by turning my back on you and leaving to live my life with Rachel. I can't honestly say that I would change that if I could, but I do regret what it did to you—to us. But you were a kind-hearted child, and you forgave me, a miracle I have always been grateful for. And when you came to live with us after your mother passed away, I swore I would never let you down again.
>
> And then I let you down again.

ROCK AND A HARD PLACE

I can't honestly tell you what it was that I had such a problem with. But if you'll indulge me here a little, I will try to explain what I can.

I have homosexual friends. I've worked with many more over the years too. And it has never affected me. When you told us that you were a lesbian, it was as though I stopped seeing you for a moment. I stopped seeing the little girl I helped to create, that I raised, that I loved, and instead I saw this amalgamation of every bad stereotype and crass porn film ever created to objectify and marginalise lesbians in our society.

And it made me afraid.

It made me afraid of you. Of seeing you and not being able to separate those dreadful images from the reality that is you.

But worst of all, it made me afraid for you.

It made me afraid of all the things you would miss without having a normal life. And yes, I do know, intellectually, that there is nothing abnormal about the life you've chosen or who you've found yourself to be. I am merely trying to explain what went through my head in those terrible few minutes. So please, bear with me and try to hear me out before you judge a foolish old man.

As a father, I always wanted you to have the best of everything I could possibly give you. I wanted you to succeed where I had failed, to love where I could not, and to have all the things that I'd wanted for myself at your fingertips. To find out that you didn't even want those same things hurt. And the hurt drove my fear to anger.

When you were born, your mother and I vowed we would never use violence when we raised you. And neither of us ever did.

Until that night.

I am so sorry, Rhian.

I have never been able to forgive myself for raising my hand to you, so I blocked it out. I refused to let myself remember what I did. It was easier to blame you for the distance between us. It was your unnatural ways that had driven the wedge into our relationship, not my own idiocy.

When Rachel showed me the video of that man striking you...two things happened at the same moment. I felt a rage and the desire to protect you more fiercely than I have since you were a babe in arms, and the deepest sense of revulsion at myself than I could ever have believed possible. I wanted to destroy the man who hurt you.

Then I realised that I was the man who had hurt you the most. The blow that despicable idiot struck was nothing compared to the blow I dealt you, was it?

Tears rolled down Rhian's face and blurred the screen in front of her. She swiped at them and carried on reading.

I can't ask you to forgive me. I won't. I know what I did was unforgivable. Yet, your forgiveness is truly my deepest wish.

I know it is a lot to ask, but would you allow me to join Rachel on one of the Skype calls? Please. Just so I can see you're all right. If you don't want to see me again after that, I promise I will abide by your wishes. I will truly do whatever you ask, my darling Rhian. I have so much to make up for. We have lost so much because of my foolishness.

Please.

Your father

Rhian wiped her face and read the missive again, trying to absorb all the details. Trying to determine the truth in them. She could picture him sitting behind his computer, tapping away at the keys with two fingers, and searching for just the right words. Words that would get him what he wanted without having to divulge too much of himself. At least that was the way it was before. But this was different. There seemed to be no hiding behind fancy words. Or attempts to confuse her with defying twists of logic. He was accepting fault. He was apologising, and he was begging her for something. Something that was tiny in the grand scheme of things. He just wanted her to let him see her face on a computer screen. But in the scheme of their things—of their relationship—this was a huge moment.

Should she agree?

Could she?

What reason did she have to believe what he was saying? Love was supposed to be unconditional, not just until you got scared or something changed and made it uncomfortable. He'd told her he would always love her. He'd also called her a disgusting pervert who he never wanted to see again.

Which was the real truth?

"Morning."

Rhian dropped her tablet to the table when she looked up, and her fingers twitched. Jayden was smiling at her and putting two cups of coffee on the table before she sat down.

"Sorry. I didn't mean to scare you." She paused. "What's up?"

Rhian swallowed and shook her head. "Nothing. I was just surprised. I wasn't expecting you. I thought everyone had gone out."

"I saw Luiji and most of the guys heading to the wall. I think there's only Brooke and Sky not going over there."

"How come?"

"Kimi said Sky's picked up a stomach thing, and no one knows what's going on with Brooke. They're ignoring her, and she's doing the same to them." She slid one of the cups in front of Rhian. "Milk, no sugar, right?"

"Thanks," Rhian said quietly. "Just the way I like it."

Jayden shrugged the comment off and tapped the tablet. "More bad news from Rachel?"

Rhian sipped her coffee and frowned. "What? No. Why?"

"I wondered if that's why you looked so upset."

"I'm not upset."

Jayden cocked an eyebrow but didn't say anything.

Rhian sighed. "I'm fine. Honestly. And no, there's been nothing bad from Rachel. Quite the contrary actually. Everything's going well on their side, so she's happy."

"And if she's happy, we're all happy, right?"

"Right."

"So why are your eyes all red? And I can see tear tracks down your cheeks."

Rhian quickly wiped her face and shook her head slowly. "It's nothing."

Jayden took hold of her hand and slid their fingers together. "If it made you cry, it's not nothing." She squeezed Rhian's fingers gently. "If you don't want to tell me, I understand. But please don't tell me it's nothing when it clearly is."

The look of gentle concern on Jayden's face was enough to make the tears well in her eyes again, but she blinked them away, determined not to cry in front of her, yet desperately craving Jayden's arms about her to chase away the questions spinning around in her head. But she could no more ask for Jayden's embrace than she could trust what her father had written. The further away from reading that letter she got, the more convinced she became that it was a ploy. Perhaps Rachel was giving him more grief about their estrangement, and after sending that message, he could always throw it back at her that he'd tried. He probably figured Rhian wouldn't answer his request. After all, she hadn't before.

She shook her head again. "I don't want to talk about it."

Jayden squeezed her fingers again. "Okay." She smiled. "You know where I am if you change your mind."

Rhian nodded, pulled her hand from Jayden's, and clasped them together on the table. "Thanks, but I'll be fine."

Jayden paused and swallowed before she asked, "So what's on your agenda today?"

"Just clearing a bunch of e-mails and checking on a few important logistical things. You?"

"Killing time, really, but I've got a couple of ideas I'd like to run by you. Challenge stuff. Any chance you could come by Adventure Trekkers this afternoon? We could grab some lunch while we talk."

Rhian nodded as she sipped her hot coffee. It really was just exactly the way she liked it. "Okay, sure. That will give me time to finish up these e-mails."

"And it gives me time to scoot to the market and pick up some groceries. Mark seems to only have frozen pizza in the house."

"And there's only so much pizza a girl can eat, right?" *I certainly seem to have lost my appetite for it.*

"Exactly." Jayden finished her coffee and stood. "See you at noon?"

Rhian nodded.

Jayden reached out and gently squeezed her shoulder, bent forward, and placed a kiss on her cheek. Rhian closed her eyes to savour the contact and ignore whoever must be watching, to pretend they were alone and that Jayden offered the kiss just to her—not to whoever was standing behind her.

The scent of Jayden's perfume lingered long after she had gone, and whoever Jayden had seen, whatever it was that had made her initiate that kiss, never bothered to show themselves to Rhian. She was glad—relieved. She wasn't sure she could have hidden the tear that traced its winding path down her cheek when Jayden walked away.

Four and a half months. *How am I going to make it through lunch, never mind four and a half months?* Somehow, knowing that Jayden wasn't attracted to her didn't help. She'd hoped it would. She'd hoped that finding out she was on her own in this thing would get her brain together and snap her out of it. Or was it her heart that was in control?

Either way, it didn't seem to matter.

———◆◇◆———

Jayden took the hamper from Isabella. "You're sure these are her favourites?"

"*Sí.* Is what I make every time Carlos bring her to dinner. She say several time this her favourite."

"Okay, cool." She fished in her pocket and pulled out a wad of cash, peeled off a hundred-peso bill, and handed it to Isabella.

Isabella held up her hand. "No, no, no. I no take your money."

Jayden grabbed her hand and pressed the bill in. "To cover expenses. I can't let you cook *and* pay for the groceries, Isabella. Please."

"Is too much."

"Then I'm in credit for next time." Jayden smiled.

Isabella sighed heavily. "For next three times."

"Fine. Now what do I need to do?"

"You want her think you cook it?"

Jayden thought about and quickly rejected the idea. "No, then I'd have to live up to that. And you and I both know that the limit of my cooking ability is frozen pizza."

"Ay, ay, ay." She pulled out a covered plastic dish. "Is ravioli. Boil pan of water, add salt, little oil, and add pasta to water for five minutes."

"Five minutes? Is that all? You sure?"

"*Sí*. Five minutes. Or will be ruined."

"Okay, five minutes. Got it. Then what do I do?"

"Drain pasta and put it back in the pan. This"—she pulled out another dish—"is pesto sauce. Pour it over the pasta, stir, and serve."

"That's it?"

"Is easy, no?"

"Sounds it." She looked at the packages.

"Okay, I must go now. Carlos is going to the airport this afternoon. I want to give him his lunch before he leave." She wiggled her fingers in Jayden's direction and let the door close loudly behind her.

"Okay, sounds simple enough. I climb mountains, I can boil water, surely."

"Do you always talk to yourself?"

Jayden looked up at the sound of Rhian's voice. The discomfort in it was so clear that Jayden wondered for just a second if this was a good idea. But she didn't have time to dwell on the thought. In her startled moment, she knocked the pesto sauce tub off the counter. She tried to catch it, managing to tip one corner with her fingers before it crashed to the ground. The lid pinged off, and the dark green, nutty sauce splattered across the floor.

"Shit."

Rhian's hand covered her mouth a she tried desperately not to laugh. "Oh my God, I'm so sorry." She rushed forward, giggling as she did so, and grabbed a roll of kitchen towels, tearing sheets off to mop up the mess. She handed several to Jayden and pointed to her pants. "You should get those pants in the wash quickly before the basil stains. That beige is a great colour on you, but it won't look good with little green stains all around your ankles."

"Doesn't matter about my pants," Jayden said, relieved that the fit of giggles seemed to have jumped Rhian out of her discomfort and the morose mood she'd been in earlier. Jayden smiled. *Then I don't care if the pants are totally ruined. It was worth it just to see that smile again.* "Be careful you don't get any on your jeans, then."

Rhian carried on soaking up the mess. "It's okay. I'm fine." She smiled over at Jayden and nodded to her legs. "Go get cleaned up. I've got this."

Jayden climbed the ladder to the loft and changed as quickly as she could. "Stupid fucking moron. So much for making a good impression," she muttered under her breath. She grabbed the nearest pair of pants she could find—a pair of skinny-fit jeans—and poured herself into them before descending the ladder again. "Sorry about that."

She stopped dead in her tracks. Rhian was on her hands and knees, cleaning up the last of the pesto sauce. At the sound of her voice, Rhian turned to look at Jayden over her shoulder, and Jayden was bombarded with the fantasy image of seeing Rhian just like that, but naked—and wanting her.

Jayden's brain slowed to a stop and desire flooded her blood…and parts south of the border as she held back the ache in her body to kneel behind Rhian and let her hands explore, to discover every dip and curve, every secret place that made Rhian squirm and writhe and call her name—

"You okay?" Rhian asked. A frown slid in place of that gentle smile.

Jayden nodded and spurred herself forward, berating herself for letting her imagination get the better of her. And worse still, letting Rhian catch her at it. She didn't want Rhian to slip back and seem as uncomfortable with her as she had been earlier…as she'd seemed in that second when she walked in. No. Something told her that Rhian really needed to relax right now. "I'm really sorry about that. I'm not normally so clumsy."

"It's my fault. I startled you." She straightened up, got to her knees, and stretched to dump the soiled paper towels in the bin. "Let me knock up a sauce to make it up to you."

"You cook?"

"I've been known to." Rhian's frown deepened as she put her hands on her hips and cocked her head to the side. "Why do you look so surprised?"

Jayden shrugged. "Probably because I can't. And anyone who can do things I can't amazes me."

Rhian stood and looked at the box, still intact. "What's in your pasta?"

"Spinach and ricotta."

Now Rhian's eyes lit up, and a smile spread across her lips. "Yum. My favourite." She pointed over her shoulder with her thumb, the other hand tapping her fingernails on the top of the pasta container. "Mind if I raid your cupboards and see what I can make to go with it?"

She only does that stuff when she's nervous. Jayden waved her hand. "Help yourself." She pulled a stool away from the small breakfast bar. "I'll just sit here and watch you work."

"Hm. I'm seeing how this works, Ms Harris." She opened the fridge and then a couple of cupboards, lifting things out, putting some back, smelling some tomatoes and a lump of cheese.

"And how's that?"

"Invite me over for lunch, then get me to cook it for you." She smiled as she plopped a carton of milk, butter, flour, and the lump of cheese onto the breakfast bar.

Jayden caught her hand. "That wasn't the plan." She ran her thumb against the back of Rhian's hand, unable to stop herself. Then she let go quickly and coughed to clear her throat. "Though I have to admit, it is working out rather nicely."

Rhian turned back to the fridge and returned with a package of bacon. "Well, since this whole lunch thing was your plan to begin with, the least you can do is help with the prep work."

Jayden grinned, crossed her wrists, and offered them as though to be shackled. "I am yours to command."

Rhian laughed and turned her face away. Had Jayden just seen the beginnings of a blush? "Yeah, yeah." She passed her the bacon slices and a chopping board. "Dice those and an onion, please."

"Dice?"

Rhian cocked her head to one side. "Yes. As in little squares."

"Okay." Jayden worked methodically, watching as Rhian grated the cheese, located the pans she wanted, set the water for the pasta to boil, and picked up the bacon from the board before throwing it into a large frying pan. She tossed the contents of the pan when she added the onion. Her movements were hypnotic, and Jayden stood next to her watching her work with the fluid grace of a dancer. "Did Rachel teach you to cook?"

Rhian laughed. "Not on this planet. Rachel's the queen of takeaways and restaurants." She transferred the contents of the pan to a bowl and dumped a few tablespoons of butter into it. "When I was at uni, I was addicted to cooking shows. Jamie Oliver, *MasterChef,* you name it. I got tons of ideas, and my housemates were always very appreciative of my efforts." She spooned two tablespoons of flour into the melted butter and stirred it together.

"You cooked for them all?" Jayden was determined to keep up the simple questions. She wasn't sure if it was the easy topics or the seemingly familiar task of cooking that was helping Rhian relax, but whatever was responsible, it was working. She was talking to her normally, her busy hands were constructive rather than fidgeting, and her smile was easy and no longer forced. The banter that had been missing since their pizza disaster was back, and Jayden was glad to see it slowly returning. *So far, so good.*

"Yup. They had to do cleanup and pay towards groceries, but I did the cooking. It was the only way to make sure I didn't die of scurvy or get bowed legs." She poured milk into the mixture and stirred slowly.

Jayden chuckled. "I lived on pot noodles and tins of soup through uni."

Rhian pointed the spoon at her legs. "How are they still straight?"

Jayden barked a laugh. "Who says they are?"

Rhian groaned and added cheese to the pan.

"That wasn't that bad."

"No?"

"I can do worse."

Rhian chuckled and added more cheese. "I'm sure you could, sweetheart, but let's not, okay?"

She said sweetheart *again.* "Okay." *And there ain't nobody here but little ol' me.* Jayden grinned.

"What's that look for?"

"What look?"

"The shit-eating grin on your face."

"This is just my face."

"Right," Rhian drawled. "And I'm the queen of Sheba." She poured the ravioli into the boiling water and put the bacon and onion back into the pan, glancing up at the clock as she did. "So want to tell me about these ideas you've had?"

"Later. Let's just enjoy a nice lunch together first." She smiled, hoping Rhian would relax a little and enjoy herself. Enjoy being here, with her. Rather than looking as though she wanted to escape at the first opportunity.

Rhian stared at her as though trying to decide what was going on... or maybe if she was going to roll with whatever was going on. Then she smiled, the shy kind of smile Jayden had seen when they'd kissed on the glacier, then nodded.

"If that's what you want." She edged a bit closer to Jayden. Was that a coincidence? She didn't see a functional need for Rhian to do that, or for the furtive but probing glance she had just flashed at her.

Perhaps a test was in order. "Can I get you a drink?" Jayden asked.

"Water will be fine, thanks."

"No problem." She touched Rhian's arm as she reached over her to get glasses from the cupboard and smiled widely at her sharp intake of breath. "Sorry," she whispered just by Rhian's ear.

"It's okay. Do you need me to move?" she mumbled.

"No, it's fine." She brushed a little closer to grab the second glass, her breasts pressing against Rhian's back for the briefest of moments before she pulled away and went to the sink. The smooth movement of Rhian's hands had become a little jerky, and her back was rigid. Jayden hoped she hadn't pushed too far too soon.

She heard Rhian swallow. Saw her shake her head and move to the sink herself where she drained the pasta, then added it to the sauce in her other pan. Her cheeks were pink when she turned to the breakfast bar and quickly served it onto the two plates Jayden had set out for her.

Jayden pulled out a second stool and waved Rhian onto it with a theatrical bow before sitting opposite her and picking up her fork. "This looks even better than the pesto sauce."

"Hm. Well, it's less green." Rhian sawed one of the pasta parcels in half with her fork.

"And much less stainy," Jayden said as she wiped a spilt drop from her jeans.

"Stainy? That's not a real word."

Jayden shrugged. "Maybe not, but you knew exactly what I meant by it."

Rhian rolled her eyes but just kept eating.

"Tastes even better than it looks," Jayden said quietly.

Rhian's cheeks coloured again. She fidgeted with her fork. "Thanks."

Jayden waited until Rhian's gaze flicked up to meet hers before she said, "No, no, no. Thank you." She hoped Rhian could see beyond the simple words to everything she truly meant. She hoped Rhian could see in her eyes what she was really trying to say to her. *Thank you for giving me a chance. Thank you for giving me the way back to myself. Thank you for showing me a future I want to be a part of.*

Rhian shrugged and took a bite. After she swallowed she said, "It's just a cheese sauce. No big deal."

The strained notes of discomfort and distance echoed through those words, and Jayden swallowed around the lump in her throat. If Rhian couldn't see what Jayden wished she could... Well, she just didn't want to.

CHAPTER 26

RHIAN STOOD UNDER THE CASCADE of cold water and let the suds run out of her hair as she braced herself against the wall. Three more days of storm had passed, and three more days of lunch or dinner or breakfast, or all of them, cooped up inside with Jayden. And hiding her feelings was getting harder and harder. Her face was forever burning when Jayden was around. The slightest comment or compliment—and there were many of those—and she coloured like a tomato. She had no control. And it was pissing her off. If she wasn't careful, her reaction to Jayden's innocent comments would give away how she really felt about her. She couldn't bear the thought of further humiliation.

Then there was the touching. The little shoulder squeeze whenever Jayden walked by her. Holding her hand, running her thumb over her wrist. God, that one drove her nuts. She was amazed Jayden hadn't felt her pulse spike under her thumb every time she did it. And she could still feel the way Jayden's body had felt pressed against her back when she'd reached over her for those glasses three days ago. Three fucking days and it felt like she was wearing a Jayden-sized jumper!

"I can't do this." She wiped water from her face and over her head, speaking to the suds circling the drain before disappearing. "I can't do this. I need to tell Rachel." She shut off the water and grabbed a towel. "Mel can handle everything here. I should go home. If I wasn't here, there wouldn't have been so many fucking problems anyway, so I should just go." She dried off. Her phone was on the bedside table next to her, and it took less than ten seconds for her to type a message to Rachel and toss the phone onto her bed. "Done."

It took less than three before the handset rang and Rachel's name appeared on the screen.

"Shit. Not done." Rhian answered the call and held the phone from her ear while Rachel got the first blast out of the way.

"What the fuck are you on about? We've got a strategy. A strategy that requires you remaining in Argentina and playing happy fucking families with the Roboclimber."

"Roboclimber? Where did that come from?"

"Doesn't matter. What the fuck, Rhi? What's happened now?"

"Nothing. I just thought this might be a better solution."

"Bullshit. I'm hanging up now. I want to see your face, so don't even think about not answering on Skype."

Rhian sighed and said, "Yes, Mother." But Rachel was already gone. Rhian opened her laptop and sat on her bed, towel wrapped around her chest, and waited for Rachel's call. She didn't have to wait even a minute.

Rachel sat, watching her through the screen. Her eyes narrowed. "Are you ready to admit you've fallen for her yet?"

Rhian didn't even try to deny it. There was no point. She'd never been able to lie to Rachel. Well, she'd never been able to lie and get away with it, anyway.

"So screw her and get it out of your system."

"Nice, Rach."

Rachel shrugged. "Okay, then make love to her and get it out of your system."

"She's not interested in me."

"Ah."

"Yeah, 'ah'."

"Must be awkward now, huh?"

Rhian nodded.

"Shit. Kiddo, if I could pull you out of there now, I would. But I can't."

Rhian stared at her and waited.

"This is already playing out. We're getting great results and a shitload of great publicity and chatter. *Free publicity and chatter.* You know how valuable that is. If I pull you now, that will dry up. Our clients won't be happy, our sponsors won't be happy, and the show's fans won't be happy."

"The show isn't even a show yet. It doesn't have fans."

"Au contraire. Check the last e-mail I sent you. It's got a hashtag trending that we didn't start, and it's getting thousands of hits—"

"That's peanuts."

"In the last hour alone. And it's climbing."

"So instead, I'm the one who gets to not be happy."

"I'm sorry."

"No, you're not."

Rachel smiled gently. "I am a little bit." She leant towards the screen. "I don't like you being unhappy."

"But me being unhappy doesn't hurt you financially. Right?"

Rachel's eyes widened, and her mouth popped open. "Wow."

Rhian's jaw clenched. She looked away.

"That bad?" The tears escaped before Rhian could stop them, and Rachel whispered, "She's an idiot."

Rhian shook her head. "Don't do that."

"What?"

"Don't blame her. It's not her fault I feel the way I do, just like it's not her fault she doesn't feel the same. Don't blame Jayden for this. She hasn't done anything wrong—quite the opposite, in fact."

"You're gonna have to explain that one."

"She's lovely. She's doing everything we could ask of her to convince the world that she's my lover. She brings me coffee in the morning, holds my hand walking down the street, takes me to dinner. Yesterday she even brought me flowers that she picked from the garden. She's respectful, considerate, kind. She's funny and gorgeous, and she's…"

"Perfect for you."

"Yeah."

"Yeah."

"Except she doesn't want me."

"I'm sorry, Rhi."

"Then let me come home."

"Oh, honey. If I could, I would. I swear. But there is so much riding on this project. So much."

"I know it's a big deal, but—"

"Rhian, if this project goes bad, we lose the company. It's as simple as that. We were struggling before. I'd remortgaged the house to fund it. It was… Well, it wasn't looking good."

"Really?"

Rachel nodded.

"Why didn't you tell me?"

"Because it's my worry, not yours. I'm supposed to be the parental figure here, remember?"

"Pft."

"Don't give me that, missy. Just trust me, okay? I know how difficult you find it to trust the truth of what people are saying to you. I've seen it in you for as long as I've known you. And yes, I know that part of that is my fault. But I have never lied to you. Have I?"

Rhian shook her head. Rachel had always been the one she could trust, the one she could rely on when everything went to shit. Not because Rachel would tell her everything would be okay, but because Rachel would tell her how shit it all was. She'd tell her the unvarnished, nonsugarcoated truth, and deal with the fallout. And she always did deal with it. For better or worse, Rachel wielded the truth like a burning sword, and as much as its wounds hurt, the cut was always clean, unlike with everyone else; it would scar but never fester.

"If I could pull you home right now without blowing this thing apart, to spare you from hurting, I would. I just don't see how I can do that. Maybe in a few weeks, we'll be in a better position. Maybe then we can get you out of there."

"And in the meantime, I'm stuck here. Pretending to be the girlfriend of the woman whose girlfriend I really want to be. And she's just playing the role you gave her—"

"Oh no. I'm not taking that one. I didn't give her this gig. She gave it to herself when she kissed you and got it caught on film. Or whatever it's called these days."

"But she wouldn't still be doing it if not for you. And technically, I suppose I started that kiss." She wiped away another tear. "None of it really helps any."

"No, I don't suppose it does, kiddo."

"What am I supposed to do, Rach? How do I do this?"

"Well, I've been in a few sticky situations in my time, but I can't think of anything that really comes close to this one."

"Helpful. Thanks."

"Sarcasm doesn't help. Look, if it were me, I'd just brazen it out. Flirt a little, have fun with it." She shrugged. "I mean, if you've already told her you're attracted to her and she's turned you down, it's not like it's going to be a shock to her if you flirt, especially if she's playing the perfect suitor. Why not just enjoy...?" Rachel lifted her eyebrow suggestively. "What? What's the head shaking and pouting about?"

"I didn't tell her I was attracted to her."

"Then how do you know she's not interested?"

"She told me she wasn't attracted to me. That she only sees me as a friend."

Rachel frowned. "Start at the beginning, and don't leave anything out."

"I can't remember it word for word. I was trying to forget it. It's not exactly a stellar moment for my ego, you know."

"Honey, now I say this with the utmost love and respect for you as a person that you can possibly imagine."

"But?"

"But you have a face and body that almost made me go Wicked Queen on you when you were growing up. I mean, seriously, you could, or rather should, be able to have whoever you want. Are you sure she's gay?"

Rhian nodded. "Yeah, I'm sure. So that sinks your theory."

"You sure she's a woman, then? I mean she's pretty tall—"

Rhian chuckled. "I know what you're trying to do, and thank you for it. But please stop. She's a gay woman who just isn't interested in me. I'm a big girl. I can accept that. I'm just finding it really hard to deal with it when she's being everything I want in a partner all day, every day, and it isn't real."

"Ah. I see."

"What?"

"This isn't a fix-my-problem situation."

"It isn't?"

Rachel shook her head. "It's a 'let-me-whine-like-a-little-girl-for-a-while-before-I-put-my-big-girl-pants-on-again-and-go-face-the-world' situation."

"It is?"

Rachel nodded and rolled her hand for Rhian to continue. "You go ahead and bitch, honey. I'm here for you." She touched her hands to her chest and looked into the camera, her face a picture of sincerity.

Rhian giggled. "You're such a bitch."

Rachel smiled. "Yeah, but I'm the bitch on your side. Always."

"Yeah, yeah. If that was true, you'd let me come home and cry like a baby."

"No, that wouldn't do you any favours."

"Making me stay here isn't doing me a favour."

"Stopping you from quitting is." She pointed at the screen. "My kid doesn't quit. And that's who you are, Rhian. My kid, and I love you."

Rhian blinked. Tears stung her eyes as she fought them back. "I love you too," she whispered, then rubbed her face and sighed. "Better take my mind off it, then. What else is going on with the world?"

"That's more like it. So let's talk about the other elephant in the room."

"What other elephant?"

"I know you got the message from him."

Rhian's jaw clenched, and she glanced away from the screen. "I really wish you hadn't done that."

"He would've seen it anyway. It really is all over the Internet, you know?"

"But you gave him my e-mail address."

"Again, he could've got that without me. So stop fannying around and talk to me."

Rhian met Rachel's gaze through the millions of pixels and thousands of miles that separated them. Her voice was quiet as she asked, "Do you know what he said? What he wrote in it?"

Rachel nodded. "He showed me afterwards."

Rhian nodded back. It confirmed what she suspected. He'd only sent it to get Rachel off his back.

"I told him he should have called you, not take such a coward's way out."

Rhian snorted a laugh. "Guess his plan failed, then."

"What do you mean?"

"The plan to get you off his back about me. As long as he sent that, he could tell you he tried, but that it's me that's the problem. That plan."

Rachel stared at her for a long time, then shook her head. "You remember a few minutes ago when I reminded you that I've never lied to you?"

"Yes."

"Remember that again right now."

Rhian frowned. "I don't—"

"Shut up."

Rhian's mouth closed with a click.

"He didn't write that to get me off his back. I haven't been on his back. Believe me, if I thought it would've worked, I would have done, but I knew you both needed to come back to each other in your own time. He showed me that message because he couldn't bring himself to say those words when he told me what he'd done. He could not force from his lips the words *I hit my own daughter* while he cried like a baby. He was too ashamed of himself."

Rhian shook her head.

"He wrote it because he loves you."

"No, he doesn't. If he did, he never would have done that."

"No, he never should have done that. I agree. And in an ideal world, kiddo, he never would have. But this is the real world. Filled with real people. People who make mistakes. People who get angry and scared and fuck up."

"That was more than just a fuck-up, Rach."

Rachel ignored her. "And we forgive them because we love them."

"He doesn't love me!"

Rachel shook her head. "He doesn't love himself, and he can't forgive himself." The hard look in her eyes softened. "And neither can you."

Rhian frowned. "I didn't do anything wrong."

"I know that, and in your head, so do you. But you still believe you drove him away. Somewhere inside you, you believe that you made him react like that. That it was your fault. I can't for the life of me fathom why, but you do. It's the only thing that even remotely explains you, Rhian. You can't forgive yourself, and you can't believe anyone else would either. You can't believe anyone would love you. Can you?"

She folded her arms across her chest. "No."

"Why not?"

Rhian shrugged.

"Is it really so much easier to believe all the negativity you tell yourself?"

"It stops it hurting."

"Does it? Really? Because this looks an awful lot like hurting to me."

She was right. It was a feeble attempt at self-preservation, and in the cold light of day, it was beginning to make less and less sense to her. The holes seemed to grow bigger, the substance of it melting like ice in the midday sun.

"I love you," Rachel whispered as Rhian buried her face in her hands and sobbed. "Ah, shit. Don't go blubbing, kid. You'll make me ruin my mascara."

Rhian chuckled through her tears and wiped her face.

"That's better."

"Your distraction was supposed to cheer me up."

"You mean you don't feel better than before?"

Rhian pondered the thought for a moment and grudgingly had to accept that she did. A little. Just a tiny bit. But she wasn't going to admit it to Rachel. "No. Worse. Now do a proper job of distracting me."

Rachel sighed. "Fine. Let's see what you do with this crap, then," she said and spent the next twenty minutes relaying everything she could think of while Rhian pulled herself back together. Eventually, she hung up to go to another meeting. Rhian picked up her hairbrush and had started to work the tangles from her hair when there was a knock at the door.

"It's open," she said, expecting it to be Mel. No one else ever knocked on her door. The hinge creaked, and footsteps echoed a couple of paces into the room.

"I'm sorry. I can come back later."

Rhian turned to see Jayden staring at her. She clasped the tucked edge of her towel and held it tight to her chest. Rachel's words echoed in her head: *My kid doesn't quit*, and *I'd brazen it out*. Maybe Rachel was right. Maybe she should try to have some fun with this. She tucked the end of the towel tighter between her breasts and shook her head.

"It's fine. Come on in and close the door."

"But you're not—"

Rhian quickly crossed the room and closed the door. "You're supposed to be my lover, Jayden. Seeing me in a towel shouldn't have you rooted to the spot like you've seen a ghost." She offered what she hoped was a disarming smile that didn't show how nervous she felt. "I'm sorry I threw you for six like that. I expected it to be Mel. She's the only one who ever knocks on my door."

"It's okay." Jayden cocked her head to the side. "Do you often let Mel in when you're naked?"

Rhian laughed. "I'm not."

"Sorry, when you're only wearing a towel toga, then."

"No. It's not often she comes calling, and I'm usually fully dressed when she does. Anyway, I doubt you came all the way up here to discuss my towel toga, so what can I do for you?"

"Oh, right. Well, I don't know if you've seen it outside, but we've got a few hours clear of the storm. It's due to hit again tonight, but I thought you might like to get out for the day? We've all been cooped up for long enough."

Rhian smiled. Great, a day out with the group. "Sure, what did you have in mind?"

"It's a surprise," she said with a wide grin. "Meet me downstairs as soon as you're dressed."

Rhian cocked her eyebrow. "Okay. Anything specific I need to bring or wear?"

"Just you."

Rhian smirked. "And the towel toga?"

Jayden looked her up and down. Slowly. The blood roared in Rhian's ears. "If you like." She stepped closer to Rhian and brushed a lock of hair off her shoulder. The tip of her finger barely grazed her skin, but Rhian felt as though that touch had covered every inch of her body.

"You might want to add shoes to the ensemble, though." Jayden's voice was lower than normal, a little husky and rough around the edges, and Rhian couldn't tear her gaze from Jayden's. Not even if she'd wanted to.

"Funny." Rhian heard her own voice but didn't remember opening her mouth to speak. The air felt thick, heavy with the aroma of apple, cinnamon, and something deeper, musky. Sandalwood, maybe. The key components of Jayden's scent.

"I try to be."

"I've noticed."

"*Ahem.*"

Jayden and Rhian spun to look at the door. The fast movement caused the towel to slip, and only Jayden's fast reflexes kept it from hitting the ground, but the action of catching it left her leaning forward with her head level with Rhian's now-bare breasts. Rhian's face burned. Her nipples were hard as pebbles, and Jayden was staring them eye-to-eye, as it were. So much for brazening it out.

"Sorry to interrupt," Mel said from the door, a snigger in her voice.

"What do you want, Mel?" Rhian said, tugging the towel from Jayden's stiff fingers, and wrapping it about her chest again.

"Just wanted to let Jayden know everything's ready."

Jayden finally managed to tear her eyes from Rhian's chest, blinking in a stupid sort of way and looking from one to the other.

"Jayden?" Mel waved her hand. "Over here, hon. That's it," she said when Jayden's gaze finally settled on her. "I said it's all ready for you."

"Right. Great. That's—yeah—great. Thanks. Erm, ten minutes?" She looked at Rhian again. "Or, like, whenever you're ready. Okay?" She didn't wait for a response. "Okay. Right, well, I'll just wait. Down, erm, stairs for you. Yeah." She practically ran to the door. "So, yeah—erm—yeah." And then she was gone.

Mel's eyebrows had disappeared into her hairline, and the laughter bubbled up. "Oh my God, what did you do to her? Hypnotise her with your nipples?"

"Shut up."

"No, no. Please, I need to know how to do that. You rendered her stupid."

"It was shock. Because of you."

"Oh no. It wasn't me she was looking at. It was definitely your tits."

"Crude."

"I'm not the one flashing my boobs to the world."

"I wasn't. The towel slipped because you came barging in to my room like a...like a... I don't know like what, but you did!"

"I did not. I knocked."

"No, you didn't. I'd have heard it if you... You knocked?"

Mel nodded, still laughing.

"Oh God. We were talking."

"I heard." She mimicked Jayden's voice and said, "'I try to be.'" Then she shifted her posture and lifted her voice an octave. "'I've noticed.'"

"Fuck off." Rhian picked up a pillow and tossed it at her. "I need to get dressed. Apparently, she's got a surprise planned for everyone."

Mel's eyebrows rose again. "Only if you promise to teach me that stupid tit trick later."

"Fuck off."

"You're repeating yourself now."

"Fuck off."

"Does it make you stupid too?"

Rhian put her hands on her hips, then quickly grabbed at the towel, mortified as it started to slip again.

Mel stumbled out of the room, tears of laughter running down her face. Rhian could still hear her laughing ten minutes later when she started down the stairs.

Brazen it out, she repeated in her head, over and over. The phrase, she was sure, would become her new mantra. Brazen it out.

⁕

Jayden gulped down glass after glass of water and tried to come to terms with what had just happened. No, *come to terms with it* wasn't the right... phrase? More like, adjust to the new reality she had. One where she'd seen, if only for a split second, the body Rhian hid beneath her clothes. Or towel toga. And, holy fuck, what a body it was. Toned abs, the curve of her ribs, the gentle flair of her hips—strong, sleek thighs—and those breasts. Oh God, those breasts. Pink-tipped mounds that she knew would fit perfectly in the palms of her hands.

She'd been close enough to see them react to her breath. To see the fine, downy hairs swish and sway under the force of air from her mouth. She'd seen the areolae contract under that same breath. And she so wanted to see that happen again. And again, and again.

She poured herself another glass and downed it.

"Is everyone else already on the bus?" Rhian asked from behind her.

"Everyone else?" Jayden turned to see the curious look on Rhian's face as she acted like nothing had happened.

"Yes. You said you had a surprise planned."

"I do." Jayden forced a smile to her lips, not sure whether or not she was relieved she hadn't arranged a surprise for everyone. That would have definitely been safer, but that wasn't what she'd been trying to achieve today. Today she was determined to spend time with Rhian in the hope they could finally regain that easy camaraderie that had been missing for a while now. Standing there with a forced smile on her lips and her hands shaking from nerves was not going to help, though. Not after the towel-toga incident. She girded her mental loins and forced herself to put the thoughts of Rhian's beautiful body aside. She would have time later to replay that image. Over and over again. Right now, she had a surprise to spring and a day to enjoy. She hoped.

She held out her hand and sighed with relief when Rhian took it without hesitation. "Come with me."

Jayden led her out to the Jeep and instructed her to get in, despite the confused look on her face. Rhian complied, and buckled her seat belt. Jayden turned in her seat, needing to get this out of the way; then she could take Rhian out for some fun.

"I'm sorry."

Rhian stared out the window. "Nothing for you to be sorry for. I'm sorry for flashing you."

"It wasn't intentional. But it was embarrassing for you, I'm sure."

Rhian smirked. "You think?"

"Will you feel better if I flash you back?" Jayden offered, hoping the comment would be taken as the joke it was meant to be and ease Rhian's embarrassment. Even if it didn't ease her own.

Rhian turned to look at her, then started laughing. "Maybe. A little."

Jayden chuckled too, thankful she could manage to seem normal. "I'll see what I can arrange for you." She chuckled and turned on the engine. "And just so you know."

Rhian waited.

"You've got no reason at all to be embarrassed." She pulled out and tried to ignore the silence. But she couldn't. Silence between them was normally pretty comfortable. This one wasn't. She finally broke down: "What?"

"A compliment?"

Jayden shrugged. "So?"

"Be careful, or you'll give me an ego problem."

"Nah. You're too nice a person to get all arrogant."

"Another one. Be careful, Jay, or I might think Mel's on to something."

Jayden frowned, wondering where Mel fit into this conversation. "What's Mel on to?"

Rhian blushed. "Forget I said that."

"Oh no you don't. You can't say something like that and then brush it off. Come on. Spill. Did Mel take the piss because of what she saw?"

Rhian shrugged. "A little, but mostly because of how you reacted."

"Me? What did I do? I was a perfect gentleman...woman, picking up your towel and everything."

Rhian giggled. "I think it was more to do with the staring and then the incoherent speech that followed."

"Incoherent...I was not. We had a perfectly understandable conversation and made arrangements to meet downstairs."

"Hm. That might have been what was in your head, but that wasn't what came out of your mouth."

"It wasn't?"

Rhian shook her head.

"Then what did I say?"

"A lot of *erm*s, and some *like*s, and a few other disjointed words. But mostly it was *erm* and staring."

"Oh God."

"Mel thinks I hypnotised you with my boobs." She giggled but crossed her arms over her breasts, shielding them from Jayden.

"Rhian, I'm so sorry. I didn't mean to make you uncomfortable."

"Not your fault. I should have put on a dressing gown or something."

"Or I should have rung instead of barging into your room."

"You didn't barge in. I let you in."

"Still, it's your private space. I shouldn't have been in there. People will talk."

Rhian laughed again. "People are talking about us anyway. They'll probably think something's weird if you don't come up to my room. So don't worry about it."

She drove a few more minutes. "But I do."

"Why?"

"Because I don't want things to be weird between us. This is already difficult for yo—for us. I don't want to add to that because I can't react like a normal person to the sight of your magnificent breasts," she drawled. *God, anything to lighten this atmosphere.*

"Magnificent?"

Jayden nodded.

"Really? Magnificent?"

"How else do you explain the hypnosis?"

"Erm, you haven't gotten laid in far too long."

"Well, yeah, I suppose there is that. But I stand by my assessment. They're magnificent, and you have no reason at all to be embarrassed. I, on the other hand, have, erm, like, plenty to be embarrassed about." She winked at Rhian, heartened to see her arms loose again and her head thrown back in laughter.

They'd crossed most of El Chaltén when Rhian turned to her and asked where they were going.

"Do you trust me?"

"With my life."

Jayden's heart raced at the unexpected words. *With my life.* Three simple words that meant everything to Jayden and in the same instant terrified her. She swallowed and plastered a smile on her face. She could only hope Rhian couldn't see just how stunned she was. She opened her mouth to speak, but the words fell silent on her tongue. She cleared her throat and tried again. "Then hang on five more minutes?"

Rhian squinted at her, but sat back in her seat and stared out the window. Her eyes widened when she saw where Jayden parked.

"Seriously? You're taking me white-water rafting?"

Jayden nodded. "You said it was something you'd always wanted to try but never had the chance to, right?"

"I did."

"Well, the Rio de las Vueltas has a class III-plus rapid section, and it's supposed to be quite a rush."

"You haven't done it before?"

"No. I thought it would be nice for us to try something new together." She took Rhian's hand and squeezed it. "Is that okay?"

Rhian grinned. "You mean the hypno-boob session wasn't enough in the way of new experiences for you today?"

Jayden laughed. "What can I say? I'm an adrenaline junkie." She got out of the Jeep and grabbed the dry bags she'd stowed for them earlier. "Come on, let's go get wet!"

Bugger. She decided it was best just to ignore the double entendre she'd just made, and the look that Rhian was shooting her, and dragged her towards the office. They were going to have a great day. She was determined. And she wasn't going to think about those magnificent breasts or *with my life* again all day. Damn it.

CHAPTER 27

"Okay, guys, when I shout 'paddle', you give it all you've got. When I shout 'down', you need to sit on the bed of the raft. And if someone goes overboard, if we're on flat water, we'll pull you back in. If we can't cos we're in a white-water section, point your feet downstream, and we'll catch you either along the way or at the bottom of the shoot. Got it?"

Dan—their guide for the trip—was handing out life vests as he spoke and leading them to the large raft at the edge of the Rio de las Vueltas. There were six of them, plus Dan, and Jayden looked as excited as Rhian felt. Her cheeks were flushed with it, her blue eyes bright and her grin as wide as Rhian had ever seen. While part of Rhian wished they were alone, she knew being with a group was much safer. She still felt raw from the morning's exposure and unsure what to make of Jayden's reaction. Seeing her so discombobulated had been confusing. Dwelling on it wasn't going to give her any answers, but rafting was going to give her a hell of a great day.

She buckled the vest over her chest and grabbed a paddle before adjusting the length for her size as Dan showed them, before climbing aboard. Jayden helped steady her as Rhian got her balance on the floating craft.

"Thanks," she whispered and took her place at the front of the boat. Jayden sat opposite her and quickly settled into place.

"You ready for this?" Jayden asked.

Rhian nodded and looked downstream. It looked quiet, calm, peaceful. She knew it wouldn't last. In the distance, she could hear the rumble of roiling, angry water that would only get louder as they got closer. "Can't wait."

"Then let's not," Dan shouted as the final members of the six-person team took their positions, and he picked up the oars he would wield at the back of the raft. "We've a kilometre of calm water before we get to the first white-water section. A gentle one to ease you all into it." He used the oars to push the boat away from the shore and edged them into the current at the centre of the river. Each of them tried out their own techniques as they ambled along at a sedate pace, slipping their paddles in and out of the water and testing the feel of the movements in their hands, the push and pull of the current against their muscles. The din of the water grew.

Cold drops splashed her as they hit choppy sections, making her gasp with frigid shock. "Christ, that's cold."

Jayden chortled alongside her. "Let's hope we don't go swimming, then."

"You can say that again."

"That."

Rhian laughed. "Brat."

"You can't call me a brat for doing what you told me to do."

"I didn't tell—"

"Okay, everyone," Dan said from the back of the boat. "We've got our first rough section coming up. Pull hard when I tell you to, and enjoy the ride."

Jayden grinned and slid her paddle into water that rippled quickly about them. The pattern across the top of the river created a V shape into the rapids. Their entry point. Dan steered them straight for the centre of it. Rocks protruded from the riverbed to the right, a wall of rock loomed from the left, and the current dragged them along faster and faster.

Rhian's pulse raced, her mouth dry. Even as they sped up, everything around her seemed to slow down as she became hyperaware of everything. Every bump against a wave rocked her from her seat and had her plunging her paddle deeper into the rough water. The energy in the boat skyrocketed to match the energy of the water around them. Laughter bubbled from each of them and danced on the waves along with the boat. It was exhilarating, and when they reached flat, calm water again, shrieks of satisfaction and accomplishment rent the air.

"Having fun yet?" Jayden asked as she reached over to tuck a lock of Rhian's hair behind her ear. "You'll paddle even better if you can see where you're going."

Rhian hid her face by wiping away the water from her eyes and cheeks. She didn't miss the way her hands trembled, and her fingers ached with the desire to reach out and touch Jayden too. The surge of adrenaline had her hyped up and wanting things she couldn't have. Her skin tingled from the merest brush of Jayden's fingers against her forehead. "Yeah, but what if I'm too scared when I see what's in front of us?" In truth, the water wasn't what she was scared of.

"Nah." Jayden stroked the water. "You're not the type to scare easily."

You scare me.

"Another set of rapids, everyone. This one is twice as big as the last one, so hang on to your paddles. And remember. If you go in, hold on to your life vest and point your feet downstream," Dan called out.

Rhian didn't remember shouting as they crashed through and bobbed over section after section of white water. She didn't remember screaming as they tumbled over a waterfall, bounced high into the air, and landed on the tumultuous water below. But she must have done. Her throat was sore. Her shoulders ached. Her head swam with images of Jayden, her head thrown back, laughing, smiling, her eyes shining brightly with pure joy as they approached another set of rapids.

"Okay, people, this is the last set. It's also the biggest!" Dan shouted over the volume of the rushing river to a chorus of shouts and cheers circling the boat. Rhian whooped right along with them. Her hand clasped with Jayden's and raised them both in the air.

"As we get through the first twenty metres or so, you'll see there's a hole on the left-hand side. It looks flatter than the rest of the water. But do not be tempted by it. There's a huge rock just below the surface, and it will rip the bottom out of this boat if we hit it. So keep right. Are we ready?"

Everyone waved their paddle to show they were and set themselves in position. Legs braced, paddles in the water, eyes front. The noise increased steadily as they got closer. The current picked up, dragging them along faster and faster, and Rhian's adrenaline spiked again. She plunged her paddle into the water, drawing it through and enjoying the pull in her arms.

The first twenty metres raced by, and Rhian spotted the rock easily from her position at the front left-hand corner of the boat. They seemed to be heading straight for it.

"Hard right!" Dan yelled over the thunder of water. "Pull hard!"

Rhian dug her paddle in and shoved against the water, trying to push the boat away from the rock, but the eddy they were caught on was pulling them harder than their muscle power could counteract.

"Shit!" Rhian shouted. Her instincts were telling her to move to the bow and throw her paddle in to help Jayden's side of the boat. But Dan had told them all to stay in their positions. *Ah well, fuck it. We're gonna hit the rock anyway. What's the worst he can do? Toss me overboard?*

She waited for the surge of water to pass and threw her weight from the side to the front of the bow, flattening her belly against the inflatable gunwale and bracing her legs across the width of the boat. She dug her paddle into the water and drew it across the front of the boat. The drag of the river was so strong, she almost lost it underneath the boat before she yanked hard and managed to lift it from the rolling, frothing water. It felt alive, writhing beneath them as she dug again and heaved with all her might.

"Keep pulling!" Dan called from the rear again. "Hard as you can, she's turning!"

Rhian didn't bother to look. She didn't have the time or the energy. She smashed the blade into the water again and again until the noise of the rapids quieted and the writhing water slipped behind them.

Rhian flipped on to her back and drew deep breaths into her lungs. Dan caught her eye and offered her a thumbs up.

"Awesome!" he shouted down the boat. "We were hitting that rock for sure before you switched. Cool." He grinned, and Rhian couldn't help but grin back. She glanced over to Jayden to see her staring at her, mouth slightly agape.

"What?" Rhian asked self-consciously.

"Thought you hadn't been rafting before," Jayden said quietly.

"I haven't."

"Well, you sure saved us all from getting wet out there today."

Rhian dipped her gaze. Her cheeks were burning. "It was a team effort. We all did our part." Out of the corner of her eyes, she saw Jayden shake her head.

"If you say so. Personally, I think you were my own personal Wonder Woman this afternoon." Jayden grinned at her and turned back to paddling the boat. All Rhian could do was stare. It wasn't that big a deal.

A few minutes later, they pulled up to the shore, where a bus and trailer were waiting to take them back to town.

Jayden took her hand as Rhian stepped from the unstable craft and almost tipped back into the cold water.

"Nearly," she said, tightening her hand about Rhian's and reaching for her waist with the other. "Don't want to break the run and go for that swim now, do you?"

Rhian shook her head, unable to tear herself from Jayden's gaze. Excitement looked good on her. "Thanks."

"Welcome." Jayden's voice sounded a little rough as a clap of thunder rolled over the mountains several miles away. They both looked up and half turned in the direction of the noise.

"Come on, then. Let's get back to the conclave before the rain succeeds where the river failed today." Jayden tugged on Rhian's hand and pulled her behind her onto the bus.

She didn't let go of my hand.

CHAPTER 28

"WE'LL BE BACK IN THREE days." Jayden lifted the last bag into the belly of the coach. Rhian was behind her, holding a flask. Jayden pointed at it. "What's that?"

Rhian held it out. "Coffee for you." She still wasn't sure what had possessed her to make it. All these little domestic things they were doing for each other were only making it more difficult for Rhian to separate the pretence from reality.

"Thanks." She took the thermos and pointed to the bench outside the hotel. "We don't leave for another ten minutes. Want to share with me?"

"I'd love to." They sat, and Jayden poured coffee into the cup.

"Mind sharing germs, or should I go get another cup from inside?"

"I don't mind."

They sat together, passing the cup back and forth. Rhian didn't want to finish the drink, or break the peaceful moment. Jayden's own slow progress hinted at a similar inclination.

When the group began to filter out of the conclave and onto the bus, Jayden wrapped her arm around Rhian's shoulders and sighed when Rhian rested her head on Jayden's shoulder. Rhian tried to block out the fact that Jayden had waited until they had an audience before offering the PDA and instead pretended no one else was there.

"I need to go," Jayden whispered into her hair.

"Be careful out there, okay?"

"I promise." She didn't pull away. Instead, she whispered in her ear, "Can I kiss you goodbye?"

Rhian closed her eyes and nodded. She knew it was a bad idea. She knew it was just for show. But neither fact seemed to stop her wanting Jayden's kiss. Didn't stop it being sweet even as she tried to swallow the bitter taste of the lie it truly was. Jayden's fingers were soft against her cheek as she eased away from the kiss.

"Maybe we can have dinner again when I get back?"

"You don't have to do that."

"I know, but there's something I need to talk to you about. Something really important."

Rhian cleared her throat but her mind was spinning. What could Jayden need to talk to her about? And not want but *need*? The way she stressed the word spoke to how imperative it was. Rhian swallowed her nerves and said quietly, "Okay."

"What are you planning for the rest of the day?"

"I thought I'd tag along with Carlos into Calafate and go visit Fen for a couple of hours while he picks up another load of camera gear."

"Give her a kiss from me, okay?"

"Sure." She smiled. "Now go and get on the bus before they leave without you." She chuckled at the narrow-eyed look Jayden threw her.

"Funny."

The doors of the bus closed behind her, cutting off the cacophony of wolf whistles and clapping. Rhian was so glad she wasn't on the bus at that moment.

The silence left in the wake of their departure made her even more glad she wasn't going to be around for the rest of the day. It wasn't just how quiet the conclave was without the contestants around. Nor the fact that most of the crew were also out on the ice, setting up their remote cameras in their high positions and establishing their eagle's nest for all the drone cameras' remote piloting. Santiago and a couple of other guides would be working with them until the show was completed.

No, none of those were the reason the building felt so quiet. It was simply because she knew Jayden wasn't going to be around for a few days. At least getting away from the conclave would give Rhian a change of scenery for a few hours.

By the time Carlos dropped her off at the hospital, it was almost two in the afternoon, and she'd brought with her a packed lunch from Isabella.

Fen was sitting in the chair beside the bed, reading a book. The spine of it rested on her cast, while the other hand held it splayed open.

"Hey, skivver. How're you doing?" Rhian rapped her knuckles against the door frame.

Fen looked up, a grin on her face that reminded Rhian of Jayden, even though the sisters looked very little alike. Fen's straight red hair and hazel eyes were so different from Jayden's mane of dirty-blond curls and her expressive blue eyes that it was almost impossible to tell they actually were sisters. The air of mischief that Fen's grin spoke of was what reminded Rhian so much of Jayden.

"Well, hello there, stranger. Long time no see."

"It's only been a week."

"A lot can happen in a week."

Rhian shrugged, conceding the fact. "Indeed. So how much has changed here, then?" She waved her hand up and down Fen's body. "Any interesting developments?"

"Well, the casts come off on Monday. Then we can start doing a little rehab to get me back home."

"What about your spine?"

Fen closed the book and put it on the table next to her. "No change."

"But I thought there was no—"

Fen held her hand up. "None they could see. And the swelling has gone down. They don't know what's going on now. All they say is time will tell."

"Shit. I'm sorry, Fen."

Fen shook her head. "Don't be. It's just one of those things, and what will be, will be."

"I don't know how you can be so…magnanimous."

"Oh, I'm not being brave or noble."

"Could have fooled me."

"Nah, I just learnt a long time ago that there was little point worrying about something you can't change. It only makes you bitter and the situation worse."

Rhian furrowed her brow, unable to stop thoughts of her dad and Jayden and all the things she couldn't change from popping into her head. Would she, and those around her, be better off if she let go of some of the stress and the worry? And the hurt. "But that doesn't necessarily mean your mind stops worrying."

"True. It is a conscious choice to not worry, and one I have to keep making. But it helps me. It lets me stay in the present and focus on what I do have and what's important to me."

"And that is?"

"My family, of course. My friends. My life."

"Like I said, magnanimous. I know I couldn't be so upbeat, not knowing what was going to happen."

"Oh, I'm not always so upbeat." She chuckled wryly. "I've spent more nights than I can count crying on Mark's shoulder in here. But today's a good day. So let's not spoil it."

"Your wish is my command."

Fen snorted. "Yeah, right. Anyway, where's my bossy sister today? Putting the troops through their paces again?"

Rhian nodded. "Yes, she's taken them out on the glacier for a few days. Final bits of training before we start filming next week."

Fen's grin was infectious. "Are you ready for it?"

"I think so. As ready as we're going to get, anyway."

"Oh, you're ready. Jayden tells me you've got everything organised like it was a military operation. Down to the second, she reckons."

Rhian snorted a quick laugh. "Oh, I don't know about that." Her cheeks heated up.

Fen watched her with a curious look on her face.

"What?" Rhian asked.

"Nothing."

Rhian's lips fell back into another frown, but she decided to let it drop.

"How is your wayward bunch of miscreants holding up?"

"Well, since Oskar shut Brooke down and Luiji fired back at Killian, it all seems to be going well. As long as we keep everything going along as it is, we should be good. The sponsors are all happy with the buzz the show's creating, and the feedback from the Twitter storm has been really good. Very positive for the show. Killian's dropped the threat of a lawsuit, so we're looking all right."

"Good."

"Yeah. Good."

"And your mother? Is she happy?"

Rhian laughed. "Rachel's never happy."

Fen chuckled. "Like that, is it?"

"Always."

"Well, what about you, then? Are you happy?"

Rhian felt the grin slide from her face and tried to catch it before it ran away entirely. "Of course," she said mildly. "Why wouldn't I be happy?"

Fen studied her a moment. "Don't know. But there's... I don't know." She shrugged. "You just don't seem your normal self. Like something's bugging you."

My dad. Jayden. Where would I even start? Rhian tried to relax her shoulders and tightened her mouth into what she hoped was a smile. "No, I'm fine, really. Just still catching up on some sleep, I guess. Probably the bags under my eyes that are making me look haggard."

Fen just continued to watch her before saying, "If you say so."

Rhian opened her mouth to tell her to stop with the judgey comments and the not-so-subtle looks but held herself in check. *I'm getting paranoid. Seeing things that aren't there.* Fen couldn't possibly know what was troubling her. Fen hadn't even seen her and Jayden together since those early days in the hospital. And she knew nothing about the situation with her father. Why would she? Rhian had come away from the conclave and the office to get a little distance and forget about it all for a little while. *Perhaps visiting the sister of your obsession wasn't the smartest move, then, dumbo.*

Obsession?

She thought about that word—about all it meant and about how she was unable to concentrate on anything when Jayden was around. And how when Jayden wasn't, all Rhian could do was think about her—well, almost all she could do. So, yeah. *Obsession* seemed like the right word. It was better than the alternative, anyway.

"Enough about me. Tell me what's going on around here. There must be tons of gossip."

Fen examined her a little longer before she relented and told her about the nurse who worked nights, was married to one of the doctors, but was having an affair with the cleaning lady. Apparently, Mark had caught them—in flagrante—in one of the empty rooms. It was one of half a dozen juicy titbits Fen had to divulge over the course of the afternoon.

The hospital was more like a microcosm of soap-opera antics than a place of healing and recuperation.

As it neared five and Rhian was getting ready to leave, Fen caught hold of her hand. "Will you do me a favour?"

"Of course," Rhian said without hesitation.

"Will you take care of Jayden for me?"

Rhian laughed and looked away from Fen's earnest expression. "I'm pretty sure your sister's more than capable of taking care of herself, Fen."

"I know it looks that way, and I know she acts like she's made of the rock she's so good at climbing, but she isn't. The last couple of years have been really hard on her. Between Nepal and our mum having to go into care, well, she's struggled."

"I didn't know your mum was in a care home."

"Alzheimer's."

"I'm so sorry."

Fen shrugged. "It was harder on Jayden. She was at home to see it happen. She was the one who had to put Mum in that place. I was over here. I saw them on Skype, learnt what was happening through text messages. Jayden lived it, and after everything else... Well, it didn't help to fix what was already broken."

Rhian tried to remember if this was something she knew or something she was supposed to know. But she couldn't think of anything Jayden had told her that explained what Fen was saying.

"I'm sorry. I don't understand."

"The earthquake in Nepal."

"The one a couple of years ago? She was there?"

Fen nodded. "She was at the Everest base camp."

"Oh God."

"Yeah, it was... I can't even imagine, in all honesty." She took a deep breath. "I don't really want to."

"Was she hurt?"

Fen shook her head. "Not physically. But what she saw there..."

"There was an avalanche, triggered by the earthquake, wasn't there?"

"Yeah."

"How many people died?"

"Nineteen. The worst single day in Everest climbing history."

"Did she… Did you both… Did you know…?"

Fen nodded, seeming to understand the question Rhian wanted to ask but couldn't form words for.

"Adventure Trekkers worked all over the world, leading climbing tours and groups. I was the static base here, and Jayden led groups, commission groups, on tours of different summits, long-distance treks—whatever came to us and caught her interest, really. Whatever kept her moving from one mountain to another. That season, she was working Nepal. They'd just finished on the Annapurna circuit, and the Everest summit was the next on the hit list."

"They?" Rhian asked quietly.

"Jayden and Rebecca."

Rhian watched Fen's face as the seed of what was coming began to germinate, and her own face went cold.

"They were supposed to be leading their expedition up to the summit the next day. The quake hit just before midday."

"Rebecca was her…girlfriend?"

Fen nodded. "They'd been together a few years." She smiled gently. "They worked well together, always moving around, always outside, always laughing and joking." Fen fell silent.

"What happened?"

"Maybe you should ask Jayden that."

Rhian studied her, then shook her head. "Why start this when you know she won't tell me? For whatever reason, you think I need to know this, so you may as well get on with it, Fen. You've come this far. You might as well finish the story now." She wiped her hands on her jeans, trying to clear the sweat from them.

"You're right. I don't think she will talk about it. Because she never has. I only know what happened from a colleague who was there with her. A doctor. Jost Clabben. When the quake hit, Jayden was with him in the medical tent. She'd gone to pick up the first aid kits and medical supplies for their expedition. When they felt the quake, they went outside to see what was going on. Jost said all they could see was the side of the mountain, and it looked like the whole thing was collapsing. It was just the ice and snow coming down, of course, and they thought that at base camp they'd be far enough away. You see, base camp is supposed to be a safe place on Everest." She shook her head. "Not that day.

"He described it like a tsunami of ice and rock crashing over them. He said Jayden saved his life by shoving him back into the med tent and under a gurney. If she hadn't, he could have been swept away by the avalanche and buried, as many of those who perished were. Instead, she got him to safety. Half the medical tent collapsed under the weight of the snow, and he told me Jay was trying to get to them, to dig them out while the avalanche was still pounding them into the ground. He had to pin her down to stop her, to keep her from getting buried too."

Rhian covered her mouth with her hand, not sure if she was holding back the sob or the nausea she felt growing in her chest.

"When it finally went quiet, she was the first one digging, trying to get to the people she knew were buried in the tent. He said there must have been tons of snow covering what was left of the medical area. Tons, and she was just scrabbling through it with her bare hands." Fen wiped her eyes. She opened her mouth to carry on speaking, but the words seemed to fail her.

"What?" The word barely made it past Rhian's lips.

"It wasn't just ice and snow and rock that the avalanche carried into the medical tent. It dragged people in with it. Dead and injured, all buried along with those who sought shelter in there." She blinked rapidly and swallowed. "Rebecca was one of them."

"Rebecca? Her Rebecca?"

Fen nodded. "She'd been out with their client that morning, helping him practice some technique or other, when the avalanche struck. Wherever they'd been, it just picked her up and carried her along until it dumped her there."

"Injured?" Rhian only managed to mouth that word. There was no longer enough breath in her to give it voice.

Fen shook her head. "Her throat was cut by her own ice axe in the violence of the avalanche. It was Jayden who found her body. In the ice. She just dug until she found someone and then pulled her out. Jost said when she turned Rebecca's body over, she just—well—it broke her."

Rhian sat, unable to move, unable to think of anything but the decimation she'd seen on TV of base camp in the aftermath. She remembered the stories of those who had been stranded at the higher camps, unable to get down because the avalanche had wiped away the ladders and ropes they needed to safely traverse the crevasses and gullies, and she still remembered the devastation of base camp all but wiped out as helicopters ferried the injured and the dead, two by two, off the mountain. Those who could walk slowly picked a path back to civilisation. But what they found was just a road to more and more destruction, death, and despair.

"That's why she disappeared from the mountains?" she whispered into the silent room.

Fen nodded.

"That's why she didn't want to do this project? That's what you meant when you said I was asking more than I could possibly know?"

"Yes."

Rhian closed her eyes and didn't even try not to cry. She let the tears fall for everything Jayden had witnessed and lived through. She let them fall for all those who had perished that day, for those who still battled with the aftermath of Mother Nature's fury. It all made sense now, Jayden's desire to do anything but this project when it had first landed in her lap. *And I made her do it. I forced it on her.*

Jayden's attitude towards her, her attitude towards the contestants, and her single-minded need to make sure every one of them was as prepared as she could possibly make them all made sense now too. Because Jayden had seen how devastating disaster on the mountain could be, even when you were prepared.

Rhian could see just how much it must have taken for Jayden to even be able to work with her in a civil manner, never mind anything more. Rhian was the woman who had made Jayden face those demons again, who had threatened her with a ruinous lawsuit if she didn't. She wondered which part of the ordeal haunted Jayden the most—her dead lover? The ferocity of the mountain? She simply couldn't imagine. The only thing she knew for certain was that in Jayden's place, Rhian wouldn't be able to forgive the bitch who put her back out there.

Does this have anything to do with this conversation she needs to have with me? Is this what she needs to talk about? Why now, though? Oh God. Did she feel guilty for pretending to be someone's lover? Did all this fake-girlfriend stuff feel like a betrayal to Rebecca's memory? Was Rhian making Jayden sell her soul to avoid bankruptcy?

Rhian had thought they were becoming good friends, but everything about their relationship had to be called into question now. How had Rhian not seen it before? She held all the cards here. Jayden must have figured at some point that she'd better be nice to Rhian, befriend her, keep the bitch happy who could sue her and her hospitalized sister into poverty at the first wrong move. And here was Rhian, blithely going on hikes with her, letting her wine and dine her…and never even noticing how all this must be killing Jayden inside.

So much was just getting more and more confusing for her. There was only one thing that seemed all too clear:

"She must hate me."

"Hate you?" Fen questioned, a note of surprise in her voice. "She doesn't—"

"I'm sorry, Fen. I have to go. Thanks for telling me. It explains a lot, but Carlos will be waiting for me." She bent and kissed Fen's cheek. "I'll see you next week."

"But, Rhian, wait—"

"It's okay. It makes sense now. Bye, Fen."

She closed the door behind herself, hoping it didn't sound as loud in the corridor as it did in her head. She pressed her hand to her breastbone, surprised to be able to feel her heart still beating inside her chest. She could have sworn it had stopped entirely. She leant back against the door trying to recover her balance as wave after wave of dizziness made the world pitch and spin. Bile churned in the pit of her stomach. She covered her mouth in an attempt to supress the urge to vomit. Tears threatened and she knew she couldn't stay there, back pressed to Fen's door.

She stumbled away and eventually crashed into the door of the restroom. She braced her arms on the vanity counter and let the tears fall. She hung her head, but still she didn't feel low enough. Her knees crumpled beneath her, and she slid to the floor. Turning so her back leant against the wall, she wrapped her arms about her knees, and sobbed until the tears dried on her cheeks and her breathing returned to normal.

"I'm so sorry, Jayden. I'm so sorry."

She'd never be able to apologise enough. She knew that now. What she'd done was unforgivable. The fact she hadn't known what she'd been doing only made it worse. How many times had she wondered to herself why

Jayden had stepped out of climbing? How many times had she promised herself she'd look into it? How many times had she ignored her own fears because she was scared of knowing?

Well, now she knew. It would make it easier to…let go? Move on?

Getting past this obsession with Jayden would be easier now. Surely. It had to. She just had to.

CHAPTER 29

"Sixteen people from all over the globe think they have what it takes to take on one of the most gruelling mountain challenges known to man." Rhian paused a beat as Angela had requested of her and cast her gaze over Jayden before pulling her attention away again. "The Fitz Roy Traverse."

"Guillaumet, Mermoz, Fitz Roy, Poincenot, Rafael Juarez, Saint-Exupéry, and finally de l'S. Five days of climbing, hauling kit, and sleeping on the mountain, spanning four and a half miles and thirteen thousand feet of snow- and ice-covered rock." Jayden read her lines into the microphone, one hand over the headphones to hold them in place. The voice recording was going to play over the opening credits while images of each peak flashed across the screen as Jayden said its name.

"In the best of conditions, it's brutal. In the worst, deadly. And every one of our competitors wants to be the first across the finish line," Rhian continued. "The first pair across gets the prize of a lifetime—a fully sponsored trip to the summit of Mount Vinson on Antarctica, the most inhospitable habitat on earth, and the title of *The Amazing Climb* Champions."

"Every one of them believes they can do it." Jayden glanced at her, then quickly looked away again.

"Most of them are going to be proved wrong."

"Cut." Angela's voice cut through their headphones. "That was really nice, ladies. Let me just check it back and see if we need another take."

Rhian held up her thumb and glanced at Jayden again. She'd been quiet since she'd come back off the ice with the group. Pensive. And Rhian couldn't help but wonder if something had happened out there that had upset her. Something else she would blame on Rhian and hate her for. Or was she just psyching herself up for this conversation they "needed" to have? Rhian scrubbed her hands over her face and pressed her fingers into her eyes.

"Hey, you okay?" Jayden asked quietly.

Rhian dropped her hands and smiled weakly. "Yeah, I'm fine."

Jayden looked at her, head cocked to the side, a frown on her forehead. "I don't believe you."

Rhian bit her lip. She didn't want to argue, not with Jayden, but she couldn't do this. Not right now. She couldn't keep doing this. She didn't know how Jayden had done it this long. "Well, I guess that's up to you. Angela, are we done here?" she asked into the mic. When Angela gave her a thumbs up from the sound booth, she pulled the headphones off and hooked them over the mic stand. She was out of the booth before Jayden could say anything else.

She ran the mile back to the conclave and straight up to her room. It was too hard. Knowing what she knew now, she was disgusted by her own insensitivity. By the way she'd manipulated Jayden into the position she was in. She was angry at herself for having put so much pressure on her. Angry at Rachel for not letting any of them back out. Hell, she was even angry at Fen for agreeing to the project and then getting herself hurt and landing Jayden in the position she was in.

She'd done things for the business before, things she'd not been entirely comfortable with. But she'd never crossed a line and forced someone to do something that hurt them emotionally, psychologically…whatever. She wanted to wash away the stench of manipulation, but it permeated from inside her, and no water or bleach could wash that away.

She leant her forehead against the cool glass of the window and stared out with unseeing eyes. She tried to swallow the urge to vomit. How do you learn to live with yourself when you make yourself sick?

"Hey."

Rhian spun around. She thought she'd locked the door. "What are you doing here?"

"I… You're upset. What's wrong?" Jayden asked, crossing the floor until she was stood in front of her.

Rhian crossed her arms over her stomach. "I told you, nothing."

"And I told you I don't believe you." Jayden wrapped her fingers gently around Rhian's biceps. "I can see it."

"I'm fine, Jayden. I'm sure you've got lots to do." God, Jayden should not feel obligated to comfort Rhian for how she felt about manipulating her. It was sick. She turned away and stared out of the window again.

"I do. But that can wait. Somehow I don't think this can."

Rhian heard the rustle of the bedclothes. When she peeked over her shoulder, Jayden was sitting on the edge of the bed, leaning back on her arms and with her ankles crossed, an expectant look on her face.

"So what is it? Is there a new problem with Killian?"

Rhian shook her head. "He's dropped the suit. There won't be any problems from him again. Rachel's plan and Luiji's help have definitely put an end to that issue."

"Good. Well, it can't be Brooke. She's been a pain in my backside for the past four days. Rachel, then?"

"No." She pressed her hand to her forehead, shielding her eyes. She didn't want to look at Jayden sitting on her bed. The expression of concern on her face looked so…genuine, so caring, that it hurt to see it. "I told you, it's nothing."

"I wasn't born yesterday, Rhian, and I'm not going anywhere until you tell me what's upset you so much."

"Fine. Then stay there." Rhian crossed the room and slammed the door closed behind her. Mel was coming out of her room as she did, and Rhian quickly ducked under Mel's arm and into her room.

"Hey, what the—"

"Sh. Please just close the door and let me hide for a few minutes."

Mel did as she'd been asked and stared at her, a questioning look on her face.

"I just need to get away from stuff for a while, and no one will look for me here."

Mel shook her head. "Fine. But I'm going to lunch. Want me to bring you something up?"

"No, I'll be okay, thanks."

Mel sat on the bed next to her. "What's going on, Rhi? You haven't been yourself for a couple of days now."

Rhian couldn't take it anymore. The questions, the emotion, it was all too much, and in a rush, it all came pouring out. "I know why she hates me. It's because I made her do this after people died on her in Nepal, and I made her go back on the mountain. And I can't help the way I feel about her, but she hates me, and she's got every right to hate me. She really does. *I* hate me now. But I really like her, Mel." Tears coursed down her cheeks as the words fell from her tongue. She didn't care that she probably made no sense to Mel. She didn't care that she was blubbering like a baby. It hurt, and she just couldn't hold it in anymore.

Mel's arms snaked around her shoulders and pulled her into a tight embrace. She stroked her hair, rubbed soothing circles over her back, and whispered soft words against her head until the sobs wracking her body eased. Mel pulled away to reach for a box of tissues on the nightstand and held them out to her.

"Thanks," Rhian whispered.

"Better?"

Rhian shrugged. "Not really." She blew her nose and tossed the tissue into the wastepaper basket. "Sorry."

"No need. Now, start from the top, and tell me why you think someone hates you."

"Jayden hates me."

Mel laughed. "No, she doesn't."

Rhian nodded and wiped another tear from her face. "Fen told me."

"Fen told you that Jayden hates you? She used that exact phrase?"

Rhian shook her head. "No, of course not. This isn't the school playground."

"Thank goodness. I was worried there for a minute."

"Sarky."

Mel just waited.

Rhian rolled her eyes. "She told me Jayden hadn't been in the mountains since the earthquake hit Nepal."

"Why not?"

"She was at Everest base camp when it was decimated by the avalanche."

"Wow."

"Yeah."

"But Fen didn't say the phrase 'Jayden hates you because you made her do the show', did she?"

"No."

"So you jumped to that little conclusion?"

Rhian stared at her. "Her girlfriend died there. What other conclusion would you arrive at?"

Mel was quiet a moment. "I'm sorry to hear she went through that. I am. But I still don't see why she would blame you for that."

"I didn't say she blamed me for that. I said she hates me because I made her do this show. Made her go back into the mountains again, made her face this awful, awful thing that happened to her, or face a lawsuit. Of course she'd despise me for it. I would." She put her hand over her mouth and bit her knuckle, determined not to cry again.

"Hon, I've seen her with you, and she doesn't act like someone who's having a hard time being around you."

"It's an act. You said it yourself."

Mel tutted. "If she's really that good an actress, she should be earning billions in Hollywood, not leading groups up mountains and freezing one's derriere off on glaciers." She cuffed Rhian's shoulder gently. "Talk to her. Let her tell you."

"No, I'm not going to make it worse."

"Make what worse?"

"The situation."

"What situation? And how can talking to her make it worse?"

"I made her do this even though she clearly told me she didn't want to. Now I know why she didn't want to. I should've done the research. I kept meaning to. I just got so busy and forgot. It just didn't seem to be relevant once she agreed. No, that's not true. Not really. I knew there was something—something painful." She hung her head. "Talking to her about it will surely only make it worse."

"For who?"

She was an utter weakling, wasn't she? "For me."

"Why? How?"

"I don't want to be the reason she's hurting. I don't want her to hate me. I don't want to hear her tell me what she's going through...what she's dealing with, what's hurting her, all because of me. I can't bear it." The sobs tore through her again, but she glared at Mel through the tears. Why couldn't she see it? Why couldn't she see what Rhian was so afraid of hearing from Jayden's lips—that it would be made all the more real spoken aloud?

Mel glared back, then laughed again, haughtily this time. "Mighty high opinion you've got of yourself there."

"What? No, I don't—"

"*I'm the reason she's hurting, she's going through it because of me.*" She mimicked Rhian's voice.

"You know what I mean."

"Yes, I do. You don't want to face her because you're afraid you'll feel worse than you already do. You feel guilty and angry and manipulative. And you feel all those things more because you genuinely care for her." Mel squeezed her hand. "Don't you?"

Rhian nodded and hid her face in a tissue.

Mel chuckled. "I've seen the way she looks at you. She likes you."

"Piss off. She doesn't. At all."

"Fine, fine." Mel took her hand and squeezed her fingers gently. "But you like her?"

Rhian's eyes stung as the tears sprang back. She nodded.

"Really like her?"

The tears began to fall. She grabbed another tissue and hid her face in her hands as she nodded.

"Maybe love her?"

Sobs wracked Rhian's shoulders as Mel wrapped her arms about her again.

"Bloody hell. Rachel's gonna have my guts for garters if you come back a mess."

Jayden could hear Rhian's sobs and the muffled conversation through Mel's door, but she couldn't bring herself to eavesdrop. Rhian was hurting, but she'd sought out the comfort she needed. That was what was important. She tried not to feel stung that Rhian had run from her in a time of emotional need, tried not to worry about what could be eating at her. She'd thought they'd made progress after the rafting trip. That they'd grown closer. That was what she wanted to talk to Rhian about. She wanted to lay everything out on the table, so to speak. To tell her how she felt. Playing games didn't feel right any more. She'd thought she'd seen something on that trip, some spark to suggest that maybe—just maybe—there was more to Rhian's feelings for her now than friendship. Rhian had had a glint in her eyes that Jayden was sure wasn't just from the excitement of the rapids.

She rested her hand against the wooden door. Jayden knew that the only place in there to sit was the bed. It was less than twenty feet away from where she stood. But she'd never felt further away from Rhian than she did in that moment.

Head on her chest, she sighed and curled her fingers into a fist. Knock, don't knock. Turn and walk away or push further, when Rhian had made perfectly clear what she wanted.

No, Jayden wouldn't push. But the way her fingers ached to reach out and hold Rhian as she cried only made her more determined to be the person Rhian would turn to next time she needed comfort. She turned and headed for the stairs.

Then the most unwelcome of thoughts crossed her mind.

What if Rhian was upset because Jayden was making her feelings obvious and Rhian didn't want it? What if she didn't want Jayden to pursue her? Was that the reason she'd run away from her? The reason she was sobbing on Mel's shoulder?

Christ, it was all getting so bloody complicated.

The air outside was cool for the time of year, and filming the first episode was due to begin in the morning. Jayden had been excited earlier. The weeks of work she and Rhian had put in so far was coming to fruition. Now all she knew was that she wouldn't be getting any sleep tonight. She needed to figure out what the hell was going on and what she should do. Should she just back off and do no more than was required for their sham to work? Or was she reading too much into Rhian seeking comfort from someone she'd known a long time?

Her mind was spinning in circles, and she couldn't find a place to begin to unravel the mess she was in. She needed to talk to Fen.

Her mobile phone rang three times before Fen answered. "Hey, back off the glacier?"

"Yeah, this morning, actually. Listen, I need some advice."

"Shoot."

"I'm not sure where to start or what's going on but Rhian's…well, she's really upset. I don't know what I've done."

Fen sighed. "She thinks you hate her."

"What the hell? Why?"

"Well, she probably thinks I told her that."

"Fen. Why the hell would you lie to her like that?"

"I didn't."

"Then why…? You better explain."

"I was going to. I was going to explain to her as well, but she won't answer my calls and won't return my messages either."

"Okay, explain it to me."

"She came to visit the other day. We were talking and I mentioned something about Nepal."

"And?"

"And the fact you were at base camp."

"And?"

"And she ran out of here saying that you must hate her."

"And what did you do when she said that?"

"She wouldn't listen to me. She said she'd see me next week, and then she was gone. It's not like I could chase after her. Look, I've been trying to call her ever since, but like I said, she won't respond."

At least Jayden knew what she was dealing with now. All she had to do was figure out why Rhian's reaction was so…extreme. She already knew that Jayden had been reluctant to pick up the reins of the show, so why would the reason behind it matter so much now?

"Did you tell her about Rebecca?"

Fen sighed. "Yes. I knew you never would, and I thought it might… help her. To see past your bitchiness and moodiness, and…well, you know, help her like you, like you want her to. I was trying to help, hon. I thought it would explain some things for her."

"Well, clearly that didn't work, now, did it? I mean, I thought we were making progress. I thought after the rafting trip we were getting closer. But now…it's like everything's back to square one." She chuckled bitterly. "Actually, it's worse than square one. She can't seem to stand being in the same room as me."

"What happened?"

Jayden quickly filled her in on the afternoon's drama.

"So what are you going to do?"

"I don't know. I don't know what's for the best or what's likely to make things worse at this point."

"Want a suggestion?"

"No. Your suggestions have done nothing but make this whole thing worse from start to finish. You need to stop interfering and stay out of it."

"Well, I'm going to tell you anyway. Carry on doing what you're doing. Ramp it up, even. Make sure you show the same if not more affection and attention when there's no one around. Show her this isn't just for show."

"I told you not to make suggestions."

"Yeah, but we both know you're just blowing off steam cos you're mad at me—"

"I've every right to be mad at you!"

"And you only really called because you wanted me to tell you what to do to win your girl round."

"Bitch."

"And?"

Jayden sighed. She didn't know what to do. Clearly Rhian didn't want to talk to her. She didn't want to tell her what she knew and—what—have Jayden explain again what had happened out there? How would that help either of them? But what about this event was tearing Rhian apart so much that she could barely look Jayden in the eye? Surely only talking to her wasn't going to get to the bottom of those details?

"Do you still want her to fall in love with you?"

"Yes," Jayden whispered.

"Do you think she's there yet?"

She blew out hard. "Given that she's crying on her friend's shoulder rather than mine, no."

"Then what do you think?"

Jayden closed her eyes and swallowed. "You don't think this is, I don't know, wrong, do you?"

"Wrong?"

"Yes. Trying to make someone fall in love with you. Manipulating her like this. It feels wrong. I mean, how is this different to Brooke continually hitting on her?"

"Wow. This is not like Brooke at all."

"She told Brooke she wasn't interested. She told me she wasn't interested. Brooke continued to pursue her, and I'm...well, so am I." She shook her head. "I think I should just back off."

"Okay, tell me this, Jay. Have you drugged her?"

"What the hell are you talking about?"

"I'll take that as a no."

"Of course I haven't. But neither has Brooke."

"I'll give you that. Have you forced her to do something after she's said no?"

"Other than trying to get her to talk to me this afternoon, no."

"Brooke did. You told me she kept feeling her up after Rhian had made it clear. True?"

"Yes, but I kissed her—"

"Only as part of the charade. Not in your private time. Right?"

Jayden agreed.

"See, different. Have you taken her out to dinner?"

"Yes."

"Taken her on an adventure activity?"

"Yes."

"Brought her flowers?"

"Yes."

"Chocolates?"

"Yes."

"Spent time talking to her?"

"Yes."

"Spent time listening to her, laughing with her, and generally being there for her and doing sweet things for her?"

"Yes."

"Now tell me...if you'd just started dating a new woman, how would you date her?"

Jayden snorted. "I'd do all the same things."

"Why?"

"To get to know her, let her get to know me, and see what develops."

"I see. And is the situation with Rhian somehow different?"

"Yes."

"How?"

"She wouldn't have agreed to the first date if I'd asked under normal circumstances."

"I wouldn't be too sure about that, Jay. She didn't look…uninterested in you the day she saw you here."

"Doesn't change the fact that a few weeks later, she told me she wasn't attracted to me."

"I'm still not convinced."

"Well, it's the truth. So much so that she wasn't even sure she could pretend to be attracted to me."

"Hey, Jay?"

"Yeah?"

"You're an attractive woman."

Jayden laughed. "You're my sister. That's just weird."

"I'm your sister, so think how hard that was for me to admit. It's much easier to tell you that you look like the Hunchback of Notre Dame."

Jayden chuckled. "Thanks for the ego boost. Me and my repulsive self need to get some shut-eye now. We're filming tomorrow."

"Right. Night, Mogo."

"Night, Fen. And thanks."

"Don't mention it."

CHAPTER 30

JAYDEN BOUNCED THE HIGHLY DECORATED jar in her hand and addressed the group. "In here are sixteen balls. Eight different colours. You'll each come up and select one. Matching colours equals your pairing for the first challenge. Everyone clear?"

A chorus of grunts and affirmations circled the base camp, and, one at a time, the climbers stood to draw their lots. Some pairs were clearly happier with their selections than others, Hunter and Lonnie, and Sky and Taylor being the happiest in the group, while Kimi looked decidedly unhappy as Brooke's partner. No one, it seemed, was happy she was still here, and no one wanted to work with her. It was the main reason they'd developed this chance game to determine the challenge pairs. No one could claim they were being targeted or not given a fair chance.

"The first challenge begins tomorrow at 0700. Pairs will then depart at ninety-minute intervals. Understood?"

Again, everyone acknowledged her.

"You have twenty-two hours to prepare yourselves for your ascent, to research your route using the materials we have here in camp, and to gather your supplies. Any questions?"

"Yeah, what are we climbing?" Brooke shouted as she leant against the ice wall surrounding the encampment.

Jayden nodded. "I was just getting to that." She looked at Rhian, hoping to catch her eye, but she refused to look over at her. Still. "This week's challenge is to summit Guillaumet and return to base camp. Teams will be timed from the moment they leave base camp until they return. Got it?"

A series of *yups* and *ayes* greeted her.

"Points are awarded not just for times, but for the technical difficulty of the route chosen. So a slower time on a harder route, for example, may gain you more points to put you ahead on the leader board," Rhian said. "But picking a hard route doesn't automatically mean you'll still beat someone who choses an easier path to the summit. It's a combination of the two factors. Think of it like a decathlon event, ladies and gentlemen. Time makes points. Distance makes points, technical skill makes points. Points make winners. Adversely, any pairs who do not complete the challenge will automatically be in the bottom four."

Jayden watched as each climber nodded, a thoughtful look on everyone's face.

"For twelve of you, when you get back to base camp, that's week one completed. The bottom four will face the climb-off," Rhian said.

Murmurs of discontent wafted on the cold wind. Even in the summer, the maximum temperature on the glacier was an average 5 degrees Celsius, and the wind was always cold.

Rhian stepped forward. "The climb-off is a series of sprint climbs to determine the two contestants up for the public vote. Voting will open at the completion of the sprints and will be open for twenty-four hours. The climber with the lowest number of public votes will leave the competition."

Jayden picked up a handful of small dry bags and handed them out, while Rhian took the other half. "In the pack, you have a watch with a GPS tracker in it, a mic pack, and a helmet and/or body cam. You must have these on you anytime you leave base camp. These are for your protection and locating you in case of emergencies as well as for recording purposes. If you do not have them with you, you could be asked to leave the program. Am I making myself clear?"

"Crystal," Luiji said as Jayden handed him his pack.

"Good." She winked at him. "Now, camera crews and safety personnel are already moving into locations to get shots of you along the way. Some will remain static, others will move with you, drop off, return, whatever they wish to get the shots they need. There are also drone cameras and cameras already set up at nest locations. Do not mess with the cameras, or, again, you could be asked to leave the program." She handed her last pack to Brooke. "Are we all clear on the rules?" Everyone answered except Brooke.

Jayden kept hold of the bag Brooke had wrapped her fingers around. "Are we clear?" she asked again.

"Perfectly," Brooke ground out through gritted teeth.

"Excellent." Jayden offered her a smile that was probably more of a grimace. She let go of the strap. "Guidebooks are on the table. Supplies are in the store tent. Remember that between the two of you, you must carry everything you need to complete this task and get back to base camp safely. That means emergency kit, avalanche gear, and basic rations at the minimum. There will be no free soloing on any of these climbs. That means gear, ropes, and helmets at any time you are climbing."

She watched the expectant faces of the group. Excitement buzzed through the air. They were ready. She was ready.

"Let's climb!"

Jayden dropped down onto the ice bench opposite Angela and Rhian. "Last team just set off," she told them. It was just after five thirty in the evening, and the last team off would have to hustle to make it to a good overnighting spot before dark.

"Great," Angela said. "We've gotten some great footage so far."

"Ang," Simon called from the other side of the encampment. He waved his arms frantically. "We've got a problem."

The three of them were on their feet and running across the slick surface as fast as they could. He stood behind a small bank of monitors they'd set up to review the drone cameras and remotely activate the body cams when necessary. He pointed to the footage coming from a drone camera: a gaping hole in the glacier filled the centre of the screen, a jagged scar on the white surface with a tiny, dark shape sprawled flat against the ice from what looked like a few feet away.

"Fuck!" Jayden shouted. "Who is it?" A knot twisted in her gut, and she swallowed back the bile rising in her throat. Not again. She couldn't lose anyone again.

"That's Kimi that we can see." Simon operated a console that looked like the controls of a toy car and zoomed the picture in closer until they could see Kimi no more than her body's length—all five foot two inches—

from the edge of the crevasse. She had her crampons and ice axe dug into the ice to stop her from moving.

"Where's Brooke?" Angela asked.

Simon zoomed out again so they could see the red-and-purple rope from Kimi's waist disappear over the lip and into the void.

Rhian stared at the screen. "Shit. This can't be happening. This can't be happening, not now."

"How far away are they?" Jayden demanded, running in her head through a catalogue of gear that was left in the store tent and gauging how quickly she could be ready to go.

"Too far," Angela said. "They've been on the ice for almost two hours now."

Jayden nodded. "She'll be cold, but she might be okay." Jayden added space blankets to the mental list she was preparing.

"No," Simon said as he zoomed out and positioned the drone towards the edge of the crevasse. The torrent of water was the first thing they could see. "Moulin."

"Fuck." Two hours under the ice-cold glacier stream would be more than anyone could survive. *I should have seen this coming. I should have anticipated this. That's the whole fucking reason I'm here. Why didn't I see this coming?* "How close are any of the other teams? Camera crews? Anybody? There has to be someone closer that can get there to help them." Blaming herself would have to wait. First, she had to do everything she could, everything humanly possible, to save Brooke. She was a pain in the arse, but no one deserved to die like this.

Angela sat at the desk beside Simon and clicked on the laptop, quickly bringing up a screen covered in little dots, the GPS locations of everyone not in base camp. "Nearest is a camera crew with Santiago, maybe an hour's hike away."

"Get me Santiago on the radio."

"Look," Rhian said, pointing to the screen.

Jayden stopped mentally berating herself long enough to follow Rhian's finger and smiled as Simon zoomed in on Kimi again and switched on her mic so they could hear.

"Damn it, Brooke, you piece of crap, stop screaming and get a Prusik on that line. Get ready to haul your ass out of there."

They didn't need to turn on Brooke's mic. They could hear her screams over the levels on Kimi's mic—and the thunderous torrent of water—loud and clear. She was clearly hysterical as Kimi secured first one, then a second ice screw into place on either side of her.

"I mean it, Brooke. I'm not dragging you out of that pit on my own."

"Good girl, Kimi," Jayden whispered to herself. Kimi was a strong, capable climber. She'd performed well in each of the training scenarios Jayden had put them through, and Jayden could see already that she was performing well under the pressure of a real-life situation. She was securing the line to give Brooke the stability she'd need to self-rescue. "You brilliant, brilliant woman." The gnawing ache in Jayden's gut eased enough for her to breathe properly. Blood rushed away from her extremities, and her fingers and toes began to tingle. Ignoring the stabbing ache, she shook out her hands, thrilled when the sensation began to return.

"Could she?" Simon asked. "I mean, all Brooke seems to be doing is screaming. What if she can't get herself out of there? Is Kimi strong enough to do it?" He glanced at Jayden over his shoulder.

"Doubtful," Jayden whispered. "Brooke's got thirty-plus pounds on Kimi. Trying to haul your own body weight out of one of those things is bloody hard work—for some, impossible."

"Can we get Brooke's bodycam on so we can see what's going on down there?" Angela asked.

Simon held the drone steady over Kimi's head and pressed a button on another monitor. Shaky footage spinning around in slow circles filled the screen. The slow turn was enough to make Jayden dizzy, but she concentrated on the cascade of water flowing over Brooke and the fact Brooke was doing nothing to help herself but cling to the rope about her middle. The fast flow of the water over her had no doubt drenched her to the core and would not be helping her focus or function, but unless she made some attempt to self-rescue, the moulin was likely to claim her for its own.

"Brooke, you fucking crybaby, you're the one who's always telling us how fucking awesome you are. Snap out of it, and show us what you're made of!" Kimi quickly tied a series of knots to secure the belay line that was holding Brooke to her and stopping her from falling into the icy waters at the heart of the glacial watermill. "Come on!"

After just a couple of minutes, she managed to free herself from the belay, now secured by the ice screws, and shuffle to the lip of the crevasse on her belly.

"Are you kidding me?" Kimi yelled into the thunderous echo of the water cascade. "You've not even got a fucking Prusik set up."

Brooke didn't answer. The screaming had stopped, but she seemed frozen. From cold or fear, they wouldn't know until she was out of the crevasse. And if she didn't snap out of it, the chances of that happening were getting slimmer by the minute. It wouldn't take long before hypothermia would set in under the ice-cold glacial water and inside what was effectively a deep freeze down there. Jayden's hands were turning cold again, the prickle of pins and needles itching her nerves in sympathy for Brooke's plight.

"Are you really just going to sit there and die?" Kimi screamed into the cavern.

Brooke didn't respond. It seemed beyond her. Just as they were beyond Jayden's help. She glanced at Rhian. Her face had gone grey, her hands were fisted against her jaw, and she seemed unable to tear her eyes from the screen. Jayden wanted to put an arm about her shoulder and tell her it would be okay. But she couldn't lie to herself, and she couldn't lie to Rhian.

In that moment, it struck her. She *had* anticipated this. That was why she had drilled them and drilled them. She'd given every one of them the best chance they could have of getting themselves out of the situation they were in. She'd taught them the skills and let them practice. Now it was up to them. They had to pull it together and save themselves. Their actions, their decisions, their will were the only things that could make a difference now. Live or die…it was their choice.

"Santiago's on his way to their location," Angela said.

"Warn him," Jayden said, her voice deep and throaty. "It might be a retrieval."

Angela only nodded. None of them said anything as they stood and stared in horror at the screens and the drama playing out. Jayden's heart went out to Kimi. She'd done everything right. She'd secured the line, she'd anchored her buddy, and she was trying to garner her cooperation. But it was up to Brooke to pull herself out, just like Jayden had taught her. Less than two weeks ago, they'd drilled this very skill, just in case the world opened up beneath them and asked what they were truly made of.

Kimi knew. It was written on her face. They could see every line of anguish through the drone's camera. She roared her anger at the futility of it, at the impotence hanging on the other end of the rope.

"Not today, you fucking useless piece of shit. You're not leaving me to live with that on my conscience." She upended her backpack and began sorting her gear.

"What's she doing?" Angela asked Jayden.

Jayden peered at the screen, edging closer to see the gear Kimi was setting aside. She watched as Kimi assembled a secondary anchor point, fastening a ratcheting Prusik to the line and anchor before adding a short-locking Prusik. She fixed a webbing strap to the secondary anchor and assembled her lines.

"She's set up a ratcheting pulley system," Rhian said in awe.

"She's going to pull her out?" Simon asked. "Really?"

"She's damn well going to try." Jayden crossed her fingers and leant closer still to the screen, wishing she could be there to help her, but pride for the tiny Japanese woman blossomed in her chest. She had heart. Stuck between the hard choice and no choice, she was going to do the only thing she could think of. She was going to try what each of them thought impossible.

Kimi set her feet on the ice and used her body weight like she was pulling on a rowing machine at the gym to inch the rope up through her system. Brooke's bodycam jerked as she rose a few inches. Kimi shuffled her hands down the rope and set herself again. She groaned as she pulled, her hands wrapped around the rope to prevent it slipping through her fingers.

"You are not dying on me today." Kimi gritted her teeth and roared again. Slowly, inch by painful inch, she hauled Brooke's body out of the crevasse. When Brooke's head broke the lip of the crack, Kimi fell onto her back, panting.

They watched, waiting, hoping Brooke would now pull herself over the edge and begin to help herself. Still she didn't. Kimi, apparently fuelled by nothing but piss and vinegar, grabbed the back of her jacket and dragged her over the bank.

"So much for you winning this thing, asshole. The rest of us should just piss off home, hey?" Kimi groused through heavy breaths as she finally wrestled Brooke onto solid ground. "Now get your wet clothes off before you freeze to death and waste the bloody effort."

Brooke still didn't move. Simon zoomed in on her face. Her teeth were chattering, her lips had a blue tinge to them, and her arms were wrapped tightly around her body.

"Don't make me strip your clothes off too, damn it. You're taking the piss now, Shields. I mean it."

It would be comical to watch the tiny climber struggle to get Brooke out of her wet clothes if the potential consequences of her not doing so weren't so dire. Frostbite, hypothermia, and death were all still very real possibilities for Brooke. But Kimi was doing everything right. She was doing everything possible to keep the woman not only alive, but whole.

Jayden had lost track of how long it had taken Kimi to get Brooke out of the crevasse, then out of her clothes, into dry spares, and under a wind shelter while she made them a hot drink to warm them both. She looked at the timestamp on the video feeds. It had to have been an hour? More? She was so proud of the young woman that she just wanted to get to her and hug her. But that would have to wait. The sun would be setting soon, and they couldn't possibly get back to camp before then. And there was no question that they were coming back to camp. Brooke looked in no state to continue across the glacier, never mind attempt a summit climb.

Santiago radioed with an update. They were safe and hunkered down for the night. They were almost three hours from base camp and would head back at first light. Brooke had, in his opinion, mild hypothermia, but she would be fine, if Kimi didn't kill her before they returned to camp. Their task failure was going to drop them both into the climb-off.

And that just didn't sit well for Jayden. Kimi didn't deserve to face the vote because of firstly an accident and then her climbing partner's inaction. What she'd achieved was a greater feat than successfully completing the Fitz Roy Traverse, as far as Jayden was concerned. She'd saved a life. She'd kept her head and saved the person relying on her.

Caught between a rock and a hard place, few others would have reacted as well as Kimi had in that situation. Fewer still would have been able to achieve it. Now she would face the climb-off and possibly the public vote. It wasn't fair. It wasn't right. And Jayden's sense of honour simply couldn't let it stand. She didn't think the other competitors would stomach it either.

But she couldn't see Brooke admitting her weakness to the group, nor Kimi admitting her act of heroism.

Everyone deserved to know what had happened. For one thing, they could all learn from it, should the situation arise again. And as the weather continued to warm, the chances of more crevasses opening up through the filming only grew. Safety was her priority. And that meant more than just preparing those out on the ice as best as she could; it meant keeping those who couldn't cope off it too, no matter what it took to achieve that. After all, Brooke had put them in the situation where Jayden couldn't contemplate ejecting her from the competition for straightforward incompetence. That was never going to be allowed to stand.

But there was always another way. You just had to be adaptable...and occasionally a little creative.

Jayden approached Angela and Rhian. "Ladies, I have a proposal."

Rhian cocked her head. "What's that?"

It was the most Rhian had spoken directly to her all day. She smiled, hoping they could get back to some semblance of normalcy. But the way Rhian quickly looked away from her told Jayden volumes. She sighed before she said, "We all know the rules. Failure to complete means bottom four."

Angela nodded a then stared, her jaw dropping slack. "Damn." She turned and looked out across the ice in the direction that Kimi and Brooke were now waiting out the night. "Kimi doesn't deserve that."

Simon squinted at them. "It wasn't exactly Brooke's fault that glacier opened up under her either."

"True, but her actions after that could have made things a lot better than they were. She was trained for a scenario just like this one," Angela said. "She could have self-rescued, or at least aided in her own rescue. Jayden's drilled every single one of us, you and me included, in what to do in that very situation. She didn't even try. She could have got herself dry and warm again without much fuss and been preparing with Kimi to complete the challenge. She isn't. She's given up."

Simon opened his mouth to make another point, but Rhian spoke first. "What's your plan?"

"Well, I thought we might let the other contestants get a look at this footage."

"With what in mind?"

She shrugged. "A training demonstration. They all deserve to see what happened here, as a demonstration of a single-man rescue technique. Big-screen it when we get back to El Chaltén."

Jayden watched her for a second and saw the germ of the idea take shape in her mind. She could see the moment Rhian realised what Jayden hoped would result from her little show-and-tell.

"Okay. A training demo."

Jayden smiled. She just hoped her instincts about the rest of the team were correct. Kimi didn't deserve to be in the position Brooke had put her in, and there was no place for weakness or sentimentality on the mountain. Hard choice or no choice. Jayden didn't even have to think about it.

CHAPTER 31

THE LAST TEAM TO ARRIVE back were Taylor and Sky, but their ascent of the most difficult climb rocketed them up the leader board and left Liv and Oskar in the drop zone with Brooke and Kimi. The bus back to El Chaltén the next morning was quiet, each contestant either asleep or talking in whispers about the expected outcome of the sprint climbs. Oskar was the odds-on favourite, as his height and reach offered him an advantage in the race-to-the-top contest that a speed climb was.

Kimi stared out the window, silently fuming and refusing to speak to anyone. None of the other teams knew what had happened. As Jayden had predicted, Kimi refused to say, and Brooke was being…vague. To say the least. Only two things that had surprised her. First was waking up in the night to find Rhian sitting on the ice bench outside their tent, weeping. She didn't know why. But she wanted to. She'd wanted to go up to her, wrap her arms about her shoulders, make Rhian tell her what was wrong. Find some way to convince her they could fix it. Together. But she hadn't. Rhian hadn't spoken to her since she agreed to show the video to the climbers, and anytime she tried to get close to her, she ran—sometimes literally—away. And Jayden still didn't know what she should do.

The second surprise had been herself. She'd half expected the incident with Brooke and Kimi to have brought back all the old nightmares, the image of Rebecca's face, the blood dripping off the ice axe, the roar of the avalanche racing for them. But it hadn't. She'd slept deeper than she had in months—years. Jayden wasn't sure exactly why, but she was sure it had something to do with seeing Kimi react to disaster, the way she'd taken

Jayden's training and utilised it. And suddenly, the pieces had slipped back together, and she saw herself again in the result.

When Carlos stopped the bus outside the conclave, Jayden stood and clapped her hands together to get everyone's attention.

"Ladies and gents, the sprints will be held tomorrow morning. Nine a.m. at the wall. I expect everyone to be there. Not just the four contestants participating. Clear?"

"Clear," came the reply from the back of the bus.

"Good. When we get off the bus, dump you stuff in your rooms and make your way back to the common room. Meeting in thirty minutes." She figured that would give them enough time to shower too, if they wanted. "We'll have dinner after the meeting. It won't take too long."

With a hum of questions buzzing between them all, everyone agreed and departed the bus. No one seemed to know what was going on. Jayden clapped a hand over Kimi's shoulder as she rose out of her seat and moved towards the steps.

"I just wanted to tell you how proud I am of you. What you did out there was nothing short of heroic. I'll never forget what I witnessed."

Kimi ducked her head, a shy smile on her lips. "Thanks. That means a lot, coming from you."

"Don't thank me. I'm thanking you. Now, go on. I'll see you in a few minutes, okay?"

Kimi nodded and scampered off the bus. Rhian was waiting for Jayden as she walked into the conclave.

"Are you sure this is a good idea?"

"What? Using what happened as a training exercise? Why not?"

"Because it's Brooke. Hasn't she already caused enough trouble?"

"Look, I'm proposing we use a situation, a real-life situation that happened out there, as a way to help keep the others safe. I'm not beaming it out across the globe to humiliate her. I'm trying to keep everyone else safe."

"But it will humiliate her. And she will retaliate."

"She signed a release that the footage filmed could be used in any way the production company sees fit to do so. This is a very reasonable way to use the footage."

"She could argue—"

"A lot of things. I know. But this isn't right. She hasn't even admitted to the group what happened. They need to know, especially if she might have to climb with one or more of them again. You're asking me to risk their lives without them knowing the risks. And I won't do that." She shook her head. "Safety is my top priority, remember? Let me handle this my way."

Rhian drew in a deep breath and nodded. "Okay. I'll send Rachel an e-mail to let her know what's happening so she can get out ahead of anything Brooke might try to pull."

"You might want to see if Mel can take the Internet offline somehow tonight too." She rolled her eyes. "Just in case."

"Oh God." She rubbed her hand over her face. "I'll get her to change the password, then if anyone tries to get on, they'll have to come to us for access, and we can monitor who has it."

"I know this is difficult. I'm sorry. I just—"

Rhian held up her hand. "I get it. I hate it too. I'm just worried about the problems she can cause."

"I know, and I'm sorry. But I truly believe they need to know what they could face with Brooke in the event she survives this climb-off."

Rhian nodded, but Jayden couldn't decipher the look in her eyes. It seemed to be a mix of compassion, loss, and something else. Respect maybe?

"I know. And I always told you that safety was the first priority."

"Thank you."

Rhian frowned. "For what?"

"For your support in this. For keeping your promise about the safety thing. For understanding why I need to do this."

"You don't need to thank me for that." Rhian ducked her head and moved away, heading for the coffee dispenser. Jayden replayed the conversation in her head. Rhian seemed so much calmer than before. Was she feeling better? Or was she just getting better at hiding her feelings? Whatever the reason, her attitude now was nothing but professional.

Climbers filtered into the room as Simon and Angela set up a big screen and a projector. The pair had been up most of the night, cutting together footage to show what happened while shortening the time lapse to less than thirty minutes.

Brooke was the last to arrive. Exactly as Jayden had expected. When she was seated, Jayden addressed the room.

"Thanks, everyone, I know you're all tired. There were some terrific climbs out there the last couple of days. But we need to go over a safety point again, and I don't have the time now to conduct more one-to-one training. Angela and Simon have helped me out with some video footage. I want you all to watch it, then we can discuss what's happened, what needs to be done, anything that could have been done differently or better, and so on. Okay?" She noticed the nodding heads around the room and the wary look on Brooke's face. "If you have comments or questions, please hold them until we stop the film."

A murmur of curiosity filled the room, and Jayden decided to just get on with it.

The drone shot captured two walkers on the ice making slow but steady progress, thirty feet apart, with a length of rope tying them together. Two seconds later, one of the figures disappeared into a newly formed crack in the ice, the jagged edges swallowing her like a great gaping maw. The second figure was dragged towards the lip, and gasps of surprise bounced about the room when the screen filled with Kimi's face as she used her ice axe and crampons to arrest her progress towards the chasm.

Kimi was looking away from the screen as every climber in the room turned to look first at her, then at the white-faced Brooke at the back.

"Damn it, Brooke, you piece of crap, stop screaming and get a Prusik on that line. Get ready to haul your ass out of there." Kimi's voice echoed around the room as Brooke's screams filled in her part.

An image of Brooke dangling on the rope filled the screen, the ice water of the glacial stream cascading over her head and thundering its way down into the moulin. Everyone stared at the screen in open-mouthed fascination as Kimi fixed her ice screws, proceeded to tie off her belay, and crawled across the ice on her belly. Jayden watched Brooke as her face went from white to grey to red. Her eyes were fixed on a point on the carpet, and Jayden could feel the angry waves coming off her from across the room.

"Are you kidding me?" Kimi's voice filled the room. "You've not even got a fucking Prusik set up."

Jayden debated hitting the *pause* button at this point. It was what she'd originally planned. But now she thought better of it. She wanted them to see what Kimi did in the face of the moment, rather than have them come up with solutions that might have been "better" or more elegant but not what they would have come up with in the real life-and-death situation as she did. So she let the film play on.

"Are you really just going to sit there and die?" Kimi screamed into the cavern. Angela had left in the full thirty seconds of the emotions playing across Kimi's face. Everyone saw it. Every single anguish-filled second. Then they all saw the determination settle on her features.

Jaws were slack with wonder and awe as Kimi dug her heels into the ice and hoisted Brooke's dead weight from the frozen jaws of the glacier.

The camera zoomed in on Brooke's chattering teeth, blue-tinged lips, and ghostly pale face. Jayden pressed *pause* as Kimi grabbed Brooke by the collar and started to wrestle her out of her wet coat.

Then she waited. She waited for Brooke to storm out of the room. Which she did.

Then she waited for the questions to start. Which they did.

"How the fuck did you manage to pull her heavy ass out of there?" Hunter clapped Kimi on the back and stared at her with open awe. He squeezed her bicep. "You really Iron Man under those little weedy arms?" The grin on his face let everyone know how much his gentle ribbing was a mark of respect.

Jayden held up her hands, and they all sat back down. "Oh yeah. The girl did good. She thought on her feet, kept her wits about her, and did not give up. I think that's the most any of us can hope to achieve in a situation like that. So why am I showing you all this?"

"To impress upon us the importance of the training you gave us?" Tomasi asked.

"That's one thing."

"So we can discuss the awesome rescue Kimi performed and figure out if there was anything that might have made it easier?" Taylor added. She was the next smallest in the group, and Jayden was certain she was wondering if she could have performed as well as Kimi in the same situation.

"Yup." Jayden nodded to Simon, and he pressed a button to bring up a few graphics she'd had him prepare. "When attempting a rescue for someone who is unable to assist in their own rescue efforts for whatever reason. Could be they're unconscious—"

"Or fucking pathetic," a voice from the back said.

"Or physically injured," Jayden continued, ignoring the outburst. "Then you need to think of how you could manage that in the pairs you end up working with. Consider this an additional part of your challenge prep. Do you have the equipment with you that you would need if you were teamed with a bigger, heavier teammate? For example, Taylor, if you were teamed with Luiji, would this ratchet system be enough for you to pull his weight up like that?"

Taylor frowned. "No. He's got seventy pounds and almost a foot on me. I'd need a more sophisticated system to be able to haul his weight."

Jayden nodded. "Exactly. Homework over the next week for you all—think about the systems you could employ in this scenario. Think about what equipment you need to add to your standard kit to do so. And then think about what you can do to avoid being in this situation in the first place."

"You mean other than staying at home?" Luiji joked.

"Always an option, Lui." She chuckled, and the room laughed with her. "Any questions?"

Oskar raised his hand.

"Go ahead, Oskar."

"Kimi shouldn't be in the drop zone. She doesn't deserve to be in the climb-off with the rest of us. What she did..." He shook his head. "She doesn't deserve to have to fight for a place."

Jayden flicked her eyes to Rhian and then back to Oskar. "I'm sorry, but the rules are very clear. Any failure to complete a challenge means the drop zone. We've tried to find a way around it, but there isn't one. Short of her winning one of the top two places in the climb-off...I'm afraid there's nothing we can do about it right now."

Kimi was staring at the floor, her cheeks burning with what? Embarrassment? Anger? Jayden smiled to herself. Probably both, if she was any judge of the young woman.

"But that's not right," Oskar persisted. Murmurs of assent gathered pace around the room.

"I'm sorry. I truly am. I think what Kimi did out there was superhuman, and if I was climbing, she's the kind of person I'd want on my team. No question. But *my* hands are tied in this."

She hoped they'd pick up on the stress she put on the word and figure out what she was asking them to do. But it was up to them now.

"I'll see you all in the morning for the climb-off. Nine o'clock, guys." She smiled at them all, caught Rhian's eye, and nodded for her to follow her to the lobby.

When she stopped behind her, Jayden wrapped her fingers around her upper arms and tugged her a little closer. "You okay?"

Rhian nodded as she leant back as far as Jayden's grip would allow. Her eyes were wide, and her breath seemed to catch as she said quietly, "I've let Rachel know how we used the video, and we've changed the password on the Wi-Fi. I think we'll just tell them it's down for the night and let it go." Rhian's tone was all business, the words clipped. Just like they had been since she'd run away from Jayden. The consummate professional. And it was driving Jayden mad.

"I think that's a good idea. Thanks."

Rhian started to pull away, then stopped. Her gaze softened as she licked her lips and asked quietly, "You okay?"

The uncertainty in Rhian's voice made Jayden realise that the consummate professional she'd being faced with was an act, one Rhian had assumed just for her. It made her heart ache and drained what little was left of her energy. "Just tired."

"You sure? I know it must have been…difficult for you."

Jayden raised an eyebrow. It was the first time Rhian had made any sort of mention of the knowledge she'd gained about Jayden's past. "Well, it wasn't fun, that's for sure. But it worked out all right in the end." A chorus of "Super Kimi" was being chanted around the common room. Jayden grinned. "I think they'll all be okay too."

Rhian wasn't meeting her eyes again. Her gaze seemed locked on the button on Jayden's chest. "I'm sorry, Jayden."

"Whatever for? You've got nothing to be sorry about."

Rhian finally looked up at her, and Jayden saw such anguish in her eyes that all she could do was pull her into her arms

"Oh, sweetheart, it's not your fault."

"Yes, it is." She pushed out of Jayden's embrace and rushed up the stairs. Jayden started to follow her.

"Leave her alone." Mel's voice was hard. "Haven't you done enough?"

"Excuse me?" Jayden turned to face her.

"Look," she said, dropping her voice to a whisper, "I get that you've made a deal with the devil."

"What are you talking about?"

"Rachel." She grabbed Jayden's arm and pulled her outside, not stopping until they were both sitting on the bench in the middle of the lawn. "I know you and Rhian have to carry on playing the happy couple while everyone's around. But can't you see what you're doing to her? Leave her alone when it's just the two of you. Haven't you hurt her enough already?"

"Hurt her? Believe me, that's the last thing I want to do."

"Then why are you playing these games with her? She might not be able to see what you're doing; she's too close. But I can. Adventure trips, meals out." She curled her lip. "First you tell her you don't want her, then you behave like you do. You're messing with her head, and I want to know why. Is this some sort of revenge for her getting you to do this project, or something equally idiotic? Because I'm warning you—"

"Whoa, whoa, whoa there. I'm not trying to get revenge on Rhian for anything. I don't know what could possibly make you think that."

"I just told you. You're messing with her head."

"I'm not."

"Then why are you acting like you're trying to woo her when you already told her you don't want her?"

"I never said that."

"Didn't you?"

Jayden shook her head.

"Really? Then why is she convinced you did?"

"Rhian was the one who said she wasn't attracted to me. So much so that she wasn't even sure she could even pretend to be attracted to me." Those words still stung.

Mel's glare softened a little. "Tell me what she actually said."

"She said she didn't think she could pretend to be attracted to me."

"Why not?"

"Well, clearly because I'm that unattractive to her. So I said not to worry, I wasn't attracted to her either, and we could just be friends, just do the girlfriendy bits when other people were around." She shook her head.

"Why am I even telling you all this? It's none of your business." She started to stand, but Mel grabbed her arm and pulled her back to her seat.

"It is my business. And you're wrong."

Jayden frowned and pursed her lips. "About what?"

"Her reason for admitting she didn't think she could pretend to be attracted to you. It's not because she finds you repulsive."

"It's not?"

"No."

"Then why did she say it?"

"She wanted to be honest with you, but you never let her finish, from what I can gather."

"Honest about what?"

"Are you really this clueless?"

"Apparently."

Mel sighed. "If you do anything, and I mean anything, to make me regret telling you this, I will personally hunt you down and string you out for the birds. Do you understand me?"

"Regret what?"

"Rhian is in love with you, you great buffoon."

Jayden stared at her. "Funny. Now tell me what's going on."

Mel glared at her. "She thinks you blame her for forcing you into the mountains after the trauma you went through in Nepal. She knows you lost your partner out there and doesn't blame you for thinking the worst of her. She thinks you're not attracted to her, or worse, that you despise her for her part in making you do this show, and meanwhile, she's in love with you. And it's breaking her heart. She begged Rachel to let her go home because it's tearing her apart to be around you every day, to have to pretend to everyone else to be what she so dearly wants to be, and then pretend to you that it's all for show. You, Jayden, you are messing with her head for reasons I can't quite fathom, and in doing so, you're ripping her to pieces."

"I think you're wrong."

"I don't really care what you think. Just stop playing games with her."

"I'm not."

"Yes, you are. We've already been over that." She sighed heavily again. "Look, believe me or don't believe me, that's your choice. But if you look at her, I mean really look at her, you'll see it. It's written on her face how she feels about you. Every time she sees you, she lights up. When you smile at her, it's like she's watching the most beautiful thing in the world, and then she remembers that you don't want her and that it's all a lie. And another piece of her dies. So, please, just leave her be." With that, Mel stood and disappeared back into the conclave.

Part of her wanted to run inside, go to Rhian, and ask her if it was true. Another part of her couldn't quite believe it and wanted to run away. Did this explain why Rhian's reaction to finding out about Nepal and thinking she'd hurt Jayden had caused such an extreme response?

She needed to process what Mel had said. Was it true? Could Rhian have feelings for her? All this time? Had she been trying to woo a woman who was already in love with her? No wonder Mel thought she was messing with her head if that was the case. Christ, this was a mess.

Jayden stood and started back to the house. She was too tired to think any more; her brain just wasn't up to it. Tomorrow. She'd figure it all out tomorrow.

CHAPTER 32

THE CLIMBING WALL WAS A massive selection of differently coloured walls with grips of all shapes and sizes bolted to the surface. Top ropes were fixed in place on the entry-level walls. The more accomplished climbers could attack routes, attaching their own protection to quick draws as they climbed. A sprint climb was a simple creature: a race to the top of an equivalent grade climb for the two competing climbers. The first to press the buzzer at the top of the twenty-metre-high wall would be the winner.

The races were set up so each climber would face the other three. The climber who won the most races was the winner. The first race was Brooke versus Kimi. They were both tied into their belay lines, Oskar on one belay—Brooke's—while Liv had Kimi's.

Jayden stood ready with an air horn to get the race under way. She waited until Angela was ready. She had guys at the top of the wall hanging over the edge with a camera to film from above, fixed cameras in locations all around the gym, and a recording helmet cam on each contestant. A soft chant began. "Super Kimi. Super Kimi. Super Kimi."

Jayden smiled and held her hand up for quiet.

"Contestants, take your marks."

Kimi flexed her knees, preparing to run to the wall and take her first hold.

"Set."

Brooke clenched her fingers together.

"Go."

Kimi was the first to the wall despite her shorter legs, and her powerful dynamic technique propelled her up the first ten feet easily. Brooke fumbled her first hold and slipped before catching up, but her longer reach ate into the headway Kimi had established.

"Super Kimi. Super Kimi."

Jayden held her hands up, begging the crowd of climbers for quiet as Kimi set herself for another huge jump up the wall. She was ten feet clear of Brooke, and the taller climber was slowing. Placing her hands and feet deliberately.

"She's given up again," a voice whispered from behind Jayden. She wasn't sure whose it was, but she had to agree with the assessment. It did indeed look like Brooke wasn't going to compete. Or was it that she knew she couldn't and so had decided to save herself for the next round? Either way, Kimi reached the top of the wall and buzzed her victory quickly and easily. She was back on the ground and releasing herself from the rope when Brooke reached the top of her climb.

When Brooke was back on the ground and she and Kimi had both grabbed a bottle of water each, Jayden turned to Liv and Oskar. "You're up next, guys. Tie in. Brooke and Kimi will belay for you too. Once the cameras are set, I'll give you the signal to race."

Liv and Oskar tied in and stood ready.

"Contestants, take your marks," Jayden said when Angela gave her the cue. Liv stepped forward, but Oskar turned to face the camera.

"It was my error on the wall that cost our team time and points. I concede the race to Liv." He unclipped his helmet and began to untie the knot on his harness.

"Oskar, are you sure?" Jayden asked. She hadn't expected him to do this.

He nodded. "I made the error. I will take the consequences of that. I won't make my teammate battle me for a safe place that should have been hers anyway." He smiled at Liv. "I'm sorry I didn't listen to you out there. You warned me that the pitch I was trying didn't have a summit route. I was sure I could find one. If we'd taken your route initially, we wouldn't have lost the four hours I spent trying to find one that didn't exist." He offered his hand for her to shake. "You win this race."

"You could have been right," Liv said. "And we could have gained a substantial lead. I agreed to take the risk with you."

"Only after I pushed it on you." He pressed his hand further towards her.

Reluctantly she took it and nodded, accepting his concession. Applause and cheers spread like wildfire around the room.

"Okay. Liv, you're still tied in, Brooke, you're up."

Liv nodded and turned back to stare at the wall while Brooke prepared herself to climb again. Both were of similar height and build. In theory it was a very even match, but, again, Brooke was outpaced as Liv hauled herself up the wall and struck the buzzer first. Brooke's hand struck less than a minute later. Climbers enthusiastically high-fived Liv as she grabbed a drink, towelled off her shoulders, and switched with Kimi again.

Kimi versus Oskar. A match everyone expected Oskar to win...but not by much. Kimi's dynamic movements and leaps up the wall made her a formidable opponent to any of the climbers in the pack, and they all knew it. They tied in and buckled their helmets in place.

"Contestants, take your marks."

Oskar turned to the camera again. "I concede this race."

Silence from the gathered crowd greeted his statement.

"What?" Kimi cried. "Why?"

Oskar turned to her. "You don't deserve to be in this climb-off either. What you did out there," he said, putting his hand over his heart, "was truly heroic. You deserve your place here. All the way." He offered his hand.

"You didn't cause me to be here."

"No, but this is my way of paying my respects. Take the win, Super Kimi." He grinned, his hand still held out to her. A soft chant began in the crowd. "Super Kimi. Super Kimi." Her cheeks blazed red, and her eyes burned with embarrassment, but she shook his hand.

"Thank you."

"Oh no. Thank you." Oskar pulled her into a hug and whispered into her ear something Jayden couldn't hear but that made Kimi slap his ribs. He leant back, laughing.

"Right. Well, Liv, I guess it's you against Kimi, then." Jayden said.

Liv shook her head. "I won't even bother to tie in. I concede the race to Kimi as well. She single-handedly dragged Brooke out of a crevasse and saved her life. I don't need a race to tell me she's a better climber than I am.

She's already proved it." She held her hand out to Kimi too, then tugged her in for a hug, laughing at the look of shock on Kimi's face. "You earned it."

The chanting grew louder, and Jake lifted Kimi up on his shoulders. Rhian stood beside Jayden and spoke softly. "This is the real reason you wanted them to see the footage, isn't it?"

"I hoped they'd be honourable enough to do the right thing, yes."

Rhian turned to her. "Let's hope the viewers see it that way when they miss out on the excitement of the races."

"Oh, I think you'll find the viewers will love this little twist. It's a one-off, after all."

"Hm. Let's hope so. Did you know Oskar would concede to Liv too?"

"No. That was a shock. A nice one. But a shock." She tucked her hand into the small of Rhian's back and bent to whisper in her ear. "I've been getting a few shocks lately."

"You have?"

"Yes. I think I need to talk to you about one of them later."

Rhian shook her head. "I'm sorry. I'm going to be busy with post-production and meetings."

"Please, Rhian. It's important."

"I can't. I'm sorry. You should take care of the final race."

Okay. This wasn't the right place or the right time to push her own agenda. No matter how much she'd tried to sleep last night, she hadn't been able to. She'd spent the whole night going over and over every interaction she'd had with Rhian, looking at them through different eyes. She didn't focus so much on the ones in public, where they could argue they were putting on a show, but on the ones where no other eyes were watching them—the ones eating dinner and talking in Jayden's apartment. She remembered every look Rhian couldn't seem to drag her gaze away from, the little blushes when Jayden made a joke, and the shy glances when Jayden wasn't supposed to be looking. Mel was right. It was all there. And it was time for them both to stop playing games.

But this wasn't the place.

Jayden quickly called Brooke and Oskar to the line, and Brooke tied in. She smirked across at Oskar as Jayden called them to their marks. Clearly, she was expecting Oskar to concede the race to her as he had to both the other girls. He didn't.

As soon as Jayden shouted go, he sprang into action and was halfway up the wall before Brooke had collected herself and climbed five feet. It was no contest. He was back on the ground and unclipped before she reached the top.

His time was slower than Kimi's race to the top by three seconds, but his concessions put him second to last on the leader board. He would face Brooke in the public vote. Given the wide smile on his face, he didn't seem displeased by the outcome. Angela and a cameraman approached him.

"Oskar, you are in the bottom two. You could be going home. Are you worried?" she asked him.

He shrugged. "It's in the hands of the people at home now. Whatever they decide, I'll abide by that. I made a mistake out there that cost my teammate a safe place into the next round. I accept the consequences of that."

"Your time was fast. You could have beaten Liv up the wall and secured your own place, maybe even beaten Kimi. It was close—"

"No. The results of this contest are right and fair. I can live with what I've done today." He glanced pointedly at Brooke. "Liv and Kimi deserve to go through, no doubt in my mind. If that means I go home after the vote, then so be it." He shrugged. "I have to live with myself after the show ends too. And I know that even if I go home now, I can do that."

"Thanks, Oskar," Angela said and moved off to interview Brooke. "Brooke, you've had a difficult few days. How do you feel about facing the public vote?"

"I have clearly been targeted by the group, and the production company has allowed this to happen because of personal differences."

Angela cleared her throat. "I'm sure it must be difficult for you. Are you concerned the public will vote you out?"

"I think the public will do the right thing and keep me in the competition. They will be able to see I've been victimised here. That these so-called climbers are clearly threatened by me and have conspired to get rid of a challenger."

"Thanks," Angela concluded and turned off the camera.

"She's deluded," Liv said from behind Angela. "She should have done the honourable thing and conceded her race to Kimi. She shouldn't be on the ice if she can't handle herself in a time of crisis. She put herself and other people at risk. There's no conspiracy. It's quite simple. No one wants to climb with a climber who's going to put their lives at risk." She turned to face Brooke before she said, "You going back out there is going to get someone killed. If not yourself, then someone else. No one wants to be responsible for that."

Jayden was immensely glad the camera was no longer recording as the shouts of the other climbers chorused Liv's outburst and the noise in the gym grew.

Jayden put her fingers between her lips and whistled loudly. Silence followed as they all turned to look at her.

"That's enough, guys. This will go out tonight. Then the voting will be open for twenty-four hours. You know the drill. Oskar, Brooke, get packed up. Whoever has the lowest number of votes will be leaving immediately from here." She looked around at the angry faces and the pouting Brooke. "And I don't want to hear any more about this. It's done."

"But—" Brooke began.

"No buts. It's done. We've dealt with it, it's over. Now move on."

They all grumbled as they left the climbing gym and headed back to the conclave. Jayden rubbed her eyes and pinched the bridge of her nose. What a day.

When she looked up, she was alone.

What a week.

CHAPTER 33

RHIAN YAWNED AS SHE CLIMBED the stairs to the fourth floor. The editing and post-production was a tedious process of tiny cuts and piecing together a timeline of images into a cohesive piece that not only made sense and told a story but told a compelling story. Fortunately, they had more than enough material. More than enough drama and excitement. Rachel was torn between ecstasy and despair at the mention of Brooke being in the first public vote-off.

She'd giggled gleefully when Rhian had told her of the results of the sprint climbs and suggested that Angela and Simon tweak the order so that Brooke's races were concluded before the concessions played out. Both had agreed and quickly reworked the session. They'd also done a masterful job on cutting some of the more damning remarks Brooke had made in her closing interview statement.

All in all, Rachel and the clients were all happy with the show that was to be released tomorrow. Now all Rhian had to do was figure out how to get some sleep. Her head hurt, and her eyes felt gritty. She rounded the landing and approached her door, key in hand.

"Hey."

Rhian jumped at the voice coming from the floor. She glanced down to see Jayden leaning with her back to Rhian's bedroom door, elbows resting on her knees and a sleepy smile on her face. She swallowed and clenched her jaw. *Not now. I can't deal with anything now, I'm too tired.*

"Long day?" Jayden asked gently, unfolding herself from her position.

"Very." Intent on ignoring her as much as possible, she brushed by Jayden and slipped her key into the door. "I need to get some sleep before—"

Jayden grasped her upper arm and stilled her. "I won't keep you long. I promise. But please just give me a couple of minutes."

She let her head fall to her chest. She didn't want to look at Jayden. Not right now. She knew she'd cry if she did—again. She hated how emotional she felt and tried to blame it on lack of sleep. But it was a lie, and she knew it. She just couldn't stand it anymore. She couldn't stand what she had done to Jayden anymore. Watching her reaction to Brooke's accident on the ice had only driven it home, and it had taken everything she had to remain professional. She'd seen Jayden shaking out her hands like she was trying to get the blood flowing in them. She'd seen Jayden's face turn grey and the ragged way her breath had shuddered into her chest. She'd held it together by only a thread. And it only made Rhian realise the hopelessness of her own situation—loving a woman who could never love her back. A woman she had only ever hurt.

"Please don't, Jayden. I can't."

"Why not? Why can't you talk to me?"

She closed her eyes.

"I'm not going anywhere, you know? If you don't talk to me now, I'll be back in the morning. Then I'll be here tomorrow. And tomorrow night, and then the next day. And every day until you do."

Rhian closed her eyes, knowing there was no way around this conversation. If she was honest with herself, she should have spoken to Jayden as soon as she got back. She owed her that much. Jayden deserved no less.

"Not out here." She pushed the door open, and Jayden followed her inside. The quiet click of the door closing behind them echoed in the small room. Rhian slipped off her jacket and went to hang it in the wardrobe. She didn't turn around. She knew she wouldn't be able to say what she needed to if she had to look at Jayden too.

"I-I need to apologise to you and thank you. And to tell you that you don't have to pretend to b-be my girlfriend anymore. I'm sorry for letting it go on so long. And I don't care what Rachel says. It's just too cruel to make you keep pretending. Not after what I've done to you."

"What have you done to me?"

Rhian crossed the room and stared out of the window with unseeing eyes. "I understand now. Why you didn't want to do this project. Why you didn't want to go out there. Fen told me. About Nepal. I made you go back out there. I understand why you hate me."

"Hate you?" Jayden was close to Rhian's back. "I don't hate you."

Tears slipped down Rhian's face. "It's okay. I get it. I'd hate me too, if I were you."

Jayden gripped her upper arms and turned her away from the window. "I don't hate you, Rhian." She wiped the tears away with her thumbs. "I don't blame you, and I don't hate you. Yes, you gave me a shove to get me back out there. But I am still a grown-up. I could have still said no, despite the threat of lawsuits."

"I'm so sorry." Rhian's voice broke as she whispered the words.

"I needed it. I needed the reason, the excuse, to get off my backside and do what I needed to do to heal. You gave me a gift. A chance to feel alive again. To be me again. I don't want an apology for that. I owe you a debt of thanks that I don't know I'll ever be able to repay."

"You don't have to be nice to me just because I'm crying."

Jayden chuckled and wiped her cheeks again. "Trust me, I wouldn't." She traced her thumb along Rhian's lower lip. "If I didn't want to be nice to you, I wouldn't."

Rhian frowned. "I don't understand."

"Don't you?" Jayden smiled, her gaze locked on Rhian's. "Really?"

Rhian shook her head.

"Then I guess I'll have to go out on a limb here and explain it to you." She slid one hand into Rhian's hair, cradling her head as she lowered her mouth to Rhian's and trailed her other hand down Rhian's throat.

Rhian moaned at that first contact. Jayden's lips were as soft and warm as she remembered. Her tongue traced the outline of Rhian's mouth, flickered against her lips, seeking an entry Rhian was only too willing to grant, even as her mind screamed at her. Jayden's tongue danced with her own, exploring every inch of her mouth. The fingers around her throat caressed the pulse point and slipped under her collar, Jayden's thumb resting at the V between her collarbones. Slowly, the kiss came to an end with Jayden resting her forehead against Rhian's.

"Now do you understand?"

Rhian shook her head. "You said you weren't attracted to me."

Jayden stepped back, tucking her hands in her pockets. "Only because you said it first." She shrugged. "You kind of bruised my ego there a little bit."

"What? That's not…" Rhian looked up at Jayden, trying to recall the details of a conversation she'd tried very hard to forget. "That's not what I was trying to say."

"Then what were you trying to say?"

Rhian pinched the bridge of her nose and made a decision she hoped she'd be able to live with. "I was trying to say I wasn't sure I could just pretend to be attracted to you because I really was attracted to you. I wasn't sure I could separate the pretence from what I really felt, and didn't want to make you uncomfortable. I knew you were upset about me forcing you into the whole show in the first place, and then I was saddling you with more of my problems. And now I know why you didn't want the project…I understand." She shook her head. "I thought I understood. And it hurt."

"What hurt?"

"I feel sick at the thought of what I've put you through, Jayden. I haven't slept since I spoke to Fen. I haven't eaten. All I could think was how much you must hate me and how I didn't blame you. I blame me. I knew there was a reason you'd disappeared off the circuit. I knew there had to be. But I never looked for it. I should've done. I should have looked out for you."

"Rhian, you didn't even know me back then. You didn't know what had happened. You have nothing to feel guilty about."

"Yes, I do."

Jayden grasped her arms and shook her gently. "Listen to me." She waited until Rhian was looking directly at her. "I don't blame you. I don't blame anyone. Was I pissed at being backed into a corner at the time? Sure. Was I scared of facing those demons again? Of course I was. But I needed to do it. I needed to get out there like I need the air that I breathe. You gave me the reason I needed to claim back that part of me. I was dying a little every day, sitting in a crummy office answering phones, and visiting my mother. I had nothing. I wasn't living. I was barely even existing. Ask Fen. She'll tell you. I'd run away from everything and everyone. I was a shell. Now I'm me again." She grinned. "I guess I do blame you for that."

Rhian gave her a watery smile. "Sorry."

"Don't be." She wiped at the tears on Rhian's cheeks again. "Now I need to make sure I'm clear on some things here. Okay?"

Rhian nodded with a heavy sigh.

"You were attracted to me back then?"

"Yes."

"And now? Are you still attracted to me?"

Rhian shook her head.

"No?"

"No."

Jayden drew in a shaky breath. "Oh. Then I'm—"

"What I feel for you now is way beyond attraction."

"It is?"

Rhian nodded.

"Way beyond?"

"Yes."

Jayden's lips slid into a wide grin. "Well, that's good, then. Because I'm way beyond attracted to you too."

"You are?"

"Yeah." Jayden took hold of her hand. "Want to know the real reason I stepped in between you and Brooke?"

"Why?"

"Because I couldn't stand her flirting with you, touching you inappropriately. Even when I could see you weren't comfortable with it, it still made me jealous."

"It did?"

Jayden nodded. "'Fraid so." She ran her fingertip down the length of Rhian's neck, from the point of her chin to the hollow at the base of her throat. Her gaze locked on Rhian's lips, scorching her with the incendiary look. "I know you're tired, but before I go, can I kiss you again?"

Rhian nodded and gasped as Jayden's mouth descended on hers. There was nothing gentle in this kiss. It was fire and rock, and it consumed her from the inside out. It was hungry and deep and held her captive in Jayden's passion. She couldn't fight it; she didn't want to. All she could do was wrap her arms around Jayden's waist and ride out the kiss. No, *kiss* was too simple a description for what Jayden was giving her. This was a promise; it was worship. It was devotion and freedom all at the same time. And she never wanted it to end.

"Please don't cry," Jayden whispered against her lips as she slowly backed away from the kiss and wiped Rhian's tears away with her thumbs again.

"Sorry," she said. "I didn't realise I was."

Jayden kissed her forehead. "I know you're exhausted, so I'm going to go now."

Rhian was torn. Part of her wanted to beg Jayden to stay. To curl up against her side and wake up beside her in the morning. Another part of her knew she wasn't ready. She needed to process what had just happened before rushing headlong into something with Jayden. She felt too much already.

"Okay," she whispered against her lips and quickly stole a sweet peck.

"Can I see you tomorrow?"

Rhian smiled. "We've got filming all day. Of course you'll see me tomorrow."

Jayden shook her head. "I meant after filming, or before. See you when it's just us. No one else around, no one else watching. Can I see *you*?"

It took a moment, but Rhian finally understood what Jayden was asking. She kissed the back of Jayden's hand and stared into her eyes. "I never pretended, Jayden. I couldn't. That's what I was trying to explain when all this got so messed up. I couldn't pretend. You've always seen me—the good and the bad."

"There was no bad."

Rhian chuckled softly. "You say that now."

"And I'll say it in a million years."

Rhian shook her head. "Yeah, yeah." She bit her lip. "I really should have talked to you about all this so much earlier, shouldn't I? I guess I have a tendency to shut down in situations like this. I find it so hard…to trust. To believe anything but the worst possible option."

"I noticed." She kissed Rhian's forehead and whispered against her skin, "We'll work on that. We still have a lot to talk about." She leant back to watch Rhian's eyes again and waited while she nodded her agreement. "Promise me you won't shut me out again?" Jayden asked, a gentle smile curling her lips.

"I won't."

"Good. Then it can all wait till tomorrow." Jayden kissed her softly, reverently, then closed the door behind her.

"Night," Rhian whispered to the closed door.

CHAPTER 34

THE ATMOSPHERE IN THE CLIMBING gym was tense. Oskar and Brooke stood on either side of Jayden, backs against the climbing wall, getting ready for Angela to give them the signal to start. Rhian already knew the results, as did Jayden, Angela, and Simon. Everybody else was still guessing.

The cameraman adjusted his angle and motioned to the guy with the microphone boom to raise it up out of his shot, then gave Angela the thumbs up. She nodded to Jayden, and Rhian crossed her arms over her chest.

"Good evening, ladies and gentlemen. Welcome to the results of the first public vote on the race to become *The Amazing Climb* Champion."

Applause, whistles, and catcalls filled the gym. Someone even shouted, "Come on, Oskar!" from the back of the room. Rhian glanced over her shoulder, but she couldn't place the voice...or the culprit. Jayden just rolled with it.

"Thank you to the members of our audience in here with us tonight. The first week has been an ordeal, that's for sure. We've had crevasses, aborted summit runs, reruns, concessions, and defeats. And most of all, we've had your support, viewers. For that we're truly grateful. But now it's my job to let you know the results of this week's public vote. We've whittled it down to two, and it's you who have decided." She held her hand in Brooke's direction. "Either Brooke Shields or Oskar Nowak." She held her other hand out to Oskar.

"And this week, the person with the lowest public vote is..."

Rhian caught the small smile that graced Jayden's lips and couldn't stop herself from remembering last night's kiss. She could still feel the heat of Jayden's body pressed against hers and the velvety softness of those lips.

"Brooke. I'm so, so sorry, Brooke." Jayden faced the crestfallen woman. The look on Brooke's face clearly told everyone that she'd expected to stay. In all honesty, there had been a lot of feedback on social media, and she'd garnered a lot of sympathy for her ordeal. But not a lot of support for her to continue in the process. Liv's damning commentary on how her actions—or, rather, lack of action—would end up costing lives had been "leaked" by Mel, via Luiji, onto Twitter. Clearly, Mel wasn't ready to forgive Brooke for her behaviour.

Meanwhile, Oskar's honourable decision to take the consequences of his mistake in place of his teammate had garnered him huge popularity.

"I'm sure this must be a shock for you," Jayden said to her.

"Yeah. I can see exactly what's happened here, don't you worry."

"Yes, well, clearly the public have cast their votes."

"Sure." She spoke with such a slur to her voice that it was clear she didn't believe that the results were truly those of the public. Jayden needed to wrap this up and fast. The results were being streamed live.

"Well, I'm sure we're all very sorry to see you go, Brooke. The place won't be the same without you," Jayden said and turned back towards the camera. Rhian stifled a laugh as Brooke stared at her indignantly.

Perfect. Just perfect, Rhian thought as Jayden wrapped up her commentary and handed her microphone back to the sound engineer. She grinned as she walked to Rhian, and Brooke slammed the door behind her. Her flight would be leaving in a few hours, and it felt really, really good to be free of her.

Jayden wrapped her arms around Rhian's waist and pulled her in close, whispering into her ear, "Have dinner with me tonight?"

"I'd love to," Rhian said and wrapped her arms around her neck. "You look so good up there on camera."

"Hm, I happen to think you'd be much better at it."

Rhian shook her head, ignoring everyone around them. This wasn't a game anymore. This wasn't for show. It was real. Jayden really wanted to do this. "Your place?"

Jayden shook her head. "I've booked us a table at La Tapera. Is that okay?"

"Sounds lovely. Do I have time to go and change?"

Jayden checked her watch and nodded. "I'll pick you up outside the conclave in thirty minutes. Is that enough time?"

"It'll do," Rhian said as she disentangled herself, and walked out the doors.

CHAPTER 35

THE RESTAURANT WAS LOVELY, THE food delicious, but in truth, Rhian barely looked around her and barely tasted a bite. She couldn't tear her eyes from Jayden. The simple black pants and deep blue silk shirt with the sleeves rolled halfway up her forearms, the top two buttons undone, was more than enough to short-circuit Rhian's brain. Conversation was scarce, but they both seemed entirely okay with the comfortable yet smouldering silence that enveloped them.

As Jayden sipped her wine, licking the drops of claret from her lips, Rhian stared and fought valiantly to prevent herself from climbing across the table and doing the job herself. She longed to taste those lips again. To feel them possess her again.

"Can we...?" Her voice cracked. She coughed and took a sip of water. "Can we get out of here?" she asked as the waiter removed their plates.

Jayden nodded, signalled the waiter for the bill, and quickly settled it. Within a few minutes, they were walking, hand in hand, down the street. The warmth of Jayden's hand in hers was as soothing as it was exciting. The heat from her arm as it brushed her own was scorching, and all she could concentrate on. Not until Jayden was leading her up the steps and into the lobby at the conclave did she realise that Jayden had brought her home.

"You wouldn't rather, erm...go to your house?" she asked shyly.

"I would, but Mark was snoring on the sofa when I left. Poor guy needs his sleep, and I'd rather be alone with you, if you don't mind."

Rhian smiled. "I don't mind." She pointed to the common room. "Want to take some coffee up to my room?"

Jayden smirked. "You're asking me up for coffee?"

Rhian blushed, then swallowed thickly, but didn't look away from Jayden's eyes. "Yes, I am."

It was Jayden's turn to swallow. Hard. Visibly hard. She threaded her fingers through Rhian's and brought her hand up to her lips before gently kissing the back of it. "I don't need anything to drink."

Rhian led her upstairs and slipped her key into the lock.

"Rhian, have you got—oh, sorry. I didn't realise you had a guest." Mel poked her head out of her bedroom door. She leant on the door frame. "Actually, since you're here, I could do with talking to you both. I've got coffee in here."

Jayden sniggered but said nothing. Clearly, the situation was for Rhian to deal with however she wished.

"Mel, it'll have to wait till tomorrow." She smiled and ducked her head, wanting to slip into the room and ignore the fact Mel would no doubt take the piss in the morning.

"Jayden." Mel's voice was low, almost a warning growl, so unusual from her normal light and airy tone that Rhian frowned and watched the look that passed between the two of them.

"Mel? Jayden? What's—"

"No games, Mel." Jayden wrapped her arm around Rhian's waist and pulled her in close. "I love her."

Rhian stared up at her, not understanding why they were talking like this, but quite frankly, she didn't care. Had Jayden really just said that? More importantly, did she really mean it?

Mel pointed a finger at Jayden. "Then you damn well better look after her."

Jayden grinned and kissed the top of Rhian's head. "I intend to."

Mel disappeared back into her room, and Rhian waited for Jayden to look at her. When she did, she saw the truth in Jayden's eyes. Still, she needed to hear the words.

"Did you mean it?"

Jayden lifted one corner of her mouth. "Oh yes. I intend to take good care of you." She tightened her hold around Rhian and pulled her into a deep kiss, one hand holding her tight to her body, the other sliding down to grope Rhian's backside. Rhian groaned into the kiss and arched her body into the touch.

She was panting when Jayden backed away and pushed open the door. "I meant the other bit."

"I know." She closed the door behind them and snapped on the light. "I meant that too."

"We barely know each other." Rhian reached for the buttons on Jayden's shirt, before toying with the top one, which was half in and half out of its hole. The heels of her palms brushed the tops of Jayden's breasts.

"Doesn't seem to matter. I know how I feel." She ran her fingers over the sleeve of Rhian's dress—slowly up her arms, over her shoulders, and her neck before diving into her hair at the back. "I like your dress. The grey matches your eyes." She scratched her nails gently over Rhian's scalp.

"Thank you." She closed her eyes and leant into the tender touch. Jayden's lips began to trace lines across her skin, from her jaw to her chin, across her eyelids, down her cheeks, and eventually claiming her lips. Rhian gripped the shirt beneath her fingers into her clenched fists and moaned at the way Jayden's hands held her head while she plundered her mouth. Possessive yet tender, passionate yet soothing. And Rhian only wanted more.

She worked the buttons until they succumbed and bared Jayden's chest to her questing hands, leaving goose bumps in her wake. She pushed the fabric from her shoulders and heard the whisper of it hitting the ground. Then all she heard was Jayden's heart beating beneath her fingertips, the blood rushing through her own ears, and her own throaty moan as Jayden pulled back and turned her around.

"As lovely as it is, it still needs to go." Jayden gathered her hair at the back of her neck and slipped it over one shoulder. She placed tiny kisses all along the nape, along the hairline, and the back of her ears. Her fingers brushed the top of the zipper. "May I?"

Rhian nodded, and wrapped her hands around Jayden's thighs, half as a means of keeping herself grounded and half to keep as much contact with her body as she possibly could.

With a soft tug at the back of her dress and the slow give of teeth, the fabric parted. Jayden's lips wandered down the newly exposed skin, slowly taking in every millimetre she bared. Rhian let her head fall forward, swaying under the attention. One of Jayden's strong arms slinked about her waist and held her up as the kisses continued.

When the zipper was finally all the way down, gentle fingers parted the garment and pushed it from her shoulders. Open-mouthed kisses, licks, and tiny sucks painted her back, and Rhian wasn't sure how much longer she'd be able to stand up.

"So beautiful," Jayden murmured against her skin, the vibrations from her lips adding to the scope of the sensations Rhian was feeling.

The arm at her waist disappeared, and her dress pooled at her feet. She pressed her back against Jayden's chest, not in the least self-conscious as she stood in Jayden's arms in her bra, knickers, stockings, and heels. She reached up over her shoulder to the back of Jayden's head and tugged her down, turning her head for the kiss she desperately needed, their height difference, for once, playing to her advantage. Jayden's hands slid over her belly, cupped her breasts, explored the sensitive skin of her hips and upper thighs, and still seemed to want more.

Rhian reached between their bodies with her right hand and managed to awkwardly thumb open the button on Jayden's pants and drop them to the floor. Jayden pulled away from the kiss a moment as she stepped out of her pants and kicked them away, her hands still roaming Rhian's body.

"Fuck me, that's hot," Jayden whispered, her gaze fixed over Rhian's head. With glazed eyes, she followed Jayden's stare. The door to the bathroom was open, and Rhian saw them in the mirror. The black satin that cupped her breasts was interrupted by a large hand as Jayden pressed and squeezed one, then dipped inside the cup of the other.

Rhian had never seen anything so erotic as the sight of Jayden's hand working her breasts under her bra. It enhanced every sensation. The gentle scrape of a fingernail over her nipple almost buckled her knees, and the image of Jayden's hand slithering down her stomach, tantalising the elastic on her hip, drew a long groan from her lips and a knowing smirk from Jayden.

She pulled at the elastic, lowering it on one side, and slid one fingertip beneath it. In and out, and in and out, setting a slow rhythm, but one Rhian was desperate to keep.

"Please," she begged.

Jayden kissed below her ear, nipped the tender lobe with her teeth, and whispered, "Please what?"

"Don't tease." She covered Jayden's hands with her own, adding another level to the visual and sensory overload while she tried to guide Jayden's hand inside her underwear.

"But teasing's so much fun." But she seemed to know that Rhian was way past teasing. She pushed her hand lower, skimming the hair at the apex of Rhian's thighs, then down further, curling her fingers to cup the wet heat of Rhian's need and play over her distended clit.

Rhian groaned and let her head fall back against Jayden's chest. She moved her feet a little further apart, trying desperately to keep her eyes open to watch. She'd never seen anything so incredibly erotic, never imagined seeing herself like this—with her lover—could be such a turn-on, but it was. Everything she saw heightened the physical response. She'd never felt so aroused before, never needed a touch as much as she needed Jayden's right then. And Jayden didn't disappoint.

She ran the pads on her fingers along the length of her clit, slid over it, and flicked the tip gently, watching Rhian's response until she settled on the one that had caused Rhian's hips to jerk the most and triggered a rush of arousal Jayden couldn't possibly have missed. If she hadn't been so turned on, she would have been embarrassed by it. Instead, Jayden's obvious appreciation had just the opposite effect. She revelled in her own lack of inhibition. It wasn't a conscious decision to bring her own hands up to her breasts and lavish them with attention, tugging and twisting at her nipples. She was beyond making such a decision. She was operating on instinct, on need, on desire.

"That's it, baby. Show me what you need."

"I don't think I can stand up." Rhian was panting.

Jayden's arm was secure around her waist. "I've got you." Her other hand continued to stroke Rhian beneath her panties, then slipped lower. Rhian cried out as a finger pressed inside her. Her knees weakened, and if not for Jayden's strength, she would have collapsed to the floor. "Keep touching your breasts. Show me."

Rhian bucked her hips against Jayden's hand and yanked down the cups of her bra, letting her breasts spill out into her hands. She pinched and squeezed as she writhed, a creature of sensation, beyond thought, existing only in the need, the desire to have Jayden take her.

Jayden's lips fastened on to her neck. Her teeth nipped at Rhian's skin before she bathed it with her tongue and plunged her finger into Rhian's centre faster.

"Oh God," Rhian cried out as the first curl of her orgasm twisted in her belly. "Don't stop."

"Never," Jayden promised and added a second finger to her thrust.

It was enough. Rhian screamed as her legs gave out, and her twitching body took them both to the floor. A tidal wave of pleasure surged through her as freely as the emotional hurricane that hit her, wrenching shudders of orgasm alongside the tears that flowed down her cheeks.

Aftershocks still rippled through her body as she lay in Jayden's arms, one hand resting at her waist, the other still buried between her thighs.

"Did I hurt you?"

She shook her. "God, no."

"You're crying."

Rhian eased her legs apart. Jayden gently withdrew, and Rhian rolled over so they were face-to-face. "I love you too, Jayden." She leant forward and kissed her—a soft kiss, an affirming kiss, one devoid of the heat from moments ago but not the emotion. Jayden whimpered as Rhian pulled back and glanced at the bed above them. "Let's move this somewhere a little more comfortable. I know I can't hold you up like that."

Jayden grinned as she rolled onto her hands and knees, then stood. "It was worth it, though." She trailed a finger along the slope of Rhian's breast and watched as the nipple hardened again. Rhian slapped her hand away and reached behind her and unfastened the hooks, quickly dropping the bra to the ground.

"My turn," she said and reached for Jayden's sports bra, then whisked it over her head and tossing it on the floor. "You. Bed. Now."

Jayden laughed. "You're bossy when you're monosyllabic."

"Get your clothes off while you're at it. See? Not monosyllabic now."

"Still bossy, though."

She grinned salaciously as Jayden stripped and climbed onto the bed. "Believe me, you haven't even seen bossy yet."

Jayden's eyes opened wide, and an eyebrow hiked up to her hairline. "I can't wait." She didn't have to wait long. Rhian kicked off her heels and climbed onto the bed before crawling up the length of Jayden's body like a lioness stalking her prey. She licked her lips and studied Jayden's body as she crawled higher, dipping her head now and then to kiss or lick some body part or another that captured her attention.

When Rhian reached her breasts, Jayden sighed as a gentle tongue licked the pebbled nipple, then grunted as teeth raked across the tender flesh, only to receive a kiss in return. Rhian's attentions wandered, never staying long enough in one place before another one caught her attention. At least not long enough for Jayden's liking.

"Now who's the tease?" Jayden asked, her voice deep and throaty with desire.

Rhian grinned up at her, nipple between her teeth, and flicked her tongue across the aching tip. Jayden threaded her fingers through Rhian's hair and pulled her up for a kiss, a deep, passionate, and emotion-filled one that left Jayden wet and wanting and desperate for Rhian's most intimate of kisses. Rhian skimmed down her body and settled between her legs. Her knicker-clad backside was in the air, tantalising Jayden with the memories of her hand playing beneath the fabric as Rhian spread her open and slid her tongue into the wetness between her legs.

Her reaction was instantaneous. She drew her knees up and rolled her head from side to side. Rhian's tongue never stilled. She licked, sucked, and kissed every millimetre of Jayden, ratcheting her desire higher and higher until there was nothing beneath her but Rhian and orgasm. She crested on Rhian's tongue as Rhian slid a finger deep inside her body and she bucked and jerked in response. Fire coursed through her, bathing her in white light and branding her with the touch that would claim her soul. Rhian.

When she finally returned to her body, minutes or hours later, Rhian was resting at her side, head pillowed on her hand, drawing lazy patterns across her skin with her fingertips.

"Hi there," she whispered, a smile on her face.

"Wow." Jayden stretched, enjoying the subtle ache in her body that reminded her just how long it had been since she had been touched intimately.

"You okay?"

Jayden nodded. "Just been a while, and that was a little...energetic, shall we say."

Rhian frowned. "Is that...is that okay?"

Jayden chuckled and pulled her into a tight embrace. "More than okay, sweetheart. More than."

Rhian sighed and rested her head on Jayden's chest. "Good. I think I like energetic."

Jayden laughed and kissed the top of Rhian's head. "I love you."

Rhian looked up at her, rested her chin on her chest, and grinned. "And I love you."

"Excellent." She slithered her hand down Rhian's back and snagged her fingers in the elastic at her hips. "Now let's get you naked and see what the rest of the night brings."

"Who's bossy now?" Rhian said as Jayden flipped her onto her back and made quick work of removing her knickers.

She grinned down at her. "I think I might leave the stockings for now." She hovered close to Rhian's ear. "I want to know what they feel like wrapped around me."

CHAPTER 36

THE REALITY TV AWARDS IN London was not something Rhian had ever envisaged being a part of her career, and she wasn't sure what to expect. Fabulously dressed people, enviable hairstyles, a plethora of fake breasts, and lots of air kissing had so far been abundant, but beyond that, all she could truly say was that the virgin mojito was better than the shrimp canapés. In truth, the conversation she needed to have with Rachel later was playing on her mind.

The auditorium was huge and seats were filling all around them. Jayden's hand at the small of her back gently guided her down the wide steps towards a waving, smiling Rachel.

Behind them, Fen eased her way down the steps with her crutches, Mark walking beside her with a drink in one hand, the other ready to help Fen if she needed it. Not that she ever did. Her back was improving day by day, and it was only a matter of time before she would be able to ditch the crutches and start giving them all hell again.

Kimi and Oskar followed, enjoying one of the perks of winning *The Amazing Climb* and attending the award ceremony with them. They would also get to meet with the team that would lead them out to Antarctica and their summit bid on Mount Vinson.

Rachel hugged her when they were finally face-to-face and shook Jayden's hand before ushering them to seats.

"Can you believe this?" she said, excitement colouring her voice. "The finale only aired two weeks ago, and we're here!"

Rhian smiled. Rachel's enthusiasm was infectious. "I know." She threaded her fingers through Jayden's and squeezed gently.

"It's been a hell of a ride, right?"

Jayden chuckled. "That's for damn sure."

Rachel glanced at their joined hands. "Rhi, we need to talk after this. Don't leave before we talk, okay? It's important."

Rhian nodded and waited until Fen and the others were sitting before following her along the row to her seat. She had no intention of leaving early. Little did Rachel know that Rhian had her own important discussion to have with Rachel. The one where she told her that she wasn't coming back to live in England and that she was in love with Jayden and moving to El Chaltén to live with her, thanks for everything, and see you later. She was pretty sure Rachel knew it was coming. Still, she was her mum, the woman who more or less raised her, and she wasn't looking forward to it.

The organisers of the event had managed to snag Davina McCall to host the show, a major coup, as the former *Big Brother* host was always a showstopper. The jokes started, the champagne flowed, and the awards were handed out: Best Female Reality TV Star, Best Male Star, Best Director, Best Sound, Best Format, *and then* Best Cinematography: *The Amazing Climb*.

Simon and Angela bounded up to the stage to collect the award, near speechless as they bumbled through a quick note of thanks to everyone involved for making it such a fabulous show. Rhian, Jayden, Rachel, and the sponsors were on their feet clapping and cheering. Sure, the stunning landscape of Patagonia gave them a vast playground for magnificent cinematography, but they still had to capture it on film. And do it justice.

The presentations continued for the best in editing, in judging panels, the best lifestyle show, and more until they got to the Best Competition Show award: *The Amazing Climb*. Rachel and the CEO of Patagonia walked to the stage to give a rather dry thank-you speech to the contestants, the people who worked behind the scenes, and to all the fans who supported the show.

Still, Rhian had tears in her eyes when Rachel returned to her seat and hugged her tight. This was the culmination of so many months of hard work. And for Rachel, years of hard work to get herself into the position she was in. She was so damn proud of Rachel.

Davina carried on with the show regardless of their emotional hug, finally calling out the winner of the best host award: "Jayden Harris."

Rhian's mouth popped open, and she twisted in her seat to wrap her arms around Jayden's neck. Jayden looked equally stunned, her arms around Rhian's back as she slowly stood amidst the applause and made her way to the stage. She accepted the twelve-inch-high golden trophy and set it down on the podium as she turned to address the audience.

"I shouldn't be here," she started.

Laughter tickled the room.

"No, seriously. Six months ago, when this project was suggested to me, I had to be press-ganged into it. I think *blackmail* is the most accurate description of the conversation, though we've taken to calling it *gentle persuasion* of late." She chuckled and found Rhian's eyes in the sea of faces watching her and blew a kiss up to her lover. "You see, a couple of years ago, I was in Nepal when the earthquake struck Mount Everest. I witnessed devastation, death, and destruction as you could never imagine. And when I got off the plane back in London, I vowed I'd never step foot on a mountain again. I'd seen their power, looked into the heart of Mother Nature, and I knew fear. I'd been humbled, bled of the confidence, or maybe the arrogance, you need to put yourself out there time after time and say, 'Not today. You're not gonna get me today.' So I ran away. I sought refuge anywhere else but the mountains." She quirked her lips into a self-deprecating smile. "I guess you know by now that I never found it, right?"

Chuckles filled the auditorium

"So there I was, six months ago, sitting in a hospital room at my sister's bedside. Fen." She waved her hand to Fen, and Fen waved back. Mark put his fingers between his lips and whistled loudly. "Thanks, Mark," Jayden acknowledged. "Anyway, she's the one who should be up here, but she took a dive into a crevasse. Broke some bones, and, well, we didn't know if her back was broken. We were totally on edge—completely at a loss about what was happening, how we were even going to tell Fen what had happened, what was going to happen—and in strolls this woman, Rhian. This woman who just turned everything upside down. She insisted I go back out there. And in doing so, she gave me a path back to the things I was missing. You see, when you know that peace that you can only find out there, it's like a drug. It calls you always, pulling you back for more. Just one more fix, one more dance with Mother Nature. And all I needed was an excuse to fall off the wagon."

Tears rolled down Rhian's face even as she smiled. Rachel wrapped her hand around Rhian's and passed her a tissue.

"Blow your nose, kiddo. Or she might decide not to come back."

"Thanks," Rhian whispered and dabbed at her cheeks with it. Rachel's hand still clung to her own as Jayden continued with her speech.

"But Rhian has given me so much more than that. Not only a path back to the mountains I missed so much, but a path back to me, to my heart. And, most importantly, to hers."

Rhian stared at Jayden on the giant screen and saw her throat work to swallow back the emotion.

"So while I thank everyone involved in this production—the contestants, producers, director, and even my clumsy-arsed sister—for making this show the amazing success it has been, I dedicate this to Rhian Phillips, because she's the greatest award, and reward, I could ever receive." She held the trophy up to acknowledge the applause of the crowd and stepped back from the podium.

Rhian wiped her face and slowly got to her feet. The rest of the crowd was already standing as they cheered and clapped, and Rhian needed to see Jayden's face again. Music was piped over the stereo system as credits to the organisers filled the huge screen at the back of the stage. Jayden walked back down the aisle, people shaking her hand and congratulating her as she went.

When she finally stopped in front of Rhian, she smiled shyly and whispered, "Hi."

Rhian threw her arms around Jayden's shoulders and kissed her soundly before tucking her face into her neck.

"Does that mean you didn't like my little speech?" She wrapped her arms around Rhian's back. Rhian could feel the smile in her words and the pull of her muscles against the side of her head.

"It was terrible," she grumbled into her. "Worst speech ever."

"Oh really? I see. Well, Miss Phillips, I'll try to do better in future."

Rhian pulled back to look into her eyes. "You do that."

"Okay, you two, break it up," Rachel said from behind her. Jayden's hand moved from her back, then her body shook as Rachel shook her hand. "Congratulations. I know there's a party after this, but could we have a few minutes before you head over there? Both of you."

Jayden looked down at Rhian, who nodded before she said, "Sure. Outside?"

Rachel led the way, the CEO from Patagonia behind them.

"What a night," the man said when they got outside. "Sorry, Scott Willis." He shook hands with them both. "Would you believe it—Best Cinematography, Best Host, and Best Competition Show?"

"It certainly makes this the perfect time to announce that the series will continue, doesn't it?" Rachel said. It was phrased as a question, but it didn't need an answer.

"Continue? You're going to do another one?" Rhian asked.

Rachel nodded. "You'll be staying in Patagonia with Jayden to work with her and oversee it all, recruit contestants, etc. Just like this last time. Obviously, we'll need bigger and more exciting challenges, but this time around, you two have a long break to come up with those things, right?"

Rhian nodded as she grasped what Rachel was saying and stared in mute shock. Rachel took her hand and pulled her away for a moment.

"You love her."

Rhian nodded again, still unable to find words.

"And you were going to tell me you were quitting to go over there and be with her."

"Yes."

"Good. Now you don't have to." She winked, and the grin spread across her face. "Of course, I'll be coming out to see the setup and to see if we need to make any changes or additions in a month or so, so make sure the spare room is made up for me, okay? I need to make sure she deserves you."

Rhian wrapped her arms around Rachel's neck. "I love you."

"I know, kiddo. Now don't get tear stains on my dress. This thing cost a fortune."

"Yes, Mother." Rhian chuckled.

"And don't you forget it." Rachel looked seriously into Rhian's eyes, and for the first time that she could ever remember, Rhian saw vulnerability there. She was truly worried she was going to lose Rhian over this.

"How could I?" Rhian asked. "You're the mum I remember, the mum who was there for me, the one who's loved me no matter what since I was a kid. You may not have given birth to me, Rach, but you might as well have.

I told you before that the only reason I never called you Mum was because I thought you'd kill me."

"And I didn't want to try and take the place of your real mum."

"Don't you get it? You *are* my real mum. When I came out, it was to you. And it's you that I've always counted on. As my mum. Not as a stepmum, my mum."

"You make me so proud."

Rhian beamed. "And that's all I ever wanted to do."

Rachel squeezed her hard again, then pulled her away, reaching into the small bag at her arm. "Here, this is for you." She held out a long thin box.

Rhian took it from her hand tentatively and pried open the lid. A braided length of white gold rested on the black velvet cushion, glinting in the light. Rhian gasped and stroked a finger down the length of it. "You didn't need to do this, Rachel."

"Not me."

Rhian looked away from the chain, frowning at her. "Who?"

"Your dad."

Rhian snapped the lid closed and held it out to Rachel.

Rachel held up her hands, refusing to take it. "I'm not taking it back."

"He can't buy me."

Rachel shook her head. "He isn't trying to. He wanted to be here tonight. He wanted to support us both. But he knew you'd go bananas if he turned up with me."

"Damn straight. He's got no—"

"He's your father, and he loves you too. He wanted you to know how proud he is of you." She pointed to the box in Rhian's hand. "That was the only way he could think of to show you how much you mean to him without being here in person."

Rhian waved the box, trying to force it into Rachel's hand. "I can't take this from him."

"Then sell it, throw it in the bin, give it to someone else if you don't want it. But I won't take it back to him."

"Take it."

Rachel shook her head. "Taking this doesn't mean you forgive him, Rhi."

"But he'll think it will, so no."

"No, he won't. He'll hope that maybe one day you can, but he knows with absolute certainty that there is a long, long way to go." She wrapped her hand around Rhian's and the box. "He's proud of you, kiddo, and he loves you. This is his statement to you. Not yours to him." She squeezed her fingers gently. "Just think about it, okay?"

Rhian stared at the box. Could it be as simple as that? Did she want it to be? She couldn't stop her mind wandering back to his e-mail. The message that still sat in her inbox. Read, but not responded to. The one she failed to forget, despite trying to on a daily basis. He hadn't tried to contact her again. He hadn't turned up tonight as Rachel said he wanted to. She could imagine that to be true. It was a great night for Rachel; of course he'd want to be a part of that. But he'd stayed away. To make it better for her. Was he really sorry? Could she really trust that?

Rachel pulled her into another hug and whispered into her ear, "Stop thinking about it. Put it in your bag, and worry about it tomorrow." She kissed her cheek and pushed her towards Jayden. "Now get going. You two have a party to go to and then a lot of packing up to do, right?"

Rhian nodded and dabbed under her eyes before she slipped the box into her own bag. She saw but decided to ignore the slightly smug grin that twisted Rachel's lips, even as tears glistened in her eyes. "Will you help me? Tomorrow?"

"Just you try and stop me." She sniffed. "Besides, I've still got so much to tell you—about the next series and the full details of your new job—and I need to get to know Jayden. And, good grief, there's a lot to sort out."

"I know." She grasped Rachel's hand, then took Jayden's in the other as Jayden stepped up to them, a question in her lovely blue eyes. Rhian kissed Jayden's cheek and smiled at Rachel again. Fen and Mark walked out the doors, waving as they approached the trio. What a circle of love and trust and friendship they'd worked so hard to create these past several months. "I know," she repeated. "There *is* a lot to sort out." A lot that was part of an exciting new future doing something she loved, with the woman she loved at her side.

"Don't worry," she told Rachel, pulling Jayden closer to her. "I'm confident we can sort everything out together."

ABOUT ANDREA BRAMHALL

Andrea Bramhall wrote her first novel at the age of six and three-quarters. It was seven pages long and held together with a pink ribbon. Her Gran still has it in the attic. Since then she has progressed a little bit and now has a number of published works held together with glue, not ribbons, an Alice B. Lavender certificate, a Lambda Literary award, and a Golden Crown award cluttering up her book shelves.

She studied music and all things arty at Manchester Metropolitan University, graduating in 2002 with a BA in contemporary arts. She is certain it will prove useful someday…maybe.

When she isn't busy running a campsite in the Lake District, Bramhall can be found hunched over her laptop scribbling down the stories that won't let her sleep. She can also be found reading, walking the dogs up mountains while taking a few thousand photos, scuba diving while taking a few thousand photos, swimming, kayaking, playing the saxophone, or cycling.

CONNECT WITH ANDREA

Website: andreabramhall.wordpress.com
Facebook: www.facebook.com/AndreaBramhall

OTHER BOOKS FROM YLVA PUBLISHING

www.ylva-publishing.com

JUST MY LUCK
Andrea Bramhall

ISBN: 978-3-95533-702-5
Length: 306 pages (80,500 words)

Genna Collins works a dead end job, loves her family, her girlfriend, and her friends. When she wins the biggest Euromillions jackpot on record, everything changes…and not always for the best.

When Abi Kitson fell in love she always knew it would go unrequited. The woman of her dreams was so close yet seemingly untouchable for so many reasons. Reasons like—they are best friends, or the big age gap, or the 'other' woman, nevermind Abi's own baggage. And even when those reasons crumble it seems luck just isn't on her side.

It's a learning curve for both of them. But what if money really can't buy you everything you want? What if the answers aren't hidden in a big, fat bank balance? What if happiness is right in front of them? They just have to reach out…

FENCED-IN FELIX
(Girl Meets Girl Series – Book 3)

Cheyenne Blue

ISBN: 978-3-95533-706-3
Length: 308 pages (87,000 words)

A tough life in outback Australia means Felix has no time for romance. When the peripatetic Josie asks Felix to board her horse, Flame, Felix is delighted as she'll now see more of Josie. But there's something suspicious about Flame, who bears an uncanny resemblance to a stolen racehorse. Felix is falling hard for Josie, but is Josie all she seems, or is she mixed up in shady dealings?

COMING FROM YLVA
PUBLISHING

www.ylva-publishing.com

SURVIVAL INSTINCTS
A Dystopian Novel

May Dawney

Civilization has fallen. Lynn, alone in the debris of a world reclaimed by nature and hiding from the threat of man, is forced to go on a dangerous journey through decaying New York City. As Lynn's feelings for her guard, Dani, grow, she's forced to face her belief that staying alone is the only way to survive.

A fast-paced dystopian adventure where love trumps instinct.

THE LAST FIRST TIME
(Norfolk Coast Investigation Story – Book 3)

Andrea Bramhall

When Gina Temple decides to go Christmas shopping for her girlfriend, Detective Sergeant Kate Brannon, in the Norfolk town of King's Lynn, everything changes. A split-second event tips their world upside-down.

In this twisting lesbian thriller, Kate's subsequent investigation leads her down a crazy rabbit hole. Meanwhile, as the two women grow closer, life keeps throwing obstacles at them.

www.ingramcontent.com/pod-product-compliance
Lightning Source LLC
Chambersburg PA
CBHW030343020726
47493CB00003B/658